Morehead City, NC
September, 2004

LIFE OF THE EAGLE

By

Richard L. Evans

for Jill with my best wishes —
Richard L. Evans

Keep hope alive — "... so that thy youth is renewed like the eagle's."

Moorehead City, NC
September, 2004

For Jill with my best wishes —

Richard L. Crowe

"Keep hope alive..." so that
thy youth is renewed like the eagle's."

LIFE OF THE EAGLE

A Novel By

Richard L. Evans

Copyright © 2004 by Richard L. Evans.

ISBN: 1-59507-038-9

Published by

ArcheBooks Publishing
A Division of Gelinas & Wolf, Inc.

www.archebooks.com

9101 W. Sahara Ave.

Suite 105-112

Las Vegas, NV 89117

All rights reserved, including the right to reproduce this book or portions thereof in any form whatsoever. For information about this book, please contact ArcheBooks at publisher@ArcheBooks.com.

This book is entirely a work of fiction. The names, characters, places, and incidents depicted herein are either products of the author's imagination or are used fictitiously. Any resemblance to actual events or locales or persons, living or dead, is entirely coincidental.

First Edition: 2004

for Carolyn
who is living proof that there really are angels
in this world

ACKNOWLEDGEMENTS

This book would not have been possible without the help and enthusiasm of many people. The author thanks all those who shared their suggestions, encouragement and knowledge. They include:

Vickey Barwick—*Vickey's House*, Beth Beswick—*Carteret General Hospital*, Allen Bryant—*First Citizens Bank*, Capt. Leland Day, Sgt. Maj. William L. Faulkner—*USMC* (Ret.), Ken Fish, Jack Goodwin—*The History Place*, Rev. Timothy J. Havlicek—*First Presbyterian Church, Morehead City, NC*, Julie Hosley—*Carteret Community College*, Gene Huntsman—*Beaufort Historical Society*, Sgt. Paul Ingalls—*U.S.Army* (Ret.)., Brian Kraus—*Craven Community College*, Mary Kurek—*Performers Network Online*, Connie Mason—*North Carolina Maritime Museum*, Robert Moore—*North Carolina Maritime Museum*, Duncan Murrell, Tu D. Nguyen, Capt. Thomas P. Palmer—*USMC* (Ret.), Sgt. Maj. Joseph Rufray—*USMC* (Ret.), Simon Sterling—*Tryon Palace, New Bern, NC*, and Col. John W. Warrender—*USMC* (Ret.).

And Barbara Casey—*The Barbara Casey Literary Agency*, in recognition that without her, this book might not have been published.

About this Book

Life of the Eagle is a work of fiction. However, all places named in the book are (or were) real. All of the Indian Tribes named are real and all of the military units named are (or were) real.

There are also many real people mentioned in the book.

To avoid confusion as to who actually lived in our history and who did not, the following were real people:

Gen. George Washington, Col. John Glover, Gen. Daniel Morgan, Thomas Paine, Gen. Henry Knox, Maj. Gen. John Sullivan, Tom Fitzpatrick, Jedediah Strong Smith, Bill Sublette, David Jackson, Gen. William Ashley, Jim Beckwourth, Jim Clyman, Major Henry, Col. Clark, Pres. Zachary Taylor, Gen. Jesse Reno, Gen. Ambrose Burnside, Gen. John G. Foster, Gen. John G. Parke, Emeline (Pigott), Gen. Robert E. Lee, Clara Barton, Pres. Abraham Lincoln, Thomas Alva Edison, Alexander Graham Bell, Capt. Alfred A. Cunningham, Cpl. Robert G. Robinson, 2nd Lt. Ralph Talbot, Maj. Emile Moses, Brigadier General Ngo Quand Truong.

All other characters are fictitious. Any resemblance between the fictitious characters in this book to anyone living or dead is coincidental.

Millions long for immortality who do not know what to do with themselves on a rainy Sunday afternoon.

SUSAN ERTZ—*ANGER IN THE SKY*

Richard L. Evans

PROLOGUE

He was the kind of man who spoke to dogs. Men found him the best of company and women adored him. People who met him at a party, at work or simply standing in a waiting line with him—anywhere—would come away feeling good about themselves after just a few words with him. Years later, people would suddenly remember something about him and wonder if he were still alive.

He is.

•

He looked down in the hospital bed at little Charee Norris. Charee had been just eight years old when she was diagnosed with juvenile acute myeloblastic leukemia. That was thirteen months ago. After the first round of the prescribed treatment, chiefly chemotherapy, and later an attempted bone marrow transplant, her parents were told that her chances of achieving recession and eventual cure were not promising. Since that time additional medical intervention including more chemotherapy and radiation, had left her tiny body shriveled, her skin a sallow yellow-brown and her spirit crushed. Now at the age of nine she was ready for her death.

He was sure he could change all that. All he had to do was take her little hand in his and wish it so.

Looking into the little girl's face brought back memories of other faces. They had all been like little Charee, near death. Her image blurred as tears filled his eyes, not for her but for the others.

He remembered them well.

He had been just a little older than Charee when he first became aware of his gift. That's what he called it at first, his gift. Later, he came to think of it quite differently.

•

The first life he touched was that of his boyhood friend, Thomas. Thomas—no one ever called him Tom or Tommy—became ill late one summer day. The two boys had explored the upstream source of a small creek that flowed sluggishly through the woods around the farm his mother rented. They had both sipped the clear water to slake their thirst.

Thomas was put to bed with a cough, rash and high fever. Fearing that the illness might be contagious, his own mother had forbidden him to see Thomas. She did not tell him what made Thomas so dangerous but he sensed her terror and knew it must be serious.

He slipped out of his room late the next night and using a tree limb, climbed into Thomas' bedroom window. There was a rising moon and it was easy. He had done it before. He could hear Thomas' mother and sisters talking softly in another room. He was sure at least one of the women was crying.

Thomas did not move or seem to know he was there. He stood by the bed and grasped his friend's hand and whispered a few words to him. The words came to him, unbidden, and he didn't understand them. He didn't think he was praying. His mother was not a "church person" and he had never attended church or been given any instruction in devotionals or prayer.

He felt Thomas's hand in his become very hot. It reminded him of the handle on his mother's iron skillet but he held it tightly, anyway. The words he spoke were the same his father had spoken to him, once. His father had held his hand in the same way he now held Thomas' hand. He didn't think about his father much, anymore. His father had left years ago—had just walked out on his mother and him. It seemed strange he should remember his words now.

Thomas stirred for a moment and then seemed to slip back into a dreamless sleep. After watching over his sleeping friend for a while, he left the room the same way he had come. He went home still terrified that his friend would die and so would he.

The next day Thomas got out of bed early in the morning and declared to his mother and sisters that he was "hungry enough to eat a horse." Thomas' mother ran excitedly to their farmhouse to tell them the good news.

His own mother asked him about Thomas with a question on her face. He had never lied to his mother or to anyone else.

When he confessed what he had done, his mother's face changed—first to anger then to something he had never seen before. A deep, grave sadness took her face down and her whole body seemed to sag with it. It scared him and he started to cry. She slapped him and then kept her hand on his cheek, forcing him to look at her.

She whispered, "Oh, Lord, oh, my Lord, boy. Don't you ever do that, again—you promise me, now—never again."

Her anger flared for a moment blocking out her despair but only for a moment. He saw her tears as she straightened up and walked slowly away. She moved as if she were carrying all the weight of the world. He was sure what he had done had saved his friend's life. Despite what his mother said, he was glad he did it.

It frightened him though.

•

Edna P. Snow liked her job as personnel director at Presbyterian Medical Center. She liked helping people find secure jobs.

She also liked sniffing out the undesirable applicants: the incompetent, the unreliable, and most of all, the thieves and sex offenders looking for easy targets. The prospect that one of the latter might slip through her finely tuned detection system had etched an almost permanent scowl on her face. No one in the Center ever remembered seeing her smile. There were those who said the "P" in her middle name must be for "Pissed."

Miss Snow (she did not like being addressed as *Ms.* Snow) was responsible for hiring almost everyone now employed at the Center. They all had experienced her scrutiny and agreed she gave a new and daunting meaning to the words, snow job. Many were sure she was the quintessential aging virgin. They were only half right. She wasn't a physically imposing person. At just five foot three inches tall and still very slender, she was considered a little old lady by the eighteen to twenty-four year-old nurse trainees. Although she was more than twice their age at fifty-seven, the thought that she might be little or old hadn't occurred to her. She lived alone but that, too, hadn't always been true. Her hair had once been long, straight and blonde. Now it was short and curled loosely. Its color had become whiter, although she liked to think of it as just lighter not, whiter. She had been a flower-child back in the sixties with many suitors. She was smart and learned quickly that free love wasn't always free. Only two men ever had a chance for her heart. Ten years ago she had taken a train to Washington, D.C. to find their names on the Vietnam Wall.

She hired him quickly—much too quickly she was sure—it violated her normally cautious routine.

There was nothing particularly striking about his physical appearance. He was above average in height but not a man who would be called tall. Through his neatly pressed dress shirt she could see he was muscular with a powerful frame. She was sure he was strong enough to handle even the largest patients. His hair was brown, his eyes a softer brown. He was clean shaven, well groomed and his necktie, pants and shoes were spotless. He obviously cared about himself.

She didn't approve of tattoos or piercings which had become so commonplace today. She couldn't see any such distinguishing marks on this young man's arms or face. The only obvious mark he carried was a peculiar scar at the hairline on his left temple. It looked quite old, probably the result of a childhood accident.

Had she known the true origin of that scar, she would have run from her office screaming for someone to call Hospital Security.

But she didn't know. She didn't know how he became marked, so she hired him to work in a modern hospital, to work in a place where people needed him most, a place where he could do the most good. She also didn't know it, but she was one of those who would need him the most.

He was very appealing: direct; even courtly—traits not usually found in one so young. She found herself attracted to him but forced that idea away. She was, after all, old enough to be his mother. That was something else that had escaped her about him—something else she didn't know.

But nothing escaped his notice as he sat in her office. He saw the utilitarian and very Spartan furnishings; the quiet efficiency of the carefully ordered space; the attention to lighting and ventilation. There was no dust and no clutter. Miss Snow's desk held no framed photos of children or grandchildren or nieces or nephews. He was sure she lived alone and had no close relatives to question what he had begun to plan for her. She was perfect.

When she said she had a position open for him, he gave her his brightest and most charming smile.

The haste of her decision to employ him as a physicians' assistant bothered her later, and she made a pledge to herself to continue to investigate his background. She checked all the easy references and documents. His birth certificate was genuine. She called the records division of the issuing hospital in Cleveland to be sure. He had a clean credit history, holding credit cards from three different lenders. Legally, she couldn't ask him about his finances, but credit checks were still easy even without permission. A poor credit history might indicate a need for money which could, in turn, mean a drug habit. Controlled drugs were too easy to steal at PMC. His documents indicated he had graduated from a high school in the Cleveland suburbs with grades in the C's and B's along with several athletic letters. He had worked as a nurses' assistant in a retirement home while attending nursing school where he had earned straight A's. Men willing to take on the duties and relatively low pay offered nurses were hard to find—almost as hard to find as trained RNs.

She didn't give any thought to how easy it might be for him, as a hospital employee, to check back files of birth certificates for children who had died in infancy; then to check the local newspapers for lists of graduating seniors of the right age, matching the name on the birth certificate to the name of the student; that done, to simply write both institutions requesting copies of the documents. Armed with a seemingly valid birth certificate, Social Security cards and drivers licenses were easy to obtain. Credit card offers would soon arrive in the mail after any employment. He had a cache of such certificates.

He knew the time would come when he would have to move on and assume another identity. A new set of documents had to be created every ten or fifteen years lest his unchanging physical appearance inspire unwanted questions. Should any of those fail, he had plenty of experience as a forger. He had once even fooled an expert collector with a very authentic-looking discharge paper from the American Continental Army copied from the original he had received in August of 1789.

Edna P. Snow had been "snowed."

•

In the dimmed light of her hospital room, Charee's face seemed almost luminous. He thought again of his boyhood friend, Thomas, and his face when he had seen it last. The face in his dreams was so swollen and blackened that it was almost unrecognizable—almost.

Thomas had hanged himself.

His friend had continued to live in the same house, never leaving his mother and sisters. Thomas' miraculous recovery from the fever had gained him a measure of local fame. He was their miracle boy, adored and doted on by his mother and four older sisters.

His sisters never married, never left the family home. Their purpose in life was to serve Thomas. But in time, his unmarried sisters grew older, and then old, with spotted, wrinkled skin and gray hair, their backs bent with osteoporosis. But Thomas remained trim, supple, with his flesh as smooth and as pink as ever—ever more the miracle boy.

Eventually, his mother and sisters died and Thomas was left alone. The care his mother and sisters had provided for him all his life died with the last of them.

Unable, or unwilling, to care for himself, Thomas tied one end of a short, stout rope to a heavy bed post and the other around his neck, then jumped out of a second-story window; the same window his boyhood friend used the night he condemned him to live.

He could see Thomas' face of death as if in a dream, just as he could the others. Again, he looked down at Charee, her tiny chest moving unevenly with her labored breathing. Could she be different? Could this be the one he had searched for—the one he had been sent to save?

•

Despite Miss Snow's afterthoughts about hiring him too quickly, he was an excellent worker with skills beyond what might be expected in one so young. The other nurses found his physical strength amazing as he lifted patients with ease. Every member of the staff had a smile for him—always returning his. The patients were even more adoring. After all, he spent most of his time with them. He was careful to devote the majority of his time to the elderly geriatric patients and to the children in the oncology ward.

He would sing with them, the golden oldies, or hymns with the old, and the latest children's TV songs or nursery rhymes with the young.

"Me, me! Come sing with me!"

Billy was only four but he was a fighter; cancer wouldn't take him without a battle.

So they sang together: "I love you, you love me..."

Old Bill liked to sing, too.

"I bet I know one you don't," came his challenge, "and I'll tell you what it is as soon as I can remember it myself."

Bill had tried to stump him for weeks—had tried to think of a song he didn't know—and failed. But he wouldn't give up either.

"How about 'In the Sweet By and By' while I try to remember the other one."

Of course, Bill knew that old hymn wouldn't stump him. He seemed to know every song anyone could remember.

It wasn't necessary for him to touch them, but he did. With his touch and his voice he gave them something he knew would bring healing, if healing were possible—healing to their bodies and to their souls. He gave them hope. Hope, like nothing else, increased their expectations of life. In time there were far fewer deaths and far more complete recoveries in the wards where his sunny outlook and gentle encouragement lifted all hearts.

The other nurses could always find him by simply going wherever they heard people laughing and singing. In time, too, Miss Edna P. Snow relaxed her vigil—just a bit. But that would be enough.

Richard L. Evans

Chapter One

ANNE

He watched his mother die.
She was dead before he knew what he was watching. She died slowly. It took a little more than half a year from the day he told her what he had done to save his friend, Thomas, to the day he heard her cough and gasp for the last time.
He went to wake her but she was so still. He tried to shake her awake. He touched her face. It was cold, as cold as the hard floor beneath his feet. He had not seen a dead person before, but he knew. She just gave up on life.
He walked to Thomas' house and told the women about his mother.
Soon people, women mainly, began arriving at the little rented farmhouse. They helped wrap his mother in her good dress and laid her body on the table near the vegetable larder. The women began to moan and cry. He couldn't understand the sounds they made—they weren't words—just sounds.
The next day, he followed a borrowed, two-wheeled horse cart bearing his mother's body along a muddy path to the far end

of the church burying ground. A spring rain soaked the earth and he had to pull his bare feet free of the cold muck with each step.

Some of his neighbors helped bury her in a place reserved for the un-churched.

He packed their few possessions in a single cloth bag, took what was left of the food brought for his mother's wake, and left.

Watching him walk away, Thomas' sisters shook their heads and wondered what might become of the orphaned boy. But they had their own boy to care for and turned back to their devotion.

Just over two years before her death, his mother had taken him to the seacoast for a few days—a rare and unexpected break from the steady drudgery of farm work. It was the only time he had ever been away from the farm.

Now he tried to remember the sound and the smell of the ocean. The memory of salt air fed his imagination. No more farming for him—he was going to sea.

He was careful not to eat much each day so it would last until he reached the coast where he was sure he would find work on a ship. The fact that he might not be big enough didn't occur to him.

Each day, just at dusk, he snuck into cow barns near the road. Strangely, the cows made no sound when he slid in their stalls. He had a tin cup and he got his breakfast before the farmers came to their barns for the morning's milking. The warm milk was sweet and the cows always seemed eager to give a little something to the quiet boy. He still had some food left four days later when he reached the coastal town he remembered so fondly.

The ships docked along the waterfront were just as he remembered them—huge, almost living things, moving gently with the changing whims of the water around them. He chose the biggest ship and climbed its walkway.

There was lots of activity on the ship. Men were moving water barrels on board. He had to dodge around them. The barrels were being stacked near an opening in the deck. He saw a tall man with a red face standing near the barrels watching the work.

That man, he thought, *must be in charge.*

He approached the tall man, saying with his best smile, "Sir, I want to be a sailor like you. I'm an orphan in need of work."

The man turned to him, seeming surprised that he had to look so far down to see the orphan.

The man crossed his arms and said roughly, "I need men, not boys," and turned back to watch the loading of the barrels.

The man's words crushed his spirit. A hard knot grew in his stomach. What would he do, now? Head down and turning to go, he noticed one of the barrels on the deck had a small pool of water forming around it. The way the men were straining as they rolled the barrels over the deck, he knew they must be very heavy.

But that leaking barrel won't have as much water in it and should be lighter than the others.

He approached the tall man and tried again.

"I'm very strong, sir. "I'll show you."

When the tall man turned again to him, he seized the leaking water barrel, gripping it at each end, and began to lift it. He was used to lifting heavy stones out of the soil on the farm, piling them up to form walls between the fields. But this barrel certainly weighed more than he did. Desperation gave him strength. He raised the barrel up and over his head, then lowered it carefully back to the deck.

"Well," said the captain, "you *are* a sturdy lad—and a wily one, as well, I reckon."

The captain had also noticed the leaking water and knew it was the lightest of the barrels.

"I believe I can use a bright lad with both those skills."

The tall man pointed to a nearby portal and said, "Go down that passageway yonder and find the galley. Ask the cook to give you something to eat. Then we'll set you up in the crew's quarters."

The captain never regretted his decision. The orphaned boy, with his ever cheerful ways, was a joy to all and a tireless worker, eager to learn everything he could about seamanship.

As the ship's new apprentice, his first lesson was with the ship's glass. He had seen similar devices in shop windows where they were called, hour glasses. The ship's glass was larger, and his first watch commander told him it timed only half an hour.

"Your duty," he was told, "is to turn the glass. When the sand in the glass runs out, you must turn it over and announce in a loud voice, 'The first glass of the forenoon watch.' You understand that? Then ring the ship's bell once. Each time the sand runs out in the glass you turn it over and announce the number of the glass and strike the bell that many times. You got all that?"

He did. What joy! What power he had—he was helping to run the ship!

On each watch his main job, other than turning the glass, was to…watch. Two other seamen were also on the watch with him. One man took the helm and held the ship's course while the new ship's boy and the other man watched the sea ahead, one to the larboard side, the other to starboard. They changed places every two glasses to help them stay alert. This changing within the watch brought him even more joy.

After the fourth glass he took the helm and actually guided the ship. For a ten-year old boy, the ship's wheel was hard to hold. The other men on the watch kept a close eye on him but did not help him. They wanted to know what he was made of. They were soon well-satisfied by what they saw. Most of the ship's crew had learned their skills exactly the way this new lad was learning his. They understood his struggle and appreciated his "grit."

After he announced, "The eighth glass of the forenoon watch," and rang the bell eight times, he was relieved by the men on the next watch. He was hooked. The life of the sailor was for him. At least, it seemed that way.

While still a boy he learned to "box the compass" by announcing clearly the names of the thirty-two points of the navigator's compass. He also learned the names of the various parts of his ship. He learned a floor was not a floor; it was a deck. A rope was not a rope; it was a line. Any ceiling was an overhead, and a set of stairs was a ladder. When his other duties were done, he walked the length of the ship touching everything he could reach as he announced aloud the name of each thing. He started with the jibboom at the bow and went all the way to the stern finally touching the taffrail. His shipmates followed his progress with amusement. Whenever he stopped, not sure what a particular part was called, he always had help.

"Those be the forechains, boy," came help from above. "And what am I standing on now?"

"That's the topmast crosstree, sir," went up his answer.

That was easy—he'd been up there himself, just yesterday.

"What sheet is this, lad?" came from a sailor in another part of the rigging above his head.

"That's the main-topgallant sail, sir," went up his reply.

"That's a good lad. You got me that time," the old tar laughed.

He was so proud of himself.

He practiced the knots all sailors used to manage the lines. He also learned the proper way to splice a line so it wouldn't part under strain. There were many days when he bled from his knees, or his elbows, or his knuckles (or all three). That was part of his education, too. The palms of his hands became so hard with calluses he could feel little with them.

He climbed into the rigging to help set and take up sail, always remembering to stay on the weather side of the cross arm lest he be blown off and overboard by the wind. His youth and physical strength made him less useful in the rigging than on the deck. That was fine with his shipmates; they were pleased to see his concentration and dedication to his duties.

One day the First Mate sent him back to the Boatswain to get some oil for the starboard running lamp. When he returned, the Mate removed the lid from the oiling tin and said, "What color is the starboard lamp, boy?"

"Why, it's green, sir." Such an easy question, he thought.

"And what color is the larboard lamp, boy?"

"Why, it's red, sir." They couldn't fool him.

"And which lamp did I tell you to oil?"

"The starboard lamp, sir."

"And what color is this oil?"

"It's red, sir." Uh, oh!

Alarm bells were going off in his head.

"Now, you go back to the Boatswain and tell him to give you the green oil for the starboard lamp." The Mate had a very stern look to him.

Returning to the Boatswain he said, "I fear I've made a mistake, sir. The Mate told me to oil the starboard lamp so I'll need the green oil, sir."

The Boatswain and three other men nearby all exploded into laughter. When he looked at them in bewilderment at their laughter, they laughed even harder.

Finally, the Boatswain controlled himself enough to explain.

"The oil for both lamps is the same, boy. It's the color of the glass that makes the lamps red or green."

There was more laughter at his expense. He was embarrassed. But he learned from it, too. Soon he was laughing with them. The delight such hard men took in him pleased him. Humor was important to them—these men who seemed always to walk around with such stern faces.

•

Years passed and he grew into a powerful and intelligent seaman, well versed in all aspects of his chosen trade. There seemed to be nothing he couldn't do with a ship—nothing that he wasn't ready to take on. Eventually, the sea would teach him otherwise.

He learned the rudiments of mathematics and how to position a ship by dead reckoning. Navigation was important. Errors could lead to another dead reckoning—his own. He learned the uses of the stars and weather signs. With a cross staff and declination chart he could measure the angle of the sun to the horizon and determine his latitudinal position. Later he learned to use a sextant. He was also shown how to use the moon and certain stars to calculate his longitudinal position. That calculation required a very complicated mathematical process that might take hours to complete. His captains were always happy to give him that duty.

At the age of fifteen he took in some other vital information. His curiosity regarding women had grown with his own developing body. When in port, he took time to observe women and girls along the waterfronts. The obvious differences between his body and theirs further fed his imagination. His teachers were his more experienced young shipmates. They were *more* experienced but not *broadly* experienced. Still, they were able to explain the basics using diagrams drawn in chalk on the deck. Their explanation was accompanied by much self-conscious laughter. The whole thing sounded to him like more ship's humor—another story about needing "oil for the starboard lamp." But he checked the accuracy of their information at the ship's next port of call—in a Cuban bordello.

They were correct.

Twenty-five years passed and he almost forgot about his healing gift and his promise never to use it.

In 1772 he signed on as First Mate of the *Anne*, a 150-ton merchantman out of London. The *Anne* had been forced into Boston's harbor by the same storm that had damaged his last ship now in for major repairs.

His new captain, Captain Davenport, gave him a quick tour of his new ship. He was surprised to find the *Anne* in good condition.

"Major portions of her hull have just been replaced," said Davenport, "as have the racks in the cargo holds. And, as you can see, everything now has a fresh coat of green or black paint."

After the captain left him to his regular duties, he began checking the ship's roster. The ship itself might be in good shape, but he noted the ship's crew numbered only eight, including the Captain. The normal complement for a vessel the size of the *Anne* should have been double that number. The lack of an adequate crew was surprising considering the main cargo he'd seen in the ship's holds—rum.

They sailed first to London, dropping anchor in the Howland Great Dock near Deptford. It was a grand sight. He counted more than twenty other ships docked there as well, their masts and cross arms creating a waving, leafless forest above the tree-lined shore—a forest in a forest. The *Anne's* cargo of rum, ivory and a variety of exotic animals including several chimpanzees was set off, and soon a very different mixture of goods came aboard.

As Mate, one of his jobs was to supervise the storage of their new cargo in the holds. More than a hundred large crates and barrels had to be stacked and carefully braced. Some contained iron bars, spoons, tankards, basins, pots and other vessels made of pewter and copper. The largest barrels held glass beads, small mirrors, and copper rings. Still others were packed with a kind of sea shell.

"What are we going to do with these?" he asked Harris, who was keeping lists of everything.

"Those are cowry shells, sir." Harris replied, "Very prized by the Africans, I'm told."

Just then a heavy barrel slipped from a lowering hoist and fell hard on the deck. The top split open. He could see it was packed with muskets. When he pulled one out, he got a dusting of brown rust on his hands. The weapon was in poor condition, not at all like the ones held in the ship's locker for the crew's protection. He cocked it and pulled the trigger. There was no spark.

"Who would want these relics?" he thought aloud.

Harris was quick to point out, "It might be just as well for us that they don't work, sir, considering where we're going."

Other crates held more muskets, pistols, powder, shot, swords, even knives. Hundreds of bolts of cloth all dyed in bright colors were stacked on top of the crates to keep them dry.

Before he signed on the *Anne,* the Captain had told him about the huge profits to be made in the African slave trade. Roderick Davenport hadn't minced words.

"The stakes are high and so are the risks. Perhaps half this crew will not return. They'll die somewhere on the voyage even if we're successful. You may not survive, either."

Fair warning, he thought, at the Captain's words.

"But," the Captain continued, "I'll still have no trouble filling a crew. That's what money can do. As First Mate you'll earn two percent of all profits. The ship's doctor will get the same, and I can guarantee you'll both earn your shares. As Captain I'll get twice that amount, and I'll earn mine, too. The rest of the crew will split another two percent among them. Each man will be required to write a will stipulating his beneficiaries. So will you. Most of them will name each other. You name whoever you wish. The officers, that is, you, me, the doctor and the boatswain can also sell two slaves each for our personal profit. You should be able to retire in comfort on your share."

Then, almost as an afterthought, the Captain added, "Or drink yourself to death."

He knew Davenport was already a rich man. The Captain had told him this would be his third voyage as skipper of a slaver.

The thought that he needed to name someone to receive his share of the profits should he not return troubled him. He had no one, no family, not even a friend to leave his possessions when he died. Finally, he did what most of the rest of the crew did—he named all the survivors to share and share alike in his portion.

Davenport was anxious for the *Anne* to finish taking on stores and be on her way.

He said, "It's already October and the best time to approach the African Slave Coast is in January. We must leave soon."

Africa was now four months away—exactly the time they had left to get there.

As Davenport had predicted, he had no trouble signing a crew. They put the English coast behind them and arrived at the Bight of Benin on the West African coast in late January, 1773.

He knew about mosquitoes, of course, but he couldn't believe the numbers and viciousness of the bloodthirsty little devils. Once in the mouth of the Rio Real at the Bight, and away from the breezes of the open seas, the heat, humidity and insect attacks became almost unbearable. His shirt and trousers stuck to his body with the first rays of the sun each day. He would not feel truly dry again for months. Every evening he found his hammock below decks still moist from his previous night's sweat. Nothing could dry out in this place. Two crewmen died of some strange disease within a week of making port.

When he'd first heard it, he had not fully appreciated the little rhyme about this place spoken by an old shipmate:

Beware and take care of the Bight of Benin
For one that comes out, there are forty go in.

The next eight months would be a test of both his resolve and his immune system. Only one would survive.

He observed Davenport as the captain began dealing with the local "trader kings" on the river. The traders were amazing. They were unable to read or write but every single detail of their business dealings was committed to unfailing memory. Gifts had to be offered even before serious negotiations could begin. But at the completion of each trade a valuable gift would come to the ship from the traders in return. It might be a young male slave or a young woman with an infant on her shoulder, both real prizes worth almost their weight in gold—if they could be brought to the Caribbean.

He was curious why the captain did not fill most of his ship's capacity at their first stop. It would have been easy and got them away from the damned heat and mosquitoes quickly. When he asked Davenport about this, the captain said it was folly to take large numbers of slaves from the same tribal area. The captain wanted groups of slaves who didn't have a common language to help them plot a war for freedom.

It was also his job to supervise the disposition of this new cargo. He understood the conventions of slavery well. His own relationship to all his captains had been essentially that of a slave to a master. He would be paid for his service but once at sea a captain's word was law and had to be obeyed without question. Any sailor who jumped ship was treated as an escaped slave. A returned sailor might be hanged as an example to other crews. There was a difference, of course. He came to the *Anne* willingly; the slaves did not.

Most of the slaves offered to the *Anne* had been taken as prisoners in the seemingly unending tribal warfare all across West Africa. Slavery was an old, well-accepted custom here, but the export of large masses of people from the entire region was depleting it of essential population. As the *Anne* moved further upstream, the crew could see miles of overgrown farmlands no longer cultivated. There was no one left to work the land.

Some miles up the river, he accompanied the ship's carpenter and a group of sailors to the interior to cut and gather wood.

The carpenter explained, "I have to build half-decks in the open cargo holds for the poor devils. The half-decks will serve as wide shelves stacked up, one on top of another. The Negroes will be shackled two together at their ankles and then have to lie side-by-side on these wooden shelves."

Other than Captain Davenport and the carpenter, the only member of the crew who had experienced a previous voyage in the "Middle Passage" slave trade was a Negro, Portuguese seaman named, Nuflo de Nino.

Nuflo was not the first black man he had seen, but he was by far the strangest. His skin was very black and had no sheen—it seemed to be covered with a light dusting of ash or coal dust which it was not. Nuflo wore a brightly colored shirt and pantaloons. This gaudy outfit was topped with a hat decorated with white bird plumes similar to the one Davenport wore as captain. Nuflo always swaggered when he walked the decks and bragged that he, himself, was a slave and he was proud of it. He said his ancestors had been sold in Portugal hundreds of years ago and that his current owner was a Portuguese merchant who expected to collect a portion of Nuflo's earnings. Nuflo swore he always sent a proper share of any prize he earned back to Portugal.

If that were so, he thought, *it was the only honorable thing Nuflo ever did.*

It took three months for the *Anne* to bargain away its London cargo. The slaves were brought aboard in small groups. He supervised the crew as they shackled their new "goods" to a fence made of wood and metal that had been erected across the top deck of the ship to provide a measure of defense for the crew should the slaves stage an uprising. The new arrivals would have to suffer the withering heat of the sun until the half-decks could be completed below.

The ship's doctor took each new arrival by their shoulders and licked a bit of their sweat with his tongue. The doctor told him he was sure he could determine the health of each slave by the taste of their sweat. Nuflo loved to watch the reaction of the slaves. Great wails of laughter would escape Nuflo each time the doctor performed his strange examination. After watching this for a few weeks, he asked Nuflo why it amused him so.

Nuflo said, "I know enough of their words to know they're terrified by you light-skinned men with your long, strange hair. They think you must be cannibals. When the doctor licks them, they think he's trying to taste them."

This sent Nuflo into another spasm of laughter.

What sort of man would take such delight in another man's terror?

He had first taken a dislike to Nuflo back in Boston's harbor. Nuflo was a malingerer, never working or giving a care about his ship. Captain Davenport explained he had paid his master a fee for Nuflo's services so technically, Nuflo was the captain's slave. Nuflo was also a linguist, able to speak English, Spanish, Portuguese, Dutch, Italian and French quite well, along with a smattering of the half-dozen West African languages. He had to respect Nuflo's knowledge of the slave trade. But it didn't take long for even that respect to die once the slaves were brought aboard. He grew to despise the black Portugee.

That was the beginning of his hate. His hate for Nuflo—and his hate for himself. The slaves were people. Certainly, they were different than anyone he had ever known, but clearly, they were not animals. They were people, and they were in desperate circumstances. No matter how often Captain Davenport and the rest of the crew referred to them as "cargo," he could not think of them as anything other than as people. He was revolted by the thought that people—people under his protection and care—were treated as cattle—or worse.

Finally, all was in place. The half-decks had been built; the shackles brought out of storage and set; a great store of yams and rice had been purchased and stored; the water barrels had been filled. Arms, mostly muskets, brought along for emergency control had been issued to the remaining crew. Three more men including Harris, his main assistant, were already dead of heat, exhaustion and disease. The most dangerous time for the crew would be the first few days sailing out of the Rio Real when they were still in sight of land, and the slaves could see that one last glimmer of hope.

There was no trouble.

They had been at sea only four days when the first slave died. It was his duty, as Mate, to see to the disposal of the body. He had not entered the hold until then—staying above to supervise activities on the main deck. When the wooden hatch cover leading to the hold was removed, a rush of putrid-smelling, moisture-laden air hit him in the face. He turned involuntarily, fighting to keep from gagging. Wellsley, Scott, and Richards standing by, armed with muskets, were watching. He had to do his duty as an officer in command. He took a deep, surreptitious breath and forced himself rapidly down the ladder. Scott would be right behind him.

Light filtered in from the open hatch cover above him and the shuttered ports on both sides of the hull. He had to catch himself with one hand on the ladder to keep from falling as he started to move across the hold's deck. His boots sank in an inch of heavy fluid rolling across the deck, and he nearly slipped down. His eyes adjusted to the dim light. As he looked around, he knew—he was absolutely sure—he was in Hell.

Hundreds of wild looking eyes were fixed on him from both left and right. The slaves were all lying on the wooden shelves built by the ship's carpenter. Each had one foot shackled to the foot of another slave. The ship's carpenter said the shackles would limit their movements and discourage a revolt. There were only men in this hold. The women and the young children were housed apart from the men in a smaller hold in the stern. He saw little clothing of any description. Most were naked.

There were three empty water barrels placed in a line down the center of the cargo hold. They were the only provision made for the disposal of human urine and feces. To relieve himself a slave would have to drag himself, along with the man who shared his shackle, to one of those barrels. Even now it was obvious this would not work. Seasickness, fear and dehydration had already made most efforts to reach the barrels futile. As the voyage lengthened, diarrhea and dysentery along with malaria and yellow fever would make it much worse. From the second week on, the lower deck would be completely awash in bloody excrement, vomit, urine and feces. He was sure the only slaves who would not find their passage across the great ocean a living hell would be those, like the one he had come to remove, who were dead. The luckier ones would die early.

The ship—both its crew and cargo—settled into a routine. The death of slaves also became routine. He would have to go down and release the dead from his shackles. Two other slaves would carry the body to the bottom of the ladder. A line would be tied around the upper chest of the corpse, and the dead man would be hauled on deck and thrown overboard to the ever-present sharks.

One night when they were both on the watch, he asked the Captain about the sharks.

"There are always sharks following the slave ships," the Captain replied. "As we get closer to the Caribbean, you'll see hundreds of them all around us. I think some of them must follow us all the way across from Africa."

After the Captain left the bridge and he was alone, he looked into the water over the stern. Even in the dim light of the moon he could see them moving just below the surface, easily keeping pace with the speed of the ship.

You sharks, you understand, at least, your role in this damned, unnatural trade. You know what you're doing here. But what am I doing here?

Twice each day in good weather, the male slaves were brought to the top deck in groups of fifty to sixty. The women and children were brought up together as another group. Buckets of water were scooped from the sea and poured on bodies made filthy by the unsanitary conditions in the holds. After the cleansing, wooden cups were filled with fresh water and a large vessel containing a thick gruel of yams and rice cooked in open metal ovens was placed on the deck. Following every meal, the slaves were forced to sing and dance. Slaves who refused to move while on deck were whipped until they did. Nuflo was always on hand, happy to do any whipping required. The ship's doctor insisted exercise was vital to hold off disease and depression. In bad weather they might still be brought up to be cleansed by the rain then returned below without food. The ship's doctor also made sure that each of his charges swallowed a cup of lime juice every other week to guard against scurvy. The crew was not accorded this protection—limes were too scarce to waste on white men.

Nuflo, the Boatswain, was entitled to purchase for his own profit two slaves to be sold in the New World. Nuflo had bought a young Ashanti woman and a Mandingo boy of about eight.

As First Mate, he was charged with supervising the changing of each watch. As he was doing this one evening, he heard several muffled cries from the foredeck. He discovered Nuflo raping the Ashanti slave woman as he held her bent forward over a raised hatch cover. Nuflo had bound her hands and was pulling the woman's head back by her hair as he penetrated her from behind. The woman's pleas only spurred Nuflo on.

The scene sickened him, and he felt an acid taste rise in his throat. He grabbed Nuflo by the short hair on the back of his neck and pulled him off the poor woman. Nuflo broke free and turned quickly as he drew the dagger he always kept in his belt.

But the Portugee froze when he saw who had interrupted his nightly pleasure. Nuflo took several steps back and slipped the knife back in his belt. The First Mate was unknown to him, but he looked strong, and he did not flinch when shown the dagger. Nuflo had not lived years at sea with hardened men by attacking another man straight on. He preferred to use his knife by surprise in a man's back. He grabbed the woman by the arm and pushed her down the hatchway to the rear cargo hold. In another moment Nuflo was gone.

Still sickened by what he had just seen, he turned and went below. He knew what else would come to sicken him—the eyes he saw every time he went down into the slave hold to take out another dead man. There were so many eyes down there staring at him—staring at him with pain and loathing. Their pain made him weep, and their loathing was unbearable.

He rolled out of his hammock and his feet landed on the deck almost without a sound.

He needed help. He needed someone he could tell about his remorse. He needed confession and forgiveness. But who would give it to him?

He had purchased an Igbo woman to sell for his own profit. He brought her up to the main deck close to the same place Nuflo had brought his slave earlier. He wanted her forgiveness. She was one of them—she could speak for all the slaves. She could tell him she understood he didn't want the money anymore—that he only wanted to get them all across the sea to a place where they would be safe.

He went to his knees asking for what only she could give him. He had never spoken sincerely the name of any deity before, but he did now.

"In the name of all that is holy, please woman, help me, forgive me."

He said it again. When there was no response, he stood and spoke again.

The woman only looked at him with the same eyes he saw in

the hold, the same pain, the same loathing. He needed redemption but got only hatred.

"What is wrong with you?" he almost screamed at her. "You must see my contrition?"

Why would she deny me even a little pity?

He seized her shoulders with his calloused hands. He shook her. He had to make her understand. She did not understand. She thought he wanted something else and brought up a knee, trying to catch him in his groin. She missed her target.

"Damn you!" he snarled.

He reached around her, grasping her wrists together behind her back as he pushed her against the line of rope forechains near the rail. He forced his legs against hers to block another attempt to disable him. His anger flashed into another passion.

"Damn you to Hell!" came only as a hoarse whisper.

With his free hand he tore aside the piece of faded cloth she wore around her hips. He loosed his own rope belt and would have taken her quickly, but she clamped her legs tightly together resisting his attack. He pushed her hard against the rope chains, but she would not yield. He raised his hand and struck the side of her head near her ear. Some remnant of sanity stayed the full impact of his blow at the last second, or he might have killed her.

The woman began to fall, but he pushed her back up keeping her standing and forced a knee between her thighs. Her eyes opened and refocused. She was tall for an Igbo, and she looked straight into his face with the same level, unrelenting, unforgiving hate. He thrust himself in her as hard as he could, now determined to hurt her for her indifference to his need. Having received no pity, he gave none.

Her face never changed—her eyes and lips never wavered. Mercifully, for them both, that part of it didn't last long.

After he exploded inside her, he continued to pin her against the ropes using his weight to keep her feet several inches off the deck. He would not let her go. He knew the knotted forechains were cutting into her back and buttocks. He wanted her to feel his power as if that might overcome her hate. He needed something, but he couldn't force it from her. No more words were spoken. No sound came from either of them.

When, at last, he felt his semen running out of her and down his leg, he pulled away from her. He used the cloth that draped her hips to wipe his leg clean. Then he pinned her arms behind her again and took her back down into the hold.

Back on the top deck he slumped to his knees again and began to sob into his hands covering his face. He didn't want anyone to see the monster he knew he had become.

He feared the memory of the slave woman's face would become part of the nightmare that was destroying his soul in this hellish place. He swore never again to debase himself. But even that oath was soon abandoned.

Observing the deterioration and sleeplessness in his First Mate, Captain Davenport gave him a small, brown bottle labeled "Laudanum." The opiate helped him drift into a restless sleep but further ate away his soul.

Late one night he stood at the rail looking at a moonlit sea. So many of the crew were now dead, he had to stand two watches every day. Ordinarily, he would have enjoyed the beauty of the ever-moving reflection of light on the dark water. But the image of men, women and children struggling for any kind of an existence just below his feet denied him any perception of beauty. He felt himself sinking deeper and deeper into the dark.

Sinking. Yes, that's what I'm doing. I'm going deeper and deeper, away from the light, away from...me...what I am, what I was...

Beneath the surface of the dark waters swam the sharks. They were waiting for him. They were waiting for everyone on the *Anne*. He was sure they wouldn't have to wait much longer. He thought what it would be like to jump into the moonlight. It would all be over quickly, quietly. On other voyages he had seen the bodies of men pulled from the ocean where they had drowned. Their faces all bore a serene look as if they were sleeping with a good dream, not like the dark one he could no longer escape. The opium was losing its battle with his nightmares, and he was losing his battle to hold on to reality.

He took a step back and raised his leg putting one foot on the top of the rail.

"Sir!" The sound came from some distance away. "Sir?"

Now the voice was right next to him. He turned and looked

into the face of seaman Richards.

"Sir, it's time to relieve the watch. I'll take it now, sir."

He nodded and went below. He stripped down and pulled himself into his damp hammock...and waited. He had come very close this time. Perhaps another time, soon he hoped, he could put an end to it. The awful dream would come on him now and carry away another piece of his soul.

Before he slept, he heard the slaves through the bulkhead. They were singing. No, not singing—he knew it wasn't singing—they were keening. That's what his mother said mourners did at funerals. He remembered how women moaned like that when his mother died. He wondered if the slaves were singing for their happy dead in heaven, or were they singing for themselves still living here in hell? Or were they keening for him?

The only things that prevented him from going completely insane were the four caged chimpanzees kept in the foremost locker just behind the bow. The chimps would bring high prices as novelties for wealthy Europeans. They were worth even more money than the slaves. The other sailors were afraid of the monkeys, but he seemed to have a special charm for them. They would scream and jump about wildly whenever anyone else entered the locker. But when they saw him, they grew calm and came to the edge of their cages making little mewing sounds, holding their fingers out to him through the bars.

He spoke to them, confessing his terrible guilt and his fears for himself and the others on board this evil ship. The chimpanzees looked at him gravely, their faces like little old men, little old uncles, showing a deep concern for him. When he touched their finger tips with his, warmth spread through him, and he felt momentarily restored. But it didn't last. He went to the forward locker several times each day to be with his "uncles."

He tried to concentrate on the work of running the ship—as if the force of his will could push the ship along faster than the wind. It was his only chance to save himself. He had to reach the Caribbean soon and get away from this ship and her damned business.

•

Near the end of their fifth week at sea a huge storm ravaged the *Anne* for three days. And for three days he was soaked through—from sweat, from rain and from the sea. Try as they might, they could not sail out of its vortex. But the storm broke on its own having proven itself their master.

Broken spars and torn sails littered the upper deck. They would have to put on all new sail. The crew's attention was therefore diverted to that task as the slaves were brought up from the holds for the first time in days. Most were ill from the tossing of the ship and several had broken bones from bouncing about on the hard wooden planks. He should have paid more attention to their condition.

A huge Ashanti man suddenly turned on Scott, the only armed member of the crew set to watch them. In seconds Scott was unconscious on the deck, and the musket was in the Ashanti's hands pointed straight at the hated First Mate—at his own heart.

In the brief moment before he charged the man, he tried to remember if he had warned Scott to load it with dry powder after the rain. The musket failed to discharge. In the commotion following his rush, two slaves were knocked overboard, one dragging the other—their ankles still shackled together. The rest of the crew started pushing the slaves back down the ladder into the hold.

Captain Davenport, having witnessed the last of these events from the bridge, ordered the Ashanti man's ankle unshackled from the other slave beside him. The shackle was then used to secure The Ashanti's wrists together with his arms now stretched around the main mast. A stout line was drawn in a noose around his neck and tied off above him so that he could not slump to the deck.

Captain Davenport ordered the crew to bring the slaves back up on deck. Each man in the crew now had a musket or pistol—all with dry powder.

The captain called Nuflo down from the rigging and, as if by magic, the Portugee produced a whip with several leather lashes, the fabled, "cat 'o nine-tails." Nuflo, enjoying himself immensely, whipped the slave's body until it bled from his ankles to his neck.

Nuflo's final blows were to the man's head bringing the lashes around to tear at his ears and eyes. When Nuflo fell to his knees from exhaustion, he turned to the man on the ship he hated the most. He held out the whip to his First Mate.

The Ashanti was released from the mast and revived with a bucket of seawater. He screamed as the salt spread in his wounds. A longer line was tied to the end of the short noose around his neck and three of the crew looped it over the lowest yard arm several feet away from the mast. They pulled the rope enough to lift the slave's feet free of the deck and tied it off. The offending slave kicked wildly for a few seconds before his body went slack; bloody foam bubbled from his nose and mouth. He was left hanging in the tropic sun for three days until his entire body was covered with a swollen, blackened crust.

And thus, another horror was added to his dreams. It mattered little anymore. One more needless, cruel death piled on a conscience already dragged down to a dark place mattered little.

Nuflo fell grievously ill the evening of the Ashanti slave's death. Perhaps it was brought on by his exertion with the whip.

Captain Davenport was very upset. He called the ship's doctor to where Nuflo lay on the deck shivering under a blanket. Ordinarily, the doctor would not assist a member of the crew. His job was to keep as many of the slaves alive as he could. Live slaves brought money; live crew members brought trouble. Nevertheless, an order from the ship's captain could not be ignored, so he bent to examine the Portugee. After a few moments he drew back and shook his head. Nuflo, he was sure, was about to die and nothing could be done about it. The ship's doctor went back to his important patients.

The captain called his First Mate to the bridge.

"Nuflo," the captain explained, "was to be our agent with the buyers when we reached Barbados. I always left the details of that business to Nuflo because he could talk to them, particularly the Dutch, in their own language. Without Nuflo we can't be sure of a good market. Now, you'll have to take on Nuflo's duties and get what you can for the slaves."

It was more than he could stand. Wasn't it enough that he was bringing these slave people across the ocean? Now he would have to be the instrument of their final disposition as well. He couldn't do it. He could barely get through each day, and he couldn't get through the night at all. Even if he could stand to sell them, how could he negotiate the sale?

He had been careful to hide his inability to read from his captain. He had relied on Harris to work the ship's manifests, but Harris was dead. There was only one thing to do. That evening, just before descending to his hammock and his nightly torture, he stooped and took Nuflo's rough hand in his. The man did not move, but he knew he wasn't dead; he could feel a faint pulse at his wrist. They were alone on deck. He had to break the promise he'd made his mother—there was nothing else to do.

He said the same words he had said at his friend, Thomas' bedside years ago—his father's words. He felt the heat grow in his hand as it had with Thomas. In another moment he dropped Nuflo's hand and went below. The only thing he shared with the slaves was their mutual hatred of Nuflo. And now he might have saved the bastard's life. The next morning Nuflo, to the astonishment of the ship's doctor, was back up to his evil, old ways.

•

He had to admit the Island of Barbados was certainly beautiful. Lush, green vegetation grew all over the undulating countryside. It reminded him of better times in other tropical paradises. The spirits of the Africans were also raised by the sight of this green land. It reminded them of home. But they hadn't seen the laborers in the sugar cane fields, not yet. That would come soon enough.

They sailed into Carlisle Bay with four chimpanzees, a crew now reduced from 16 to nine and 354 living (more or less) negro slaves. Nuflo was over the side and into the skiff almost before the anchor had set. He made for shore even though there was no particular hurry. Fresh water was brought aboard, and the slaves, all of them, were brought up from the holds. Captain Davenport told him that now that they were in this strange territory, there was little fear of a revolt. Double rations of food were given to all and they were encouraged to drink all the water they wanted. This double feeding would be repeated for the next three days.

When Nuflo returned, he brought with him a half-dozen plantation slaves. They moved among the new arrivals, answering questions in their own languages. They were brought out to the ship to calm the fears of the new arrivals, particularly that their new masters might be cannibals. Early on the third day, the slaves were given cups of palm oil and instructed to rub it over their bodies. They glistened with a healthy—albeit false—glow. A short time later the main buyers came aboard.

He watched as each slave was examined thoroughly. Every square inch of skin, inside mouths, ears, genitals, everything was scrutinized carefully. Even their anuses were probed. Observing this, he turned with a quizzical look to the captain standing next to him.

The Captain saw the look on his face but turned away saying, "Some slave captains pack the anuses of slaves suffering dysentery with oakum to prevent the bloody discharge from running down their legs, exposing their illness and making them much less desirable."

The Captain turned back to him. "I, of course, would never do such a thing."

He couldn't be sure, but just after the captain finished speaking, he thought he saw him wink.

Captain Davenport had been, from the first, a mystery to him. Why would a man who was already wealthy beyond any reasonable measure continue to command a slave ship? The answer, he thought, must be that the captain had always been a seaman and thought of himself as nothing more. The fact that his was a slave ship was of little consequence to him. Other than the necessary navigation and operation of the *Anne*, he kept himself away from the real necessities of the trade. He never went into the cargo holds. He never meted out discipline himself. He was almost never present when the slaves were on the upper deck. He bought but would not sell his human chattels—someone else must do that. As the First Mate, he was the captain's open hand—Nuflo was his fist.

The Negroes were divided into three groups. The people in the largest group were those the trader/broker would purchase directly from Captain Davenport. The trader hoped to resell them either on Barbados or on one of the other islands. A few would eventually be sold in the American colonies further to the north. A second group of about thirty were deemed "trash" slaves—those that were too sick or too weak to survive the harsh working conditions on the plantations. The people in the third group were the slaves belonging to the officers of the *Anne*.

He could see his Igbo woman among those in the third group. He had been advised back in Africa to choose Igbo slaves because their agrarian skills would bring a higher price from the Caribbean planters. The woman was staring at him with the same cold dignity he wished he could forget. He later sold her and his other slave for an excellent price, twenty-three pounds each. The trader paid twenty-one pounds each for the 314 "choice" slaves. Captain Davenport was well pleased with the sale. The cost of the goods traded in Africa worked out to just under three pounds per surviving slave—a tidy profit indeed.

The "trash slaves" were loaded in small boats the next day and taken to an open market place several hundred yards on shore. He went along with Scott, Wellsley and Nuflo to supervise the sale.

Another round of examinations by a large group of local residents was followed by an explanation of the terms of the sale delivered by Nuflo at the top of his voice: first in English, then in Dutch, and finally in French. It was to be a "scramble." At the sound of a bell anyone present could purchase any slave they caught and held for two pounds each. The slaves were huddled together with the buyers all around them. The bell sounded and the ensuing riot justified its name. In the end all the slaves were taken.

On the way back to the ship, he asked Nuflo why those people would buy weak and sick slaves.

"Those fools," howled Nuflo, "they will try to heal them and then fatten them enough to sell for household slaves. Bah! Most of them will die anyway. I told the Captain we should just dump them overboard."

That was Nuflo, he thought. He knew he could always count on Nuflo to be Nuflo.

The next few days proved to be as hard as any he had seen. His deteriorating mental condition was affecting his physical strength—and even his sight. He smashed his thumb with a hammer and fell off a ladder, taking a piece of flesh out of his knee. The pain barely penetrated his senses. He had to concentrate as never before to accomplish even simple tasks. But the completion of his work would mean the end of this terrible voyage and the beginning of another—one fit for men of conscience.

The half-decks in the holds had to be ripped out and the whole of the ship's interior hull thoroughly scoured with lye and hot vinegar. The wooden planks from the half-decks were sold ashore. He was told that stout building wood was scarce here and it would probably be used to build casks for the Island's second leading product: rum.

New racks to support their next cargo were prepared. As that cargo came aboard, he tried not to think about where the wood used to build the casks he was handling had come. He never drank another drop of rum in his life.

•

Eleven days later they were ready to lift anchor and sail with the tide; but they missed that tide. Nuflo was not aboard. He was sent ashore to find him. Local inquiries turned up nothing, and he was about to return to the ship when he saw a flat-bed cart pulled by a tired, old horse coming directly toward him. On the cart lay a body. Only a body—the head was missing.

He recognized the dagger still thrust in its belt. It seemed, according to the story he pulled together from those present, that Nuflo had walked about a mile inland where he spotted a comely slave woman working to gather fresh cut sugar cane. As he approached the woman, one of the nearby cutters recognized Nuflo from the ship that had brought him to this misery the year before. The cutter spoke briefly to the woman who then turned to the approaching Nuflo with a welcoming smile. The cutter held a razor-sharp machete.

•

Richard L. Evans

The *Anne* set sail for Virginia in the American colonies. That night the nightmare changed again. The eyes of the slaves were still there, but there was something new. The look of shocked surprise on Nuflo's face almost made the dream bearable.

Chapter Two

TITUS

The *Anne* was stopped by three British warships as she sailed into the mouth of Chesapeake Bay. The British boarding party told them England was preparing for war with "a bunch of rebel fools." The Royal Navy was patrolling the coast boarding and checking ships that might carry vital stores for the rebels. He noted the looks of disgust on the faces of the British naval officers when they realized where the *Anne* had been. By then, he was well beyond shame.

Captain Davenport charted a course north to the fine, deep-water port at Baltimore.

"We must repair the hull in colder water away from the Caribbean," he explained. "In warm waters those bloody little teredo worms bore right through a wooden hull."

The *Anne* had been given a double hull with horsehair packed between two layers of heavy planking. As Mate, it was his job to supervise the replacement of much of the outer hull. He then set the crew to repainting the entire ship with the same black and green colors he had noticed when he first came aboard in Boston—in what now seemed a lifetime ago.

He couldn't work as he once had—his strength giving him pleasure in hard work. That was now impossible. He was sinking deeper into depression and consuming more and more of the opiate syrup, lacing it with whiskey. His cargo of human misery was gone, but no matter, their memory would not leave him. The night before the *Anne* was to sail for England, he failed to return. Two men had followed him as he stumbled out of a tavern. Captain Davenport found him later that night unconscious on the dock. He had been beaten, robbed and left for dead.

He awoke quickly. There had been a sharp cry—a scream, he thought.

He opened his eyes but it was dark: the darkness of night, not the darkness of the hold of a slave ship. He was thankful for that. The sound was not repeated. He tried to sit up but the pain between his eyes put his head back down on...a pillow? He lay still trying to remember why he might be in a bed with a soft pillow and not in a damp hammock.

He began to drift back to sleep when a shaft of bright light fell across his face. A door had opened. There was a low rustling, and then a hand touched his forehead. He reached for the hand and opened his eyes squinting in the light.

The hand remained on his forehead and its owner spoke, cooing softly.

"It's all right, everything's all right, now."

It was a woman's voice.

When he awoke again, he saw the clean light of morning coming through an open window. The light danced off plain white curtains blowing gently inward with a breeze. He looked around the room. Other than the large bed he had slept in, it was furnished like an elegant parlor. He found a slop jar beneath the bed and relieved himself. A mirror hung on a wall above the headboard.

What an odd place for a mirror.

He positioned himself to look into it and was shocked by his appearance. His skin was tanned so deeply it was darker than the color of many of the Negroes he had helped deliver to Barbados.

He had lost weight—a lot of weight—it showed in his face. His mid-section was sunken, and every one of his ribs stuck out. He used water from a pitcher and several towels to help his appearance, but a sour taste remained in his mouth. He wet his hair enough to keep it out of his face then found the clothes he had worn the day before. They had been washed and folded neatly. He dressed and reached for the only door to the room.

Before he could move the latch, it was opened from the other side by a young woman.

"Oh, well, you're up. My name is Margery."

Hers was the same voice he'd heard in the night. She was the prettiest girl he'd ever seen.

She led him out of the bedroom into a wide, double-sided hallway then down a long stairway. At the foot of the stairs he looked up over twelve feet to the floor above.

They entered a large room. It was decorated with paper glued to the walls. The paper was painted with bowls of fruit in a repeating pattern all around the room. The colors were muted in contrast with the bright colors he saw in the large paintings hung on all the walls. The scenes in the paintings were beautiful landscapes of places he didn't recognize: forests and hills of black and gray-green were painted under red, pink and yellow colored skies.

In the center of the room was a huge, highly-polished table. There were a dozen ornately carved chairs around it. He sat as he was told and within minutes was served a meal by Margery and two other young women about her age. No one else was seated with him at the table.

When he asked about that, Margery replied, "It's a little early for us around here."

He could see that the sun was already well up and would have inquired further, but he was hungry, hungrier than he had been in months.

He ate everything: slabs of salt bacon, four or five fried eggs, biscuits with thick, whitish-brown gravy, and a dish he had not tasted before. It looked like oatmeal but tasted like corn. Margery told him it was "grits." He was sure he had misunderstood her, so he asked again.

She said with a little laugh, "You ain't from the South now

are you, darlin'?"

No, he wasn't but the way she said it, he wished he were.

After breakfast, Margery told him, "Miss Lucille wants to see you."

She ushered him into a small room in what he thought must be the back of the house. Margery left immediately. A woman of about forty rose from a chair behind a giant desk facing the door. She introduced herself as Miss Lucille. She was a large woman, not fat, just big. He thought she was pretty. Her hair was dark with just a hint of gray at her temples. She was stylishly dressed in somber colors, dark grays. Every hair on her head was combed perfectly in place. Her eyes never left him. He thought she was judging him—making up her mind about him.

"And this," she said pointing to a man seated behind the door he had just entered, "this is my man slave, Titus."

He turned to the man but stepped back instinctively. The man was short, just over five feet tall with a round, completely bald head. He was almost as wide through his shoulders as he was tall. His arms coming from those massive shoulders were long for his body and thickly muscled. They were easily the size of a man's legs. The man wore a short waistcoat over a clean, white shirt. The hands emerging from his shirt sleeves were huge. All this he saw after his initial shock. The first thing he had noticed about Titus was that he was a Negro.

Titus nodded but said nothing.

Miss Lucille lifted a cloth bag from the floor and placed it on the desk in front of her. He recognized his kit.

"Captain Davenport left this for you," she said. "He also left this."

It was a letter. He recognized his name on the paper. Miss Lucille handed it to him without comment and sat down motioning to him to sit in the only other chair in the room. He unfolded the paper—a page torn from a ship's log. He stared at it helplessly. He could read a sextant, a chart, a log, a tide table, the stars—sometimes he could even read a seaman's heart—but here were lines of words written in script across a page. A tremor shook his hands, and he put the paper down on the desk. When he thought he could, he picked it up again. He started to say something, but stopped when a huge, dark hand gently took the letter from his.

Titus read the letter aloud:

> *My good friend,*
> *You have served me well as my first officer. Indeed, you are as good a seaman as I have ever known. But the humanity you discovered in yourself has left you incapable of further service to me.*
>
> *I am leaving you safe with a dear, old friend. You may find her circumstances somewhat unusual, but she is a fine lady of kindly instincts. I am also leaving in her care your personal belongings and your share of the profits from the Anne.*
> *Fair winds and Godspeed,*
> *Roderick Davenport*

He looked at Titus, surprised. His voice and intonation were those of a well-educated man, not something he thought possible of a Negro.

Miss Lucille produced a heavy, cloth bag, the type that was used on shipboard to hold sand for counterbalance. She turned the bag upside down and emptied its contents on the desk. There were dozens of gold coins. Just two of those coins could support a man for a year.

"He paid you your share of the profits from the *Anne*. I took one of these coins to pay for your keep here for one week."

The price seemed a bit steep to him but he was not in a position to bargain.

"After that," she continued, "you're on your own."

Two hours later, when the "nooners" began to arrive and were taken upstairs by their "regulars," he realized where he was—he was in a whorehouse. "Miss" Lucille wasn't a "miss," she was a "madam."

●

His addiction to opium was total. He could not function without it. But he was in the wrong place for that. It was a firm rule of the house, enforced with no exceptions by Titus: there would be no drugs or spirits on the premises. Miss Lucille ran a respectable business, and drunks, or those only temporarily soused were turned away at the door. Fortunately, Titus was a master of the art of addiction control and withdrawal. Many of the soiled doves who found their way to Miss Lucille's were already afflicted, so Titus was almost constantly purging someone of their devils. Now Titus would have a new patient.

He was moved out of the main house to an outbuilding containing just a few narrow beds. A cold withdrawal would have been impossible for him were it not for Titus's bulk pinning him to the bed each night and holding his head over a vomit bucket for days. He felt as if nails were being driven into every square inch of his flesh. He would have done anything to anyone to get the drug he knew would stop the pain—at least for a while. But he could do nothing; he couldn't even move—not with Titus on top of him.

After a week of drug deprivation he improved enough so that Titus's bulk was no longer needed to keep him down. Then he found himself relying, more and more, on Margery.

He awoke from his nightmare toward the end of that first week to find himself inside her. Her touch had aroused him as he slept. After that she would come to him every night after her shift in the house was over, wiping the sweat from his face and cooing to him softly. Sometimes he would wake from his nightmare to find her holding him, lying in the bed with him. Sometimes she held him gently, comforting him as a mother would her child. Sometimes she held him fiercely, as a passionate lover. Sometimes they made love. He would spend hours with his mind moving back and forth between sleep and a motionless passion. When he moved to ease his position, she moved with him in a strange embrace—a languid dance of love.

He wondered why she came to him. Perhaps she needed to give him the genuine love she dared not give her clients. Titus forced him out of his addiction, but Margery gave him a reason to come back from his insanity. Margery's gift was love: genuine love, the kind of love that is only possible when shared. He knew love for the first time in his thirty-six years.

Margery's unconditional love helped ease the pain he still felt over his unforgivable treatment of the slave woman aboard the *Anne*. He had raped that poor woman, not out of a need for sexual gratification, but out of his need for something else entirely. He wasn't sure, even now, what he expected from the Igbo woman. His unknown need had driven him deeper into a desperate depression. He began to understand what he needed then was what Margery was giving him now.

No one ever forgets his first love. And so it would be with him. And so it would be with her.

After three weeks he felt he could make it through most nights alone. But he was happy that Margery would not have it that way. Titus slept in another room only a few feet from him and on his bad nights he would wake up looking into the concerned faces of two angels: a lovely young woman shunned by most of society, and a man whose race he helped enslave, kill, torture and rape.

He spent those nights in one of eight small beds set up behind the house in what was originally intended to be a barn. Many of the beds were occupied by the girls during their menstrual periods when they were forbidden to work. Strangely, almost all the young women would find themselves "visited by their redheaded cousin" at the same time of the month.

He now rose each morning well enough to move about the house and yard. He was not used to inactivity and began to help with the daily chores where he could. The first job he took on was collecting and emptying the slop jars from the upper rooms. He also did what he could to keep the dining room orderly.

One of his favorite jobs was heating large pots of water for the ladies' baths. Miss Lucille took pride in her merchandise, and each girl in the house was required to bathe at least twice a week.

He gathered and split wood which he placed in a large, iron, cooking stove. The stove was located in another small outbuilding near the old barn that served as their kitchen. Summers in Baltimore were much too hot to have the kitchen with its constantly burning wood stove in the main house. A covered walkway led from the kitchen to the rear door so food could be transported in rainy weather. The "ladies" bathed in one of two very large copper tubs placed in the old barn. He hauled hot water from the kitchen to the tubs.

The girls took delight in displaying their wares for him in what they thought were their most alluring poses. He was often invited to join them in the tubs. But he was taken. Margery had his heart.

Weeks passed and he took on more jobs. In the evenings he stationed himself with Titus on the upper hallway in the main house. Any trouble would be taken care of quickly and as quietly as possible.

Titus liked having the company. Titus also liked giving up most of the cooking chores after teaching his new protégé how to cook for a dozen or more at a time. The last job he took on was one Titus was most happy to give him. He became the house abortionist.

Girls came and went at Miss Lucille's. Most thought, or at least hoped, one of their regulars would marry them and take them away to live like proper women. It happened, but rarely. If a girl stayed on for many years she would eventually age out and have to find other work usually as a laundress, charwoman or cook. She might also die or go mad from a sexually transmitted disease. Most of them just drifted away living by their wits on the street. Others would drift in from the street. One of those was Francie.

Francie found herself beached in Baltimore City by a sea captain who made some extravagant promises which included taking her away from her job in a Charleston brothel. Francie was the kind of girl who might well turn a man's head. She was beautiful and very blonde—a true blonde as she was happy to prove to him during her ablutions at bath time. She was easily the most beautiful girl in the house. He had to admit she was even prettier than Margery. Francie was also firmly fixed on him to be her beau.

His favorite job, which he enjoyed even more than delivering water for bath time, was emptying the slop jars each morning. He simply dumped the contents of the vessels in the muddy ditch along the side of the unpaved road in front of the house. It was not a chore most would care for, but he was always careful to empty the jar in Margery's room last. Some days it might take him more than an hour to find her jar, particularly on those days when he searched for it in her bed—with her there to help him. The only problem he had was getting out of Francie's room first.

She would try to trap him.

Usually, he could sweet talk his way out, but sometimes he had to just toss her aside on her bed. She liked the physical attention, such as it was, much more than his sweet talk. Her screamed comments concerning the beasts in his ancestry followed him down the hall to Margery's room.

Margery always wore a small, gold, Christian cross on a narrow chain around her neck. She never took it off. It was the only thing she ever refused to remove for him.

She taught him the mechanics of sex and sex games. He was amazed at the variations possible with different sexual acts—and the variations on the variations. He had not thought of the uses that could be made of the whole body for sexual gratification. He thought genitalia were all they needed. But Margery knew well how to add to his pleasure; she knew the many places on his body waiting for erotic stimulation; she taught him how to stimulate her body, too. He wondered if the young sailors who first taught him the facts of life knew about all these other things.

He doubted it.

Margery taught him more than the mechanics of sex. She taught him the pleasures of a simple caress, a soft kiss, a whispered endearment. She taught him to do everything with love. Eventually, he learned to love her for more than she could give him and for more than he could ever think to give her.

He had been living in Miss Lucille's for three months when, one day, he laughed. Margery was very put off by his laughter because it came at a particularly climatic moment. So he stopped laughing. But a wonderful thing had happened—it was the first time he had laughed in almost a year. Making love to Margery was a catharsis—her love brought his soul back from madness.

And so one day he told her, "I do love you—so much more than I can say."

Late one morning while they were both catching their breaths in her bed, he asked Margery about Titus' disappearances each week. He noticed that every Sunday morning Titus would go away for hours, usually returning an hour after noon and leaving again for several hours in the early evening. Miss Lucille's did not cater to the trade on Sunday. This rule came from Titus not Miss Lucille. It was difficult enough holding off the threat of the religious community without openly going about the business of sin on the Sabbath.

"Oh, that," she replied, "Titus has his own church where he preaches every Sunday morning and then he goes back for Sunday school at night. It's a negro church about two miles west of here. I asked him if I could go with him once. He said he thought I'd make his flock nervous. I guess I would be the only white woman who could go and not have my reputation suffer. Hell, I'm already a whore."

She thought for a moment.

"I'm a whore to everyone but you. With you I'm a real person. I'm just another girl with her lover. I know when you touch me, you're touching more than my body; you're touching all the rest of me—whatever you call it—my soul. No one has ever done that for me. No matter what happens to us, I'll always be with you."

Most mornings, long before it was time to empty slop jars, Titus would shake him awake and motion for him to follow. He would shiver in the early morning chill, moving over a grassy area to the small, flat-bottomed boat Titus kept tied up to a tiny pier a hundred yards or so from Miss Lucille's place. One of them sat in the boat while the other heaved it from the pier and then jumped in at the last moment to keep its momentum. They wouldn't go far. They didn't have to. The shore dropped off steeply, and deep water was only a few yards out. If the wind was right, they could catch a half-dozen striped bass—called "rockfish" by the locals.

On those mornings when the fish weren't biting, they went crabbing. The fabled Chesapeake blue crab was a delicacy greatly appreciated by watermen, slaves, and prostitutes alike. Titus taught him to pick up the crabs from the rear so they could not use their terrible claws to pinch his hand or fingers.

He failed his first lesson. He gripped a crab exactly as Titus had shown him, but another crab in the box took a firm grip on the soft tissue between his thumb and forefinger. Titus roared with laughter at his pain. He had to break off the crab's claw to remove it. He bled for ten minutes.

During some of their crabbing expeditions, he noticed Titus remove certain crabs brought up with their fish bait and put them in a cage-like structure tied to his little pier. The cage was made of heavy wire and measured about two feet wide by eight feet long. It was tied to the pier with a line long enough to allow it to rise and fall with the tide, so it "floated" just below the water line. He wondered about those crabs for weeks before he was offered the absolute worse looking but best tasting dish of his life.

The crabs Titus placed in his cage were "peelers." Titus held up one for his inspection, placing the crab flat on his upturned palm. This would be a dangerous way to handle a crab at any other time of its life, but this peeler was helpless, its body completely flaccid. He touched the back of the soft crab, and it felt like a piece of paper. Titus explained that from time to time blue crabs would outgrow their shells. The shell would split and fall away with a whole new version of the crab emerging. Titus fried his soft shells to a golden yellow-brown. Everything was eaten: body, fins and claws. After Titus's fried soft shell crabs, nothing would ever taste as good.

Titus also raised vegetables on a garden plot Miss Lucille owned a few blocks back from the waterfront.

His early days on the farm with his mother had convinced him that farming was the last thing he wanted to do. He liked to help eat it, but he was sure he wasn't going to help raise it. He watched Titus as he spent many an afternoon bent over in his garden, sweat dripping from his chin as he hummed contentedly.

•

He and Titus were resting in the boat. They had caught enough fish to last two days at Miss Lucille's table. They were just drifting with the current enjoying an idyllic, early spring morning.

He was squinting up at some high, puffy clouds when Titus said, "Do you remember that first day in Miss Lucille's office? You couldn't read the letter written by your captain, could you?

How much schooling have you had?"

"I grew up on a farm. There wasn't time for schooling. But I can read a little. Names and numbers and such."

"A man should know how to read," Titus replied. "I'll teach you. We'll start tonight."

Lessons began after supper. They sat on his bed in the old barn. They had an hour or two before the evening customers began arriving, Titus lifted the lid of a secure metal box and removed his most precious possession, his Bible. Its cover was leather and had once been red but was now a muddy dark orange. Age and use had removed most of the gold leafing on the edges of the pages. Titus opened it with care—with reverence.

He came to love the bible stories, particularly those in the first part of the book called the Old Testament. He had seen more of the world than most men of his day could ever hope to see. Yet, he had not thought about how the world he knew had come to be as it was. He was fascinated by the miracles described all through the Bible. He was most attentive to the stories of Jesus healing the insane, the lame, the blind and particularly, the sick. Could any of this be about him? He had met no one else who could heal sickness with just the touch of his hand. Jesus had done it and so could he.

"Jesus," Titus told him, "was the Son of God."

That would explain how Jesus could do it. But what could explain his power to heal? Titus's Bible gave him no answer.

He was also beginning to feel strange about his age. Counting back the years, he judged he must now be about forty. Other men his age seemed older. He looked and felt as young as he had twenty years ago. The stories in the Bible about Abraham and Moses and Noah spoke of men living for hundreds of years. Was he like them—made to live on by God for some purpose? Was he part of some divine plan? He didn't think so—not after the evil things he had done on the *Anne*.

The concept of evil had not come into focus for him until his sessions with Titus. It was now clear that he was capable of doing things that were surely against the will of God. Titus believed what the Bible said about all men sharing the sins of the first people—the people in the very first book, Genesis. He also asked

Titus about the sins of adultery and prostitution. After all, Titus was largely responsible for the daily operation of Miss Lucille's house.

Titus said, "Our Lord Jesus came to save all of us, both slaves and freemen. Do you remember the story of Jesus' birth? Do you remember the part about the angels coming to earth to tell people that a savior had been born in Bethlehem? Do you remember who they told first?"

Titus was quick to answer his own question. "The angels came from heaven to tell poor shepherds abiding in the fields, that's who. Shepherds! Not the Roman Emperor or the King of Israel or the Pharisees or generals or senators or any other powerful people. They came to shepherds—poor working people—some of them were even slaves. And Jesus lived with sinners. Tax collectors were despised by all the Israelites who had to pay taxes to the Romans. They were hated by all the so called, good people, of Jesus' day. But Jesus took one of those tax collectors, Matthew, and made him a disciple. He saved Mary Magdalene, a harlot, and she was the first one to see the risen Lord after he was resurrected from the grave. My Jesus made himself a servant to those sinners, and I take comfort from that."

Titus stopped talking, but it was obvious he wasn't through. He squinted, seeming to look at a distant thought, working out what he wanted to say.

"Now let me say something else to you," he spoke again. "You told me about your sins on the slave ship, that you're sorry for them. Yet even now you fornicate with Margery, and she with you. She is not your wife and you are not her husband, so your union is not sanctified by God. But our Lord Jesus also told us we have to 'love one another.' I know what you and Margery do is done in love, not like the other things done in this place. So I've said nothing about it. My judgment doesn't matter. God will judge us all at the end."

Titus paused again, considering his next thought.

"One more thing you should know: I never pray for God's help—I pray only for God to lead me. If I just ask God to 'help me' then it would be to do what I think is right, not what God knows is right. You just pray to God to show you His way and you will be set right. God will show you what to do if you ask to be led to it.

"You are not like any man I have known," Titus went on. "I believe God has a special plan for you—God means to use you for something important. I felt God's hand on my shoulder in Miss Lucille's office that first day you came here. God wanted me to help you.

"Do you remember the stories about Jacob? Jacob was not a good man. He did bad things, too. He lied and he used other people to get what he wanted. He even had to run from his own home to escape the wrath of his brother. But even so, God chose Jacob for something important—to lead God's people. God saw something in Jacob that even Jacob didn't see himself. But before God blessed Jacob, God wrestled with him. God wrestled Jacob and he even hurt Jacob's hip. But Jacob would not let God go; he would not give up, and when he asked God to bless him, God did it. I think you must wrestle with God, too. And when you do, you mustn't give up. You mustn't give up on God. Do you understand?"

No, he didn't understand. But Titus' could see he was already struggling with God. His wrestling with God had begun on the slave ship. Neither man had any idea how long his struggle would last—or how God might finally bless him.

Days later, after another long talk about his guilt and his nightmares, Titus told him, "God has already forgiven you. Jesus took on your sins and died so that your sins would die with him. You have been forgiven. Now, you must forgive yourself."

Then Titus repeated his words slowly, putting spaces between them: "You must...forgive...yourself."

Those words from Titus, his dear friend and great teacher, would stay with him forever.

During his evening lessons he tried to pull Titus's life story from him. It wasn't easy. But, over time, he was able to put much of it together. Titus was born on a plantation in Carolina far to the south. It must have been a big operation on the Tar River.

Titus told him, "My mistress schooled all the children on the place—her own son, a neighbor's child and four of us plantation slaves.

"I loved my mistress—she was all the mother I ever knew. My birth mother was sold away just after I was born. But my master, my mistress's husband, now he was different. He did not approve of his wife teaching 'little Nigras' to read.

"That was the first time I heard that I was a Nigra. I remember.

"When I was twelve my mistress died in childbirth, and my master sold me the next day to another farmer up in Virginia. That man set me to work keeping accounts, but then he decided there was not enough work to keep me busy in the house. He put me out in the cotton fields with the other hands. It only took one lash of the overseer's whip to convince me I didn't need to work out there. So I ran away. I was caught just outside Baltimore where Miss Lucille bought me for my bounty price.

"That was before Miss Margery was born."

Seeing the question in his eyes, Titus continued, "You did know that Miss Lucille is Margery's mother?"

No, he did not, not until that moment.

He discovered another of Miss Lucille's best-kept secrets, too. Titus was not at his accustomed post on the upper floor of the house one evening but arrived well after dark with a group of five Negroes. The Negroes were put to bed in the spare beds set up in the old barn. They stayed in the barn for two days, never coming out. Titus fed them himself, and no one else was allowed in the barn. Then they were gone in the night—led away by another Negro he had never seen before.

Nothing was said by anyone about this. A week later, it happened again. It continued to happen at odd intervals the entire time he stayed at Miss Lucille's. He wasn't unusually bright, he knew, but he wasn't stupid either. Titus and Miss Lucille were helping runaway slaves escape to friendlier places, probably in the North. If no one was going to say anything, he didn't see why he should say anything either.

The days passed in a sweet harmony of useful work and learning and love. Each morning, Margery used his body teaching him how a woman should be "handled." Each evening, Titus used his mind teaching him his ABC's and the history, poetry, and glorious lessons of the Holy Bible. Margery taught him to love. Titus taught him to love God.

Then the sickness came.

One of the girls came down with what everyone thought was just a bad cold. But in four days she was dead, her lungs filled with fluid. Shortly after that, almost everyone else fell ill. Everyone, that is, except Miss Lucille who had lived through an influenza epidemic as a young girl, and Titus, and him. It appeared that most would recover but Margery did not get better. Nothing Miss Lucille or Titus did for her worked.

He was afraid.

He remembered the fate suffered by the last person he had tried to save. But he was losing his Margery.

The evening of the fifth day of her sickness he waited until they were alone. She was still burning with fever and didn't know he was there. He could not allow the woman he loved more than life itself to die without trying to save her. He took her hands in his and said the words he hoped would heal her.

He left her and went to his own bed and fell to his knees asking God's mercy and the life of Margery. He would regret those prayers.

The next morning Margery had recovered completely. It was thought a miracle.

•

There was a lot of talk about war with England. Most of their information came from the girls who got it from their customers. Miss Lucille, still in the profession though less active now, had one particular "friend" who came to her quite regularly—several times each month. Like some others, the fellow was not interested in the usual exchange but merely wanted to talk to someone who would listen to him. His wife thought him a fool and dismissed anything he said as nonsense.

Miss Lucille had perfected all the tools of her trade, especially the most important one, that of being a good listener. This man came to her only for her ears. The news seemed to point decidedly in favor of war. Miss Lucille was delighted at the prospect. Her business was well-positioned to profit from large numbers of men sent to places far away from home (and wives).

Late one evening in early June, a British naval officer arrived at Miss Lucille's. The officer spied the beautiful Francie and soon climbed the stairs behind her. Titus watched him closely but let him pass. He didn't seem to be drunk. Minutes later a scream came from Francie's room. Both he and Titus rushed down the hall, but he was closer and so was the first to burst through her door.

The officer had one hand on Francie's throat and was using the other to beat her with a closed fist. Dropping Francie, the officer turned quickly to the dresser behind him, snatched up a pistol, and aimed it at his heart. The pistol failed to fire as he charged the man. He saw the officer swing the pistol wildly. It struck him in the left temple, knocking him on top of Francie who was still on the bed. He was only stunned.

He forced himself up from the blackness crowding his mind just in time to see the officer cock the pistol and pull the trigger again. This time it fired. He heard two loud explosions: the first was the pistol shot; the second the sound of the officer crashing backward into a chest of drawers. The officer struggled to rise from the floor, the pistol still in his hand. Titus lay motionless across the officer's legs, blood already spreading across the floor. The officer was cocking the pistol again.

Fed by a murderous rage, he leaped on top of the officer closing his fingers around the man's throat and jamming his thumbs into the officer's windpipe. He held him, crushing his voice box, until there was no more movement beneath him.

Several candles had been knocked over, but he could still see that blood was everywhere. Some of it was dripping off his chin, flowing down from the gash the pistol had opened high on the side of his head. But there was much more blood than could come from his single wound.

Titus still lay unmoving on top of the officer's legs. There was a lot of blood beneath his body. The officer had re-cocked his pistol and fired just as a second man charged through the door. Titus had launched himself at the man but was probably already dead when he smashed into the officer driving him back against the chest.

Titus was shot through the heart.

He fell back in horror. Francie was screaming hysterically.

The shot had caused the other customers to suddenly remember their wives and sweethearts. All the other rooms were emptied of gentlemen callers in less than two minutes.

Miss Lucille arrived, sized up the situation, realized a cool head was needed and took over.

"Trudy! Agnes! Kit! Get in here!"

Miss Lucille was shouting orders even as she used a pillow case to bind up the wound still dripping blood from his head.

When the frightened girls arrived, she said, "You three and Francie wrap poor Titus in that small rug by the door and drag it down the stairs and out to the old barn. Move now, quickly!"

There was no room for any rebuttal in her voice. Francie, still sniveling and coughing, complied. Margery also arrived with several others, and they and Miss Lucille helped him carry the dead officer to the back yard. Miss Lucille and the rest of the girls went back in to clean up Francie's room.

He found the barrow he and Titus had used to bring vegetables from the garden. He tried not to think about Titus. He loaded the body of the officer in the barrow and pushed it to the little pier where Titus's boat was tied.

He returned to the house and loaded the barrow with a strong fishing net and three large stones from around the outdoor fire place. Returning to the boat, he placed the officer's body in the net and loaded everything in the boat. Rowing slowly and as quietly as he could, he moved well out from shore. There was a deep hole about fifty yards out. He tried to find the landmarks he had learned to use as reference points during the day. It took some time, but the dark was his friend tonight. He rolled the body over the side of the boat tying the fishing net to the side fore and aft. Then he placed the three stones in the net hoping the weight would not pull the boat over on its side. He closed the net, tied it off and released the lines holding it to the boat. It disappeared in the cool, brackish water of the Chesapeake Bay. For months afterward the local watermen commented on how unusually sweet the crabs tasted that year.

He used the barrow to take Titus' body to the garden. There

was a small stand of trees in the far corner where he buried him under their spreading branches, still wrapped in the rug.

Exhausted both physically and emotionally, he collapsed and slept on top of the grave until the sun was well up and other gardeners had begun to tend crops near by.

Returning to Miss Lucille's, he bathed himself quickly in cold water, changed his clothes, gathered his kit and went to say his good-byes. He knew when the dead officer failed to return to his ship, they would come looking for him. He was sure someone would remember seeing him go into Miss Lucille's. He couldn't stay. He would be a threat to Margery, Miss Lucille and the girls. And his neck would surely find a noose hanging from a Royal Navy yard arm.

No one said much.

The weight of Titus's loss was too heavy. Margery gave him the small, gold cross that hung on the thin, gold chain around her neck. She kissed him quickly and ran away in tears. Miss Lucille gave him his bag of gold coins. He took out just two of them and gave it back asking her to use it for a headstone for Titus' grave and to help the runaway slaves. She also gave him Titus' Bible. She handled it just as Titus had, with great reverence.

In another minute he was gone.

It took three days for the British to trace the officer to Miss Lucille's. They searched all the rooms in the main house and all the out buildings but could find no evidence to suggest foul play. No one knew anything about it. No one except Francie who panicked at the first sight of her inquisitor's uniform. She told him everything and even gave him the name and a description of the man she had seen strangle the officer. After the Navy officers left, Margery threw Francie into the street.

Two days later, as Margery was taking her usual bath, Francie and two of her new friends crept up behind her. Her friends held Margery while Francie slit her throat.

•

That same night he reached the border separating Maryland from Pennsylvania. He found a dry area under a low bridge where he could sleep. His nightmare returned. A new face was there with the others—a face he loved dearly. He knew she was dead. The wound at his temple was healing rapidly, but the hole in his heart would never heal.

Chapter Three

PATRIOT

He avoided large towns. At night he lay hidden under bridges or in groves of trees. He crossed from Pennsylvania into New Jersey and chanced stopping late that night in a place called Trent Town. He walked carefully through the streets looking at posts and trees to see if a wanted bill had been printed seeking his capture. Finding none, he took a room over a tavern, then sat drinking a few ales with the tavern's other customers. He noticed most of the other men in the room were drinking rum. His stomach turned at the thought.

All the talk was about "the rebellion." It was loud and disputatious. A man holding a beer stein came to his table.

"Mind if I sit here a spell, young feller?"

"No, not all," he said.

As the man set his stein down on the table, he noticed his hands were discolored with reddish brown and black stains.

The man saw him looking at his hands and laughed softly saying, "I'm a cobbler by trade. Can't ever seem to get the dye off these hands. What happened to yer head there, young feller?"

He told him he had slipped down in the street. The cobbler gave him a knowing laugh.

"Everybody living in town knows to watch yer step. Now that it's summer, we have to hold our noses, too."

The man laughed again and said, "I've not seen you here before. You passing through?"

"Yes," he replied, "I'm a seaman on my way back to my ship."

"What ship would that be, young feller?"

"The *Anne*, out of London."

"And where will you catch her? New York?"

"No, I'm on my way to Boston."

"Boston! Well, you be careful going thataway. There's trouble aplenty up there."

The cobbler rose and moved to another table. The cobbler sat with his back to him, but it was obvious the cobbler was reporting what he had learned. Glances came his way as the cobbler spoke.

Yes, it's important in these times to know who is in the room when you speak your mind.

As more rum was consumed, loud voices were raised all around him. There was a lot of rancor between the Tories who supported the colonial government and the rebels who wished for greater autonomy from the English king. Some were even called "revolutionists." They were also called scoundrels and traitors. Other words, too, flew all around him. He heard words like, dog and swine and idiot, and saw raised fists above faces red with anger.

Several times he made ready to jump out of the way of a fight. He didn't understand why the rebels wanted to break away from English rule. Surely, they didn't believe they could oppose the power of the mighty British Army. He knew nothing of the high taxes or other deprivations those who favored the rebel side said were so burdensome. But among them, only the most vigorous of the "insane rebels" wanted a wider war. But a wider war had already begun—and it was raging exactly where he was going. The safest place for him, if he was to escape the British hangman, was with those insane rebels surrounding Boston.

Summer was almost gone before he reached the approaches to Boston. He found a half-dozen, rough-looking men guarding the road. They called themselves, militiamen.

When they learned he was looking for a ship, one of them said, "He must be one of Glover's boys. Take him over to the Colonel's regiment."

"Who?" he asked.

"Colonel John Glover," repeated his guide. "He's the commander of a regiment of fishermen from up around Marblehead, on up the coast. Ain't you from there?"

"Close enough," he said.

The company of other watermen sounded good to him. He had no taste for their cause, but he had even less taste for what the Royal Navy had in mind.

Colonel Glover was not at his headquarters. He was met instead by a burly Lieutenant who said his name was Grim.

Here was a man whose physical presence matched his name.

Grim had steely gray eyes set deep in a face made of skin the color and texture of brown boot leather. He wore a dark blue pea coat and baggy, white trousers that ended just below his knees. A brimless, brilliant red sack cap was set squarely on his head.

Grim looked him over with a look that suggested he might be having trouble digesting his lunch. The Lieutenant was a man of almost no words. When asked, he gave Grim the names of the ships he had served from his boyhood—including the *Anne*. His answers to a short quiz on marine navigation must have satisfied Grim because the Lieutenant grimaced and nodded "yes." He was in. Not with great fanfare or enthusiasm but "in."

Exactly what he was "in" worried him.

He didn't expect to be welcomed by the other men in Glover's regiment and he wasn't. He'd heard of Marblehead. He knew what mattered to people along the coast, too. Marblehead was a small fishing village a little north and east of Boston. The two places were close enough in distance, but in outlook and character they might just as well have been on opposite sides of the Earth. He wasn't from Boston, but that didn't matter. What mattered was that he wasn't from Marblehead.

His new shipmates spoke even less than Grim. This wasn't done as a discourtesy; they just didn't speak much at all. Their humor was droll, and he suspected they were another "oil for the starboard lamp" bunch. He had served on shipboard with other men like them: men who were hardened in body and spirit by the harsh conditions they faced every day of their lives. He had been glad to have them on his crews—he knew he could count on them to be as stern in the face of adversity as they were with him.

They all wore close variations of the uniform Lieutenant Grim wore except that most of them were shoeless. He was soon outfitted in like manner—for a price. When asked his name for the enrollment, he lied. It would be better if his true identity was not recorded should he ever be captured by the British. It was the first time he used an alias. There would be no turning back.

He had been in camp only a little over a month, still waiting for action when a small group of fresh troops arrived, backwoodsmen from Virginia. They carried the long, thin rifles earlier contingents of frontiersmen had used to demonstrate their amazing skills as marksmen. They wore leather shirts, moccasins and leggings, all trimmed with fringes made of deerskin. Most wore feathers stuck in their broad-brimmed hats.

The Marblehead Regiment seeing this group of gaudily-dressed men began to hoot and shout schoolboy insults at them.

It was still September, but a light snow had fallen the day before and had begun to melt. Soon snowballs were flying from both sides. As they usually do, one thing led to another and soon there were skirmishes between leather clad men and men in floppy, white trousers with dark blue coats. He felt obliged to join the fracas out of a desire to prove himself to his new shipmates. He ran forward toward a lanky Virginian. The man might have been tall and skinny, but he was very strong.

They had only started to grapple when he felt a hand grip the back of his collar, and he was thrown backward to the ground. When he looked up, he saw the Virginian was also on his backside. The other man was not looking at him but at a large figure wading through the throng of struggling men, throwing them aside as easily as he had the two of them.

From behind him someone said in a hushed voice, "That's General Washington!"

As the General strode through the skirmishers, it reminded him of a drawing he had seen of Moses parting the waters of the Red Sea. He remembered Titus reading his Bible in the candlelight and how excited he got when he came to the story of thousands of slaves being led from bondage. The melee broke up quickly. The General strode back past him, mounted a dappled gray horse, wheeled around and rode away, never once looking back.

He got to his feet and looked at the man he had tried to wrestle to the ground.

The other man smiled in a wide almost toothless grin and said, "'Name's Homer Davis, what's yours?"

He answered in kind, giving Homer his new name. He said, "I've seen other men with rifles like yours. I'd like to try one some time."

The Virginian smiled again and said, "Meet me here tomorrow and you can try mine."

Homer Davis, like the other long-riflemen, was a crack shot. The next day, a dead leaf no bigger than a man's thumb was stuck to a tree trunk more than a hundred yards distant. Homer cut the target in two with one shot. The Virginian then held the rifle out to him.

"Go on, take it," Homer said.

He did.

"Now," Homer began giving instructions, "hold out yer hand. This is how you load her up," he explained as he poured a measure of black powder in his own hand before transferring it to his pupil's open palm. "Down the barrel, that's it. Good. Now take a patch and wrap the ball. The wadding'll make her tight. That goes down next. Then ram it in good with the rod."

He did as he was instructed.

Homer then demonstrated how to set his feet for a good firing foundation.

Then he said, "Now you jus' got to prime her and yer all set. Sight down the barrel and center the target. Aim a little high cause the ball'll drop a bit at this distance. You got that?"

He did.

"Oh, yeah, I almost forgot; you got to take in and then blow out yer breath real slow and easy like while yer squeezn' on the trigger. Don't pull it; jes' squeeze her off. You got that?"

He did.

"Okay. You see what's left of that leaf on the tree, yonder?"

He did.

"Take yer shot, then." Homer stepped back.

The double explosions of both prime and powder caused him to lose sight of his target for a moment. When he looked again, he saw that a good portion of the lower part of the leaf was gone. Homer Davis and a handful of his friends standing by pounded him on the back and declared he must be a natural and would be welcomed in their company any time he could get away from those sailor boys from up North.

Two days later he was assigned to a vessel optimistically called a ship. It wasn't much bigger than a fishing boat. It had been commandeered by Colonel Glover along with two dozen others like it. He was going to war.

Lieutenant Grim told him, "We're going to stop things coming into Boston by sea. We're now privateers."

It was a long speech for Grim.

Three weeks later they took their larger fishing boats loaded with men and supplies to Manhattan Island in New York. The siege of Boston was over.

He hoped the next battle would be as easy.

•

He was just rolling the last barrel of powder up a loading plank when a man high up on the dock shouted and pointed behind him. A large fleet was sailing in—all British ships. He saw what must have been a 64-gunner coming in with more than 150 other ships. They were followed by still another hundred ships, all loaded with redcoats.

"They'll be Hessians with them, too."

Lieutenant Grim was also eying the fleet and looked even grimmer than usual if that were possible.

The waving masts and yard arms of the Royal Navy anchored in the harbor reminded him of the glorious sight he had witnessed at Howland Great Dock aboard the *Anne*. But this fleet had better than ten times the waving timber he had seen in London. The moving forest created by the British ships obscured the countryside behind them. He had a very uneasy feeling that he was in the wrong place at the wrong time.

Days later he and his shipmates thought they were finished ferrying men and supplies across the East River from Manhattan. The Continental Army was going to defend the city from a ground attack. They were resting in their fishing boats on the east bank of the river when the unmistakable sounds of cannon and mortars came to them from the south and east.

The fight had begun.

Nothing seemed to change on the battle lines for several hours. Then men started rushing to the landing docks in disorganized groups of two or three. Then it got worse; they came sixty or seventy at a time. Some were almost completely covered with mud and grass. Some were wounded. Lieutenant Grim started shouting, and his crew began rowing the ragtag army back across the East River to Manhattan. It didn't take a genius to figure out that the British forces were driving the whole army back to the river in a panicked retreat.

Back and forth he rowed, returning the demoralized Americans and their equipment across the river until a heavy downpour shortly after dusk forced them to lay up for a few hours. Just after midnight the skies cleared, and they were again in action. Everyone in his boat kept a sharp eye peeled to the south where they knew the Royal Navy waited. They couldn't understand why the British didn't sail up the river into them. Only a few of those terrible gun ships, sailing among them, would doom both them and the retreat. But the British seemed content to stay where they were.

They worked the river all night. Just at dawn a thick fog rolled in covering them from the gunfire of the first British troops to arrive on the Brooklyn shore. The Marbleheaders had just loaded the last of their men trapped against the river before disappearing into the mist.

The magnitude of the disaster was obvious to everyone on the rebel side. Men lay scattered about in bunches. They were dirty, disorganized, dispirited and exhausted. But not the Marblehead men who sat together in small groups around open fires.

He felt the muscles in his legs, arms and back ache from the exertion of the last twelve hours. He had done well. The entire Regiment had done well. He saw Colonel Glover moving among his men patting their backs and shaking their hands. The Colonel seemed to single out the older men for his greatest praise. He thought he understood. As sore and as tired as he was, the men who were in their forties, fifties and even their sixties must be in even more pain by now. He hadn't given any real thought to his own age. That he was fast approaching forty meant little to him. He still felt like a man of twenty-five.

No one near him said much. It seemed to him that his shipmates must be even too tired to give him their usual glowering looks. He had started to relax a bit when Lieutenant Grim stepped into his group. Grim moved among the men, shaking hands and congratulating them for their success just as the Colonel had done among the other groups. Then Grim looked directly at him and did something he thought he would never live to see: Lieutenant Grim smiled.

He was afraid for a moment that the creases the smile caused in the Lieutenant's face would dislodge large chunks of his leathery skin, and they would fall off. The smile didn't last long—just long enough for Grim to be sure he saw it. The man sitting to his right touched his arm and handed him a spoon and a bowl of hot soup. The man sitting on his left tapped his shoulder lightly. He, too, had been congratulated. No military decoration could equal the honor he had just received.

The warmth of the soup coupled with the warmth he felt in the company of these brave men spread through him. As he spooned the soup into his mouth, he was sure it was the best tasting thing he had ever eaten. Then he remembered Titus and his fried soft-shelled crabs. He stood quickly, turned and stepped away from the others. He didn't want them to see the tears in his eyes.

Within a week the Regiment was moving again. Colonel

Glover ordered his boats up the Hudson to escape the trap posed by the British fleet. He was issued a rifle, powder, packing and shot. He went with Lieutenant Grim and about 150 men marching eastward, crossing the Bronx River to help protect the "back door" for the Americans' retreat from Manhattan. They were still moving east when they ran into an advance unit of Howe's Army.

The British had decided to come in that back door.

He crouched behind a low stone wall and tried to remember what Homer Davis, the Virginia sharpshooter, had told him about marksmanship. He steadied himself in a comfortable position ,making a good solid firing base by kneeling on his right knee and steadying the rifle with his left elbow on his left knee. He brought the rifle up and sighted, took a deep breath, released it slowly and told himself to "squeeze, don't pull," the trigger.

Other rifles were being discharged around and in front of him. He wouldn't have noticed his shot was away had it not been for the recoil. He glanced in the direction he had aimed and saw a green clad soldier falling off on his side.

He reloaded as fast as he could, saying the steps aloud: "Tear the cartridge with your teeth; put powder charge down the barrel; put in packing and ball; ram it home with the rod; level rifle and then prime pan with fine powder; finally, cock and aim."

With practice he was able to fire his rifle three times each minute. He sighted down the barrel, breathed, released his breath and squeezed off another shot. Another green coat went down. He was loading again when he heard Lieutenant Grim growling somewhere behind him to fall back. For the next hour he ran from stone walls to trees and back to stone walls always falling back but taking a terrible toll on the British regulars. He ran out of green coats and started dropping red coats. He knew, of course, there were men wearing those coats, but he didn't think about it—not until many hours later. He was just doing his job like rowing a boat or carrying out slops.

The Marbleheaders had to transport a few boats as best they could over rough roads often just dragging them along. They were running ahead of the advancing British forces—running south to who-knew-where. At one spot a high place in the road caused his crew to strain, trying to force their boat over the hump. They all stopped to rest.

He said to no one in particular, "What's the big hurry? Let's just leave this here until tomorrow and try it again."

Lieutenant Grim came around the side of the boat. "You want to stay here?" Grim said to him.

It didn't sound like a question.

"A week ago the British were a week behind us. Today, they're two days behind us. Why don't you just stay here and wait for them. When they get here, you can try talking them to death."

The boat was over the hump in less than a minute.

He learned from the other men that Lieutenant Fredrick Grim had fought in the war with the French and Indians. That was why he was their officer. He never heard any of the men speak to the Lieutenant using his given name. No one dared. Grim was tough but fair—the perfect definition of a good leader. Nobody liked him, but they all respected him, and that respect saved their lives more than once.

Reaching the Delaware River, just up stream from Trent Town, they foraged for all the boats they could find to move what was left of the American Army into Pennsylvania. For some reason that no one on the American side could understand, the British didn't follow.

•

In mid-December it seemed to him that the American experiment in revolution must soon end, perhaps along with his escape from the gallows of the Royal Navy. He had read a tract called *Common Sense* circulated in the American camps beginning back in Boston. He saw its author moving with the troops along the march from New York. A captain from one of the Connecticut infantry regiments pointed him out.

Thomas Paine didn't look like much of a solider—small and slender of build—but the captain said he was probably the most valuable warrior they had. His pen was, indeed, mightier than any sword.

But how mighty a weapon would be needed to save this ragged army?

For the next week he and the other Marbleheaders were put to work "collecting," sometimes by force, a number of specialized boats built for the river trade. They were called Durhams—large, flat-bottomed boats between forty and sixty feet long. To pole the boat, he stood at the bow, set one end of a twenty foot pole on the river bottom, and moving along a narrow walkway built over each gunwale, he walked back the entire length of the boat, pushing the boat forward by pushing the pole backward. He then lifted the pole from the water, walked back to the bow and repeated his steps. One misstep and he would be swimming in near freezing water.

On Christmas Day, December, 25, 1776, he was ordered to standby his boat. Maybe, he thought, someone had come to their senses and they would be allowed to escape down the river and go home. Exactly where that would leave him, he didn't know.

Shortly after nightfall men and arms began arriving to be loaded on the boats. It looked like his wishes were about to come true. But that sweet, little daydream came to an abrupt end when the order was given to pole the troops across the river.

Across the river? That's where the enemy was!

Across the river he went—many times that night. It was cold—very, very cold. Ice floes in the river were continual hazards. Cannon and horses were loaded and moved over the water. He saw men marching to the boats with no shoes. Some had wrapped rags around their feet, but many walked over the frozen ground with bare feet. But they moved on. Silently they came, their breath forming little clouds of steam in the air as they moved.

Who were these men to give themselves for what was surely a lost cause?

He couldn't understand them.

He had just landed back on the Pennsylvania side of the river for one last load when he saw a tall figure he recognized from the siege at Boston step into another nearby boat. It had to be General Washington. Another officer stepped in the boat behind the General. That officer was hugely fat, and when he sat near the stern of the boat, it lurched dangerously to one side.

He was sure he heard the General shout to the officer, "Don't swing your balls, Knox, or you'll swamp the boat."

He could hear a dozen, half-suppressed guffaws from all around. It helped him regain some of his enthusiasm for poling through the ice and fog one more time. When his last load was ashore on the New Jersey side, he helped the rest of the crew beach the boat. The Marblehead fishermen needed rest, but that was not to be. They moved along a road close to the river with troops commanded by General Sullivan. The cold winds cut through everyone like knives. They had five more miles to cover that night.

Their orders, given during the march and passed along from man to man, were to march past Trent Town on the river side and secure a bridge across a creek just south of the town. If the Hessian troops tried to escape the main attack, they would have to cross at that point. The sun was well up by the time they got to the bridge.

In just moments he heard gunfire coming from north and east of the city. Sullivan's troops split, moving up both sides of the creek. He recognized the town as one where he had stopped on his way to Boston more than a year ago. He wondered if the cobbler was still supporting the English king.

It wasn't long before the defenders of the bridge came under fire from what appeared to be a disorganized group of blue-clad Hessians running at them. The fight was on—but not for long. The Hessians fell back, running eastward right into General Sullivan's trap. Part of the army under General Washington and General Greene had attacked from the other side of the town, surprising and trapping the enemy.

The battle at Trent Town was over in less than two hours. The American Army had defeated a professional British force. He couldn't believe it. Men who had crossed that nearly frozen river and marched all night in freezing cold had won a decisive victory. For that victory the American troops got the honor of marching back to the ferry landing that afternoon in a driving snowstorm. Captured Hessian troops were loaded on some of the first boats to cross the Delaware back into Pennsylvania.

He watched as a contingent of Hessians stood stiffly at attention in the center of his boat. They were short, thick, heavily muscled men wearing what a few hours ago were impeccably clean uniforms with very high collars. They wore their hair long and braided in a single "tail" trailing from the backs of their heads. The collars made their braided hair stand almost straight out. Ice was beginning to freeze to the sides and bottom of the boat, so he and the other Marblehead fishermen began to jump up and down to break if off. The commander of the Hessians was advised of the problem and quickly gave an order. The Hessian prisoners also began to jump up and down on the boat in perfect "step," the whole company jumping up and down at once. The sight of all those braided tails flying up and down in unison brought smiles to the watermen and the American guards. He wasn't sure, but he thought he saw a trace of a smile flicker across the Hessian commander's face. No ice stuck to their boat.

A few days later the army moved back across the river to a defensive position east of the town. There was much discussion among the Marbleheaders about what they should do next. All their enlistments would end with the new year, 1777 and most of the men wanted to go home. They thought there was money to be made raiding British ships. He wasn't so sure. He had gone to sea to make a lot of money on the *Anne* and had gone mad for it.

On the morning of December 31st General Washington spoke to the assembled regiments and asked the men to stay and fight just one month longer. The General rode back and forth in front of the assemblage. All he could promise was a ten dollar bonus for those who would stay. The General spoke of the hardships they had already borne for their country, their wives, their homes and all they held dear. Finally, the General asked those who would stay to step forward.

He thought about what he had done and what he had seen. He had seen men with no shoes board shallow boats to cross an ice-filled river then walk over frozen ground for miles to fight a superior enemy. He'd been told the only two deaths suffered by the army at Trent Town were two men who had not been shot by the enemy but who had frozen to death during the night march on the city.

Why? Why would men not fall away and huddle for warmth?

Richard L. Evans

He knew there were some things men would fight and die for: wealth, land, fame, or women. He knew that men would also sometimes fight just because they were in the company of other brave men. But here was something new to him. Here were men who were willing to suffer great deprivation, even death—for what? He thought he knew what it was: an idea. In the old world what counted was *who* a man was. But in this new world it would be *what* a man was that counted.

Thomas Paine had written:

>*These are the times that try men's souls. The summer soldier and the sunshine patriot will, in this crisis, shrink from the service of their country, but he that stands it now, deserves the love and thanks of man and woman. Tyranny, like hell, is not easily conquered; yet we have this consolation with us, that the harder the conflict, the more glorious the triumph.*

Many of the men in the other regiments volunteered. Only four men from the Marblehead Regiment stepped forward. He was one of them. Against his will; against his wishes; against his own common sense, he had become a patriot.

•

There were other battles and other defeats.

The Marbleheaders were gone, so he was put in an infantry regiment. Forced marches, usually to escape destruction, were their orders for many days. There was a fiercely bloody battle near Paoli in the mountains. After that the army played fox and hounds with the advancing British. Sometimes they were the fox and sometimes the hounds. He waded through chest-high freezing water and pushed through densely forested hills and valleys.

The two armies came face-to-face again under a cast-iron gray sky on a muddy field laid between two low mountains. The enemy advanced in neat formations, their bayonets flashing even in the dim light. The rattle of their weapons and the muffled cadence of thousands of boots striking the ground together came to him. Many would fall here. This, he was sure, would be his last battle.

The lines drew up.

He heard men all around him cursing under their breaths—fear mixed with rage.

Without warning, a fierce wind suddenly blew down the valley and across the field, knocking men down and tearing banners from their flagstaffs. He knew what it was—a northeaster. It pushed a drenching rain that went through his coat and every bit of his gear. Not a shot could be fired from either side—no one had dry powder. Still the British moved forward with fixed bayonets. They were so close he could see the same fear and rage on their faces he knew was on his. The Americans had nothing to match that British steel. The American Revolution was about to end in a place called White Horse. But the British never got to the new American Army. Try as they might, they could not advance against the force of those terrible winds. The men fell, slipping and taking others near them down with them. More curses and oaths were voiced but were not heard on the American side—the wind took them away. Orders were given and both armies withdrew.

He was wet, cold, muddy, exhausted, but alive.

In early October he was again marching toward another battlefield. Germantown was just a few miles north of Philadelphia. It was to be a surprise attack. By the end of the day he would be dead tired and twenty miles in the opposite direction.

There was no surprise.

It was another "glorious defeat." But as exhausted as they were—marching like zombies—the retreating men all around him were not at all discouraged.

He heard many voices saying things like, "Don't worry, boys. We'll get them next time."

To his further surprise, his voice was one of them.

They kept moving west away from the enemy. He found his old friend, Homer Davis, the Virginia rifleman from the siege at Boston. They walked together. Homer had just returned from Saratoga.

"Up thar in New York." Homer said, "Oh, yeah, that feller Gentleman Johnny Burgoyne sent his soldier boys out thinking they would whup up on us unwashed backwoodsmen. Ha! We set up in the trees and picked off all thar officers before they could even get close to us."

That wide, nearly toothless grin was back.

It was one of the first days in December when they stopped at another place deep in Pennsylvania. There was a small stream on one side of the road and a sloping hillside on the other. It was alternately sleeting and snowing. Homer saw an old woman near a stone house. She was bent over collecting deadfalls for her fire.

He called out, "Old Mother, what be the name of this place?"

She looked up and said, "Valley Forge."

They made camp on a level, heavily wooded area at the top of the hillside above the road. Exhausted men slept on the frosty ground next to campfires the first night. With daylight came orders to build houses—this was to be their winter camp.

During the next few weeks he learned to use an axe with increasing skill. He watched as expert woodsmen felled trees, trimmed limbs and logs to size, carried the logs to the houses then cut notches to custom fit each log in place. His dexterity with an axe would serve him well for many years to come. A thousand huts were built with trees cut from the campsite. Logs had to be locked together. Mud was hauled from the banks of the stream below the road and forced into the spaces between the logs.

Men complained bitterly that there was no source of water, no spring, on the high ground where their camp was building up. All water had to be carried up the sloping hillside. Roofs were crudely thatched. Each cabin was built to the same specification: a rectangle fourteen feet by sixteen feet with one door and no windows. A stone chimney and fireplace was built on the wall opposite the door. The floor was uncovered. First it was dirt, then mud, then worse. The winter would be spent in smoke-filled quarters lying on ground kept wet by the leaky roofs over their heads.

Homer went to his commander, Daniel Morgan, and asked if his friend could be enlisted in the regiment. They had talked it over on the road before coming to camp. Men were leaving every day—walking or dead. The request was granted. He had begun the war as a seaman from Massachusetts. It looked now like he would finish it as a rifleman from Virginia.

There was precious little usable clothing in the camp. Men

shared what they had. Sentries were given the best coats and hats from each cabin and often stood guard standing on their hats to keep their bare feet off the frozen snow. His Marblehead peacoat, now in tatters, was the warmest coat in his cabin and was used every night by a different sentry. The men left sleeping in the cabins were almost naked.

Life in his cabin was a little better than in most. Either he or Homer were out during the day using their talents with a rifle hunting what little game was available in the harsh winter. Sometimes he would bring in a squirrel, or if fortune had truly smiled on him, a rabbit. They each brought down a deer in the same week so many could be fed a little meat. The hides were scraped and eventually sewn into the pants and shirt he would wear for the rest of the war.

Homer came in one evening with a beaver he had shot on the bank of a distant stream. The fur pelt was a blessing. After that, every man from their cabin assigned guard duty was given "the beaver" to wear in any way he wished. Some wore it as a hat, but most stood on it in the snow to keep their feet warm.

The beaver's tail was roasted and some of the men ate it. But when God made the beaver, He took pity on the beast. In His infinite mercy the Lord made sure men would hunt the beaver only for his fur coat. Those who tasted the meat of that poor beaver soon came to look on roasted rats as manna from heaven. Compared to beaver, a toasted rat hung over an open fire by its tail until cooked was a thick, juicy cut of prime beef. No self-respecting rat would ever be caught dead in the same stewpot with a beaver.

There was another source of meat. "I found another one four cabins over," Homer said, poking his head in their door.

"I'm with you." The two of them went quickly to Homer's "find."

So many horses had died of cold and starvation that they had to be buried in shallow ditches. Rain or melting snow would often uncover the corpses and men were required to recover them.

Most men raised with horses were disinclined to eat horseflesh. They seemed to feel that horses were in some way their friends.

He and Homer had no such associations and were happy when they found a horse that hadn't been dead too long. The meat was stringy and had a decidedly "gamey" taste. But it was meat—and it wasn't beaver.

One evening just before Christmas, he remembered some of the carols Titus had taught him. He began to sing "Joy to the World." Most of the other men were sleeping so he began singing very softly. He was surprised on the second verse to hear a sweet tenor voice join him. He looked around and saw Homer Davis smiling his nearly toothless smile as he sang. In just a few moments most of the others in the cabin were also singing, some even harmonizing.

They also sang, "While Shepherds Watched Their Flocks by Night." Someone had a harmonica and played under their voices. They would sing after their meager supper each evening. Homer was a real surprise. He knew dozens of hymns and other songs. Homer admitted that his mother had dragged him to church as a lad. He had loved the singing.

"But the rest of it," Homer said, "was turkey feathers."

It occurred to him that he had no idea what Homer meant by "turkey feathers." He had never been inside a church in his life.

They were invited to other cabins to sing and encourage others to sing, too. One of the most favored hymns spoke to their own wintry plight with the words:

O God our help in ages past, Our hope for years to come,
Our shelter from the stormy blast, And our eternal home.

Returning to their own cabin one night, he told Homer about a ship's doctor and his theory that singing and exercise helped keep people healthy. He didn't elaborate further.

His nightmares came with much less frequency at Valley Forge. The misery of daily life left him emotionally as well as physically exhausted.

Conditions in the camp continued to worsen with more cold and less food as 1777 turned into 1778. The rotting bodies of the horses polluted the stream waters and typhus, cholera, dysentery, scurvy and other diseases began to take many good men. Seeing the cabins with men lying cold and naked in their own waste reminded him of the hell in the holds of the *Anne*. The human misery was the same, just 100 degrees colder.

The ill were sent to crude hospitals, often set up in barns or farmhouses. The doctors and nurses trying to treat them were almost completely wiped out themselves by the diseases. Four men from his cabin were diagnosed with typhus. Only one ever returned. That man told the rest of them that if they became ill, they would be better off to just curl up by their fire and "take what would come."

At the end of February a large number of hogs, goats and cows were driven in from the countryside. A few days later wagons loaded with food began to arrive.

When the line of wagons stalled in front of him, he approached the muleskinner holding the reins of an uncovered wagon.

"Where'd you find all this food?" he asked.

When the driver turned to him, he saw he had a huge plug of tobacco in his cheek. The driver had to speak around his plug.

"All over the place. Them farmers sure weren't happy to give up supplies for the army even after we paid 'um. I got a friend, he's two wagons up ahead there, he had to point this musket at a farmer to get his wagon loaded."

The driver shook his head in mild disbelief and continued, "I've heard, too, of farmers refusing to grind grain already paid for and of some who burned their wagons or broke the wheels to stop us from bringing in our loads."

The wagons ahead of him started to move again. The muleskinner nodded a farewell and turned forward as he spit a big, brown squirt of tobacco juice. The juice splattered against the hind quarter of the nearest mule. The mule jumped and the wagon lurched forward and moved on.

So much for the popular revolt.

•

Summer came again and he went with Morgan's Regiment north and west to punish the Six Nations of Indians. Homer

Davis, who had been an Indian fighter in the French and Indian Wars, taught him about Indian tactics and how to fight them. At first he didn't like killing Indians. He could understand killing redcoats—they were the enemies of freedom—but the Indians were fighting to keep what lands they had, their own lands.

In late July they came upon a recently abandoned Indian encampment. He moved forward cautiously. Homer, walking beside him, stopped suddenly, reaching out and grabbing his arm. At Homer's feet was a round, blackened object. It took him a few seconds to realize it was a human head.

The company silently spread out, rifles at the ready. In another hour they had found twenty-five burned bodies, only the bodies—all men from their regiment. They had been skinned, burned and then beheaded. The company could find only twenty-three heads. The heads were scattered over a wide area as if they had been flung about in sport. They stayed at that terrible place only as long as it took to bury the remains of their friends, then moved on with a new and deadly resolve.

It was almost dark when a strange scream came to them on the wind. No one had heard an animal that made such a cry. His nose gave him the answer—even though his eyes refused to believe it. Ahead, through the trees was a huge, flaming torch.

A man's body writhed, seeming to dance in the flames. His captors had tied the man's hands near the top of a pole then set him afire. The Indians surrounding the burning corpse were jumping and celebrating their victory. They didn't notice the approach of their victim's comrades—until it was too late.

He discharged his rifle then leapt forward with the others. Morgan's men all unsheathed their long knives. No Indians were taken captive that night, and none escaped. He never again had any qualms about killing Indians.

•

In the fall of 1781 at Yorktown on the Virginia coast of the Chesapeake Bay, General Cornwallis surrendered and British military action ceased.

Homer Davis went home to his farm in Virginia.

Some, including General Washington, still thought the war was not over, that the British would fight on with new troops. He had no place to go so he stayed on. But the militia regiments dwindled away after Yorktown. Men returned to their homes and families. After another eight years he, too, took his discharge even though he had no place to go.

He returned to Baltimore.

The streets were still as he remembered them, unpaved and muddy. He found the place where Miss Lucille's house had once stood. The house had been burned sometime during the war, and the lot where it had been was now empty.

He walked back from the street to the garden plot where Titus had labored over his precious vegetables. Two new buildings had taken part of the land, but he could see a group of large trees behind a house at the back of the lot. He remembered burying Titus under the branches of those trees. As he approached, he saw an iron fence had been erected around the trees protecting a small cemetery.

The cemetery had only four markers. The gate was unlocked and he stood looking at the headstones. One of them was newer, larger and of a slightly different design than the other three. Each of the stones had a Christian cross carved in its center. His eyes moved from left to right. The first stone was one of the older markers. It was inscribed, "Margery Deneraux." Below her name were the dates, "b. November 17, 1752 - d. June 11, 1775." The second stone was the largest one. It was more ornate. It was inscribed, "Lucille Deneraux" with the dates, "b. January 18, 1733 - d. January 22, 1789" below her name.

He had missed finding her alive by eight months.

The third stone had only one name. It read simply, "Titus." A single date, "d. June 4, 1775," followed the name. The fourth stone was his. His name had been carved in it followed by "d. June 6, 1775."

Obviously, Miss Lucille had tried to throw off the British Navy by pretending he was dead. Perhaps his running away to war had not been necessary after all. He smiled for the first time in weeks. Few men get to see their own gravestones let alone their own graves.

Richard L. Evans

He stayed in the graveyard the rest of the day. He pulled weeds from around the stones and the fence, sweat dripping from his chin just as he remembered seeing it drip from Titus' chin as he worked among his beloved plants. Sometimes tears were mixed with his sweat.

Finally, he sat on the ground and looked at the sky, his back resting against his own gravestone. He tried to picture Eternity in this place. He heard a muffled rumbling. Thunderstorms were brewing in the south. Birds chirped indifferently but insects took up the slack. The sound of a dog barking and a few faint voices from the waterfront drifted to him. He felt a slight breeze cool his face as it dried up his sweat.

Near dark he stood and walked behind Miss Lucille's grave and placed his hands on the tops of Margery's and Titus's headstones. He bowed his head and recited words he had memorized years before, words he remembered Titus saying in a deep, wavering voice:

"Bless the Lord, O my soul: and all that is within me, bless his holy name. Bless the Lord, O my soul, and forget not all his benefits: Who forgiveth all thine iniquities; who healeth all thy diseases; Who redeemeth thy life from destruction; who crowneth thee with loving kindness and tender mercies; Who satisfieth thy mouth with good things; so that thy youth is renewed like the eagle's..."

He couldn't remember the rest of it.

He closed the gate behind him and never returned.

Chapter Four

PESHEWA

He went looking for his friend, Homer Davis

Homer had spoken often of the little farm his family worked close to the upper regions of the James River near Lynchburg in the Virginia mountains. The Davis place was easy to find. Everyone he spoke to knew where it was.

Homer's family said he had tried farming for a year "but just didn't take to it" and had gone back into the wilderness over the mountains.

He packed his kit. He would have to travel light. Gunpowder was stowed in a waterproof pouch. Titus's Bible with Margery's cross sewn inside its cover was secured in another pouch at the bottom of his leather pack. He traded his army uniform and boots for new buckskins: a shirt, pants and two pairs of moccasins made in a mountain tailor shop. He put on his three-cornered military hat and went west.

Autumn touched the leaves of the hardwood forests with a brilliance he remembered from his childhood. For days he moved through a waving sea of red and gold, touched here and there by patches of evergreen.

It was mid afternoon one October day when he climbed near the crest of a tall hill where he found a break in the forest. A rock slide had taken out a swath of trees about twenty yards wide.

He looked back to the east at lines of hills forested with tens of thousands of brilliantly colored trees. Clouds animated them with rolling blue shadows. Sometimes the shadows went high on the hills, sometimes low, sometimes disappearing, then rising and rolling again. The scene reminded him of the paintings on the walls at Miss Lucille's—those wild landscapes had been so strange to him—the red and orange skies over bright leaves. Now he saw them spread before him. Remembering those paintings brought other memories. He remembered how Margery looked the first morning he saw her. She said she would always be with him, and she was right. He felt her presence sitting with him watching the glory of the earth and skies. When the sun went down behind the hill at his back, his old friends, the stars, began to peek out of the dimming twilight. At last, in the darkness that wasn't darkness, they were fully arrayed in the great arching vault of heaven.

He was at peace.

His days in the great forests were precious gifts. He spent early mornings squatting amid the dense woodland foliage as the night mists slowly lifted with the warming sun. Condensed water dripped from his hat, shoulders and body, and he was as wet as if a shower had just come over him. By the time the sun was above the horizon, he would be nearly dry again as the water returned to the air—cool steam. There were long days when he just sat still watching life around him. He saw grasshoppers leap and fly briefly as they sampled blades of brush and bush. Butterflies, ants, beetles, tiny moths and dragonflies danced or struggled over open meadows and darkening forests. He knew he should be part of it. He belonged to the earth as well as to the sea. He watched death, too. One life fed on another in a seemingly unending cycle. He knew he should be a part of that cycle, too.

But he wasn't. He lived on.

He kept moving west until the days became winter-cold. He

found a cave. After checking it carefully to be sure it didn't house a sleeping bear, he moved in for the rest of the winter. Homer Davis had shown him how to set snares for small animals, and he lived on fire cakes and rabbit stew just as he had at Valley Forge.

Whenever the weather permitted, he walked through the forests near his cave to contemplate what was, or should have been, his fate. He had plenty of time to think. He had all the time in the world. He knew he was now fifty-three years old. Looking at his face in a clear, still, icy pool, he saw the same man reflected there he had seen aboard the *Anne*; the same man whose face was reflected in the little mirrors he traded for slaves; the same man he had seen in the mirror over Margery's bed at Miss Lucille's; the same man he had seen at Yorktown in his Army uniform. He knew he didn't look or move like other men his age.

He pulled the knot from the deerskin strap holding his hair behind his head. He looked at his hair as it fell around his shoulders. There was no hint of gray or white in its light brown strands. His beard was still dark, almost black—a young man's beard. He had the agility of a man half his age. And he had always been strong, stronger then most men he met. His strength had not diminished.

Why? Why do I live on, unchanging?

On two occasions, guns had been pointed directly at him—first by the slave on the *Anne,* then by the British officer at Miss Lucille's—yet both weapons failed to fire, preserving his life. *Why?*

Was it chance—just good luck that saved him? Or was it something else?

The British officer had struck him with his pistol before pulling the trigger again. Unaccountably, it fired the second time, killing Titus. The scar on his temple had not changed or faded in all the years since that terrible night in Baltimore. It was as distinctive now as it had been then.

Titus's Bible told of two brothers, Cain and Able. Cain carried a "mark" given him by God after he murdered Able. Was the mark he now carried—the scar left by a man he murdered—his "mark?" He had murdered that officer in a rage, just as Cain murdered Able. All through the war he had been exposed to gunfire—had seen men standing next to him fall silently with terrible wounds. Yet, he was untouched. Titus had spoken about the mark and the sin of murder first brought to the world by Cain. The mark was put on Cain by God to prevent other men from killing him.

Was it God's intention to prevent other men from killing me, too?

And what should he believe of his gift of healing? He had used it to save three people: Thomas, Nuflo and Margery. All had died anyway, and in horrific ways. Was his a gift or a curse? He thought about what his mother had said, and how she had looked when he told her he made Thomas well.

"Oh my Lord, oh, my Lord, boy."

That was all she said.

She looked so stricken when she said it. He didn't understand it then, and now he was afraid there was something dark in it, something he'd better try to understand.

He was tracking through the forest one winter day that first year in the wilderness when he thought he heard something. He stopped to listen. New snow had fallen for several hours, and the woods had taken on that strange, almost pure silence it got after a windless snowfall. There was no birdsong, no rustling of dead leaves or dry bushes—the snow insulated the sound of the moving branches. He stood and listened—listened in the silence. He thought he could hear something: a faint voice whispering to him in the hushed forest. If only he could hear it more clearly!

He looked for the answers to his questions in the only place he was sure would have them—the only place he trusted to have them—Titus's Bible. He read for long hours by a small fire at the mouth of his cave but found nothing. He was sure the answers were right there, right in front of him, but he couldn't see or hear them. It was as if something didn't want him to know what he was, and what that might mean. Not yet.

•

The passing of the years got away from him. He tried to mark them but the seemingly endless forests made keeping time irrelevant. Time, after all, is not a natural phenomenon. Time is a man-made thing used only to measure mankind's passing. The earth rotates.

Man says, "Ahah! I can use that."

The turning of the earth and the turning of the seasons is noted by almost all living things, but only man tries to codify them, to bend them to his uses. When humankind ends, time will end. Then the earth will be what it was before, and all of man's minutes, weeks, fortnights, eras, centuries and millennia will add up to nothing. So, he wasn't worried by not knowing what year it was.

For him, the only really important "times" were dawn and dusk (light and dark) and the food times: berry bush times, wild apple and plum times, ducks and geese time, hungry bear time, fish run time, baby animal birthing time and honeysuckle time. There were also the times of the moon, the growing up and dying down times, and the wet and dry times.

In the middle of a hot and dry time he discovered, quite by accident, another strange ability. He was fishing in a large impoundment formed where a quiet stream had been blocked by an old rock slide. It was only a little more than knee deep, and he could see fish, some quite large, moving about the water. He cast out a fishing line but his hook became snagged several yards from the bank, and he waded out to free it. As he reached in the water, a fish swam right up to his hand and stopped as if it were waiting for something to happen. He slowly reached out his hand and took the fish in it. The fish made no effort to escape, and he picked it up out of the water. Two pounds of brook trout made a fine supper that night.

After that, whenever he wanted a fish dinner, all he had to do was kneel by the water's edge and wiggle his fingers in the water, and he would soon have his choice of several fish. This "trick" worked wherever he went. It also worked with birds. He could whistle a little tune, and in minutes birds would land on his hat and shoulders, chirping away with him as he sang the old songs from his days at sea and at war. He valued their company as much as any he could remember.

Sometime later he was following a game trail close by his latest camp when he saw a rabbit sitting very still and very alert about ten yards ahead. He stopped, put his rifle on the ground, knelt down and held out his hands as he did when catching fish. The rabbit stirred but didn't run. On an impulse he began to sing one of the old hymns Titus had taught him. To his great surprise, the rabbit turned and slowly hopped to him, stopping only inches from his fingers.

"What on earth?" he said to himself.

He couldn't remember ever seeing such strange behavior by a wild animal. He stopped singing and stood up. The rabbit still didn't run away.

Finally he said to the rabbit, "Go on, now, I'll see you another day when I'm hungry."

The rabbit waited until he was finished speaking, then calmly hopped away into the brush.

"Oh, fine," he thought, "now I have another mystery to ponder."

But he remembered to thank God that night in his prayers.

He was pondering these mysteries—instead of paying attention to the trail as he should—when he almost walked out on an open hillside above an Indian village. He stopped quickly and turned to leave, but something below caught his attention. The people who lived in the village had cleared a large area close on the flood plain of a sluggish river. The charred remnants of trees lay about.

That must be how they cleared the land.

He saw women working in big, well-tended gardens. It was early summer, and he could see the fresh green sprouts of new plants thrusting up through the soil. There were no men in sight so he assumed they were in the forests, hunting. He watched the women farmers from the cover of a large thicket of locust trees. He thought they must have lived on this land for a long time. Their homes were permanent structures built of logs with tightly thatched roofs. Watching the women made him uneasy—a young man's juices still flowed through him.

He started to move away but as he did, he startled a large deer. The buck lowered its antlers as if to charge. Instinctively, he raised his rifle and fired.

Now, he had two problems. He almost never killed large animals such as the buck that now lay dead a few yards away. He couldn't eat all the meat the animal would provide, unless he worked to preserve it, and that would require his presence in one place over several weeks. And why should he work to preserve meat when fresh meat from smaller animals was almost always available?

His second problem was very straight forward: the Indians would have heard his shot and been warned of his presence. How would they react? He didn't have to wait. Even as he turned from the dead deer, he could see more than a dozen men hurrying out of the village and up the slope toward him. They were all carrying muskets or rifles—the home guard had turned out.

He got under the deer and managed to center it on his shoulders behind his head. It was a very large buck, and it was all he could do to raise himself up and stagger into the open with the deer. The men from the village were now very close to him, but when they saw him step forward, they stopped. He took a few more steps toward them and flung the deer to the ground in front of him. He smiled, hoping his smile was a gesture of friendliness and not an invitation to battle. It worked. The Indians lowered their weapons and smiled back at him. He turned slowly and eased back into the forest cover. Retrieving his rifle, he moved as swiftly away as he could trying not to make a sound. He looked back later from a higher elevation and saw the men carrying the deer back to their village. He took pride in noting it took four of them to manage the carcass.

•

It was early morning a month later. The sun had not yet appeared but there was enough predawn light so he could find his way. He was moving again to the west when he smelled something that caused him to freeze where he stood: smoke. He turned his head, first one way, and then another until he was sure of the direction of the smoke. Smoke meant one of two things: a natural fire which might be a big forest fire, or men. Both were serious threats.

Moving cautiously, he approached the source of the smoke. It was a campfire, very small and well-covered. The builder of the fire did not want it noticed. Ordinarily, he would have just slipped away and not bothered whoever it was who didn't want company. But something, he didn't know what, made him get closer. He stayed low in the brush until he could see a man sitting by the fire. The man was turned in profile so he saw his face clearly—an Indian but not of a tribe he recognized. He was about to turn and go when two more figures came out of the forest opposite the seated man. Another man and a woman approached the fire. The woman was quite different in appearance from the two men. She was darker and her features were much softer. Her hands were tied together at the wrists in front of her, and there was a leather strap tied tightly around her neck. The other end of the strap was held by the second man as he pulled her along. The whole situation became suddenly very clear. She was their prisoner—a slave!

He slipped back a few yards. It wasn't likely they could smell him with the smoke from the campfire in their noses, but he didn't want to chance being noticed. Now he couldn't just slip away; his conscience would never let him do that. The woman was a slave and he couldn't simply abandon her, not after what had happened to him on the *Anne*. Negotiation was not an option. He had nothing to bargain with, and his chances of surviving a fight with two against one were very poor—unless, of course, he could take them by surprise.

He made a decision.

He watched them leave their campsite moving in the same direction he was—west. They were following a game trail, and he thought he knew where it would lead them. He took a course parallel to theirs, racing through open forest when he could, trying to outdistance them. It was just after noon with a high sun when he came on the game trail he thought they were using. He stayed several yards off the trail following it until it rounded a large boulder and then to an open area covered with other loose boulders. He dropped his pack and placed himself behind the rock where the trail turned. They would have to pass right by him, and he could take them from behind.

He waited.

Within minutes he smelled them. He hoped they couldn't smell him, too. He pulled his axe from his belt and placed it on the ground at his feet. After checking the powder charge in his rifle's pan, he steadied himself just as Homer Davis had taught him.

The first man came around the boulder holding an old musket in the crook of one arm and the end of a leather strap in his other hand. The woman followed. Then the second man appeared. He was armed like the first man and was also holding the other end of the leather strap tied around the woman's neck. She was controlled from both front and back.

He waited until the first man, the man farthest from him, mounted a rock before he fired. The ball tore through the Indian's backbone in the center of his shoulders, exactly where he aimed. He waited only until he felt the recoil of his rifle before he dropped it and scooped up his axe. He had spent many hours practicing throwing his axe as a form of recreation. Now his skill would meet a desperate test. He leaped forward toward the turning figure of the second Indian. The man raised his musket to fire but the Indian woman had taken hold of the strap tied to her neck and pulled it, yanking him off his target. By the time the man recovered, it was too late. The axe smashed into his chest just below his throat. Both Indians were dead before they hit the ground.

He drew his knife and jumped forward to the nearest Indian making sure he was dead. Then he checked the other man. The woman was caught between the two dead men, nearly pinned to the ground by the straps around her neck. She looked up at him, terrified.

He held up his left hand, still holding his knife in his right, and tried to assure her he was not going to kill her, too. He smiled. It had worked with the Indians back at the village, maybe it would work with her. It didn't. Then it occurred to him she might be afraid he had something else in mind for her, and a smile would not calm that fear at all. He moved to both Indians again and used his knife to cut the straps holding the woman down by her neck. She stood and backed away from him, still fearful.

He turned to the muskets the Indians had been carrying. They were very old. They reminded him of the weapons Captain Davenport had traded for slaves in Africa almost a hundred years ago. They must have been used in the French and Indian Wars. Homer Davis had told him about them. The dead men also had steel knives thrust in their belts, probably from the same source. There were a number of scalps tied to their belts—something the white man had taught the "savages." He pulled a knife from the belt of one of them and stepped to the woman indicating to her that she should hold out her arms—they were still bound at the wrists. He used the knife to cut the leather bindings, freeing her hands. She took a step backward but didn't attempt to run.

He dropped the knife at her feet and went back to where he had dropped his pack and rifle. He turned and watched the woman as he reloaded his rifle and checked the prime. She didn't move. Finally, he pointed to the knife on the ground and then to his belt and then to her belt. She picked up the knife and put it in her belt. He thought he saw her relax a little.

He shouldered his pack and looked questioningly at the woman. He pointed in several directions trying to get her to indicate which way she wanted to go. She pointed back the way they had come. He nodded in that direction and took a step forward. The woman held up one hand to stop him and then went to where the first Indian lay. She was wearing a leather shift which came to just above her knees. She suddenly raised it up on her thighs, squatted and urinated on the dead man. She did the same to the other Indian. Then she stood, spit on the ground in disgust and began walking in the direction she had just pointed.

Not someone. I'd like to have for an enemy.

He put his rifle across his shoulders and followed her. They walked for the next six hours stopping only once. When they did, she stepped off the trail and squatted again behind some trees.

"Oh, *now* you're going to be modest!" he whispered to himself.

He turned his head and stepped behind a tree to relieve himself, remembering the little etiquette his mother had taught him long ago before the Colonies became States. The woman waited for his return. He took a canteen from his shoulder and offered her a drink which she accepted.

They stopped near a clear flowing stream. As she pulled up handfuls of tall grasses to twist into soft bedding, he went to the water and worked his fish-catching fingers-in-the-water trick. She hadn't finished half her bed making when he held out a large, squirming fish to her. She took the fish in her hands and looked at him with a question on her face. It was apparent she had no idea what to do with it.

He turned and cut a small sapling with his knife and skinned the bark from it. He cut it in two pieces, one much longer than the other. He tied the two pieces together. He then cut off the fish's head, gutted it and spread it wide using the two sticks cut from the sapling, crossing them to hold the fish open, butterfly style. A short time later the fish was roasting over an open fire, held up by the longer length of the sapling thrust in the ground. The green wood did not burn easily. After their meal he gave her one of his blankets, and they bedded down several feet apart.

The woman still had her knife tucked in her belt but would not need it. His memory of the slave woman he raped on the *Anne* was still vivid in his memory, and he would never consider doing such a thing again. He had studied her as they moved along the trail. She carried herself well, upright and with dignity. She wore her hair long, almost to her waist. It was straight with a single braid falling in front of her left shoulder. Her figure was clearly feminine, but she would not be thought beautiful in the world he had known—certainly not as compared to his lovely Margery.

The Indian woman was dark: hair, eyes and complexion. She had good teeth and seemed very strong. She was also very intelligent. She had picked up everything he tried to tell her from his gestures or expressions alone. He was surprised when she didn't know what to do with the fish—how to prepare or cook it. But she enjoyed eating her share of it. She might decide to kill him while he slept. He would have to take the chance. Once, he did awake in the night with the woman kneeling over him. He must have had another of his nightmares. When she saw he was all right, she went back to her bed on the ground.

The next morning he showed her how he caught fish. As they ate their breakfast, he was pleased to see her regard him with what he thought was a heightened respect. He wasn't sure why that was important to him, but he liked it. The woman said very little and he couldn't understand any of the words she used anyway. They communicated with their hands, with head movement and facial gestures.

As they stood to leave camp that morning, the woman turned to him and pointing to herself said, "Peshewa."

He was sure it was her name. He pointed to himself and told her his name—not his birth name—but the name he had used in the war. She repeated the sound of his name. He liked hearing it. He repeated the sound of her name. She seemed to like that, too.

They traveled together in this manner for another week. He brought in game or fish, and she gathered wild fruits, nuts and roots to eat. Most of what Peshewa brought in he had never seen or thought to eat before. But everything went down well (and stayed down). He had to admit to himself that he liked her company. He liked having another human being to share each day.

As they moved closer to where Peshewa wished to go, he began to recognize the country. They were moving back to the area he had left a month ago. Later, he was sure the familiarity of the country must have been running through his mind, distracting him from the trail. He also had to admit he was distracted as he studied Peshewa's buttocks and the backs of her legs. Her legs were heavily muscled but smooth and womanly.

How else could he not have smelled the bear?

They were about halfway down a small ravine with a trickle of water in it when a large brown object appeared above the brush along the stream bed at the bottom of the cut. They both stopped. The brown object suddenly rose up until it was every inch of ten feet above the ground. The object was the head of a very large bear.

He had no time to think; he just took three quick steps getting in front of Peshewa, pushing her behind him. As the bear dropped to its feet and began to charge at them, he jumped up on the trunk of a fallen tree next to the trail so the bear was sure to see him.

He raised and spread his arms over his head and yelled, "Ho, Bear!"

The bear stopped its charge fifteen feet in front of them. He wasn't sure what to do next, so he began to sing. The song that came out of him unbidden was a song all the men had sung together at Valley Forge:

Way up on Cinch Mountain,
   I wander alone;
I'm as drunk as the devil,
   Oh, let me alone!

The bear growled, opened its mouth and bared its teeth but made no move toward him.
He continued to sing:

I'll eat when I'm hungry,
   En drink when I'm dry;
If whiskey don't kill me,
   I'll live till I die.

The bear now rose up on its hind legs and extended its front paws mimicking his stance. Even though the bear was slightly downhill from him and he stood on a log, the bear's head was still taller than his.
He kept on singing:

Rye whisky, rye whisky,
   I know you of old,
You rob my poor pockets
   Of silver and gold.

The bear remained standing but now cocked his head right and left, listening.

Rye whisky, rye whisky,
   You're no friend to me.
You killed my old daddy,
   Goddamn you, try me.

He knew more verses but he stopped singing. The bear dropped to the ground on all fours.

Trying to sound authoritative, he said, "Go on now, bear. We won't harm you. Go on, be on your way."

The bear turned and walked slowly, almost casually, away, back down the ravine and across the stream. He lowered his arms only when the bear finally disappeared in the trees up the opposite slope.

"We won't harm *you?*" he muttered. "Did I really tell a bear *that?*"

He heard a low whistle of air as Peshewa exhaled behind him. She must have been holding her breath the entire time. Her exhalation was followed by a series of gasps as she tried to take in air through her constricted throat. When he turned to her, he saw two eyes even wider than they had been when he killed her captors and came toward her with a knife. She stared at him for a long moment, then raised her hand in his direction.

Pointing at him, she said in a hushed voice, "Pele'thi!"

He jumped down from the log and retrieved his rifle. He couldn't remember dropping it any more than he could remember when his knees had become so wobbly. He indicated to Peshewa that she should continue leading. But she shook her head, "no," and pointing ahead, indicated that from now on he would walk in the lead. Somehow this pleased him. He didn't know what "Pele'thi" meant but that she had said it pleased him, too. Peshewa never called him by any other name.

They reached their destination in four more days. It was, as he suspected, the same village where he had killed the deer almost two months before. He stopped at the edge of the forest and waited for her to walk ahead. She was well down the hill leading to the gardens before she noticed he was not following her.

He thought she might just go on home and that would be the end of it. But, no, she turned and ran back to him taking his arm and pulling him gently with her. By now their presence had been noticed in the village, and a growing number of people were coming from all directions toward them—including half a dozen men from the forest behind them. He knew, of course, they had been trailed for the last half-mile but could think of nothing to do but stay with Peshewa.

Peshewa was greeted with great emotion, laughter and tears.

She moved from one to another—the main focus of the moment. But he, too, was watched. He was watched closely but not directly. One of the things he had learned from his brief contact with other native peoples was that staring at a person you did not know was impolite. He did the same, looking at them but keeping his eyes over their heads or at their feet.

Peshewa led him into the village. He was given food and something to drink. The drink was a kind of hot tea which he enjoyed. He was shown to one of the shelters and was left there to rest for the remainder of the day.

That evening the whole village gathered in an open area in the center of the shelters. Everyone sat on the ground in a large circle. There were now more than 200 in attendance. Many more men had come in, and there were dozens of children. He was led to a leather blanket spread on the ground and was seated next to their head man, Wesecahnay. They all waited expectantly, and he was not sure what, if anything, he should do. But it wasn't long before Peshewa moved to the center of the circle and began to relate the events of her capture and rescue.

She was amazing. He couldn't understand her words, but he understood everything she was saying because her acting was so elegant. Of course, he already knew most of the story, anyway. She had been taken by surprise while in the forest gathering nuts or fruit. She fought them but they tied her hands and neck. They walked for ten days, then, "bough!" (the sound of a rifle) and one captor dropped. She pulled on the strap holding her neck and, "whump!" (the axe striking the other captor's chest). She fell, mortally wounded.

Her audience cheered, "Ahhhhhhhh!"

Their attention was directed to him as she described his leaping out and cutting her neck and wrist bonds.

"Ahhhh!" another cheer.

His fish-catching, finger wiggling was demonstrated next which brought out a long "Ohhhh!" of awe from all assembled (except him, of course).

But she was just getting warmed up.

She froze with a terrified expression on her face, turning around to everyone and said in a low, dramatic voice, "Muga!"

It had to be the first sight of the bear.

Little children hugged their parents and men straightened up, sitting taller. Then she imitated his leaping up on the log and then his song. She hadn't gotten his words, but the tune she sang was nearly perfect. Back and forth she went. First she was "muga," then she was him on the log, more singing, then she was the bear, "muga" again. Finally, the bear walked away. She straightened up from imitating the walking bear and turned to him again.

She pointed at him just as she had in the forest and said, "Pele'thi!"

Now there were "Ahhhhs" and "Ohhhhs" all around him.

He smiled. Who wouldn't? After all, he was the hero of the story.

•

He lived in the Shawnee village for another three months. He took part in the festival of the corn in August after which everyone could harvest and eat their corn. Soon after that many more crops matured and the living was good. He saw Peshewa almost every day but only briefly—she had women's work to do in the gardens, and he had men's work, hunting and fishing.

The children followed him out of the village to hold the fish and small animals he called to him. He also went with the men for bigger game: deer, bear, elk and the few remaining buffalo in the woodlands. In the evenings he would read his Bible, again with children sitting near him, as he acted out the stories he read. His acting wasn't nearly as good as Peshewa's, but the children were polite and accorded him their complete attention. He learned a few words and phrases, enough to know that the whole tribe would soon move to winter quarters further to the west.

Fall had again tinged the leaves when Peshewa began making a point to see him several times each day to teach him words and phrases.

One in particular seemed very important to her: "Ni haw-ku-nah-ga."

He memorized it without knowing why. She also touched his beard on several occasions with obvious dislike. The other men, the Shawnee, had almost no facial hair, so he decided to shave his beard as he had through most of the war. He used his pack knife to hack off most of it, and washed what was left before scraping it off with his skinning knife. After a few days the damaged flesh recovered and tanned to match the rest of his face.

Late one afternoon Peshewa brought him a set of deerskin clothes made of a fine, doe hide. The skins had been sun bleached and cured with animal brains to make them very white and very soft. She gave him leggings, a breach cloth and girdle, vest and a short jacket. She brushed his hair until it shone. She showed him how to wear bracelets of silver and shells high on his arms. There were also ankle bracelets tied up with small bells and more shells.

Then she disappeared.

Two hours later the mystery of her disappearance deepened when the younger unmarried men came to get him. They, too, were dressed in their finest white doeskins. They moved to the open area in the center of the village and began to move rhythmically to the sound of several drums, rattles and a set of hollowed wooden logs which were struck with a stick. As they danced they formed a straight line.

He fell in with the others.

The bells and shells at their ankles set up a pleasant pulsing sound. Soon, young women came into the circle through the crowd surrounding the ceremony. Each positioned herself in front of a particular man. No woman danced in front of him until Peshewa arrived. She was resplendent in a beautiful white shift decorated with porcupine quills, bird feathers and shiny metal beads. She smiled at him broadly.

He looked down the line of men and saw that none of the men were smiling, only the women. He contained himself and concentrated on his dancing which consisted only of shifting his weight from one foot to the other in rhythm with the other men.

A man at the end of the line began a chant.

"Ya ne hoo wa...ya ne hoo wa no...ya ne no hoo wa no..."

All the men joined and sang the chant three times then stopped as the women took up the same words. Each group sang the chant alternately. The two lines of dancers came closer and closer together.

Peshewa began to move wildly, throwing her head back and around so that her hair flared out in a wide arch. She twisted her body about in increasingly sensuous movements. The line of dancers continued to move toward each other. At first they had been several feet apart—then they were only a foot apart. Now they were close enough to touch each other with their bodies.

He used his body to touch her breasts and her belly. She did the same, feeling his chest and his belly. As they danced, the other couples spoke to each other, offering compliments, he thought.

Peshewa said, "Oui-shi e-que-chi."

He said, "I have never seen your hair so bright and shiny."

He was new to this.

The dance continued for several more minutes before the rhythm slowed and the dancers slowly came to a halt.

All around him he heard men and women all saying, "Ouisah meni-e-de-luh."

He started to say the same thing, but Peshewa shook her head, "no," and said, "Ni-wy-she-an-a," and nodded to him.

He thought it must be his cue, so he repeated the phrase she had insisted he memorize.

"Ni haw-ku-nah-ga."

That seemed to be what she wanted him to say because she smiled very broadly as did most of the other dancers near them. She seized his arm and led him to a specially decorated shelter—one he hadn't noticed before. She pulled him through the entrance. He suspected that he had just been married, but he couldn't be sure. A half hour later Peshewa had convinced him he was.

•

When the rest of the tribal group moved off to their winter camp, he and Peshewa did not go with them. They walked due south for two weeks.

He remembered a protected place near a good spring with an open area ideal for a garden. He wanted a place where he might find peace in the company of his good wife. Years from now she might be old and have to leave him in death, but he would deal with that when the time came. Now he needed a place where he might rest at least part of each day. He was sure he would need to rest often because Peshewa was an insatiable lover.

He remembered his dear Margery as a girl who loved to make love, but Peshewa was far more voracious in bed. She couldn't seem to get enough of him. She was like a kid in a candy store—and he was the candy: maple sugar cakes, lemon drops, liquorices, taffy—he might be the only thing in stock but everything tasted good to her.

Curious, he had observed the other Indian husbands and their wives. They all seemed to go through each day in a normal fashion with no discernable physical contact between them. Peshewa always found a way to touch him whenever and wherever they were: a hand on his arm; her shin against the back of his leg; the brush of her buttocks against his side. Could she be the only Shawnee woman with such a sexual appetite?

He had asked one of the older children who were always around him in the village what "Peshewa" meant. The child used a stick to draw a likeness of an animal in the dirt. The little girl scratched out the shape of a wildcat.

•

Together, he and Peshewa built a log shelter on the order of the one he had helped build at Valley Forge. Peshewa knew how to thatch the roof so that, unlike the ones at Valley Forge, rain and melting snow did not leak through it.

Spring came and he helped her clear a level area for her garden. She planted her rows carefully, making sure they were lined up east and west in the traditional Shawnee way. One summer afternoon the sun was very warm so Peshewa shed her shift—working naked in her garden. She bent over her plants as he watched her in profile. Sweat dripped from the tip of her nose and he was reminded of Titus working the same way in his beloved garden. Their images blurred and blended before him causing him to laugh to himself.

Here was Peshewa working the soil: Titus with tits!

She caught him smiling at this thought. Seconds later he was pinned to the ground by a sweaty body while grubby hands worked to remove his breach cloth. The woman knew what she wanted, and she wanted it any time she could get it.

Peshewa's first crops came in with the fall months, and she went back to the Shawnee village. On her return, she said little about her trip or the rest of the Shawnee people. But she did keep him very busy making up for lost time.

Some things would never change.

But things did change. There were two very big changes. The first one they named Ruth and the second, a year later, they named Ester. Peshewa liked the stories he told her that came from the Bible, but she had no interest in learning about the one he called, "God."

The Shawnee knew there was a supreme being looking after the affairs of men, a creator named "Kokumthena." Kokumthena was the "Great Spirit," the grandmother of all men, weaving her ethereal basket in the heavens. When her basket was completed, there would be no more need of mankind or of this temporal world—end of story. But Peshewa liked the biblical names from the ancient world.

So, for the next four years, Ruth and Ester ran around, over and through their adoring parents. He had never known such continual joy as that he shared with his "girls." Even his nightmares died away.

Each year, after her harvest was in, Peshewa would travel back to her tribe just before they left their summer village. The sixth year she returned with a big bundle on her back and an even bigger smile on her lips. She opened the bundle in front of him and drew out a huge, full-length robe. The robe was made from the hide of a single buffalo, a white buffalo. She lifted it up and put it over his shoulders. There was room for all of them to crowd around him under his beautiful new robe. And that's what they did. It was a moment he would cherish all his life.

Spring came once again, and he set to work with Peshewa to get her garden ready for another year. The garden was now almost five times the size it was their first year and still getting bigger each spring. As they worked in the cool of the early morning, they heard a shot—a single rifle shot.

He ran the few steps to his rifle while Peshewa ran back to their house with the girls. The shot had come from the east near a shallow river where water from their spring would eventually flow. He moved quickly but silently using his nose and ears to find what his eyes couldn't see through the high brush and trees. He stopped and bent low in the tall grass.

Then he smelled him.

He watched the man from cover. The man was moving along a game trail, coming toward him. He couldn't be sure who had fired the shot. Perhaps the man had been shot by another, or perhaps the man had fired the shot himself as a call for help. He waited. The man stopped, listening. The man's rifle was still in his hands, and he could see that the flint was down. Minutes passed but there was no movement in the nearby forest. The man continued forward, stumbling past him. He heard the man moan. He followed him until the man was just on the edge of the woods very close to his home. Suddenly, the man blundered forward toward the house. He raised his rifle to fire, but the man fell before he could squeeze the trigger. The man didn't move.

He called to Peshewa to stay inside the house and stepped to the man's side putting his foot on the barrel of the other man's rifle, just in case. The man's hair was white, his skin wrinkled but it was also…he inhaled sharply…the man's face was nearly black, and was covered with small, dark blisters.

Small pox!

He would have jumped away as soon as he saw the pox, but something else caught his eye. The man's face, even though it was swollen and dark, was familiar. He looked closely. He hadn't seen that face for many years, but there could be no mistake—the man was Homer Davis.

Impulsively, he picked up his old friend and carried him the few steps to the door of his house. At his call, Peshewa opened the door. He put Homer on their bed. Peshewa immediately put the white buffalo robe over the man to warm him. When she saw Homer's face, she turned quickly back to him, a question on her face. She had not seen small pox before. He could only shake his head in resignation. He had seen it many times; his friend would not live much longer. Homer's eyes opened. They widened as he recognized his friend from the war. Homer raised his head and tried to speak but fell back, dead.

Only then did the enormity of his mistake strike him. He had brought small pox into his home where his wife and children had no immunity! He put aside his sorrow at the passing of his friend and gathered his precious daughters in his arms. He sat on the edge of the bed and put one on each knee, wrapping his arms around them and taking their little hands in his. He repeated the words he remembered from his own childhood, the words he hoped would save his children. Then he stood and took Peshewa's hands in his. They knelt together on the floor facing each other. He repeated the healing words again. It was all he could do.

He buried Homer at the far edge of the garden away from the house. He wanted to put a marker on his friend's grave, so he walked to a place several miles down the river where he knew there were many large, flat stones. He found one that was almost a perfect rectangle of the right size. It was smooth and flat on one side, so he could scratch Homer's name and the year on it. He began to carry the stone back home but stopped only a few yards from the stream. He couldn't remember what year it was!

He tried to count the years backwards to 1789 as he started walking again. Distracted by this effort, his nose failed him again. He blundered on a small black and white object on the trail, almost stepping on it. The skunk, too, was so surprised it unleashed the most potent defensive weapon in the entire animal world. The little dark animal scurried away secure in the knowledge that it would not be followed. But the target of that weapon was anything but secure. In less than a second the whole focus of his world had changed.

He stumbled back to the stream and tried to submerge himself. The only way he could escape the terrible odor, his terrible odor, was to hold his breath underwater. That wouldn't work for very long. Staying in the near freezing water as long as he could, he stripped off his clothing and rubbed every square inch of himself and his clothes with sand from the bottom of the stream. The worst of the sticky fluid had hit him low on his legs. That's where he concentrated his efforts. Finally, he could stand the cold water no longer and stood on the bank wringing out his clothes and jumping up and down to get warm.

He had been gone from his work in the garden most of the day. He hung his wet clothing on low tree branches and went hunting for something to bring home for dinner. Finally, his clothes were dry and he picked up the flat stone for Homer's grave again. He walked to the gravesite and dropped the stone calling for Peshewa. There was no answer. He straightened up and looked toward the house.

Then he saw them.

Ruth and Ester had been killed by a single blow each to the back of their heads. Peshewa had been stabbed in the back and scalped. They had tried to run from the house to where they thought he would be. He sat on the ground. He didn't know how long he sat before his mind began to function again. Whoever had murdered his family might still be near, and he would be a perfect target for them. He didn't care. He held back his grief. He fought it. There would be time to grieve later. He had other things to do first.

He used the flat stone intended for Homer's grave to dig a larger one next to it. He took care to orient it east and west as was the Shawnee custom. He laid Peshewa in first and then placed his little girls with her, one on each side with her arms around them.

He didn't have time to line the grave with stones or bark, and he couldn't cover it with small logs before piling on the earth as her tribesmen would have done. He just covered them with the garden soil that had been worked so lovingly by Peshewa. Night had fallen, and he slept on the mounded earth until the first light. There would be no nightmare this night—his sorrow was too deep.

His heart was empty, but his soul was filled with fire—murderous fire. He took only his rifle, powder, shot, axe, knife and one canteen. The murderers had taken everything useful from his house. He found their foot prints at the edge of the yard. There were at least two of them. They must have been following Homer, looking for an easy kill when they found his family. But this was his country, and he knew where they were going.

It was nearly dusk two days later when he found them.

There were three of them. He moved to within ten yards of the man nearest him. He was sure the remaining odor of the skunk would cover his own scent. One man was seated on a log, facing away from him looking at a small fire. Another was seated across from the first man on the other side of the fire. That man was also seated on a log and was wearing the white buffalo robe Peshewa had given him. He could barely see the third man who sat on the ground to his right, also facing the fire. He recognized their features and their dress. They were of the same tribe that had captured Peshewa.

Peshewa. He couldn't let himself think of her, not yet.

He should have taken his time and planned his moves, but his blood was up. He shot and killed the first man, the one closest to him. Immediately, he was on his feet, his axe in his left hand and his knife in his right. The man in the buffalo robe stood, bringing up Homer's rifle to aim at him. He ignored him. Indians were notoriously poor shots, and he would have to take his chances. He leapt instead toward the third Indian just getting to his feet, slicing through the man's throat with his knife.

He heard the rifle fire and thought in the second he had left, "This is it."

But as the Indian stood to fire, the buffalo robe caught on something behind the log. It held him, momentarily pulling him off his target just as Peshewa had pulled one of her captors off aim when he first rescued her. The man jerked upright to free himself just as his rifle fired. The ball went high—too high.

He was driven back as the rifle ball grazed high off the left side of his head. He went down but rolled away, coming up quickly still holding his axe. The man in the buffalo robe dropped the rifle and ran toward the forest. His axe should have killed the fleeing Indian but stuck, instead, in the only tree between them. The Indian ran on, disappearing into the woods.

He started after him, but blood from the wound in his forehead blinded him and he had to stop and staunch the flow with his hand. He cut a piece of leather off the vest of the second man who now lay dead at his feet, blood covering his face and upper body. He wiped the blood from his knife on the rest of the man's vest. He used the leather to improvise a bandage for his head wound. It was in the same place the British naval officer had hit him with the pistol back in Baltimore.

It was his "mark of Cain," opened again with two new murders. He retrieved his rifle, loaded it and pulled his axe from the tree. He began to run after the other Indian, holding his axe in one hand and his rifle in the other. He ran for two more hours before the moon set, and he could no longer move through the trees safely. Stumbling over a rock or fallen tree in the dark could mean a broken leg or foot. That would allow the other man to get away—something his rage could not allow to happen. As he waited in the forest for dawn, he concentrated on the pain from the wound in his head. He could not allow the emotions pushing him so hard to well up and weaken him. Not now.

He followed the other man for three more days. He knew he was getting closer each day because the man had abandoned all his earlier attempts to cover his trail. That took time and did nothing to slow the chase. He had a very good idea where the man was going, and he ran hard, barely looking at the trail.

They were in more open country now, crossing a series of low ridges where the trees did not grow well in the rocky soil. The third day he saw the object of his raging hate. The Indian was close to the top of the next ridge. After a few strides, the Indian disappeared over it. By the time he reached that same place, the Indian had crossed a small stream at the bottom of the ridge and started up the opposite slope. As he watched, the man stumbled, picked himself up, and stumbled again.

He lay down, steadying his rifle. The man was not more than 300 yards away. It would take a good shot—but he was better than just good. He took a breath and released it slowly, his finger tightening, not pulling, on the trigger. In another second the murderer in the buffalo robe would be dead.

But there was no sound of a rifle shot. Slowly, he moved his finger away from the trigger. He lowered the hammer on the rifle and watched for another few minutes until the man reached the top of the ridge and started down the other side.

As he sighted down his rifle, laying its sight on the broad back of the Indian, he had seen something else, something very interesting just on the other side of the ridge ahead: smoke—lots of smoke hugging the ground. The Indian's tribal campsite must be just there, over the last ridge. The Indian had stumbled several times climbing the slope.

Was he tired? Or was he sick?

He would soon be with his tribesmen—tribesmen who would all admire his new robe made from the single hide of a white buffalo—the same white buffalo robe that had covered Homer Davis as he lay dying of small pox. Small pox was unknown in this part of the forest—until now.

He turned and moved swiftly back to the camp where he had killed the other two Indians. He recovered his kit including Titus's precious Bible with Margery's cross inside. He picked up Homer's rifle where the third Indian had dropped it and started back home. Then he remembered something. He returned and took care to urinate on the bodies of both dead Indians, then he spit on the ground. He, too, was not a man anyone would want for an enemy.

He marked both Homer's and his family's graves with flat stones without names or dates. He liked the Indian attitude toward history. What had happened in the past had happened—and could not be altered. Exactly when, or in what order events had happened was, therefore, unimportant. All that mattered was the memory and the lesson.

There was only an hour left before nightfall when he turned away, again moving west. A light rain had begun to fall.

Peshewa would like this soaking rain.

He had gone less than a mile. "Peshewa!" her name exploded in his mind. The grief he had been holding back broke through. He fell to the ground, lying on his side. He drew his knees to his chest in a fetal position, covering his head with his hands as waves of sobs swept over him. He would have vomited from the convulsions but couldn't—he hadn't eaten anything for days.

Much later, when he could, he stood and threw his head back, letting the rain strike his face and mingle with his tears as he screamed a long aching howl into the night. Soon, another voice joined his. A wolf a short distance away took up his call. Then another took up the call, then another and another. Dozens of wolves from all directions, some near, some far, took up the sorrowful cry. Man and wolves together, howled a mournful keening.

Richard L. Evans

CHAPTER FIVE

JEDEDIAH

He inhaled, then let it out slowly as he squeezed the trigger. It was second nature now. The rifle ball exploded out of the barrel and the Blackfoot brave kicked forward in a complete somersault spraying blood across the tall grass. The horse the Indian had been leading jumped sideways a few steps then steadied. The sound of his shot echoed from the mountains all around him. He had lost count, but he thought this one was about the twentieth man he had killed since he left the valley of the Ohio River and the grave containing the only family he was sure he would ever have. They were all Blackfoot Indians. This was the only one he hadn't killed in self-defense.

This one he executed for the crime of murder.

He had found a trapper's body, what was left of it, and followed the horse's tracks until he was sure which way the killer was headed. A man on a horse should have outdistanced him easily, but the horse was loaded with beaver pelts and traps, so the Indian walked ahead of the horse—and died for his greed.

He stood over the man he had just shot in the back and thought about what brought him to this place: a place where one man killed another for the skins of animals—or just for the hell of it. He thought about his journeys across the vast, grassy plains and the cold, beautiful mountains.

It had been a long time.

•

The familiar forests were behind him—the forests where the wolves took up his sorrowful cry. The forests gave way, grudgingly at first, to scrub bushes and coarse grass. Now it was just grass, grass for as far as he could see in every direction. It reminded him of his days at sea with no land in sight. He used the same navigation aide he used at sea to keep him on course. Before noon, he kept his shadow in front of him. After noon, he kept the sun in his face.

There was so little to see, so little variation from hour to hour, that he turned off that mental energy and turned again to his long search for himself. What was he? Even more important, what was he supposed to be? Why did he carry the mark of Cain? Why did he only succeed in killing those he tried to heal? Why did he live on when everyone else died?

The same questions returned again and again, and he was no closer to the answers. He remembered the snowfalls in the forest. He remembered the silence that wasn't exactly silence, the silence that had a voice he couldn't quite hear. The sound of his legs swishing through the grass gave him the same sense of expectancy. Perhaps the voice would speak more clearly here.

But another sense broke through his consciousness: smell. He smelled smoke. Smoke in the grasslands usually meant danger. If he could smell smoke, it meant it was coming on the wind and that meant the source of the smoke was coming, too. He put his face in the wind and saw it. It was wide and the smoke was not drifting up; it was hugging the ground—moving fast. He looked around quickly. Old survival skills, like finding a river or a cave, wouldn't save him here.

He brought his rifle off his shoulder and plugged the touch

hole with a twig so that it wouldn't fire the main powder charge and ball when he pulled the trigger.

He kept the twig in his pouch along with some dry tinder for just such an emergency. And this was an emergency.

Working fast, he tore up handfuls of the driest grass near him and twisted them into makeshift torches. He pulled back the hammer and put a pinch of dry tinder in the rifle's pan and pulled the trigger. The tinder flared up from the spark and he lit one of his torches. He lit the others with the first one and began setting the prairie grass downwind on fire. His only chance was to follow close behind his new burn and hope the big, fast, deadly fire behind him would die of "starvation" when it reached the place he had already burned. His fire began to shoot up and move away quickly.

He ran after it feeling the fresh, hot ashes through his moccasins. If that were all the heat he'd feel this day, he'd count himself lucky. The smoke was intense. The fire behind him was getting very close. His eyes stung but he kept them open; he had to keep running in the right direction. Finally, the smoke got in his lungs and he had to stop to breathe. He looked behind him through watery eyes at a clearing sky. The only fire still burning was his and it was going away. His feet hurt. His eyes hurt. His lungs hurt. He thanked God.

The prairie held other surprises.

Massive thunderstorms and lighting strikes drove him to low places where he crouched, making himself as small a target as he could. Flash floods followed those storms to drown the unwary who stayed too long in low places. After surviving at sea for years, it would have been a strange twist to drown on the dry plains. At sea he was also used to cyclones called waterspouts. They were nothing compared to the giant windstorms on the plains. But the most deadly thing on the prairie was the plains buffalo

He had hunted the Eastern buffalo in Kentucky, Indiana and Illinois. His beautiful white robe had been made of a buffalo hide. That robe was made all the more precious because buffalo were becoming hard to find in the woodlands west of the Appalachians. The plains buffalo were a different story. They were larger and lived in huge herds. They were tougher, stronger and dumber than their Eastern cousins. That made them all the more dangerous. They were unpredictable.

He had heard stories of hunters shooting buffaloes straight through the heart and then having to run for their lives, trying to dodge the animal they'd just shot as it charged after them. A large buffalo might run for a half mile after taking a shot in the heart. Professional buffalo hunters shot a buffalo through the lungs, not the heart. Shot through the heart, it would panic and run, causing all the other buffalo to run with it. Shot through the lungs, a buffalo would stand still before keeling over and dying. He didn't care about how to kill lots of buffalo. He had no desire to kill more than one buffalo at a time.

There came a time when he was happy to kill just one.

The sun was well up one morning as he went downstream following a small creek bed hoping it would lead him to a tributary of the Platte. The short brush crunched underfoot with a frost that hadn't yet melted in the near freezing air. Sunlight glinted off ice that was just forming on the edges of the creek. The water in the stream began to move from side to side.

Peculiar.

Then he felt it under his feet. The earth was vibrating with a high frequency. The sound came next. He ran up the side of the slope away from the water. He assumed a flash flood was racing down the stream bed.

But as he ran he thought: *It's much too loud—there couldn't be that much water.*

When he reached the high ground above the stream, he saw it. As it got closer, he saw that it wasn't an "it," it was a "them." Thousands of "them" were running so close together they made an "it" It was a huge, rolling shadow racing over the prairie toward...him!

Like his experience with the prairie fire, there was nowhere to run and nowhere to hide. He dropped to one knee, checked his firing cap, pulled back the hammer and took aim. The earth shaking under him caused his rifle sight to jump up and down wildly. He only had time to say a quick prayer and fire. It must have been a very good prayer.

Richard L. Evans

The buffalo nearest him stumbled forward and began to roll over and over. Just before it rolled over him, it stopped. It was still kicking. He leapt forward and flattened himself against the back of the beast. He pushed his rifle against his chest and ducked his head in both hands. Other huge bodies began falling in the dirt on both sides and behind him. The buffaloes behind the one he shot couldn't turn away from the fallen bull and began piling up around him. He was part of a new island, building in the middle of a dusty brown and black tide passing over the prairie—and over him. He tried not to breathe. Dirt and grass were kicked on him, and the air around him became a brown semisolid. The body of the buffalo he lay under continued to jerk and pound his body into the earth. The animal was dead but was now being kicked by other charging beasts.

He didn't know how long it lasted: one minute; five minutes; thirty minutes; time became irrelevant. All he knew was the dirt, the pounding his body was taking, the roaring sound of thousands of hooves striking the earth and the smell. Oh, God, the smell! The smell was worse than the smell in the hold of the *Anne* with its pitiful slaves.

Then it was over. Just like that.

The sound receded. The earth stopped shaking and the dust began to settle. He tried to pull himself from under the weight of the great beast. One of his legs was pinned securely, and he had to use his knife to dig out the soil under it before he could pull it out.

He stood and checked himself. Nothing seemed to be broken. His rifle and pack were still with him and were undamaged.

He walked back to the stream bed he had run from earlier. The stream was a muddy smear from the bed all the way up the other slope where the buffalo had run. If he hadn't run up the bank, he would probably be just a reddish streak mixed in with the wet earth. He went back to the dead buffalo. There were actually three dead animals. Two others had been trampled by their own kind after piling up behind the one he shot.

He dined on "fat cow" that evening and for several days more. He took part of the hide with him to repair the bottoms of his moccasins. Buffalo hide was the toughest material to be found on the plains. He was lucky the buffalo weren't "wearing" him on the bottoms of *their* feet.

When he told what had happened to him that day to other frontiersmen, they only smiled at him and told him how much they enjoyed his "tall story."

Snakes were almost never a problem. They would always move away if given a chance. In all his travels in the wilds he was bitten only twice. Both times he had come upon the snakes too quickly for them to escape, and they had struck in self-defense. His immune system took care of the venom quickly. He thought of snakes as his "lowdown brethren." He never attacked snakes, killing them for no good reason as he saw other men do. He had a lot more trouble with scorpions. They liked to crawl up to him at night.

•

He thought the lower Ohio was wide until he saw the Mississippi. He paid a ferryman to take him across to the western shore where he turned north, going upstream. A frontiersman he met back in Kentucky told him to find a trading place called St. Louis.

"That would be the best place to start if you're dead set on going to the high mountain country. That's where the beaver are, for sure, but this child wouldn't go back there on a bet."

That was the first time he heard a grown man refer to himself as a "child."

At St. Louis he found a merchant trader who gave him a lot of good advice about what he was about to do and where he should go to do it. All the other new arrivals were going up the Missouri—going after beaver, to get rich.

He already knew about getting rich.

He was after something else.

The merchant showed him a rifle that was both familiar and strange.

"This is what we call a prairie rifle," the merchant said. "It looks a lot like that flintlock you've been carrying on your shoulder, but it differs in two important ways."

He could see one of the differences right away. When the merchant held up a rifle ball, he saw the other.

"Yep, this is a Hawken rifle," the merchant continued, "fires a fifty caliber ball out of a thirty-eight inch barrel. It packs a lot more killing power than your flintlock—drop a buffalo at 400 yards. You'll also notice that it fires with a percussion cap rather than a flint striking a steel flange. No need to prime the pan, just drop in the cap, pull back the hammer and squeeze her off. You load her the same way you're used to with your old flintlock."

He knew about the Hawken rifle. He also knew that a lot of the mountain men still preferred a flintlock for its lighter weight and simplicity. All a man needed with a flintlock was powder and ball. The Hawken added the need for percussion caps which were not easily made in the wilderness.

"I have two flintlocks," he said.

He showed him Homer Davis's Kentucky rifle.

"That's a fine piece, too my friend, but my advice is to take the Hawken."

"I'll need to try it first."

They walked outside a few yards to the rear of the merchant's store. The wilderness started right there. He took the rifle and the ball from the merchant and measured a powder load in his hand.

"A little more," said the merchant, "remember you're driving a lot more weight with the Hawken's fifty caliber."

He measured out more powder in his hand until the merchant nodded.

"Packing?" he asked the merchant as he loaded the rifle.

"Some like it. It helps to wipe the barrel, too, but unless you've got one hell of a long shot, I wouldn't bother." He bothered. He used a patch to pack the ball as he had been taught by Homer Davis.

"How about that single dead limb sticking out of that tree down there?" He pointed to a half-dead elm tree standing out from the others He knew it was every bit of 650 yards away, but he wanted to hear what the merchant would say.

"Who do you think you are, Colonel Boone?"

The merchant had his doubts—more about his sanity than his marksmanship.

"I don't believe the Colonel himself would take that shot."

"I'll take the shot for a small wager. If I hit that dead limb from here, we trade my rifle for this Hawken, dead even. If I miss, we trade both my rifles for this one."

The merchant knew a good bet when he heard one.

"Done," he said.

Pulling back the hammer, he said a little prayer hoping God would take special care of his friend Homer Davis up in heaven. Seconds later he was outfitted with a brand new rifle.

He traded Homer's rifle for two pistols of the same caliber as the Hawken—there was no sense worrying about having the right size ball when in danger. And having to use the pistols would mean he was in danger.

The merchant invited him back anytime he had something good to trade and particularly anytime he wanted to make a few extra dollars "behind the store." He explained he had some friends in St. Louis, betting men, who wouldn't believe that shot any more than he had.

He started up the Missouri but not the way most men did—most men went by boat. He was in no hurry and wasn't looking for company. He liked the freedom to go anywhere his feet might take him. He started walking.

The merchant had warned him about the Arikara Indians. The Arikara were infamous for attacking river traffic from their fortified cities along the river's banks. They were hostile, brave and tough. He didn't think he'd care to know any more about them. When he came into their country, he took a wide detour away from the river. He had a lot of time to think about it. The Arikara were 600 miles up river.

It wasn't until he was well up in the highlands near the Yellowstone that he was first attacked. His attackers were Blackfoot Indians. He was also warned back in St. Louis to avoid the Blackfoot country.

"Why are they called, Blackfoot?" he asked the same merchant who had outfitted him.

"They rub wood ashes on their moccasins. It turns them black. No one knows why they do it. Least ways, no one I know. None of them other Indians do it. But, stay away from them as much as you can. The Blackfoot are warriors, always fighting with someone, the Sioux or the Crow to the east or the Flatheads to the west. I've had mountain men tell me they even take on the Kiowa. There's been some that could trade with them, but they didn't stay so long as to wear out their welcome. Stay away from them."

The merchant added, "You've also got the Pawnees to the west and south. They're big trouble, too. Of course, if you really want to die in the worst way—and I do mean the *worst* possible way—you can take on the Comanches or the Apaches."

He tried to follow the man's advice. It didn't always work.

It was the constant threat of attack that caused him to adopt some of the safeguards he used back in the eastern forests. He set his campsites in low depressions surrounded by trees where possible. He built fires only when necessary—always using dry wood which burned with less smoke and always in a low place so the wind would not carry the sight or smell of smoke very far

If he built a cooking fire, he didn't sleep near it. He would move his blankets thirty or forty yards off from the fire and lie under the trees. He also tried to put a rock face or ravine behind him away from the fire. He didn't want to be surprised from that direction. If he had fresh meat, he staked it near the fire. Grizzly bears or wolves sometimes came during the night looking for a treat.

Indians, too, liked to attack at night, particularly on moonlit nights. Away from the fire he might escape detection. If not, he would have his attackers lit by the firelight with a safe background to protect him. He could kill them out of the dark. Now that he was in Blackfoot country, he moved cautiously and set his camp carefully.

He saw them way off down a long, grassy slope.

They were just coming out of a grove of cottonwoods. There were four of them mounted on horses, each leading two other loaded horses or mules. They didn't appear to be Indians. He couldn't be sure, but he thought they saw him, too. They weren't trailing him. He had come from the south; they were coming from the north.

He turned his horse, the horse he had taken from the Blackfoot brave, and rode slowly on up and over the top of the slope. He set his camp another four miles higher up in a ravine. It was a good campsite—a small forest well protected on two sides with a cut behind him he hoped would be a backdoor in an emergency. Night was about to fall when he heard the call.

"Ho, there in the camp!"

He responded from his cover away from the fire.

"How many are you?"

"Four. I'm Fitz, Tom Fitzpatrick."

He'd heard of Fitzpatrick. He was famous as a mountain man.

He said, "Come on in Tom Fitzpatrick."

As they came in, he saw them more clearly in the firelight: trappers, loaded with gear. He stood and came toward them. They weren't surprised when he came out of the darkness rather than near the fire. He showed them where his horse was so they could tie up their horses and mules, too.

"Your horse didn't give you any warning of us," said one of the men.

He was tall, the tallest in the group. He was also angular in build and looked to be strong. Like the others he was young, not more than thirty at most.

"I told him not to," he told the stranger.

There was a little laugh from the other three men. But it was true; he had.

"I guess you saw us when we broke from the trees."

It was the same tall man.

"My name's Jed Smith."

That was another name he had heard before: "Captain" Jedediah Strong Smith. Despite their apparent youth, these men, Fitzpatrick and Smith, had the best of reputations among their fellow fur trappers. The other two men introduced themselves and after hearing their names, he knew he was in very select company. The others were both rather tall men, too—not as tall as Smith but much taller than the Irishman, Fitzpatrick. Their names were Bill Sublette and David Jackson.

He had shot a buffalo three days before and packed as much of the meat with him as he could. When he set this campfire, he had staked up two large roasts to cook. It was late spring but still quite cold in the mountains. They could see he expected them.

Soon they were all seated a few yards from the fire eating "fat cow"—the best meal a mountain man could get—and drinking a little coffee the trappers had packed in. Mountain men were usually close with information about themselves. But that night, in the company of others like themselves, they were very open. He found them charming, like grown-up kids. He said little and listened a lot.

They had bought out General William Ashley's fur company, and were bringing supplies to their trappers in the upper reaches of the Missouri River. They were also scouting the high country, looking for new beaver valleys. They had all been through this country before.

"Why don't you come join our brigade?" asked Bill Sublette. "You can make some good money, and we'll stand for all your supplies."

Sublette thought he was recruiting another independent trapper.

"That's not what I'm after," he replied. "I've had money, and I know what it can bring. I'm after something else."

"What's wrong with money?" asked Fitzpatrick.

"Let me ask you something," he replied. "Have you ever seen those mountains that rise above that sweet plain covered with wildflowers over near the Yellowstone? The Tetons, I've heard them called. Have you ever seen them when the sun was low behind you and lit up the snow caught in the crags of those mountains? It makes the whole sky look like its being eaten by an animal with giant, fiery teeth. And those yellow flowers in the valley! I've sat in that waving sea of golden flowers. I've sat there and felt the power of something so enormous I couldn't describe it…the power of God, maybe."

They all had seen them or some others like them.

He went on, "If you get way up in the mountains, you can watch while a rain cloud moves along the slope down below you. And sometimes after it rains, you can see a rainbow. If you're high enough above it and the sun's just right, you can see almost the whole rainbow, the whole circle. You've all seen that?"

They all nodded that they had.

"If you had enough money, could you buy that rainbow?

Could you buy those mountains and that snow and that sunshine?"

There was no reply.

"Look at the stars. If you had the money, could you buy even one of those stars? Of course not, but look at all the multitude of stars we have tonight, and they're all free—no charge. Me, I don't have to buy those snowy mountains or even one of those brilliant stars—I don't have to buy them because I already have them. They're mine for as long as I want them. They're gifts God has already given me."

He half-laughed, "What would I do with money? What could I buy that would be better than what I already have? Could I buy a better evening than this one? Could any of you?"

There was still no reply. They were all thinking.

"A millionaire couldn't buy anything better than this. I'm already living as well as any millionaire—so I don't need the money."

Again, they all nodded in agreement. But he knew tomorrow they would be on their way looking for more beaver streams to make their fortunes.

They settled in, taking that sure comfort men find in the company of other men like themselves. Pipes were brought out and smoked.

He looked at "Captain" Jedediah Smith as he sat illuminated by the fire light. He was called "Captain" because he always took the lead in any group of men. Even skilled mountain men like Bill Sublette and Fitz followed Jed's lead on the trail.

As he watched Smith, he noticed a peculiar scar, a long thin line running across part of his forehead and into his hair line. The hair around the scar grew unevenly. Jedediah Smith had obviously let his hair grow long to cover the scar running over his head. One of his ears also appeared to be slightly angled from his head. The other three men present knew the reason for Jed Smith's unusual appearance, but he would have to wait awhile to learn about it.

Smith reached in his pack and pulled out a book. The book was covered in black leather with gold leaf along the edges of the pages: a Bible.

He reached into his pack and retrieved Titus's Bible. His eyes met Smith's.

"I see you're a Bible reader, too," said Jed.

"Yes, for years now. But I'm still working at it—I'm still wrestling with God."

"That won't end, I do believe. But it's good you do it. Too many just give up on God. Things don't come their way or work out the way they think they should, so they blame God for all their troubles.

"Some others believe God is like a rich uncle ready to hand out favors in need.

"You just keep struggling and you'll be all right."

That evening, he found a kindred spirit and made a good friend in Jed Smith.

The evening ended with stories told all around, and the stranger the story or the bigger the lie, the better. The best story teller by far was Tom Fitzpatrick. Other than himself, he had never met a more accomplished liar. He did it out of his need to keep his secrets—Tom Fitzpatrick lied for the shear pleasure of it.

The moon was well up when it came his turn to entertain. He told a true story.

"Did you ever have one of those days," he began, "when it just doesn't pay to roll out of your blanket? I had one like that about a year ago.

I was up on one of those high, level places up toward the Big Horn and had crossed a shallow river, wide but shallow. I thought I was following a buffalo trail. Next time, I'll look more closely at the trail. I was actually trailing a bunch of Indians who were trailing the buffalo—a Blackfoot war party—Gros Ventres, I think. I came up over a low rise and found myself looking at about two dozen braves. They were a couple of hundred yards ahead of me.

"It's a good thing they're not mounted," I thought.

"It would have been even better if they hadn't seen me, too."

The men chuckled.

He went on, "Now, there are times when it's best to stand and fight. But that wasn't one of them. I turned around and started running. Imminent death can give a man a real kick. I knew my only hope was to get back across that wide, shallow river and pick them off as they slowed down to wade through the water after me. But that meant I had to beat them to the river by a wide margin so I could get across before they did the same thing to me.

"I took a chance and glanced back over my shoulder and saw I wasn't going to make it.

"As I turned forward again, I—*Whoa!* I yelled and took a quick step to one side. My mind caught up with my instincts a half second later. This huge, brown and yellow thing had risen up out of a low trough in the ground right in front of me. Grizzly! Where did that big fellow come from? I had dodged him, but that wasn't necessarily good news. I'm thinking, if he decides to chase me down, I have no chance. Nobody can outrun a grizzly bear. But at least that griz will kill me a lot quicker and with less pain than those Blackfoot.

"My brain wasn't helping me much. But, behind me, that old bear sure was.

"I guess I had come up on him so fast, the griz had not seen me coming and was surprised to see a little, scared animal whiz past him. But old Griz, he did see that other bunch of black-footed little animals running at him from the same direction. He must have decided he'd had enough of that nonsense. That bear went after them, not me. Most of the Indians decided to take a more circuitous route to the river. But a couple of them were too close to the bear to do anything but die. The diversion gave me enough time to cross the river, drop to one knee, level my rifle and kill the first Indian to the river. Three more were floating facedown in the water before the rest of the party decided they'd have to hunt me down another day.

"From that day on, I've been attacked every time I came anywhere near the Blackfoot. I've never shot another grizzly bear, though. Old Muga and all his family are my friends."

Then he told them the story of how he escaped being trampled by the buffalo herd. They didn't believe that one, either.

"You said Muga? Do you speak Shawnee?"

Jed Smith was curious.

"Yes, some. I was married to a Shawnee woman some years ago. She was killed."

He said nothing more.

After a few seconds the other men understood that was all he wished to say. Mountain men respected a man's privacy.

"The Shawnee are a fine looking people," said Tom Fitzpatrick easing away from an obviously sensitive subject. "Almost as good looking as the Shoshone."

He learned later that "Old Tom" had taken a Shoshone wife at one time, so he should know.

He was curious about the sexual appetites of other Indian women. He wasn't sure, but he felt Peshewa's ravenous desires were not all that common. Not knowing how to ask, he was about to let the subject drop when the others began talking about a fellow named Jim Beckwourth.

The story, as they told it, was about this fellow, Jim Beckwourth.

Jim was born in Virginia, the son of a black slave woman and a white plantation overseer. Jim had come west seeking his fortune as a fur trapper but soon found other ways to make money that were a little less demanding but every bit as dangerous. He traded with the Blackfoot for a time, had even been adopted by them as the long, lost son of their chief. He was said to have married at least one, and maybe more, Blackfoot women. And according to his companions, "Old Jim" was quite the ladies man.

Tom Fitzpatrick said, "He left a sweetheart back in St. Louis when he went in the mountains. He spoke of her often, even after he married that crazy Blackfoot woman and them eight Crow wives."

"There was actually nine of them," said Jackson.

An argument broke out about the exact number of Old Jim's wives.

He had to know, and he might never have another chance.

He asked, "Did Old Jim ever talk about the...um...Indian women...their...um...sexual attitudes?"

The other men looked at each other with gentle smiles. Every man there knew about the "...um...sexual attitudes" of most Indian women.

Tom Fitzpatrick broke the silence saying, "Old Jim, he said

they was all willin', sure enough, but he got a lot more exercise trying to keep peace betwix his eight wives than he ever got under their blankets."

"There was nine."

David Jackson didn't give up easily.

Before they left, he asked them what year it was. They said it was 1826. He'd lost a year somewhere. How much time you've already lived doesn't seem so important if you think you still have lots of time left.

Jed Smith said he was organizing a party to explore the western side of the mountains.

"There are sure to be a lot of beaver that way."

Jed showed him a map of the whole region. The place where he wanted to go was blank. No one had ever mapped it.

"I could use an experienced traveler like yourself," Jed said. "Meet me at the summer rendezvous at Willow Valley if you're interested. I need someone who knows how to draw a map."

•

The annual summer rendezvous was a new but growing tradition among the mountain men. A different place was chosen each summer where a combination market, festival and free-for-all attracted hundreds of trappers. They would bring their entire yearly stock of beaver, otter and deerskins to sell to the major fur companies. The proceeds of their sales would then be spent immediately on well-watered whiskey and gambling. Impromptu contests of marksmanship and courage, often ending in the death of one or more contestants, were held.

The gathering also attracted large numbers of friendly Indians. The Indians would set up small villages around the area marked off by the mountain men. Many marriages with Indian squaws were arranged and consummated on the spot. Fights usually broke out both before and after those marriages.

He arrived at the rendezvous a little early. He wanted to learn all he could about Captain Jed Smith. He knew the mountain men loved to talk about their heroes and that the whiskey would lubricate their already subtle minds. He got the story about

Smith's scars from a fellow named Jim Clyman who, as luck would have it, had been there.

"We was sent out by General Ashley and Major Henry," Clyman started, "to scout ahead in the area of the Yellowstone River. That was right after them Arikara tore us up real bad coming up the Missouri. It was a miracle that this child got out of it alive. But Jed, he survived it, too, and led us out. That was when we started calling him Captain.

"Well, we come upon this big stand of cottonwoods down by a little tributary of the Yellowstone. It looked to be a good place to set up camp for the night. Captain Smith, he was in the lead there, leading his horse through the tall brush up front. All of a sudden here comes a griz—she just pops right out of the brush about the middle of our line. Scares the very bejesus out of us, but don't come on us. She wheels and runs right along side of us until she comes up on Jed at the head of the line, and she jumps him real quick.

"We all ran up there and started in shooting that bear every way we could. By the time we killed it, old Jed he was in a pretty bad way. The griz had his head in her mouth and had torn most of his scalp off. One of his ears was just hanging down, you know, by just a piece of skin. The bear had clawed his side and leg pretty bad, too. None of us could think what to do. But before long, old Captain Smith he sits up and starts giving orders. This one go down to the river and fetch water. That one set up a tent.

"Then he turns to me and says, 'Get a needle and thread from my pack and sew me back up.'

"Well, hell boy, I don't want to do that, but what else could this child do? I told Jed my stick didn't float thata way, but he said I had to do it. I washed the blood off his head and cut away all the hair I could and then proceeded to stitch him up. I told him I didn't think we should try to save his ear, but he had me sew it back on anyways. He sure didn't want to go off with just the one ear. I must have put a hundred stitches just in that ear alone. Ten days later he gets up from his bed in that tent, and off we go again like it was nothing. End of story."

After hearing Jim Clyman's account of his Captain's encounter with the grizzly bear, he decided to go with Jed Smith into the great unmarked territory west of the Rocky Mountains.

When he saw Jed later, he just said, "Lead on, Captain."

•

Everyone agreed the only good thing about the unmapped country they were traveling through was the scarcity of Indians. Even that good fortune almost ran out one parched afternoon.

The heat of the day forced them to travel more often at night than during the day. Jed's party had stopped to find shade below a rocky outcropping, and most lay in shallow trenches dug in the sand to escape the heat. He was kneeling to sketch the position of a distant range when he heard a low whistle. Low whistles always mean "pay attention." It was Jed Smith motioning to him to get down. As he did, he saw Jed point across an expanse of desert scrub to a place about a mile off. There, walking slowly, was a large war party of Indians leading their horses—Comanche. He tried not to even breathe. All eyes followed the slow progress of the Comanche warriors until they passed out of sight.

There were a number of Indian tribes no one wanted to tangle with. The Comanche were at the top of everyone's list. Capture by those braves who had just walked across their line of vision would mean a death more torturous than anything any of them could imagine. They had all heard the stories. Stories of men peeled like grapes, then set to burn with flaming rods thrust into their bodies. The Comanche squaws were very inventive.

After another month the horses all died. They ate them. The water barrels were empty. There was no more jerky, flour or salt. He had heard of other trappers in similar, desperate circumstances, starving when there was no game. There was a story, true or not he didn't know, about a man who was so hungry he roasted the buffalo hide on the bottom of his moccasins and ate that. He considered it. One of the men brought in a raven. They ate that. Another man brought in a vulture. They ate that, too.

Less than a month later and very near starvation, he sat looking at a land so green he wasn't sure at first that he really saw it. They had crossed a great, dry basin and a brutal desert occupied by the Mojave Indians. The last of their water was gone. But Captain Smith got them to the western slope of the San Bernardino Mountains where southern California lay before them.

After resting at a Spanish mission for several weeks, they moved northward through one of the broadest and most beautiful valleys any of them had ever seen. Eventually, he stood on a low hill overlooking the ocean. His seafaring eye lit on the most nearly perfect natural harbor he had ever seen.

"What is the name of this place?" he asked using signs of the Indian who was serving as their guide.

"Yorba Buena," the Indian said.

He made a mental note of the place. He wanted to return someday.

"Yorba Buena."

He repeated the name so he wouldn't forget it.

They turned east to the American River region, then came to a halt. Jed Smith said it was time to go back across the Sierra Nevadas to report his mission at the coming rendezvous of 1827. Jed left with three men.

After agreeing to meet Smith at this same place in another eight months, the rest of the party set out to trap beaver. Having no interest in hunting beaver, he continued northward and then westward alone, back to the Pacific coast. He, too, agreed to return in eight months to meet his good friend, Jedediah. Everyone was sure the "Captain" would make it back. But he didn't.

Chapter Six

WILLOWY

He was tired. He had wandered for years. That was the best word for it, "wandered." He had no direction—no destination. He walked on through shortening days until it started to turn cold again.

He came to a wide river and followed one of its small tributaries up a lovely, forested valley. He passed an Indian village. He didn't recognize the tribe, but they nodded and smiled back when he smiled at them. He kept going until he was well up the valley. A high, level elevation overlooked miles of green forests with silver strings of water running through them. There was a spring nearby. This was as good a place as he would find, and there he rested.

In another month he completed a cabin. It was like the one he and Peshewa had built together. It had her strength, but he doubted it would ever have her loving touch.

He began watching the Indians that lived down the valley, the friendly Indians he had passed coming to his new mountain home. He watched them take salmon from the river in woven fish traps and gather nuts around oak trees. He gathered some acorns himself and tried to find a way to eat them. It was impossible. They were bitter. Even when he did manage to get them down, they upset his stomach. The Indians were welcome to all the acorns they could find—they would have no competition from him. He found game and other roots and plants plentiful so he didn't need oak nuts. The salmon, like the other fish, swam to his wiggling fingers.

He killed two deer with a single shot—the ball passing through one, killing it—then injuring another. He had to put down the second deer to end its pain.

On a whim, he carried a large portion of the venison to the Indian village as a gift. As he walked between two lines of deerskin covered huts, he was met by a large group of people. They were of all ages and both genders. He was relieved. If they meant him harm, the "welcoming party" would have all been warriors.

He stopped, and one of the Indians stepped forward. He held out the venison he had wrapped in a doeskin. The whole village broke into smiles and his gift was accepted.

He was led to an open area and when all were seated with him, he was offered a bowl of *uh oh...acorns*. They had been mashed and cooked as a kind of mush. He was a guest. It would be impolite not to eat what they offered, so he did. It wasn't so bad—it was better than beaver and only a little worse than roasted buffalo hide from the bottom of his moccasins. Whenever he had more meat than he could eat, he took it to the Indian village.

He marked the passing of the seasons but forgot the number of the year again. One day he was surprised to see two women from the village walk into his home site. One was young and rather pretty. The other was much older, perhaps in her fifties. She was much more like the others of her tribe—short, with thick arms and legs. Both women were stoic, unsmiling. He had learned a little of their language, and he used the universal sign language of the plains Indians to fill in the gaps where he didn't know the words. They had come to live with him. They were "gifts" from their chief. The chief was concerned about him—that he had to work with no woman to help him. The whole village felt sorry for him and wanted to do something to make him happy. A young man should not live alone. The older woman was to work for him. The younger woman was his wife.

He had lived alone since Peshewa was killed. He had remained celibate for years. Other Indians had offered him squaws as wives but he always refused.

Most squaws understood that their lives would be easier living with a mountain man than it would be living with their own kind. He remembered something one of his early shipmates had told him years ago. The sailor said it was an Old Russian proverb: "Women do all the work, men do the rest." He was sure the American Indians had adopted the Russian model for their social organization. The Indian braves hunted, fished and made war—they had all the fun. The Indian women did everything else—all the hard work. Now, he had two women who expected to divide the labor.

He didn't want to live with these women, but he knew he absolutely could not send them back. That would be a terrible insult to people he had grown to like and who were thinking only of his welfare.

He made room in the cabin for "Willowy." Willowy was the older woman. Her name wasn't exactly as he pronounced it, but that was as close as he could come to it. His "bride" was Ollia. Ollia and he slept at one end of the cabin with Willowy at the other. Sleep was primarily what he did in bed. Ollia was not enthusiastic about her "wifely duties."

With two more mouths to feed, he had to bring in more food. He spent many days away from his campsite, waiting mute and unmoving among the giant trees of the Pacific forests. The deer were cautious of the strange, human creature so he had to use stealth and surprise to kill them. He knew he could whistle and birds would come to accompany his vigils, but their presence thwarted his deer-hunting. He didn't try to call the deer to him. He thought that unfair to "friends" who fed and clothed him.

The misty mornings and the dusty afternoons reminded him of his days of wandering in the eastern forests. One clear morning he waited at the edge of a stand of giant evergreens. The sun was up. Soon it would burn off the morning chill as it always did in spring. Spring always surprised him. One day there would be a light dusting of yellow pollen and the next day green shoots and budding flowers would appear, as if keeping an appointment he couldn't time—and spring would be all around him in only one soft day.

He sat on a thick bed of tiny, dead leaves fallen from the trees above. In the pine forests they were called "needles," but here they were smaller and softer. He was looking over a meadow that must have been created years ago by a wildfire or windstorm. Without the cover of trees, warm sunlight reached the sleeping seeds waiting in the earth below. Now the meadow was a young yellow-green. It was a place where deer came to feed on the new growth and where he came to feed on the deer.

He looked up at the tops of the giant trees more than a hundred feet above him.

"You big fellows are much older than I am," he said.

There were no deer in sight, so there was no reason not to speak to the trees spreading their branches over him. He often spoke to the other things that shared their world with him.

"You were standing here the day I was born, weren't you? Oh, yes, you were smaller then but still pretty big trees, I reckon. I wonder if you'll still be here when I'm finally gone—when I find death. I wonder, too, if you know God in the same way as me."

He had kept track of his age and knew he was older than any animal in the forest. But he wasn't as old as the trees.

He wasn't one or the other—not animal and not tree. He really didn't belong here. There was no place where he belonged. There were no people he could call his own. The people he knew were all dead or would some day die away from him, leaving him alone, alone with his memories and bad dreams.

When the salmon were running, Ollia, Willowy, and he caught all they could and smoked or dried them. The women were very impressed by his ability as a fisherman. They tried wiggling their fingers in the cold waters as he did, but all they got for their efforts were cold fingers. The salmon would last only part of each year, so he began taking more deer from the forests. It grew into a small business as the women skinned the deer and then prepared the hides for curing and trading. There were things he could not provide for himself. He got lead for shot and gunpowder by trade. Deerskins were his money.

Late one afternoon he spoke with Willowy as she was scraping fat and muscle from the back of a deerskin. Ollia was off in the forest gathering acorns—which they ate and he didn't. He questioned her about herself and about Ollia.

Willowy had been married three times. Her first husband and their only child, a son, had drowned—swept away together by swift waters while fishing with their woven baskets. Her second husband went hunting in the forest and never returned. Her third husband had fallen off a cliff. He lived for a month before succumbing to his injuries. During her recitation about her troubled life, she continued to work without any outward sign of emotion.

He asked her about Ollia. He thought she seemed so sad, so distant. Willowy told him Ollia had been promised to a young man in their village before the chief sent her to him. He asked her if she thought Ollia wanted to marry the young man—did she love him? Willowy nodded, "yes."

It took them another week to bale the deerskins for travel. He put a small, leather bag of stones he had gathered in his shot pouch. The two women hoisted the packs of deerskins and followed him down the valley to the Indian village. He would have carried a pack of the skins himself but knew if the Indians saw him carrying a heavy load, it would reflect badly—not on him—but on Willowy and Ollia.

The skins were piled in the village. As they were being examined by the chief's two wives, he asked Willowy to point out the young man Ollia was supposed to marry before she was sent to him. Once he saw him, he knew he should have guessed his identity without asking. The young brave had eyes only for Ollia, who kept her own eyes on the ground. He maneuvered through the villagers until he stood next to the man. The chief raised his hand above his head and nodded in his direction, indicating that his skins were all acceptable. His trade goods accepted, he called Ollia and told her to stand at his side. He took her hand in his, a symbol he knew of a married couple. He had "paid" for Ollia with the deerskins. She was his. Suddenly, he gripped the hand of the young man next to him. He took a step back and brought the hands of the young Indians together in front of him. He was giving his "bride" to the man she desired.

He watched the chief to be sure this was acceptable. The chief smiled broadly. Now he was almost where he wanted to be—*almost*. He went to the chief and gave him the small bag of stones he had collected during his deer hunting trips in the forest. The bag contained obsidian. Obsidian was more valuable than almost anything here. It would be shaped into arrowheads. The chief accepted the stones but with a question on his face. The question soon turned to a very broad smile when he saw what his mountain friend wanted in return—he was holding Willowy's hand in his. Seeing this, the chief raised his hand, first in a fist, then with his index finger extended, tapping his forehead. He couldn't be sure if the chief meant his was a wise decision or that he must be a fool. But Willowy was now his wife.

When they returned, Willowy moved out of the skin-covered hut she had built for herself next to the cabin and into her new home. The huts the Indians built were never meant to be permanent structures. When one became too dirty to be lived in, it was simply burned to the ground and a new hut built. It was an interesting concept in housecleaning. An idea, he was sure, many women all over the world thought of often.

That evening at the cooking fire he set about preparing the meal. He had only just started when he was pushed sternly away by "the woman of the house." The look on her face told him she would now do all the cooking. After dinner Willowy took out her pipe, filled it with something, took a puff and offered it to him. He took one puff and gave it back. He wondered if she might be smoking dried acorns.

He stood, stretched and went inside the cabin. It was a warm evening so he stripped and slid under a single deer hide. A short time later, the cabin door opened and closed. There was a rustling sound and the hide was pulled back, momentarily. A naked body touched his. By morning he had a new appreciation of experience.

Willowy was a revelation—a triumph of substance over form. He was very happy. He understood exactly what the chief meant when he tapped his forehead. His only wish was that all his future decisions would be as wise as the one to take Willowy as his wife. She continued to make him happy for the next twenty-four years.

•

As the years passed, he wondered why Willowy never questioned his unchanging face. She changed from an older woman to an old woman but never seemed to notice his perpetual youth.

He came, finally, to understand that Willowy thought nothing of her own appearance, so she was unconcerned by his. How she looked was not of interest to her. She arose each morning and went about her duties. By the end of the day, she had accomplished all that the day demanded. She was happy. The only thing that could make her happier was his reach for her at the end of the day. He was no fool. He reached for her often. He would never look at older women in the same way again, no matter how long he lived.

She died in his arms late one evening. He buried her near the cabin and packed up his kit. There was nothing here for him anymore. He was no closer to the truth about himself, and his nightmare was still with him. He remembered the place where he had seen a beautiful natural harbor, a place called Yorba Buena. He turned and began walking south. He didn't wipe away the tears running down his face. They weren't for Willowy. They were for him…now that he had to live on without her.

Richard L. Evans

CHAPTER SEVEN

THE SOUTHERN CROSS

He smelled the ocean. He wouldn't actually see it for days but the scent of salt air took him back to his earliest days at sea when the child became a man. Good days with good men. It lifted him. His spirits returned as they were in the best of times with Margery, Titus, Homer, Peshewa, Jed and Willowy. His head came up and his senses revived. He walked for days with the sun on his shoulder and the stars on his hat.

Then he smelled something else. It was still the sea, but there was so much else with it. He came up on the same low hill he remembered from the past. It was the same hill where an Indian pointed to a nearly perfect bay and said it was, Yorba Buena.

And there, ahead of him, it was...yet it wasn't.

This time he knew what year it was: 1853. In just over thirty years an almost pristine, salt water bay, surrounded by green forests, had become something very different. The water was still there but little else. Later that week he would learn the thing before him, whatever it was, was now called San Francisco.

He walked through streets deep in mud and animal manure. There was activity all around him. Some of it seemed almost frantic. There seemed to be no organization to it. Men shouted at each other and at their mules. New houses were going up everywhere. He wondered how the builders could determine where they should go. He saw no indication of a civil government. The "savages" he had seen on the plains and mountains all set out their settlements in good order, but these "civilized" men seemed to have no idea what they were doing. There was no time for forethought here. The whine of sawmills and the rapid explosions of many hammers followed him down the streets.

When he arrived on the quay running along the waterfront, he was forced to believe what his eyes did not believe from the hill above the bay. Until he was there, that close, it didn't seem possible.

He remembered the masts and arms of the ships he had seen at the Howland Great Dock near Deptford before sailing to Africa on the *Anne*. He remembered the virtual forest of masts and cross arms of the mighty armada he had seen in New York's harbor when the British fleets—two of them—had come in with Lord Howe's Armies. But the sight before him in San Francisco Bay overshadowed those memories by a factor of a hundred. The denuded hills around the bay were blotted out by the swaying timber. Over 500 ships of all descriptions: barks, brigs, schooners, brigantines, sloops and clippers were anchored in the harbor.

He noticed the forest of masts seemed to have some leaning, "dying trees," too. He had to get closer and get better angles to notice that many of the ships were sunk or sinking. A few even had chimneys where they should have had masts—steamers. The ships had been abandoned—left to rot where they rode at anchor.

One ship, docked close by the quay, was different. It was of a design he didn't recognize. But it was a beauty and built for speed. It looked like it was in fair condition. He guessed her at about 250 feet and she probably ran around 800 tons. She had a deep draft, maybe 15 or 16 feet. That would make her stable, even with all that speed. There were barnacles and grass visible along her waterline. She hadn't been hauled and scraped in a couple of years. Her name, *The Southern Cross* was painted just under the monkey rail near the bow. He walked back and forth on the quay admiring her.

Hungry, he went into a waterside restaurant. When he saw the prices the restaurant had posted on a slate just inside the door, he backed out. He counted all the coins he had accumulated over the last twenty-five years in the mountains. He had just enough to buy two restaurant meals in the city of San Francisco.

As he turned away to go back to the hills where he could provide his own supper, he heard a low whistle. The whistle came from behind him, from the water's edge. He turned to see a man lounging against a tall piling. The man was looking directly at him. There was no mistake; the whistle was meant to draw his attention.

The man might have been handsome if he weren't so big: big hands, big shoulders, big feet, big nose. It was obvious that this big fellow had watched him as he turned around in the restaurant. The man motioned to him with a nod of his big head to come over.

"Donald Yarborough," the man said by way of an introduction.

He had to think for a second about what name to give the man back. He decided not to use the one he'd used in the mountains. Deceit was a habit. He gave him a new name.

"No luck in the gold fields, huh?"

Donald Yarborough seemed friendly enough.

"No, I've just come in from up north—up near the Columbia," he replied.

He wondered what this man thought he could sell to someone he just saw back away from a meal because he didn't have the money.

"You came over the Oregon Trail, then?"

"No," he replied. He really didn't want to tell this total stranger anything until he knew what he wanted from him.

"From the look of you with that Hawken on your shoulder, you must be a mountain man. That right?"

"Yes."

"That mean you've never been to sea?"

"I've been to sea."

"Served a ship, you mean?"
"Yes."
"River or ocean?"
"Ocean."
"See this one here, the one behind me?" Again, Yarborough motioned with his head.
"Sure. It'd be hard to miss. A beauty."

Of course he had seen the ship behind Donald Yarborough. No real sailor would walk here and not notice *The Southern Cross*.

"I watched you from the bridge as you walked her over. She's 243 feet and 780 tons. She was built in New York for the California trade. You see how sharp she is? That's for speed, my friend. Speed is the name of the game. *The Southern Cross* can do fourteen knots even with no strong following wind. You put a lot of thought into the look you gave her. If you're looking for work, I'm pulling a crew."

He turned his head to look up and down the quay. Then he looked up at the deck of *The Southern Cross*. Not another seaman was in sight.

"I'd have to say, you don't seem to be having much luck."

"Not today. But tomorrow a train is due in from the fields. They'll be plenty of men broke and plenty of men rich enough to book passage back to New York."

He only had to think about it for a few seconds.

"I know my way around a merchantman. I've served plenty of square riggers."

Donald Yarborough smiled.

"Come on, I'll buy you breakfast and we can talk. You can pay me back in three years when your contract is up."

Yarborough didn't smile when he said he could repay him. He was pretty sure Yarborough meant what he said. He liked that.

The rest of that morning was devoted to his education about gold, San Francisco and *The Southern Cross*. Gold, lots of gold, had been discovered in the American River country in 1848. Donald Yarborough had sailed into San Francisco Bay in late 1849.

"I was among the first to arrive from the East Coast," Yarborough said. "I'd read newspaper accounts telling of solid gold six inches deep in the stream beds. A man, they said, could easily pick up $40,000 worth of gold in a day. I jumped ship. So did every other man on board, including the captain. Navy ships came in and lost most of their crews, too. You might notice there aren't any navy vessels anywhere near here. They stay well out to sea, so they won't lose any more crews to the gold fields. An entire army company disappeared into the wilds, officers and all. That was when the United States was still at war with Mexico before California became a territory."

"California's a territory?"

It was the first he'd heard of it.

"You *have* been in the back woods, haven't you? Mexico ceded Upper California to the United states four years ago."

"How much gold did you pick up off the ground each day?"

It couldn't have been very much. Yarborough wasn't dressed that much better than he.

"At first, I did all right. I panned in the upper streams. Eventually, I got very close to the Sierra Nevadas, way up there. When I came down, I thought I had a fortune in my pockets. And I did, too. That is, I did until I tried to buy something—something like food or an extra blanket. I came back here to San Francisco.

"You can go up there and try your luck if you want to, but a good seaman can do pretty well rounding the Horn hauling the lucky ones back East and bringing the next wave of fools back out here. That's what I do."

"Tell me about San Francisco."

"You mean what's happening here now? Just look around. But look quick because tomorrow it'll be different—there'll be another new opera house or a couple of more saloons. There'll also be, maybe, six more new graves in the cemetery over to the west side of the bay. You'll hear the shots at night. I'd keep those pistols in your belt there loaded and half cocked if I were you."

"No police? No law? No courts?"

"Not to speak of. Not yet. Things are getting better, though. There are a lot of people here who've made good and have a stake in law and order. It'll come. What they really need now is a fire fighting brigade. Too many places just burn to the ground. The whole city'll go up in smoke one day."

Yarborough rose and put enough coins on the table to pay for their meals.

"Come on, I'll give you a tour of your new home. Bring your kit. If you sign on now, you can stay aboard."

•

Donald Yarborough, as it turned out, was not the captain of *The Southern Cross*—he was the First Mate. The captain's name was Watson Brownlee. Captain Brownlee kept a low profile. He didn't see him until they prepared to make way.

"Sheets fore and main tops'ls! Let go aft! Let go for'ard! Ease her away boys. Two points to larboard, Mr. Yarborough."

The captain walked the main deck on the dock side of his ship, watching in four directions simultaneously. Where Yarborough was big, Captain Brownlee was small. Small, that is, in stature. His voice was powerful, and there could be no mistake about who was in charge. As he watched the captain supervise the sometimes hazardous procedure of slipping away from the dock, he noted the captain had a strange gait. One side of his body seemed to move ahead at a different speed than the other. Brownlee had to constantly adjust his direction to keep in a straight line. He knew of only one thing that could cause a man to move like that—booze. He was sure the Captain had been "nipping." He had signed on to sail 13,000 miles over open ocean around Cape Horn with a drunk.

A crew, of sorts, had signed on. There was a cook, a carpenter, a sail maker, and two stewards to see to the needs of the passengers. Besides the Captain and Yarborough, that left him and seven others to run the ship—a very thin crew, indeed. Two of his shipmates had only last names, Brown and Quick. He wondered what they might be running from. Their appearance made him think it might be just as well that he didn't know.

However, two days before they were scheduled to leave, another ship sailed in—or more properly, steamed in. The *California* ran from San Francisco to the west coast of Panama and back. The coal-burning, side paddle wheeler could move in a straight line over the ocean in almost any weather.

Richard L. Evans

The short route to the East was across the narrow isthmus to the Caribbean Sea where another steamer, the *Panama*, would complete the voyage to New York or Boston. The short route took only eight or nine weeks, even with a stopover in Havana. The sea route around South America was much longer: four to eight months. But the short route took a traveler through some of the worst areas in the world, swarming with mosquitoes carrying malaria and yellow fever. It was also swarming with thieves and cutthroats looking to do their "gold mining" the easy way.

Nevertheless, at the sight of the *California*, two thirds of their passengers cancelled off *The Southern Cross* and booked passage on the steamer. They were left with sixty-one passengers. None of them had paid the top price of $500 for a first class cabin. Even so, at $200 a person plus payment for its cargo, *The Southern Cross* would make a good profit on the voyage. All they had to do was get there.

They had been out only three days when it became apparent theirs was not a good crew. He was one of the few men on the ship who knew even the rudiments of seamanship. Some of them had only been to sea as passengers. His knowledge and experience put him right behind First Mate Yarborough. He was made Second Mate, like it or not.

Except for the immense fog banks where the cold current flowing down from the north met the warmer waters farther out to sea, the conditions were almost ideal for sailing. The good weather lasted for twelve days, and they made good progress south and east.

Although Captain Brownlee was using the instruments to position the ship, his own experience from years ago gave him a good idea of the direction and speed of his vessel. Each day brought them closer to the Equator and to an area of much less dependable winds. It was summer and they were also coming into an area made very dangerous by storms. In the Atlantic Ocean they called them, "hurricanes."

With so few men available to work the sails and do the normal maintenance required at sea, they were divided into just two watches. Yarborough took command of one and he took the other.

That meant every man was above deck at least twelve hours each day. He was below in his hammock when the first rain squall hit. He thought little of it until the sound of the rain was joined by a strong roll from the larboard quarter. The wind had picked up and swung around from the southwest. When he added everything up, it totaled trouble.

On deck things looked and felt better, but he could see a major front coming with the wind. It took only an hour for things to get much worse. The Captain took the wheel and both watches were called up. The passengers were told to stay below and to brace themselves for some rough treatment as the ship would probably be bounced around in the sea. Bolts securing the hatch covers were locked down. The crew on deck lashed themselves to solid elements. He tied himself through the larboard ladder just below the bridge. It would give him something to brace himself against the wind.

He went over the situation in his mind, checking both the pros and cons. It was an old habit from his previous sailing days. His captains had told him to always be prepared, to "keep sharp" in times of trouble.

Okay, this ship is well-built and has certainly held together through this kind of weather before. It also has a deep draft giving it stability in heavy seas.

He knew the most danger would come from large waves washing over the decks, then, powerful winds—a gust of wind could lift him up and throw him overboard into the sea, and finally, debris falling from the ship's rigging striking him. There was nothing here he hadn't faced before.

He directed his attention to the seas ahead of the bow and to the straining sails above. The rain and wind increased minute by minute.

He didn't see the wave that broke over him. It came from the stern, up over the bridge and then down on him. As he tried to recover, his feet went out from under him, or to be more precise, the deck went out from under his feet. The ship veered sharply to his right, to the starboard, slamming him against the ladder where his line was tied.

There was an explosion.

Richard L. Evans

He heard what sounded like a small cannon. The foremast had snapped below the foretop gallant and was swinging with the ship's motions, threatening to take out more rigging as it did. He swung up on the ladder in time to see the captain recovering control of the wheel. The wave must have surprised him, too, and knocked him down. Turning back toward the bow, he saw Donald Yarborough with two men, Brown and Montford, working their way up the rigging to the broken mast.

As the captain brought her back into the wind, the ship steadied, and the three men reached the broken mast and began cutting it away. Minutes passed, and it looked like they would come out of it with no other damage.

Then, another surprise wave, one of those huge mountains of water called a "green one" by seasoned sailors, struck the ship from the other side knocking the Captain off the wheel again. The ship swung violently to larboard. They rode into a long trough between two mammoth swells, slipping sideways and out of control.

He saw it coming and hoped the men aloft saw it, too. He wrapped both arms around his ladder rail and braced himself for the impact. The wind drove *The Southern Cross* into the leading swell, and she lurched a full thirty degrees to starboard. The starboard rail went underwater for only a second, then she straightened back up going over ten degrees the other way. He shook the salt spray from his eyes and looked at the foremast again. The broken top of the mast, the sail and all the rigging were gone. So were the three men.

The sea was going to hit them again unless the ship was brought around. He cut his lashings and leapt up the ladder. The captain was trying to get to his feet by the starboard rail but seemed unable to rise. There was no way to know how much time he had to right the ship. The swells that were pushing her to destruction came at odd intervals. He jumped for the wheel and pulled it as strong and fast as he could to starboard.

Another wave slammed into them but only after *The Southern Cross* has started to turn. The wave actually helped her stay upright. He had her moving with the wind now, the sea swells following. He scanned the water both ahead and astern looking for Yarborough, Brown and Montford. He had no real hope for any of them. Even if he saw them, there was little that anyone on board could do to help them. He would be lucky to hold the ship where it was. He saw no one in the jumbled waves.

He kept the bow with the wind, so they rode the huge swells fore and aft like a giant seesaw. First they would dip violently downward as the swell came up from behind—the stern clearing the water. Then the bow would rise completely out of the water as they crested the wave. Running with a following sea made the ride up and then down the swells a little slower. He had to hold fast to the wheel when the stern, and therefore the rudder, came momentarily out of the water. In that brief moment the rudder could be taken by the wind forcing them back sideways in the troughs. Or it could be much worse—the rudder could be lost— and with it all their lives.

Fourteen hours later they sailed out of the heavy seas into a relative calm. The sun came out and stayed out for the few hours before dusk. The passengers were allowed on deck; most of them came through the storm quite well, their few injuries were only slight. No one spoke about the men lost to the sea. A heavy melancholy fell over the ship's crew. Captain Brownlee disappeared into his cabin.

The sun went down.

The sea has no agenda, no regard for men—whether highborn or low-born. Whether a man is a good man or bad does not interest the sea. The sea is neutral. It exists and that is all it does. Use it or don't use it; live on it or die in it—it makes no difference to the sea. The sea was not created for a thinking man. A man who thinks he can use the sea—that it will always work for him will fail.

He had grown up on the sea. The sea was his first workplace and in a very real sense, his first love. Anyone who lives with the sea learns to be wary—always and in everything—wary. Watching the water isn't enough. Watching the daytime sky isn't enough. Watching the stars isn't enough. He had to be wary because the sea can be very subtle with its warnings. Sometimes there is no warning. A giant swell can suddenly come out of a sea so calm it looks like a huge mirror. Where did it come from? No one knows. Where is it going? No one knows that, either.

Other things matter, too. It's important to notice the presence of birds—how they fly and in what directions. It's also important to notice the absence of birds. That goes for the other creatures of the sea as well. And why are there great expanses of the sea where there seem to be no creatures at all? No one knows. The sea simply moves on—a force having no consideration for men—none at all.

The sails and rigging lost to the typhoon were replaced. He had Stewart, the ship's carpenter prepare a replacement for the damaged part of the foremast. It took him and the remaining crew three days to complete the repairs. Smooth seas and a light westerly wind helped them.

He had taken charge of the ship. The captain did not appear at any time during those days—not since he lost the wheel in the storm. The storm had almost certainly blown them off course, but he thought he knew the correct heading to sail and held to it.

Shortly before noon on the fourth day, he knocked on the captain's door. He had to have a sighting to establish their position. He knew he could just keep going east until he eventually bumped into something, but a good seaman is particular about what he might bump into at sea. When there was no response to his repeated knocking, he tried the door. It was barred. Stewart examined the door and said there was no other way to open it except with an axe. He set Quick to work with that tool, and the door soon fell open.

The Captain was dead.

"Lor' Jesus!" said Stewart, "he's drunk his self to death!"

It did appear that Stewart's pronouncement was correct. The captain lay on the deck below the wooden shelf that served as his bed. There were no outward signs of injury. But a tortured mind must have driven Watson Brownlee to consume the contents of far too many of the rum bottles now littering the cabin.

No one on the ship blamed Captain Brownlee for the loss of Yarborough, Brown and Montford—no one other than the Captain, himself. Indeed, as the second mate he was the only one except Brownlee who knew the captain was not in control when they were hit by the wave. The wave all but took him down at the same time. The captain, even cold sober, could not have prevented the tragedy. But here he lay—dead—a man with too many storms and too many waves broken over him.

He met the crew on the bridge around the wheel. They were now without a captain or first mate.

He asked, "Is there anyone who thinks himself qualified to take command of this ship?"

When there was no response, he said, "To look at me you might think I'm not old enough to have enough knowledge or experience to command *The Southern Cross*. That is not the case. I assure you, I can navigate this vessel anywhere on this earth where there is deep water. But I cannot do it without your duty. I will take charge only if I have your word, each of you, to support me and to follow my commands."

They all agreed. What choice had they?

He organized a ceremony of burial at sea. Most of the passengers were already on deck. There was no way to hide the truth from them. The two most important of the ship's officers were dead. Their fate at sea was now in the hands of only the number three man in the crew.

Rodriquez took the helm and was instructed to keep *The Southern Cross* into the wind. A portion of the main rail was removed. The center of the ship usually had the least roll. The body of Captain Watson Brownlee had been sewn into a length of sailcloth and weighted at the feet. It was laid on a plank at the edge of the opening in the railing. The American flag was lowered to half mast. No one on board was a minister or knew the Captain's religious persuasion. It fell to him as acting captain to perform the service.

He stood before the assemblage and tried to remember the elements of other burials at sea he had witnessed. He held Titus's Bible and read several passages he thought appropriate. He ended his Bible reading with the last line in St. Matthew: "…and, lo, I am with you always, even unto the end of the world. Amen."

He closed the Bible. He stood for a few moments in silence, then invited those assembled to pray with him.

"Almighty God, we commend to you the soul of our recently departed, Captain Watson Brownlee. We commit his body to the deep, sure in the hope of the resurrection to eternal life through our Lord, Jesus Christ. Amen."

He nodded to Porter and Stewart.

The two seamen raised the inboard edge of the plank, and the Captain's body slid into the sea.

At noon he took a sighting using Captain Brownlee's sextant. He also used his previous experience to determine their position with respect to longitude. His first notation in the ship's log was the position of the Captain's burial in the sea. He meant to send that position along with the Captain's personal belongings to his family in Rhode Island—if he ever saw Rhode Island.

A crew that was very thin in numbers to begin with was now four men fewer. Now they were only eleven. Two were little more than stewards, serving the needs of their passengers. Another was the cook. That left only himself, Stewart, the carpenter, Quick, Rodriquez, Porter, the sail maker, Schoner, Marks and Helvgaard. Two watches would have to be stood, each with just four men.

Thin, very thin.

They would have to sail with full sheets from now on. They were too few to risk men above. But which way should they sail—back to San Francisco or on around the Horn? He was now the captain, and he would decide. There was little to be gained going back. It would be the Horn.

After taking command, he stayed on the bridge almost without pause. He went below only to plot a new course on the chart with each sighting and to make entries in the ship's log. Stewart built a low shelf several feet from the wheel where he could catch a few fleeting moments of sleep each day and night. He told Stewart to brace it well. He knew his life would depend on its strength.

Three days after the burial of Captain Brownlee, a group of men approached him as he stood on the bridge. The men said they were a delegation from the rest of the passengers. One man, a Dr. Roderfer, spoke.

"We had expected the ship to turn north after the loss of our captain. Returning to San Francisco seems the safest solution to our problem here. But we note that we are still on a southerly course. Would you explain that, sir?"

Dr. Roderfer ended his question with a word usually used in civility or denoting respect. But his use of "sir," was not civil nor one of respect. It was a challenge.

"Dr. Roderfer, I'm pleased the passengers are keeping up with the operation and direction of the ship. I'm also sure you must know that Cape Horn and thence, New York City lies to the south, not to the north."

Dr. Roderfer tried to interrupt him, but he continued.

"Further, *The Southern Cross* is not without a captain. I have assumed command, and I assure you I am qualified to fill the office. I hope that you and the other passengers will do your utmost to help me bring our ship home."

He didn't know about the other passengers, but Dr. Roderfer showed no inclination to help him do anything except return to San Francisco. The next day the Doctor returned leading about a dozen men. They had armed themselves with wooden legs pulled out of stools to be used as clubs.

"Sir," it was that insulting use of the word again, "turn this ship back on a course for San Francisco, now."

He was pleased to see Rodriquez, Stewart, Porter, Marks, Schoner and Helvgaard closing in from behind the threatening passengers with Dr. Roderfer. Quick was at the wheel. They, too, had armed themselves with clubs and chains in support of their captain.

He had expected something like this and had taken the precaution of loading his two pistols, placing them just under his sleeping shelf on the bridge. He had sold his Hawken rifle in San Francisco, but it would have been much less useful than the pistols, anyway. He said nothing but turned and picked up his pistols. Very casually he checked the cocking action and then slowly, with great deliberation, slid them in his belt. Nothing was said. Dr. Roderfer had his reply. The men turned and went below. The incident was not repeated.

The passengers were restricted to their cabins. They were permitted on deck no more than six at a time. This he knew would only be necessary for a few more days. Very quietly, without any fanfare, they had already crossed the Equator. In another week it would make no sense, even to Roderfer and his friends, to turn back.

Nevertheless, he kept his pistols at hand.

Sailing in the southern Pacific brought on new problems. The star patterns he was used to seeing in the northern hemisphere gradually changed as they moved farther south. Polaris, the North Star, went over the horizon and didn't return. The prevailing winds were from the southeast, and he was now working against a strong, cold current coming from the south toward the Equator. It was not only strong, it was wide. He could avoid sailing against it by taking a very southerly course, staying perhaps a thousand miles from the South American coast, or he could stay very close in to use its counter currents. But staying close to the coast meant exposing his ship to attack by seagoing criminals who had taken to calling themselves "privateers" but who were really nothing more than pirates.

His was a very valuable and therefore desirable cargo—gold rushers returning home from the mines and presumably carrying their treasure home with them. There was also the matter of the U.S. Government shipment of gold he had discovered in Captain Brownlee's two locked chests. They had been hidden behind a false panel under the Captain's bed. He would not have noticed the panel had he not sailed as cabin boy with two captains who kept their valuables in exactly the same place. He found the key to the locks at the bottom of one of Captain Brownlee's rum bottles as he was pouring it over the side late one night. His aversion to rum continued to be a blessing.

He took the short course, close to the coast. He needed to stop and go ashore to calibrate the ship's chronometer. The moving deck of a ship would not allow him to make the delicate celestial measurements he needed. No chronometer measured the passage of time precisely. It could provide an accurate reading only if one knew the magnitude and direction of its imprecision. If a chronometer gained (or lost) as little as two seconds each day, after only a few days his determination of the ship's longitude would be off and would only get worse with each succeeding day. On a long ocean voyage, tiny, seemingly innocent errors in positioning soon became big, mean errors. Knowledge of the exact plus or minus error of *The Southern Cross'* chronometer had gone into the deep with Captain Brownlee.

He turned east keeping the Galapagos Islands just over the horizon to their north. He had studied the charts and made his decision.

They dropped anchor just off Bahia de Caraquez in Ecuador. The area was remote yet had good stands of timber close to the sea. He needed that timber. What he didn't need was official recognition of his presence by government agents. The remoteness of the Bahia de Caraquez served both purposes.

They rode at anchor for three days while hardwood was cut and shaped into thick timbers and heavy beams. Some passengers had to move out of their cabins and into new quarters so that the timber could be placed correctly, bracing and strengthening the hull. The ship had been built primarily for speed. That meant her structure was kept light, too light—in his mind—for the pounding she would have to withstand rounding the Horn.

Fresh water and even more importantly, fresh fruits were brought aboard. They sailed again, changing course to take the long passage, well out to sea. He stayed on the bridge continuously.

His days and nights merged. His nightmares came so often the seamen handling the wheel no longer woke him in their concern for him. They couldn't be sure if he was sleeping or had slipped into a kind of delirium. It became his normal behavior.

He'd heard of the "roaring forties" and the "screaming fifties" from some of the old salts he'd sailed with as a youth. First the winds "roared" and then they "screamed" as they increased in power and speed. In the southern hemisphere at a latitude of about forty degrees south, the only land area all the way around the globe that could block the winds and currents was the very southern part of South America. Having nothing to block them, the winds grew fiercer and fiercer away from the Equator. The West Wind Drift was the west-to-east current stopped by nothing. Ocean swells could grow as they moved all the way around the globe before they hit a ship. That was the good news.

The watch was cautioned to look sharp for the large ice floes common in very southern waters. It was the Antarctic spring so new floating "islands of ice" were breaking off the main ice shelf each day. The sun all but disappeared behind a cloud cover that rarely broke. Ice formed on every exposed part of the ship, lines, rigging, masts, decks, sails—everything. His breath froze on his beard but he stayed on deck.

Navigation had to be reduced to the old trick used by early travelers to the New World. Once they arrived at the right latitude, they just kept going due east or due west. He intended to move due east through the open waters of the Drake Passage south of the little island of Cape Horn.

The passengers were instructed to stay below where they had to listen to the screaming wind, the moaning of the twisting hull and the crashing of ice being smashed on the deck above their heads. Given surging waves and ice covered decks with winds strong enough to sweep a man to certain death in a freezing sea, everyone else was happy to stay below.

He stayed at the helm, lashed to his sleeping shelf. Going from west to east was much easier than going the other way. Going east was merely brutal.

There was no horizon. The giant ocean swells created the impression of being surrounded by mountains on all sides. The color of the sky and the color of the water were the same except where the wind sheared off the tops of the waves blowing white foam everywhere. The ride was exhilarating. He might have enjoyed it if it weren't threatening to kill him at any moment. Night made it easier. He couldn't witness the power all around him—it just took him along in the dark.

He feared losing consciousness. He had to remain in control, to steady the helm. Words came to him—words he hadn't heard in many years:

If I take the wings of the morning, and dwell in the uttermost parts of the sea; even there shall thy hand lead me, and thy right hand shall hold me.

It was true; another's hand held him.

Eight days later they were in the Atlantic, far enough north and east to roll in a moderate sea. In another week the decks of *The Southern Cross* would be nearly dry and her damaged sails replaced. He went below and slept.

They were going "home."

They put in for fresh water and fruit at Montevideo. Rodriquez recruited two more experienced seamen which made working the sails safer. The two new men spoke only Spanish, but they understood basic marine commands in English perfectly well. The ship also picked up a mail pouch bound for the United States. He put it with the one from San Francisco.

Once in the sea lanes north of the Equator, he made sure the watch kept their eyes sharp for other ships. The frequency of shipping here increased the danger of piracy.

He set the crew to ripping out the bracing they had installed to strengthen the ship before their passage by Cape Horn. Now he needed speed much more than strength. And a lighter ship would be much faster. The timbers were placed on deck close to the rails so they could be jettisoned quickly to lighten the ship. He hoped that wouldn't be necessary. If he could save the timber, it would add to the profitability of the voyage. Tropical hardwoods would bring a high price in New York City.

Once the extra bracing was removed, he set the crew to a new task: they drilled daily in setting and taking up sail to make the ship not only fast but highly maneuverable. Pirates would have fast ships, too. If he couldn't out run them, he'd have to out maneuver them. All of these precautions were unnecessary. They were not threatened.

Standing by the forward rail just before dusk, he noticed a large school of sharks swimming along side and keeping pace with the ship. They reminded him of the sharks that had followed the *Anne*.

"Sorry, my old friends," he said softly to them. "You won't find this ship as rich a source of food."

He wondered if any of the sharks in the water could be the same as those he saw eighty years ago. He had heard that sharks didn't die of old age. As long as nothing else, including their own kind, got them, they just kept getting older and bigger. He doubted any of these "old friends" could be the same ones he started to leap to so long ago. He also wondered if his little fishing trick using his fingers would work with them as it did with fresh water fish. He didn't think he'd try it.

"Perhaps, some other time," he whispered to himself.

The Southern Cross sailed into New York harbor four days before Christmas, 1853—143 days out of San Francisco. He watched from the bridge as the passengers departed quickly, including a stern-faced Dr. Roderfer who spoke not a word.

After making final docking and security arrangements for his ship, he found the owners of the shipping company. They were very grateful for his service and agreed to allow him to buy out the remainder of his three-year contract with the proceeds from the sale of the tropical lumber.

He went first to Rhode Island to find the family of Captain Brownlee, returning his personal property including his sextant. He went next to Boston where he did the same for the families of Donald Yarborough and John Montford.

For the next eight years he crewed on a number of coastal vessels. He'd had all he wanted of deep water sailing.

•

In the spring of 1861 he went into a barber shop for a shave and clip. He knew the barber well. He had been coming to his shop for the past three years—whenever he was in New Bedford, usually about twice each month.

Once in the chair he asked the barber, "From my looks, how old do you think I am?"

He tried to keep his voice and manner casual as if he were just making conversation. He didn't want to hint how important the barber's answer might be to him. The barber was an older man, experienced in the world as barbers are often forced to be. The man was good at distinguishing truth from little prayers or simple bravado.

The barber thought for a moment, then said, "I've wondered about you, trying in my mind to answer that very question. By the look of your hair and your skin, most people would guess you to be about twenty-five, maybe even thirty. But your eyes are old.

You've seen a lot—too much, maybe."

The barber stopped speaking and turned away, pretending to concentrate on mixing the shaving soap—embarrassed by his thoughts about another man's secret life.

Yes, my eyes have seen a lot—too much, that's for sure.

He picked up a day-old newspaper lying in the next chair. A headline had caught his eye. The story detailed a tragic accident at sea. *The Southern Cross* had gone down off the coast of Scotland with all hands and the loss of 194 passengers, mainly immigrants headed for the United States.

Everything dies someday.

He hoped it was true.

Richard L. Evans

CHAPTER EIGHT

FRANK and SILAS

He had traveled thousands of miles and crossed two oceans. He had been close to death so many times that he had lost track of the number. He had lived a long, seemingly unending, life. He had a gift for healing.
Why?
He was no closer to the answers than he was before he even knew the questions.
He was dining in a small waterfront restaurant one evening in early July, 1861, when a well-dressed man stopped beside his table and asked politely, "Are you one of the crew off that steamer that docked here the day before yesterday?"
He said he was.
The man asked if he could speak with him for a moment. There was an empty chair across the table. The man sat down and introduced himself as Colonel Clark. Clark explained that he was raising a regiment that would be a part of the Union Army fighting in the cause of freedom, to free the slaves.

"I want to raise a regiment made up of sailing men like you," he explained. "Such a unit could prove very useful in military campaigns along the southern coast, if you see what I mean?"

He did see what the Colonel meant and said so.

Two weeks later he signed up, got a $200 enrollment bonus and a brand new uniform. A month after that, he and his new army mates were shipped to Annapolis for training.

Despite his efforts to hide his familiarity with drill and tactics, he was soon singled out as one who knew what all this training was supposed to accomplish. No one else knew much about it—not even the officers. He had lied about his war experience just as he had when he gave them a new name. He was offered and accepted a commission as a Lieutenant in the new 21st Regiment, Massachusetts.

He spent the first few weeks in camp trying to pull together a fighting force from Colonel Clark's other recruits. The young men were very enthusiastic about the coming glorious war they would fight against the "Johnny Rebs." He knew all too well of the "glories" they would find in searing pain, blood and death. The British, the Hessians and the Indians had taught him those lessons well. But the men were in such high spirits he kept his foreboding to himself. Instead, he listened to their bragging about their coming exploits and joined in singing their patriotic songs. He hoped they could sing them with the same enthusiasm in a year or two. The men were all sure the war would be over in three months, six at the outside. He had no such illusions. He'd heard it all before.

Soon after their training began, he noticed a man in his company who looked familiar. There was something about his carriage, the strength of character he exuded and his steady, steel-gray eyes. Although the man was obviously a raw recruit to infantry training, he had a mature attitude. The man also had three chevrons on each sleeve—another sergeant with no training in military drill or warfare. The sergeant introduced himself as Frank Grim.

"Grim! Was your…let me see he would have been your great-grandfather…was he in the Marblehead Regiment?"

"Yes, sir! He was a Lieutenant with Colonel Glover."

A wide grin spread across Frank Grim's face.

It was the second time he had witnessed a Grim's grin.

"Was someone in your family in that regiment?" the sergeant asked—obviously delighted that an officer would associate his own family with the famous Revolutionary regiment.

"No," he said.

Technically, no one in his family had served with Glover— just himself. He had become such an accomplished liar that sometimes he could even deceive himself.

"I just read a lot about them. Are you from Marblehead?"

"Yes, sir. My people have always been fishermen."

Over the next three months he grew to like Frank very much. In many ways Frank was like his great-grandfather, the man he had known as Lieutenant Grim. But Frank was more affable, more easygoing. Frank loved to sing and was a fine storyteller. The story he most liked to tell was how his great-grandfather had rowed both Colonel John Glover and General George Washington across the Delaware on Christmas Day in 1776. Frank became very animated each time he told his story, acting out gasping for breath in the frigid air and the pain of pulling on a heavy oar with frozen fingers. His family pride was very evident.

It amused him to hear Frank's version of a night he remembered so well, himself. Of course, in his memory he saw Lieutenant Grim standing on the New Jersey shore all night directing the unloading of the boats. Colonel Glover was on the Pennsylvania side, supervising their loading. No one rowed any of the boats—they had to be poled across the water due to the ice floes in the river. But he had to admit, it was a better story the way Frank told it. Time and Grim family pride had made the night colder, the river wider and the whole operation much more dangerous.

He also learned that Frank's family had carried on Lieutenant Grim's devotion to his country in other times of military need. Frank's grandfather had fought the British again in the War of 1812, and his father had fought the Mexicans with General Zachary Taylor. Now, here was Frank in still another war.

He asked Frank about his family, the family he had left behind in Marblehead.

Frank said "I have two, fine young sons at home, such good boys. Zachary is eight, and he's already an accomplished net mender. Daniel is six. Daniel's a little devil at times, but I wouldn't trade him for all the tea dumped in Boston Harbor. They can already read most of the books their mother brings home from the school. We get most of them after they're donated by wealthy people down in Boston. Laura, that's my wife, is the school mistress and…well…she's just a whiz at everything."

Frank paused, a little embarrassed by his own enthusiasm. His love for his family just poured out of him. He was delighted to talk about them.

"I had to think awhile before joining up and having to leave them," he said at last. "But the holding of slaves is an evil, and I just had to fight against it. I write to Laura almost every night. And she writes to me, too." Frank showed him some of her letters. "I always make sure they're easy going with news and amusing stories about the other men in the regiment."

Frank laughed then at some unspoken thought. He wondered what Frank said about *him* in his letters.

They were drilling in a large field, practicing advancing as a company in line of battle when they heard someone screaming from the direction of a nearby road. It sounded like a woman's voice. He detailed Sergeant Grim and two men to investigate the disturbance. They were camped in an area known to have many southern sympathizers. Frank returned an hour later to report that an accident had taken the life of a little girl. She had run out in front of a supply wagon being drawn by a team of mules. The driver was unable to stop in time. Frank was very upset, on the edge of tears.

That night, after supper, he asked Frank about it.

"You saw the child who was killed today?"

"Yes, sir. She was just three or four years old," Frank said in a stern, military way even as his eyes moved down and away, looking off to the side.

"Have you never seen death before?"

He was concerned for Frank and for the men he would lead. The death of friends was something they would surely have to face.

"Oh, yes, sir," Frank said quickly.

Then he paused, taking particular care about his next remark.

"Laura and I had another child, a little girl. She was about the same age as that little girl in the road today. Our little Evelyn died, too."

Frank's words came out flat. He was controlling the emotion in them, sitting on them so they wouldn't escape and take him down.

Several minutes passed. Both men were silent. Frank obviously didn't want to talk about it, and he couldn't talk about it. He couldn't tell Frank about his own little girls, killed by Indians so many years ago. He would have to reveal too much about himself to do that. Nevertheless, he understood why Frank had not mentioned a third child before. Some things can be made better by talking about them—and some things can't.

When Frank spoke of his dead child, he saw his great-grandfather's hardness come into his face. But he knew, like his great-grandfather, the hardness was there only to protect a tender heart.

Frank's family became very real to him, almost as if he was a distant relative. He came to think of himself as, perhaps, an old, long-lost uncle. When he was alone with his own petitions to God, he said a prayer that his country would not have to call on Frank's sons to fight as it had four previous generations. He also asked God to grant Frank's family his safe return.

In early January, 1862, the regiment was attached to General Reno's 2nd Brigade as part of General Burnside's Expeditionary Corps. As Colonel Clark had predicted, they were to attack the Confederacy along its long coastline. The regiment captured a rebel fort on Roanoke Island but he saw no action. His company remained behind the rest of the regiment as part of the reserve force.

They camped further south on Hatteras Island for several weeks. A number of the men came down with a mysterious illness that produced a very high fever. The fever was followed by convulsions and death. Four men of the regiment were already dead when Sergeant Frank Grim went down with the fever. Two days later, late in the evening, he bent over Frank's feverish form in the infirmary tent and took one of his hands in his. He could not allow a man he'd come to love as he would a son to die so young.

•

The western banks of the Neuse River rose up in places more than fifty feet above the water.

Not land that would be easily taken if the Confederates wanted to defend it.

Night would fall soon, and that might help. A steady downpour had already drenched them, and it was dark by the time he stepped off the steamship, *Northerner*. Colonel Clark said their landing site would be a place called Slocum Creek on the North Carolina mainland. There was no creek that he could see. Actually, he couldn't see much of anything. He knew he was going in the right direction only because the water became shallower as he moved forward. Then it was just mud.

The company formed up. Names were called and answered in deliberately hushed voices. They began to march away from the river. The rain made it difficult to get an accurate heading, but he sensed they were heading first west then north. They moved over ground that had already been used by many boots. He tried not to slip down in the uneven slop. After about two hours they came to a railroad track.

The clouds overhead parted briefly and he could see that the rails seemed to run north-south and they were moving northward. Dawn came but the rain continued to pelt down on them. They followed the tracks for two rainy days, always looking both left and right for signs of snipers. They camped just before dusk the second day. After a cold, wet supper, he was briefed by Colonel Clark.

"The rebel forces have not run as we hoped," the Colonel explained, "but have fallen back to a defensive line less than a mile ahead. Our brigade will form the left flank of the Union attack. We'll control an area roughly just east of the railroad to a large impoundment of water to the west. We can't outflank them in that direction. The water is too wide and too deep, so it's not going to be easy. General Foster's brigade will attack on a wider line on our right. They'll have the river on their right and some support from the Union gun ships moving up the Neuse. That end of the Confederate line is anchored by a fort with a number of thrity-two pounders. Foster's boys won't have it easy over there. To our front will be a line of breastworks backed by artillery. There's a swampy area on our west but we won't have to worry about crossing it. We'll have to cross about two-hundred yards of cleared ground straight ahead where we'll be directly exposed to their fire."

The Colonel finished and moved on to the next company. It didn't sound like they were in for an easy time, either. His 21st Massachusetts would be to the right of the railroad tracks, about in the center of the whole battlefield.

Dead center.

Just before dawn, the rain stopped and a heavy veil of fog hugged the ground. As he waited for the order to advance, he saw his commanding general, General Burnside, with several of his aides, step out of the forest line. A single artillery shot from the Rebel side caused them to step nimbly back into cover as a cannon ball whizzed past their heads. Within minutes the order to attack sounded, and lines of blue-clad men stepped forward.

He stayed ahead of his men. Almost immediately he was wading in and out of pockets of shallow water that had collected in the uneven ground. The high spots were easier to negotiate, but the brush was not thick here and offered little cover. His company had to wade in the swampy waters and then duck or crawl over the higher ground. Spring had not yet arrived, so there was little vegetation to hide their advance.

Gunfire opened up to both their right and left, but strangely, they did not come under fire for several minutes. He kept his men moving forward, wondering why they were not being fired upon. He could see the enemy's defenses ahead. Two lines of breastworks had been thrown up with trenches dug in front of them. On his left were a series of crescent-shaped works. On his right the breastworks were in a rather straight line stretching to the river, perhaps three quarters of a mile away. But the two fortifications were not on the same line. The one to his left was angled back away and behind the one on his right. Directly ahead, the Rebel line took a sharp angle backwards to join the two parts. There was also a low earthen building with a rounded roof anchoring part of the line directly ahead of him. He fixed on that building as his objective.

When the Rebs finally did open up, he understood why they had waited and his heart leapt. The sound of the enemy gunfire ahead was not even. They were firing many different types of small arms—shotguns, fowling pieces, rifles—probably even some old flintlocks, too. They must be militia, and militiamen would certainly mean a mixture of trained and untrained men. Most of them would be green troops, not yet bloodied in battle. Their arms would be less effective than those of the regular army.

When he was within a hundred yards of the Rebel line, he ordered his men to increase their pace forward to double quick time. As he did so, he was careful to place himself directly in front of Frank Grim. He wanted Frank to live, and if that meant his own death, then so be it.

He moved swiftly, crouching and jumping from mound to mound over the low places. Coming to the top of a slope, he slipped down on the wet grass and slid back until his feet sank in a pool of cold, dark water.

Frank moved on ahead of him. He yelled at Frank, telling him to stop, but he knew Frank wouldn't hold back anything. He was just like his great grandfather. Once on his feet again, he reached the top of the slope. Sgt. Frank Grim lay a few feet ahead of him. Most of the left side of Frank's head was gone.

He fell to his knees beside his friend.

"Dear God," he shouted, "Here's another one I tried to save—and killed with my touch."

He dropped his pistol. Rage and frustration took his reason. He stood and raised his hands above his head in supplication to God.

He screamed, "Enough! Oh, God, I've had enough of this life."

He turned to face the rebel lines and began to run at them, yelling, "Come on, do it now! Do it now!"

He ran into, and then out of, another low, water-filled depression. He heard a sharp crack and felt himself driven backward down the slope he had just climbed.

His world went black.

When he awoke, his first sensation was that of sliding—but sliding upward. He realized he was being pulled up by his backpack. In another moment he was sliding down but sliding backwards this time. The movement stopped and he tried to open his eyes. He couldn't see out of his left eye. What he could see with his right eye was a grayish tan coat smeared with a dull red color. A column of brass buttons ran up the coat and there were black patches sewn across the tops of each shoulder. The man wearing the coat was staring into his eyes and saying something. He was distracted by the man's appearance. It took him several seconds to understand what the man was saying.

"Gotcha now, blue-belly. Thought you could just die out here and nobody would notice, huh?"

The man was wearing a short-billed cap the same color as his coat. Waves of very blond hair fell from beneath his cap to his shoulders. And his eyes! His eyes were the bluest he had ever seen. He thought where he might have seen a color like them before. An image of a cloudless day with a high sun shining on the shallow seas near Grand Bahama Island came to him. Only that high sun could make the water look as blue as this man's eyes.

He felt it as the Confederate soldier wiped the side of his face with a handkerchief. The amount of gore he saw on the handkerchief should have come from a large wound, but he had only a mild sensation of pain. The Reb held a canteen to his lips, and he was instructed to drink as the man supported his head. He blinked away a red haze and was able to see with both eyes.

The man kept talking. "What's your name there, Union boy? What outfit you with?"

He answered both questions.

"My name's Silas Rose, 33rd North Carolina. You fellas about had us whipped when you broke through those militia boys. They run like rabbits, didn't they though? If it hadn't been for those boys in the 7th North Carolina and, of course, my boys, you might of had us good."

The soldier took a breath and laughed. The smile stayed on the Reb's face the whole time he spoke. He thought all Southerners were supposed to be slow talkers. This man could outtalk anyone he had ever known. That, he thought, was what fear could do to a man. He should know.

The Confederate was still smiling and talking.

"Hold your hands together 'till I can get'm bandaged. Looks like you been shot through both hands."

The man wrestled the pack from his own back and pulled out a pair of socks.

"Make a fist around each of these," he said as he balled them up and forced one of them into each of his hands.

Pain shot up both arms as he pressed on the soldier's socks in his hands.

"I bet that does hurt a goodly amount," his benefactor said, cheerfully. "I've got to tie them on somehow, though."

In another moment the Reb had torn two strips from a flag he also pulled from his pack. His hands were soon wrapped with the strips to hold the socks in them.

"You pretty near drowned there blue boy." The Rebel soldier, Rose, was still speaking. "If it hadn't been for your backpack holding your head out of the water, I wouldn't have me a prisoner—just a dead Yankee Lieutenant. What's that book you got in there, anyway? What ever it is, it saved your life."

Silas made another bandage from his flag and wrapped it around the wound on his head.

They continued to talk for some time. Silas Rose did most of the talking and he did most of the listening. Silas was from out West in the piedmont.

"Up," he said, "around Alamance way."

When it was his turn to speak, he asked Silas if he was descended from the Regulators who challenged the colonial Governor, William Tryon back before the Revolutionary War. Silas was so stunned at the question, he stopped talking for an entire second.

"You know about the Regulators!" he gasped. "I sure am and damned proud of it! How'd you know about them? You must be an educated man. I'll bet you can read, too."

He assured Silas that he wasn't that well-educated. He had just been around longer than he might think. Mixing a little truth in with a big lie wouldn't hurt.

Silas picked up the flag he had cut to hold the bandages on his captive's hands and head.

"I got this from one of them fellas over in the 35th North Carolina. That's the other outfit that turned tail when your boys broke through. He said it was made special for him by a lady friend down in Morehead City. He said her name was Emeline, but he wouldn't tell me her last name. Probably afraid I'd take her away from him." Silas had a good laugh at that—his own vanity.

"He lost it to me in a game of poker. Just look at the needlework on this—and it's made of silk, too. The best 'Stars and Bars' I ever saw."

He examined the flag Silas held out to him. It was, indeed, beautiful workmanship. It was a shame he had had to cut it—and to help a "blue-belly" at that.

All the while Silas bound his wounds and they spoke, the battle continued to rage. Artillery fire, the cracking of rifles, the screams of wounded men and dying horses carried over the battlefield all around them. Then there came a rush of running feet over wet ground. Silas peeked over the top of their ditch then slid back down, quickly putting on his backpack and taking up his rifle. The rifle in Silas's hands was of a newer model.

When he asked about the rifle, Silas said, "Oh, yeah, this is one of them new Enfield's from England. I guess your Navy boys can't stop everything."

With that, the talkative Reb with the golden hair and clear blue eyes stood up and said, "I got to go, Yank—looks like the fight's coming back this way. You'd better hold on to my flag for me. I want to show it to my folks when I get back home. Now, you stay right where you are. I want your word you won't try to run away or surrender to any other Johnny Reb but me. How about it? Do I have your word on it?"

He did. In no time, Silas Rose was over the top of the ditch and running with a wild yell, still smiling.

He eased himself down on his back and drew his hands up to his chest, resting his elbows at his sides. Now that he was alone, he became more aware of the battle around him and the pain in his hands and his forehead. He drew in the familiar smell of acrid gunpowder smoke mixed with the slightly sweet smell of the swamp. The sky was still cloudy, but no rain had fallen since last night.

"Last night" seemed so long ago.

He couldn't be sure with the clouds obscuring the sun, but he judged the time to be about an hour before noon. There were more shouts and running feet going past his ditch—this time the other way, he was sure. Another half-hour passed and the gunfire, both rifle and cannon, from his right toward the river seemed to move away to the north and then all but ceased. There was still a lot of firing to his left across the railroad tracks. He thought of Frank Grim. And he thought of God. He closed his eyes. He needed to sleep.

"Lieutenant? Sir?"

He opened his eyes and looked into the familiar face of Corporal Rogers.

"Sir? Are you all right?"

He saw Rogers' eyes grow wider.

"Good God, sir! You look a bloody mess."

Corporal Rogers was not famous for his sensitivity.

"Help me up, Rogers. I think I can walk."

He looked at his hands and arms. Blood had soaked his uniform through both sleeves from the elbow down. His hands disappeared into the bloody bandages Silas Rose had bound up. He almost dropped the Confederate flag Silas had left in his care.

Corporal Rogers shouldered his rifle, and they made it up the slope to the field.

Looking at the reddish stains on his coat, he asked, "What kind of place is this Corporal—all this red mud and that low building with the arched roof over there?"

The Corporal looked down as if for the first time and said, "Looks to me like a clay pit for making bricks. That building yonder must be the kiln for firing them, sir."

As they moved back toward the railroad tracks, Rogers began to give his report.

"We all saw you and Sergeant Grim go down. Then you jumped up and started running toward the Rebel lines even without your pistol. We heard you shout: 'Come on and do it,' so we all jumped up and started to run after you. When you were shot down just like Sergeant Grim, it just got our blood up to where we couldn't stand it, so we charged them even faster and started yelling like a bunch of wild Indians. You would have been proud of us, sir. Every one of us—yes, sir! Every damned one of...oh, excuse me, sir...every one of us ran at the Rebs. And they broke and they all ran. Every one of them; they all ran. They were just militia. But when we went over their breastworks even the regulars on the right ran, too. We were behind that whole line on the right flank, sir!"

Rogers took a deep breath, then continued.

"We'd of had them for sure, but the next group down, they turned their line and took us on from our right. Then we got hit from the left; I think from a bunch of reserves. They pushed us back down past where you were, and so we had to regroup almost back where we started.

"Then them Pennsylvanians and the boys from New Jersey and New York on our left sort of come our way to help us out. They weren't doing anything where they were. They couldn't cross that swamp in front of them, so they decided to come our way. We threw the Rebels back through that same hole in the line, and this time we stayed. The rest of them Confederates, all of them, all the way to the river had to fall back or we'd of had them for sure. Then we turned with Parke's Regiment...oh, yeah...Parke's boys joined us after we got though that hole again. Then we turned west and got behind that bunch on our left flank."

As if to confirm Rogers's report, the firing from that direction suddenly died away to almost nothing.

"Then I came back to check on you and Sergeant Grim. The Sergeant's dead, sir. We need to get you to the surgeon, but I'm bettin' that won't happen 'till we get to New Bern."

They reached the railroad tracks and began walking north. Another hundred yards up the track they approached four dead men in tannish-gray uniforms spread out on one side of the tracks. One of the men was smeared with red stains. That man had suffered a grievous wound. Most of his left leg was gone. As he neared the fallen man he could see the man's cap had fallen off revealing long, wavy, blonde hair. His eyes were still open. They were the bluest eyes he had ever seen. Silas Rose was still smiling, even in death.

He knelt down and closed Silas's eyes with the tips of his fingers.

Then he stood and turning to Corporal Rogers, said, "Help me unfold this flag."

Together the two men spread Miss Emeline's flag, with the three strips cut off, over the still body of a man from "up around Alamance." Some of his own blood leaked around his wounded hands and spotted the flag. A little of Silas's blood had not completely dried, and it, too, stained a spot on the flag.

Both stains were the same color.

Richard L. Evans

CHAPTER NINE

MILLICENT and CLARA

By the time they reached New Bern, it was dark. It took another hour before he was assigned a billet in a private home on a wide avenue appropriately named, Broad Street. An artillery captain introduced him to the house's owner, Mrs. Willis, and left.

He was exhausted.

As he looked around, he was sure he was in Mrs. Willis' parlor. The room was large and beautifully decorated and had several overstuffed chairs. He knew the carpet he was standing on must be a real oriental rug. It covered almost the entire floor. He started toward the plainest chair in the room. The woman said nothing but moved to block his path, then motioned to him to follow her.

He was led to a side porch with three rocking chairs. He sat in the first one he came to. The woman went back inside the house. Minutes later she returned carrying a large candelabrum with a dozen lighted candles and what appeared to be a sewing basket. She set them down on a small table next to him. She left again but soon returned with a bowl of water and a large kitchen knife. He must have started at the sight of the knife because she stopped and spoke for the first time.

"As much as I'd like to, I'm not going to kill you with this. That coat you're wearing won't come off over your hands the way they're bandaged. I'll have to cut it off you. It's ruined anyway—no great loss to me, I can assure you."

She pulled up another rocker and began to cut his sleeves from his wrists to his shoulders. She was very meticulous, taking care not to cut either him or herself, washing the knife from time to time.

Despite his tiredness, he watched her face as she worked. She had dark brown eyes. Her hair had once been dark, too, but was now liberally streaked with gray and white. He thought she might be pretty if she smiled. That was something he didn't expect to see. He thought she must be about fifty. Her plain, black dress was well-made but cut conservatively even for those days. She had apparently lived well, so she could be older, maybe even sixty. She unbuttoned the sleeves of her dress at her wrists and rolled them up a few inches.

Probably to keep from getting my gore on her clothes.

Her expression suggested she really didn't want even to touch a Yankee soldier but was doing so only out of Christian charity—and to keep him from soiling her furniture.

With the sleeves cut, she helped him remove his coat and then began to remove the bandages from his hands. He noticed she moved carefully and with considerable skill. As each hand was exposed, she washed it gently using a small piece of cloth from her sewing basket. Then she dressed both palms using a small wad of raw cotton secured by a cloth strip wrapped completely around each hand. She washed his arms to remove the dried blood. She took the bandage from his head and touched the wound lightly with a dampened rag. A clean bandage was wound around his head.

The dark expression on her face never changed, and she spoke not a single word. As she stooped to pick up the old bandages fallen on the porch floor, she stopped, then carefully raised a strip of silk to the candlelight, examining it closely. The strip was unmistakably part of a Confederate flag. Her knife was still on the table next to her hand, and he launched immediately into the story of how a man named Silas Rose had saved his life on the battlefield. She looked at him with a mixture of disgust and disbelief, but she made no move for her knife. Instead, she led him back into the house, holding the candelabrum high ahead of her. He climbed the stairs behind her and was shown to a bedroom at the front of the house.

"This was Captain Willis' room," she said and left.

He lay on the bed and was asleep in seconds.

He awoke the next morning surprisingly refreshed. He must have gone deep into sleep. There had been no dreams for his nightmare to distort. He found a pitcher of water and a towel. He used his thumbs and fingertips to hold the towel as he bathed. He was also able to pick up the slop jar using his open hands from below and carry it down the stairs and outside to an outhouse in the backyard.

A large, ferocious-looking dog approached him as he was returning to the house. The dog let out a low growl and bared its teeth. He began to speak to the dog, and it stopped moving toward him, closed its mouth and sat, looking at him quizzically. He walked to the dog, knelt down and began to pet it using his forearms. The dog licked his face.

"Who are you, Lieutenant?"

Mrs. Willis was seated on a chair on her back porch. Apparently, she had been there as he crossed the yard and was confronted by the dog. He wondered if she would have intervened if the dog had attacked him. He was willing to bet she wouldn't.

Mrs. Willis repeated her question as she rose and came down off the porch toward him.

"Who are you, Lieutenant?"

The dog left him and jumped happily around her, wagging its tail even more vigorously than it had for him.

"I'm what you see, ma'am. A man shot through in battle, trying to make sense of it. That's all."

She squinted at him, not buying his simple explanation, never mind the truth.

"My dog has never allowed anyone except me to approach

him, let alone pet him. So I have to ask some questions, don't you think? Here I have a Yankee soldier forced on me by an enemy army bent on destroying my society. He comes into my home with pieces of a Confederate flag holding bandages on both of his hands, makes himself useful carrying slops out of the house, and to top it off, makes friends with my dog. I'd also like to know just how a man, who is supposed to be attacking an enemy holding a weapon, is shot through the middle of both hands. Mr. Lieutenant, we are going to have a talk—right after breakfast."

She turned away from him and said over her shoulder, "Come on Lad."

It took him a moment to realize she was talking to her dog.

It had been a long time since he had eaten anything other than what the army provided. He could pick up a cup using both his palms but couldn't grip a fork or spoon without pain so she fed him. Breakfast was wonderful and would have been even better if he hadn't spent most of it planning what he was, and was not, going to tell Mrs. Willis about himself.

"Those were the best grits I ever tasted, Mrs. Willis."

He thought he might start the conversation on a high note, even if it was a lie. Titus could make better grits—for that matter, so could he. But he needed every advantage he could muster.

"What's a Yankee know about grits?"

Mrs. Willis was curious but her expression proved she was not buying the compliment.

He explained that he had been a sailor since the age of ten, and had spent some time with friends in Baltimore while recovering from an illness. He didn't tell her it had been almost 120 years since he first went to sea or that his friends in Baltimore had all lived in a house of prostitution or that his illness had been an addiction to opium.

After all, there were some things one just didn't mention in a social conversation.

He told her about his friend, Frank Grim who had recovered from a dire illness only to be killed on the battlefield. He told her the truth about going insane with sadness and rage at Frank's death and how he had raised his hands to God as he turned on the Confederate lines. Then he repeated his story of how a Rebel soldier had helped him—had probably saved his life after he was shot. He also told her about the Confederate flag and how he had left it draped over the body of his slain new friend. It was the first time he had called Silas his "friend."

The last time he had shaved was the morning the regiment boarded the steamer to attack New Bern. The stubble on his face felt bad, and he was sure he looked even worse. He couldn't control a razor and asked Mrs. Willis if she would help him shave. She left the room and returned minutes later with everything the job would require. She had heated water in a cooking pot which she set on a hot pad. Within minutes warm lather covered his neck and chin. Mrs. Willis began sharpening a straight razor on a leather strap. Watching the blade in her hand gave him a momentary queasiness in his stomach, but he remembered how she had resisted killing him last night with a knife.

He asked her, "Have you shaved men before?"

"No," she said, "I've shaved only *one* man before. Whenever Captain Willis came home from the sea, I would shave him every day. Don't worry; I won't cut too much off your Yankee face."

She was too much a lady to put the word, "damn" in front of "Yankee." But he was sure she thought about it.

She was skillful with a razor—just as she had been with a knife. As she worked, he noticed the sternness in her face relax. She seemed to enjoy what she was doing.

Perhaps, she was remembering good times with her husband.

He used the lowering of her guard to draw her out. She began to talk. She never referred to her husband by any name except, "Captain Willis." He had been the captain of a whaling ship but died at sea when a late summer storm drove his ship aground near the Ocracoke Inlet on the Outer Banks. That was the big storm of 1853; he had heard about it. He remembered coming through a typhoon in the Pacific about the same time. He also knew the Outer Banks were "the graveyard of the Atlantic."

Her nursing skills came from tending all the gunshot wounds, accidental and otherwise, around New Bern. She was also a midwife, and helped deliver many children including three born to her slaves. At one time she owned four slaves but had to sell them after her husband's death. The only reason she had agreed to take him in was the money the Union Army promised her.

Mrs. Willis finished shaving and washing his face, then sat at the table facing him. She reached out and took his hands. She removed the bandages she had applied the night before and turned his hands over, palms up.

"You have remarkable powers of regeneration," she said. "I've tended to many injuries as serious as these and wouldn't expect to see this degree of recovery for several weeks." She paused then continued, "These are the stigmata."

He had not heard the word before, and he looked at her questioningly.

"The mark of God." she said, "Your hands have the same holes in them our Lord Jesus had after he was crucified and raised from the dead. You have been marked by God."

•

It was three days before he saw the regimental surgeon. Corporal Rogers had brought him a new uniform, and Mrs. Willis had helped him bathe so he would not soak his bandages. She also "loaned" him one of her husband's shirts. His hands were doing much better, and the bandages Mrs. Willis used now barely restricted their use. But it was still painful to close his hand or to grip anything.

The surgeon, Major Fulford, apologized for not seeing him for so long but explained he was still setting up a more permanent hospital while tending to the most seriously wounded. His biggest concern now was the spread of infection in their wounds. The Major, too, was surprised at the degree of healing that had occurred in his hands. He thought his scalp wound was taking longer to heal due to the presence of so much scar tissue from a previous injury.

Before he left the doctor to return to Mrs. Willis', he asked him if he might be assigned to the medical service of the regiment. The Major thought his wounded hands would recover soon enough for such duty and promised to speak to General Reno about it. Three days later he got his orders—the assignment he requested.

Richard L. Evans

Mrs. Willis had been treating him with a bit more civility since declaring him, "marked by God"—civility, but not friendliness. He was still the enemy, and now that God seemed to be on his side, she redoubled her efforts to freeze him. He fought her coldness with his warmest smiles, his best manners and help with any job he could manage around her house.

One afternoon, shortly after his daily shave, and still trying hard to warm her with a subject he thought might work, he asked her about her dog. Lad had adopted him not as a second master but as a friend. The two of them spent hours in Mrs. Willis's backyard throwing and retrieving a stick. Mrs. Willis watched from her chair on the porch. At first, Lad expected him to pull the stick out of his mouth but seemed to sense his pain when he tried to do it and learned to drop the stick at his feet.

"What kind of a dog is Lad," he asked, "I don't think I recognize his breed?"

She said he was a "sooner."

When he said he hadn't heard of such a breed, he thought he saw the beginnings of a smile flicker on her face.

But she twisted it away saying, "He'd sooner be one thing as another."

A few days before he was to leave New Bern, he asked her for another favor. He wanted to write a letter to the family of Silas Rose but couldn't hold a pen tight enough to control it properly. He asked her if she would write the letter as he dictated to her. She said nothing but left the room returning with paper, a bottle of ink and several pen nibs. She sat and looked at him expectantly. He began to tell her what to write speaking slowly, taking care with his words.

"To the family of Silas Rose, 33rd North Carolina Regiment, C.S.A. I am writing to you today with a heavy heart, but I must inform you of my friend, Silas Rose's death."

Mrs. Willis stopped writing before the word death.

She looked at him and asked, "Are you sure you want to use the word 'death?' Perhaps you could say, 'passing?'"

He thought about it, and then said, "No, death is what happened, and saying it differently won't make it easier; write 'death.'"

He continued, "I met Silas on March 14, 1862. It was an early spring day a few miles south of New Bern. We were in a battle together where I was shot and grievously wounded. Silas pulled me to safety, bandaged my wounds, gave me comfort and stayed with me until the battle once again demanded his service. Before he left me, he spoke lovingly of you, his family, and his life and friends in Alamance County.

"He died a short time after leaving me. He fought to his last breath for his beloved country and for the family he loved even more. Silas left in my care a Confederate flag, a beautiful banner with the stars and bars in blue, red and white. After the battle, I found my friend where he had fallen and placed the flag over him as a salute to a fallen comrade in arms.

"Blessed is he who lays down his life for his friends. Even more blessed is he who lays down his life for his enemies. I am a Union soldier.

"I am sure in my prayers that God has had mercy on the soul of your beloved Silas, for surely God loves such a man. And I pray God will give you His comfort, sure in the knowledge that we will meet again someday on the other side.

"I am yours in deepest sympathy and respect."

He paused and Mrs. Willis looked up at him.

"Don't write my name. I'd like to try to sign it myself."

She helped him hold the pen between his fingers and thumb. He moved the pen slowly over the paper, trying not to let the pain show on his face.

After he signed his name and his Regiment, he asked her, "Do you think a letter sent to just 'The family of Silas Rose, Alamance County' will reach them?"

Mrs. Willis nodded, "Yes, I'll see to it."

"I'd like to write another letter," he said. "I want to write a family in Marblehead, Massachusetts. Will you help with that one, too?"

"Of course, I will."

When the letter to Frank Grim's family was finished, she took both his hands in hers across the table.

"I've heard you cry out in the night. God has marked you for some purpose in your life. I cannot tell you what it is, but you must remember this calling. Jesus took away your sins, and God has forgiven you for whatever troubles your dreams. Now, you must forgive yourself."

He was stunned. She had used the exact words Titus had used so many years before.

"You must forgive yourself."

She asked him if he were a Christian. He thought about his answer for several minutes while she waited patiently. He was a liar, a slaver, a rapist, an abortionist, a dope addict and a murderer many times over—yet he had been forgiven all those things.

Finally, he said, "I can't be sure. I'm not baptized."

His answer seemed to satisfy her.

She said, "I've known the most evil people imaginable who still declared themselves to be 'Christians' at the top of their lungs."

He asked her, "Do you believe in angels?"

"Of course I do," she answered quickly. Still holding his hands, she looked into his eyes and said, "My name is Millicent."

Five days later he was prepared to leave. Corporal Rogers brought him a cloth bag to hold his extra clothes and kit. Millicent sewed a cloth belt on it so he could carry it over one shoulder and not have to carry it with his hands. He gave her his best smile and said his thanks for all her care. She said nothing but kissed him lightly on his cheek. Then she smiled at him through her tears.

He was right—she was pretty when she smiled.

•

The 21st Massachusetts, with its new medical officer, was refitted and on its way north. The flesh on the backs of his hands closed and grew over with scars that were barely discernible. His palms, however, would always have deep holes in them. As long as he kept his hands partly closed, no one would ever notice his "marks from God."

He was moving west through the Maryland countryside as part of the Army of the Potomac. Six months had passed since the battle at New Bern. General Lee had brought the Confederate

Army into western Maryland and everyone knew a clash of arms would soon follow.

The men no longer sang the rousing fighting songs they had enjoyed so much at the beginning of the war. Too many had seen too much suffering. Too many friends were gone. They still sang but now they sang sentimental, reflective songs.

Many are the hearts that are weary tonight,
Wishing for the war to cease;
Many are the hearts looking for the right
To see the dawn of peace.
Tenting tonight, tenting tonight,
Tenting on the old campground.

The Federals broke through a gap at South Mountain in western Maryland and two days later approached a small farming town near the Potomac River. Sharpsburg was on high ground, a half-mile on the other side of a small stream named Antietam Creek.

The morning of September 16, 1862, dawned in clouds and mist. The weather reminded him of a similar morning just that past spring when he had charged a Confederate force, trying to kill himself. A light rain had fallen during the night and a low fog hugged the ground. Surgeons and orderlies were bustling about the field hospital, preparing for what they feared would be a very busy day. Tables were set up to treat the wounded; boxes of bandages rolled by volunteer ladies' groups were opened and set out; bottles of chloroform and other antiseptics were set on other tables; surgical tools and supplies were unpacked. All was made ready for a battle. They thought they were prepared for whatever would come. Twelve hours later, they would realize how woefully unprepared they were.

Dawn had not actually lit the sky before the sound of rifle fire came to them from a stand of woods to the north of the town. The Union offensive had begun. For the next three hours most of the sounds of fighting came from that same direction, the right flank of the Union forces. At times the sound of individual rifles could not be distinguished from the continuous roar of firing.

Richard L. Evans

Cannons on both sides were also firing so rapidly they created a sound like unabated thunder. Even though his regiment was stationed on the left flank, downstream from the fighting, casualties began arriving at an alarming rate. Other field hospitals had been overwhelmed so quickly some of the wounded had to be carried as much as two miles southward to his unit.

When the sounds of battle grew even louder, he knew the Army was now attacking the center of the Confederate lines much closer to Sharpsburg—much closer to a middle bridge over the creek and much closer to him. By then, his hospital, too, was overwhelmed by the dead and the soon-to-be-dead.

The surgeons and their staffs left the hospital and moved forward. Their only real hope of saving men with terrible wounds was to get to them sooner. They, therefore, had to go to them and not wait for the wounded to be brought back. They crossed the creek to the battle.

He went with them. There was nothing for him to do at the field hospital, so he carried a folding table and a set of surgeons' tools, hoping to help one of the doctors. He was directed to turn to his right, to go up the slope from the creek to a farmhouse. It was well out of his IX Corps area but was apparently where he was needed most. As soon as he set up his table, a wounded man was laid on it by two other soldiers. The soldiers disappeared immediately going back to the battle. Most of the wounded man's left foot was gone.

"You'll have to take that one." A voice came from his left.

When he looked that way, he saw a surgeon standing over another wounded man.

The surgeon gestured to him with a nod and said, "Get a tourniquet on the upper leg and use the saw with the larger teeth to cut just below the knee. You'll have to take it off."

His mouth opened, but he couldn't speak.

"Do it! Do it, now," the surgeon yelled.

He found what he needed in the surgeon's tool pouch but hesitated.

The wounded man, a young private from a Wisconsin regiment looked at him and said, "Oh, good Jesus, sir. What will we do, now?"

"That's just what I was thinking, son," he replied.

Then there was another voice. Someone was standing at his side. He was startled to realize it was a woman's voice. She was telling him exactly what he must do. She spoke calmly but with authority. He looked at her. Dark hair, pulled back and knotted behind her head, framed a pleasant face. High cheekbones set off dark eyes that looked at him steadily.

She smiled slightly, reassuringly. "You *can* do it, and you *must* do it."

For the next nine hours, until the sun went down and he could no longer see to work, he sawed, cut, sewed, cauterized and bandaged so many maimed men he could not guess the number—and he really didn't want to know. Around the two tables where he and the Army surgeon worked that day were piles of severed arms, legs, hands and feet.

He went back to the field hospital where lanterns had been lit. The army had run out of candles. The lanterns had been brought to the battlefield by a woman, a private citizen, along with four wagons of other supplies.

More wounded men were being brought in by volunteers who crept over the darkened battlefield listening for the cries of the wounded. He worked on until after midnight. Finally, he took a clean uniform from his kit and stripped off all his clothing. His old uniform was stiff with dried blood, soaked through from his neck to his toes. He bathed his arms and face in a water basin and put on his fresh clothing.

"You did well, today."

It was the same voice he had heard on the battlefield.

Turning, he faced the woman who had helped him with his first patient. She looked older than he had first thought. He guessed her age at about forty. She extended her hand, not in the usual fashion of a woman with her palm down, but with her palm open like a man expecting a handshake. He shook her hand and gave her his name. Her hand was strong and he was sure she must be used to hard work.

"I'm Clara Barton," she said. "You have a natural talent for surgery. I hope you will consider getting some formal training when you can."

Then she moved on, working up and down the rows of wounded men. She gave comfort to all and water to those who could have it. There were few beds so most of the men lay on blankets stretched on the ground. As she moved from man to man, she spoke to them, touching each briefly. She put her hand on their heads or shoulders or arms. The effect the combination of her voice and touch had on the wounded men, was immediate and sometimes dramatic. Perhaps it was the sound of a woman's voice—the comforting sound of a sweetheart, sister, wife or mother. Those who could smiled and seemed to be lifted in spirit. Those who were only sleeping relaxed and went deeper into a healing calm. She was giving them the one thing they needed more than anything else: hope.

He felt he was watching a whole series of small miracles. He wanted to make those miracles, too. He had heard of Clara Barton: the "Angel of the Battlefield," they called her. That day, he believed it.

God had given him long life; Titus had given him direction; Silas had turned him from death back to life; Millicent had shown him his life had purpose, and now, Clara had shown him what that purpose was—he was a healer.

The next morning he had another responsibility as medical officer. He left the maimed men in the hospital to the doctors' care and took another group of volunteers with him on the battlefield. He carried a staff with a white flag indicating, he hoped, that he was a noncombatant looking only to help the wounded and remove the dead.

He tried years later to describe what he saw, but there were no words for it. Everywhere he looked, he saw death. Men and horses strewn over the farmers' fields, in places resembling cornstalks or sheaths of wheat cut down for harvest and set in neat rows all facing in the same direction. Some had been torn apart; others appeared just to be sleeping. He set his volunteers to loading the corpses on horse-drawn wagons to be buried on a level elevation just east of the town in a place soon to be called Cemetery Hill.

Early in the afternoon he realized he could have saved the trouble of carrying his white flag. Both the Union and the Confederate Armies had declared a truce to see to their wounded and bury their dead.

He saw only a few men wearing dusty gray uniforms. Most were Rebel doctors and some of their walking wounded. They, too, were moving over the battlefield looking for any of their wounded comrades who might still be alive. There were far too few of them. They would never be able to remove all their injured and their dead. He turned to Rogers, now Sergeant Rogers, and sent him back to IX Corps headquarters to ask for more men and wagons. They would have to help the Confederates bury their dead.

As he watched from the hill, he saw the Confederate soldiers pause, then move to one of their party who was pointing at something farther down the slope. All the Confederate men and doctors just stopped and stared. His curiosity aroused, he walked toward them. As he did, he noticed the far slope of a hill rising across from whatever it was that had caught the Rebels' interest.

The slope was covered by hundreds of bodies, all wearing blue. He was within a few yards of the Confederates when he saw what they were staring at. A low road, sunk down below the level of the fields joining it on both sides, ran for about a half mile toward the creek. The road was filled—no, more than filled—with the bodies of more hundreds of men, most wearing gray. They were piled on top of one another, as many as four or five men deep.

"My God!"

Even though he whispered it, one of the Rebel soldiers turned to him. He recognized the black stripes along the top of the man's uniform shoulders. The soldier was wearing the same black patches Silas Rose had worn. He stared at the other soldier for a long moment and then asked, "33rd North Carolina?"

"How'd you know that?" the soldier asked.

"I saw your black patches at New Bern last spring."

"Yeah," replied the soldier, "we was there. So were some of those boys," he nodded toward the road. "Some of them was in the 35th North Carolina. They was the ones that ran away with the militia at New Bern. You'd of never of got us if those boys hadn't run then."

Richard L. Evans

The soldier thought for a moment and then said, "They didn't run this time, though." Then, after another moment and in a much softer voice, he said, "Sure wish they had."

Many are the hearts that are weary tonight,
Wishing for the war to cease;
Many are the hearts looking for the right,
To see the dawn of peace.
Dying tonight, dying tonight,
Dying on the old camp ground.

CHAPTER TEN

SYLVIA

The war was over. President Lincoln had freed the slaves and been shot. The country was still divided with terrible animosities on both sides—some that would only get worse with time. But he had no doubts about what he was going to do. He was going to be a healer. He was going to medical school.

The medical school at the University of Pennsylvania was one of the best in the country. Many practicing physicians of the day were not certified, and some had no formal education in medical matters. He didn't want to be one of those. He applied to Penn and was accepted, even though he could produce no evidence of any previous schooling. He was worried about what he might learn in a real school—learn about himself. He had never been in a classroom until he walked into his first class at Penn.

The sea, the wars and the wilderness taught their lessons differently—they were never abstract, and the laboratory work always came ahead of the lecture. First you got the answer—then you got the question.

Richard L. Evans

His concern was groundless. After one semester he was almost at the top of his class. The other medical students, with few exceptions, were young and fell victim to the distractions of their youth. The only thing youthful about him was his looks. He'd seen and done far too much to ever be young again.

Not having money was a problem. Only the elite of the day were expected to attend professional schools—those who had patrons or whose families had money. He had no patron. He would have to earn his way.

He used what little money he had to buy new clothes and a pair of buttoned shoes. The shoes hurt and made him wish he'd kept his army boots or even better, his moccasins.

He applied for a job with the school as a cook. He wasn't asked to supply references and a good thing for that. He was a very good cook, though. He served his apprenticeship under Titus and his journeyman work with the colonial army, the Western mountain men and the American Indians.

He was such a good cook he was soon assigned to the faculty staff dining room. This was a particularly good job because it came with a room of his own. Most of the professors lived close by the campus, but they and their families were served lunch and dinner every day except Sunday at the Faculty House. A free lunch has the same appeal across all social and intellectual lines.

He was always busy—going to classes, studying, working in the laboratories, and cooking left no time for other activities. If there had been time, though, he had more than enough offers from a number of the faculty wives for "other activities."

Late one afternoon he was preparing salad plates for the evening meal. He was bent forward over the preparation table when he sensed the presence of someone else in the kitchen. A hand touched his buttocks. The hand squeezed him lightly. From the corner of his eye he saw it was his anatomy professor.

"Well, professor, how nice of you to come by," he said. "Would you please remove your sinistral metacarpal and phalanxes from my left posterior gluteni?"

Nothing more was said about it. He had been approached with similar proposals by other men and found that "no" said in a pleasant and non-threatening way always saved the situation for everyone. Penn might be a Quaker sponsored school, but most of the faculty and students were not Quakers.

His talent as a singer emerged soon after his employment. He had acquired the habit of singing softly to himself as he wandered through the wilderness. It wasn't long before every evening meal was followed by a songfest under his direction. The faculty's families were always invited to join them for the evening meal. Some of their wives could play the large upright piano that dominated the parlor of the Faculty House. With the added attraction of musical performance afterward, more and more families joined in the evenings' pleasures.

The children all learned one of his old songs and were always invited to sing it sometime during each evening.

There were men on the faculty who were opposed to the presence of children in the parlor of the Faculty House. They were even more opposed to having children sing in the place. The obvious fact that their wishes were completely disregarded led him to his first lesson in the subtle power of women in that society.

The civil and criminal laws of the day placed all power in the hands of men. A married woman could not hold property in her name alone. But the women had learned the power of something else—something very personal—and they weren't afraid to wield that power. Women had no vote in public affairs. But in private affairs there was no need to vote.

So the children sang almost every evening. The song they liked best was "Yankee Doodle Doodle Doo."

Father and I went down to camp along with Captain Goodin,
And there we saw the men and boys as thick as hasty puddin',
CHORUS:
Yankee Doodle doodle doo, Yankee Doodle dandy,
 Mind the music and the step and with the girls be handy.

There were six more verses, but the children rarely got that far—they would dissolve in giddy giggles every time they came to the end of the chorus and sang, "and with the girls be handy."

He took away many fine memories of those evenings...so far away from slave ships, murderous Indians and sunken roads.

There was another memory he kept from those days, too. Her name was Sylvia.

His professor of pharmacology, Dr. Morgan, and Mrs. Morgan had been coming to the evening singing for some time. He thought them childless until one evening in November they brought their daughter, Sylvia. At least, he thought they brought her. Mrs. Morgan was a striking, auburn haired woman. In the presence of her daughter, however, no man in the room noticed her at all. Every other woman in the room took an instant dislike to the daughter. She was just too beautiful to be liked.

Sylvia Morgan was only fifteen when he first saw her. When he looked into her all-knowing, green cat's eyes, they made him wonder where she had spent those fifteen years. Dr. and Mrs. Morgan had lost all control over their daughter, their only child, at least twelve years before. Sylvia did what Sylvia wanted to do, and went where Sylvia wanted to go, and crushed anyone who got in her way. No one "brought" Sylvia anywhere.

He asked her if she were related to the famous Revolutionary War hero, Colonel Daniel Morgan. She was, but only distantly. "Distant" was the operable word with Sylvia—at first. She made it clear in their first sixty seconds that she was blindingly intelligent and did not suffer fools. That was good for him, actually. He had lived too long to think himself a fool and had been with too many beautiful women to make a fool of himself over this girl. He made *that* clear in their second sixty seconds. It was a mistake. His resistance attracted her. Sylvia decided he was to be her man.

He was in big trouble.

Sylvia became a fixture at the Faculty House. When she wasn't in the dining room for lunch or dinner giving the men an eye test and the other women ulcers, she was in the kitchen, helping. Her "help" usually amounted to positioning herself opposite him at the preparation table, then leaning over to reach for something, carelessly allowing the top of her dress to fall open just enough so he could appraise her cleavage. Or she might "accidentally" bang her knee on a table leg and produce real tears of pain.

"You're learning to be a doctor. You should examine this knee."

This last was spoken as she propped her foot up on a chair facing him, and then slowly raised her skirt well above her "injured" knee and even more slowly, rolled down her stocking to reveal the "damage." All of this, of course, was supposed to have an affect on him. And it did. But he had been resolute in the face of dangerous adversaries before and usually managed to suppress any uprising.

Sylvia was brilliant; there was no question. She had attended school for exactly one day. She came home that afternoon and announced she would not be returning. She was six at the time. She read, instead, every book, pamphlet, map, periodical or other reference she could get her hands on. She also had a photographic memory. Having read all the textbooks he was to study, she was an invaluable source of study help. That is, when she kept her hands, arms, behind, breasts, belly, legs and feet off him. He worried she might be another Peshewa, and he didn't have the time nor the energy for that. Not now.

Crossing the campus one day with Sylvia cooing at his side, he observed another student, a handsome, young fellow, following her every movement.

Nodding in the fellow's direction, he said, "You might like to talk to him. Judging from his total concentration on you, I'm sure he'd be an easy conquest."

"They all are," she said.

He didn't doubt it. While he watched, the young man, with his head turned in Sylvia's direction, walked into a tree.

"Look at that," he said.

"Yeah," she said, "another one."

Sylvia could be so cold.

It did no good to bring up her age.

"Lots of women my age are already married and have children," she said.

It also did no good to use any tactic that led to a contest of wills, logic or intellect. Sylvia would always win. By the end of his junior year she was almost nineteen. He could hold out no longer.

It was early evening of the summer solstice, the first day of summer. He lit two gas lamps even though a red dusk still shown through his window. Sylvia was at his door exactly on time, the time they had set earlier in the day. She was flushed, almost glowing, he thought.

As soon as the door closed behind her, she said, "Shall I take off my clothes?"

This girl does not fool around.

"No," he said, "I'll do that."

"Oh, good," she said as she closed the few steps between them.

He took his time. It was ritual—like the unveiling of a new bride. With each garment he took from her, he took off one of his own. Their bodies emerged slowly from their clothes, exposing his scars and her perfection. They were both covered in perspiration—the primitive mating response. He shivered but not because he was cold—it was the sight of Sylvia glimmering in the fading, golden light.

It had been a long time since he had made love. Sylvia, her perfect body now fully exposed, might have intimidated him were he a younger, less experienced man. But he was more than up to it. He was sure she could see that.

He turned her toward the bed. But Sylvia turned back, looking him up and down coolly with just a twitch of a smile turning the corners of her perfect mouth.

Damn it, she's just here for a lark—something to write in her diary. He saw it and hated it. *Well, not this time, sweetheart.*

He stepped through her maddening smile and embraced her lightly, his body just touching her breasts and thighs. His erection pressed against her stomach. He didn't know if she had any detachment left, but he didn't. He was ready. He picked her up roughly and carried her to the bed.

He was about to throw her on the bed, to take her hard and fast. But something in her face stopped him. Was it a hint of fear? Not knowing, he put her down gently on the bed and lay next to her. He touched her face and neck. He moved his fingers lightly along her arm and down her side to her hip. She started to speak but he put a finger to his lips stopping her.

"First, we have to talk about babies," he said.

He was sure she had learned how girls became pregnant early in her life—probably at a far younger age than he.

"Don't worry about it," she said.

"Oh, yes we must worry about it, my dear, sweet Sylvia."

Was it possible she didn't understand the potential consequences of what they were about to do? He was as well-prepared as possible, but what he had was no better than what had been available back at Miss Lucille's. Nothing was reliable. Only abstinence was a sure thing, and that was no longer an option.

"I can't have babies," she said. "When I didn't start bleeding when my father thought I should, he took me around to all the learned doctors here. I'm infertile. I'll never have children. Now, can we just get on with it?"

Can we just get on with it?

Her words touched a nerve. That's all that mattered: "just getting on with it." She would never have children, and it didn't matter. That was Sylvia, all right—that door was closed; so don't look back; just get on with opening another.

"Now," he said, "I want you to do to me what I'm doing to you." His hand moved to her breast.

"Oh!" she said.

That's better, he thought.

It was the first time he'd heard her say something with emotion. She did as she was told and put her hand on his chest, moving her fingers through his chest hair.

He slid his hand down and across her belly reaching between her thighs. She did the same to him.

"Whoa, hold on there," he said quickly. "Don't squeeze those."

"Why? Does that hurt?"

"Yes."

"But you squeezed my breast?"

"Yes, I did. But did it hurt?"

"No, it felt good."

"Well, when you squeeze those, it hurts."

"Oh." She smiled her little winner's smile as she released him. But she found something else. "Can I squeeze this? It's much harder."

"Yes."

"And it's getting bigger, too. How big does it get?"

"If you keep squeezing it like that, you're going to find out."

"Oh, good."

He rolled her over on her back and pushed her legs apart. Her musk floated up to him, the aroma heightening his anticipation. But Sylvia had one more little surprise for him: she was a virgin.

He pulled away, startled by the discovery. She had been so sexually aggressive he assumed she must have taken other lovers.

"You've never done this before?"

"No, I've waited for you, my sweet doctor."

Her smile widened.

"I'm not a doctor, not yet."

"But you'll always be my first, my first lover and my first doctor."

Then she laughed. It should have been a merry laugh but it wasn't. It was the laugh of a conqueror.

Slow and easy.

He made his first thrust and felt himself slide into her, breaking through. Sylvia moaned once, but that was all.

"Are you all right?"

"Yes," she said, "I thought it would hurt more, but it didn't. Can we do it some more, now?"

He began again, coaching her as he moved. Soon, they were moving together. She brought her knees up as he instructed and began to match his thrusts with hers, raising and lowering her pelvis, matching his rhythm.

Sylvia was round and soft everywhere she should be round and soft, but she was no delicate blossom. She was strong and used her strength well. Even concentrating as hard as he could, he couldn't hold himself back for more than a few minutes.

"Oh, that's so warm," she said.

Her enthusiasm couldn't match his, though.

He continued his job as cook at the Faculty House. The days were his, but the nights were Sylvia's. Every night she arrived at his door exactly on time. From eight to twelve each evening they did a new dance of the amours. All the research she had done, all her reading over the years about sexual intercourse—and a lot more—could now be tested and evaluated. She had to know how everything felt; no possible sensual experience for any part of her body was to be omitted or taken halfheartedly. At times he was sure he had stepped into some alien world of sensuous nonsense.

Their joining had been properly conventional the first few nights. But Sylvia would never be content with mere convention. Somewhere in her exhaustive research she had read that pain increased sexual pleasure. That wasn't true for him. He had experienced lots of pain, and none of it had ever given him pleasure. But she insisted he prove it to her.

He tried to hurt her, just to please her. He used leather straps to bind her wrists and ankles together before whipping her and taking her roughly, simulating a rape. But it was too close to what he had done to the Igbo woman on the *Anne*. He couldn't finish it, and he couldn't tell her why.

Her pain was physical—his went much deeper. It had been many years since his cruelty on the *Anne*, but the memory was still sharp, as sharp as any razor. She said he wasn't cooperating, that "he didn't love her enough." That part was true. He didn't love her, and he knew she didn't know how to love him. She seemed incapable of loving him. He wanted to teach her more.

He wanted to share his love of God with her. She had read the same Bible he had—every word—yet those words meant nothing to her. It was as if she gave every word she read in every book the same weight; none were more important than any of the others. She knew them only as markings on pages—just thousands of meaningless marks on thousands of meaningless pages. She couldn't love herself, and she couldn't love him. So how could she love God? She got from him only what she wanted, nothing more, and he did the same to her.

None of the other women he had known in love: Margery, Peshewa or Willowy were as beautiful as Sylvia, but they all gave him much more pleasure. Sex as an expression of love was a precious gift. Sex without love was not a gift—it was just sex. But that was all Sylvia wanted.

She had read a lot about bondage, but it was hard for her. She had to trust him. She had never trusted anyone before, certainly not her parents. Having control over everything else in her life, relinquishing control of her body could stimulate her to near ecstasy. It was up to him to take her the rest of the way.

He didn't like it. He didn't want to hurt her, but he didn't want her to enjoy it too much, either.

Perhaps, too much pleasure, like too many warm, sunny days in a row, might stifle her enjoyment. Could there ever be too much pleasure for Sylvia? He had to try.

He lashed her wrists to the headboard and her ankles to each end of the footboard leaving her on her back, her legs spread wide on the bed. Then he introduced her to something Sylvia hadn't read about: a long, narrow feather from the tail of a pheasant. She smiled when she saw it, not aware of his intent.

He said, "I'll wipe that smile off your lovely face soon enough, my dear."

He started with her ribs. "That tickles," she giggled.

Her giggles turned to a low moan when he moved the feather up a few inches. As the tip of the feather touched her nipple, it shrank and hardened. She moved, trying to escape the feather's brush, but she couldn't escape. The feather didn't stop until both her nipples were standing hard and upright. The feather moved down. It moved slowly over her belly.

"Oh," she said, "that tickles, too."

The feather continued moving, around her hip to the inside of her thigh. She shivered. Down it moved, down, almost to her knee, then back up.

Sylvia yelped, "Oh, oh, no!"

He moved his face close to hers, asking, "What ever happened to, 'Oh, good'?"

The feather continued upward. Now it brushed over her labia following the line where her lips came together. She twisted again, but the feather followed her movements. He lifted the feather and examined it.

"Damn," he said smiling, "you've gotten it too wet."

But that was all right. He had another, and now he used his fingers to spread her labia until he could see the object that would soon become the center of her universe. He brought the end of his new feather to its tip. The feather moved, alternating between being flicked slightly and moving in tight, little circles. Sylvia twisted and thrashed about for a moment before losing control. She screamed, her hips twisting wildly, but he kept the feather moving with her. Her efforts to escape made no difference. He was relentless.

At last she gasped, her whole body going rigid—her torso lifted off the bed, supported only by her heels and shoulders. Her muscles convulsed and then she collapsed, moaning between long inhalations. Again he moved until his face was next to hers.

He whispered in her ear, "I believe I saw a pheasant in the bush."

Even though she was working hard to take in more air, she still managed to curse him between gasps. Sylvia knew some very imaginative curses—even some he hadn't heard before. Most of them involved parts of his body and his body's orifices along with a whole array of items to be inserted or affixed.

He thanked her for her intense interest in his future activities. Then he held up his hand so she could see he was holding six more feathers.

"I read," she began in a way that usually meant she wanted to try something new, "that holding your breath during intercourse increases your climax."

So it had to be another contest to see who could hold their breath the longest and have the more intense orgasm. She "won," of course. She always did.

As they rested after a particularly strenuous round of copulation, he remembered a question he had long wanted to ask her. She was such a mental phenomenon; he thought she might have read about Jedediah Strong Smith.

"Yes," she said, "I have."

"Do you know what happened to him, how he died?" he asked.

"Why do you want to know about him?" Sylvia never gave anything away for nothing.

"My father used to talk about him," he lied. He knew he had to be careful what he told her. She never forgot what she saw, and she never forgot what she heard.

"Smith was an explorer out West," she said. "He was killed in 1831 by Comanches in Arizona while he was leading a bunch of settlers west."

So, his good friend had been on his way back to his men. He

never doubted it. That was one more mystery solved. But he knew Sylvia couldn't help him with the other mysteries in his life. Only God could do that.

He had to rest and recover after each new encounter. While resting between positions, she held him close to her body, almost as if she were afraid he might run away. Those became wonderful moments for him. It was in those moments he asked her about the other things she had read, the thoughts of poets and philosophers, warriors and politicians. There were so many books. She told him all of Homer's stories and many other ideas from the ancient world. He was fascinated by Hippocrates and Galen, both early physicians—healers like he wanted to be.

In the wilderness the only book he had was Titus' Bible. Crossing the Continent he had to read the signs around him, not a book, just to stay alive. At sea and at war there had been little opportunity to read. But now a whole new world was opened to him. All the rest of his life he would remember Sylvia's only real gift to him, a gift more precious than any he would ever be able to give her—the gift of human striving for knowledge.

Night after night, strange delights most men only dream of came to him. Sometimes she came to him dressed alluringly, and sometimes she came undressed alluringly. And sometimes he undressed her. Sylvia, the she-devil, was learning where he was weakest and how to use his weakness. He felt like he was just a boy again back on the deck of his first ship, standing the watch. He was on duty. Only then he had been in control. Not now.

The eighth glass of the midnight watch. Ding-ding, ding-ding, ding-ding, ding-ding—then he could sleep.

Would this summer with Sylvia never end? But after his "watch" was over and his "duties" done, precious sleep would take him.

It hadn't been long into Sylvia's experimentation with all things sexual and her own personal exploration, when she discovered the holes in his palms. He explained how it had happened in the war. They were sitting up in bed, facing each other. She took his hands in hers, and he thought for a moment she would tell him how sorry she was he had been injured. For just that moment he forgot who she was—what she was.

She was a witch.

Sometimes she was a good witch and sometimes she was a bad witch. Men recognized this and were fascinated by the gorgeous witch. Women recognized it too but they pronounced Sylvia the "witch" with a "b."

She took his hands and brought them to her bare breasts inserting her nipples in the holes.

"Squeeze them," she said.

He didn't think that was what God had in mind when He marked him in the battle at New Bern. It didn't matter. After that, whenever they walked together in public, she would take one of his hands in hers, slip a finger in the hole in his palm and smile wickedly at him.

As the summer wore on, he thought he might actually survive Sylvia's demands on his body. That feeling was reinforced when she failed to come to his room three nights in a row. Then on the fourth night he was awakened from his usual bad dream by a warm, naked body snuggling next to his. By the time his mind threw off the dream and he realized it was Sylvia in bed with him, he felt a second warm body slide in next to him on the other side. That body, too, was naked.

He started and would have jumped from the bed, but Sylvia held him, speaking quickly.

"It's all right. It's just my friend, Elizabeth. I've told her so much about you she wanted to...um...meet you. We've known each other since we were little girls—but I had no idea! She's shown me some new things, and now she'd like to do you, too. Oh, my sweet darling, you can't imagine how wonderful it feels to make love to a woman." He was sure he knew—without having to imagine anything.

He would have taken Elizabeth's hand and introduced himself, but they were already so intimately acquainted he thought there was no need for a handshake. Elizabeth had already found something else of his to grasp.

Sylvia was still speaking, "How would you like two for the price of one? You know, as nice as Elizabeth is, she still doesn't have what you have."

He was glad to hear that. Both women had gotten very busy

with him even as Sylvia spoke. He did what he could. He didn't want to disappoint Sylvia. Or Elizabeth. The doctor was in.

He wasn't surprised by Sylvia's use of Elizabeth. Sylvia's ambitions went far beyond a few steamy weeks with one man.

Why should she limit herself to only half the world's population when she could screw everybody?

•

Sylvia slept very well, too, that summer of 1870. Her physical needs satisfied, her prodigious mind took over her energies. She borrowed $1,000 each from her father and two other professors. She invested the money in her father's name. She saw the possibilities of the next American Revolution: industrialization. She rolled the money over many times, always, at least, doubling it.

In a few years she invested in a new company, building a system based on an invention by a man named Alexander Graham Bell. A few years after that, she did the same for an inventor by the name of Thomas Alva Edison. She saw steam powered land vehicles and recognized the potential, not so much of the vehicles themselves, but of the other products and services that would be needed in the coming automotive age: better roads, bridges, tires and fuel storage. She saw clearly the coming movement of workers from the farms into the cities to take up new jobs in new industries. She knew just what to buy and where to invest.

Twelve years after her first investments, Sylvia had made her father into that rarest of fellows: a wealthy academician. She bought off her other first investors after three more years, at seventeen times their original investments.

Her mind was such that she could keep everything in her head—all her accounts, where the money was, who was responsible for what, and how much was available at any time for further investment. She needed no books, so she created no records. Nothing was ever put in her own name. She was immune from prosecution for any of her questionable business manipulations. The laws were written for Sylvia Morgan.

He faded from her world. Having gotten from him what she wanted, Sylvia went looking elsewhere for excitement. He waved to her from the platform as her train pulled out. He had helped arm her with some potent weapons. The knowledge first given him by Margery and later embellished with so many nuances by Peshewa and Willowy was now hers. She had a legacy of love but knew nothing of love. He prayed for her. He prayed for those she'd surely use, too. He watched as her train disappeared down the tracks. He thought that would be the end of it.

He was wrong again.

After his years of medical school at Penn, commencement exercises came and went. He held a diploma in his hand, testifying that he knew enough to be called a physician. By the end of the day he had two more diplomas—two rolled documents left carelessly about by two of his classmates. They would apply to the College and get replacements. He applied too, and was also given a duplicate of his own diploma. That gave him a total of four diplomas—one to use now and three he could alter slightly as needed in the future. If he stayed for twenty years in each place, he could be a doctor for the next eighty years.

As he thought about it, he was already the oldest living doctor on the planet. He was 133 years old.

•

He went south.

For nine years he worked at his own practice, then joined the staff of a teaching hospital. Life was good if the heat and the "skeeters" didn't get you.

He was about to celebrate his seventeenth year as a doctor when a telegram arrived: Sylvia would meet him at the train station at 11:00 am Saturday.

Not, "Would you be so kind as to meet me?" but, "Be there!"

He was there by 10:30.

Sylvia stepped off the train. He had tried to prepare himself for the disappointment. After all, it had been seventeen years. What could have happened to her in seventeen years? Wrinkles, fat—who knows what else? And there she was. He couldn't help it—his heart jumped and started running madly. He wasn't alone. There must have been twenty other men on the platform. After her third step, there were forty-two eyes watching every sway and ripple as she came toward him. Of course Sylvia had changed—for the better.

She took his arm, and they walked to the horse-drawn cab he had waiting for them. She told him she had been investing in his name. The law still prevented her from investing solely in her own name. Now, she needed his signature on some documents. She thought he was the perfect silent partner. She knew he cared nothing for wealth so would probably not try to cheat her. She also knew he would remain loyal to her if things ever got out of hand. And, finally, his position as a successful and respected physician would lend legitimacy to her operations.

Finally, she said, "Oh, yes, by the way, how are you?"

He had tried to reserve a room for her at the best hotel in the city but was told she had already reserved a suite for herself.

They sat across a table from each other in the hotel lounge. He had questions. She had one question. They took hers first.

"Why haven't you changed in twenty-one years?"

"I've changed," he said.

"You've let your hair grow longer, and you have that nice beard, but nothing else has changed. Why not? Is there something wrong with you?"

"Of course not. I grew the beard and let my hair grow..." He had a bad, old feeling that he was in way over his depth.

"...So you would look older." She finished his sentence for him. "When we first met I was fifteen. You had been in the war, an officer in the war. You had to have been, what, twenty-eight, thirty? That was twenty-one years ago. Giving you the benefit, twenty-eight and twenty-one make you at least forty-nine. You're probably in your fifties. You don't look a day over twenty-five. Are you going to tell me why you still look like you did twenty-one years ago, or do I have to screw it out of you?"

The bad witch was back. He couldn't believe how quickly she pegged him. He had to either take her on—take on that indomitable will—or confess. He decided to confess—a little.

"I do have a problem. I have a condition. It's not very common, actually it's very rare, but it slows the aging processes. I can't tell you why, and I've never met anyone who could tell *me* why. Believe me I've tried to understand it, but I can't. I thought I might discover the answer in medical school, but they don't know, either.

"I have to move on, I mean, I have to change my identity every fifteen or twenty years. If I don't, people begin to notice it and start asking questions, questions I don't know how to answer. That's why I never told you."

"Can you give it to others? Are you contagious?"

"No."

"Are you sure?"

He knew how her mind worked. If he could slow down the aging process in others, it would be worth...he couldn't even begin to estimate what it might be worth. The sum would be astronomical.

"I'm very sure," he said. "It just kills other people." He wished he were lying about that.

Sylvia had already calculated what his "condition" would be worth on the market with great accuracy.

"Too, bad," she said.

She had also run his condition through her memory of hundreds of medical texts and had come up with nothing. He was telling the truth.

She sat regarding him. She liked it. He would be even better as her partner in another way. His need to change identities every fifteen to twenty years would give her opportunities to diversify her operations. And knowing his secret would give her even more leverage with him.

"I'll make you a deal," she said. "I won't say nor do anything to reveal your little secret if you'll allow me to use all of your *identities* for my investments. All you'll have to do is sign some papers from time to time. I'll make you the three or four richest men in the country."

"No deal." He had been thinking, too.

"What do you mean, no deal?" *Who did he think he was?*

Apparently he had forgotten the last time he tried to say, "No" to her.

"I want more," he said.

"How much?"

Now they were in her arena, and she was the champ.

"No, no," he said, "I know the old rule in bargaining that says the first person to name the price, loses."

"So, what is it you want?"

Oh, she was going to have such a good time taking him—him with his high moral ideals about "love" and "God."

"I'll tell you my price and there will be no negotiation. It's take it, or leave it. You said a little while ago that you thought I would remain loyal to you 'if things ever got out of hand.' You're right about that. But I think the same thing goes for you. You're a good witch, Sylvia. You can be whatever you want to be with everyone else, but with me, you're always going to be a good witch. You would remain loyal to me, too, even if 'things ever got out of hand.' So, here's my price: Half."

She frowned and started to speak, but he held up a hand and stopped her.

"I want half of all gross profits to be donated to good causes. You can reinvest the rest or do whatever you wish with it. That's it. That's my price."

"What causes?"

"I'll give you a list."

"What makes you think I'll accept your...*deal*?"

She said "deal" like it was something too dirty to touch.

"I know something about you that you may not know yourself, my good witch. You and I, the two of us, are alike in one important way: you don't care about the money any more than I do. It's the getting it that makes you wet."

She sat, thinking.

Finally, she said, "Deal."

This time she made "deal" sound as sweet as a little tinkling bell. The woman had talent.

They talked on for most of the afternoon, catching up on each other's lives. His life was very boring. Hers wasn't.

She had married twice. Mr. Youngblood and Mr. Fine were very wealthy men. Both had, unfortunately, died of natural causes within a year of their marriages to Sylvia.

"Natural causes?" he smiled.

"The most natural of causes," she smiled back. "I made them

very happy."

"And they helped to make you very rich." He couldn't help himself.

"I could have bought and sold them both," she said, "I married them so I wouldn't have to."

It was getting late in the afternoon.

"I've been thinking," she said. "I have to wait until Monday for a train to take me back…" She reached across the table and took one of his hands in hers, "…and I've just had this wonderful idea. Do you remember the old nursery rhyme that went: 'There was a little girl, who had a little curl, right in the middle of her forehead. And when she was good, she was very, very good, but when she was bad, she was horrid'?"

"No." He'd never heard it.

"Well, I'm a lot like that little girl. When I'm good, I'm very, very good, but when I'm bad, I'm marvelous! If there's anyone on this good earth who should know that, it's you."

He'd noticed when she first got off the train that there were several long pheasant feathers adorning her hat.

Coincidence?

He didn't think so.

She led him up the stairs to her suite. She was smiling. One of her fingers was thrust in the hole in his palm.

The next day, Sunday, he rented a horse and buggy and took Sylvia to a place he had found several years before. He went there often to get away from his problems as a healer and as a loner. It was a small public park a few miles from the city. Wooden picnic tables and benches had been placed under the protecting shade of a grove of huge live oak trees. He had prepared a picnic lunch for them and carried it in a wicker basket. A slow moving river curved around the park running on two sides with a grassy bank. The grass under the trees and near the river had been cut, scythed down the day before. The smell of the fresh-cut grass along with the cloudless, sunny sky made the day seem nearly perfect. Sylvia's presence in a soft yellow dress that billowed out in the light breeze completed the dream.

She made it a perfect day.

After lunch they sat on the river bank, talking. As they spoke, his eyes were drawn to a group of people who began arriving on the other side of the river. The river was only about fifty yards wide at this place, so he saw them clearly.

Many of the people were dressed in white cotton robes. He pointed them out to Sylvia, and they watched together as those dressed in robes began to wade into the river led by a tall, thin man. The man had removed his shoes and coat before wading in ahead of the rest. He wore only a collarless shirt and his pants held up by dark braces. The people wearing robes came to the center of the river where the water came up to their hips and stopped. The man motioned to the robed person nearest him, a girl of about fifteen or sixteen, to come to him. He spoke a few words to her. Neither he nor Sylvia could hear what the man said, but the girl crossed her arms in front of her body, placing her hands on her shoulders. The man stepped to her side and placed one hand behind her head and used the other to pinch her nose closed. He then tipped her over backward in the water until she was completely submerged. He brought her back up immediately.

"Baptism: He's baptizing them." He turned to Sylvia and asked, "Have you been baptized?"

"No." She was not impressed.

They continued to watch in silence as the others wearing robes were baptized one by one. While still sitting on the bank, he removed first his shoes and then his coat, collar, tie and shirt.

As the last of the newly baptized came up from the water and turned to the other shore, he rose and walked straight down the bank and into the water. He was being pushed along by a force he didn't understand. His legs were working, but they were not following directions from him. The baptizer heard him coming through the water behind him and turned around, mildly surprised.

"Will you baptize me?" he asked the man.

"Are you a Christian, brother?"

"Yes, I am."

"Do you accept Jesus Christ as Lord and Savior of your life?"

"I do."

The man looked into his face, seeming to seek reassurance.

"All right," he said, "cross your hands in front of your body."

As Sylvia watched from the riverbank, the baptizer held his head and nose just as he had the others and said something she couldn't hear. The baptizer then pulled his head back over and under the water. After he was pulled back up to his feet, the baptizer said something else to him.

Her lover was facing away from her so she couldn't see his face. There was a momentary pause, then she was astonished to see him raise both his hands out and above his head. He said something to the baptizer who fell back, almost falling under the water. The man caught himself, quickly turned and half swam, and half ran, churning the water until he reached the other shore. He snatched up his clothes and ran back away from the river with the rest of his "flock" close behind. They all soon disappeared into the woods on the far shore.

He turned and waded back to her.

"What in God's name just happened out there?" she asked.

"He wanted two dollars," he said.

He stood in front of her on the bank, his pants soaked; water dripping down from his hair and beard, pooling around his bare feet.

"He wanted two dollars for baptizing you?" She was incredulous. "I've never heard of such a thing."

"Neither have I. Maybe it's the going rate, but it made me angry. It took away part of something that should have been a sacred moment in my life. I felt I was drawn to him to be baptized."

"What did you do that made him jump back and run away?"

"I raised my hands so he could see the holes in my palms and said, 'Get thee behind me, Satan!' I wish I hadn't done it, now."

Sylvia looked up at the dripping man in front of her, water still running down his face. She smiled. She smiled her very brightest and most lovely smile, the one she reserved for special people.

As she smiled, she shook her head slightly and looking into his eyes said, "Jesus Christ, my ass!"

•

Richard L. Evans

He never saw her again after that weekend. Whenever she needed his signature on documents, they would arrive by special courier. Whenever he moved and changed his identity, he mailed her a letter marked "personal and private" with his new name and address on the return portion of the envelope. The envelope would contain a single piece of paper which would either be blank or have the names of some "good causes" on it. He tried to update his list from time to time. Nothing else would be written on the paper. He would get an envelope addressed to him by return mail. It would contain the same piece of paper he sent her. If there had been names on the paper, they would now have a check mark next to them. That was all. It was their code.

Sylvia kept her bargain. Sometimes she more than kept it. Year after year, decade after decade, "good causes" benefited from Sylvia's generosity. Even during the worst of the early days of the Great Depression in the 1930's, many soup kitchens were opened and kept open secretly by Morgan Investments. Mortgages were bought up and forgiven in the same way to preserve the homes and farms of many deserving families and institutions. Factories were kept running to pay workers even though they wouldn't turn a profit for many years. Scholarships for promising students were provided when no other funds could be found.

Sylvia could be such a good witch.

Chapter Eleven

HEALER

It was time for him to move on again.

His unchanging appearance would soon draw unwanted questions. The only thing he feared more than God was being found out by his fellow men. He was certain he would be imprisoned, or worse, committed to an asylum as insane. He might spend decades in such a place before anyone believed him. And, what would the world do with him then? No, he had to leave. More friends and colleagues would have to be left behind without a word, with no "good byes."

He severed all contact with everyone. Everyone, except Sylvia. Another hospital in another state would soon certify a new doctor—a new, young doctor with a new name and a new medical diploma—and a very old secret.

The one thing he hadn't counted on in his scheme using the extra medical diplomas he had filched at graduation was that he might come across another doctor who had been in the same class as his bogus identity.

"That's funny," Dr. Small said, "I don't seem to remember you at school."

"I was actually a year ahead of your class," he thought fast, "I had an accident just before graduation and had to finish in the fall of your senior year."

When he said the word, "accident," he pointed to the scar on his forehead. He thought it worked, but he caught Dr. Small looking at him questioningly several times after that, as if he were trying hard to remember him. Four months later he left the hospital in Cincinnati and Dr. Small's scrutiny.

A newspaper headline had caught his eye.

Barton Appeals For Help With New American National Red Cross.

Of course he remembered Clara Barton. She was his inspiration to become a doctor. The article under the headline quoted Miss Barton as saying she hoped many trained, medical personnel would volunteer for the newly renamed service. She mentioned her need of doctors in particular. He knew doctors and other medical personnel would have expenses that would have to be paid out of donations. Clara Barton got another doctor and Sylvia Morgan got another letter.

Wherever he was sent by the Red Cross, he went to church. He had been introduced to God by Titus when he was almost forty years old. It had been another 100 years after that before he finally accepted Jesus as his Lord and Savior with his baptism. In all that time, he had never been inside a church. He remembered Homer Davis talking about how most of what he got in church was just "turkey feathers." Unlike Homer, when he finally did start going to church, he discovered he had a real taste for "turkey"—feathers and all.

He didn't marry again. He could have. There were many unmarried women wherever he went—older women. Willowy had taught him the joy of loving an older woman, and he could have had his choice of one of the widows left from the war, or even one of the spinsters who never found husbands because the war had depleted the available supply. But he couldn't do it. He couldn't leave someone he loved, and he wouldn't take a woman in lust. One Sylvia in a lifetime was enough.

His evenings were usually spent alone. The pages of Titus' Bible flickered in the lamplight for long hours. Sometimes he just let it fall open hoping some divine force would lead him to the passage he so desperately wanted to find. He was given a lot of valuable direction—but his questions remained unanswered.

"What am I?" And, "What am I to God?"

The answers were not in the Bible. They were not in the quiet snowfalls of the forest, the grassy plains, the high mountains, the deserts or the open seas. The answers did not come to him in the roar of battle or in the silence of the dead. But the answers were always with him; they went with him wherever he went.

He could not hear the voice within him because he was not listening with his heart. The "voice" first spoke to him on the slave ship. He knew it was there but could not understand it, and that failure led him into madness and near death. But the voice, the spirit, was still in him. His salvation depended on understanding the voice. To hear it, to know the spirit, he needed others listening with him. The voice spoke to all hearts. The spirit lifted all hearts. And the voice of the spirit spoke loudest in church. He couldn't understand it, but still, the spirit led him, guiding his hands and his mind as he treated the ill and comforted the dying. He recognized it and welcomed it.

•

In 1917 he went to Europe with the American Expeditionary Forces to help win the "war to end all wars." He was commissioned a surgeon and sent to France, very close to Belgium.

The wounds and other injuries he saw were horrible. It was unusual to have a patient with only a single bullet wound. Multiple wounds from both bullets and shell fragments were much more common. He could do little for those attacked by chemical smoke—mustard gas inflicted burns to eyes, skin and lungs. Men, even good men, could not endure life when their feet and legs were submerged for weeks on end in stagnant water at the bottom of muddy trenches. Raising one's head even a few inches above the top of a trench was an invitation to a sudden and very messy death. Some men were simply driven mad by the dirt, insects, poison gas, and the stench of death all around them.

Then came influenza. During the height of the epidemic in 1918 and 1919, he saw more people die of influenza than from combat. He did what he could to save them, but many still died—choked to death by their own fluid-filled lungs.

There were few ways to escape the despair he found in this place. One of them was Yvonne.

Mme. Yvonne Jardinier was the widow of a French artillery officer killed four years earlier defending his country in the first battle of the Marne. There were many, newly widowed women in France, most of them quite young.

Yvonne was different. She owned and managed an inn close to the Army hospital. Because she appeared to be somewhere in her fifties, she was thought much too old by the other medical officers who gathered in the tavern on the first floor of Mme. Jardinier's establishment each evening. The other officers went after the young women.

He, of course, knew better. Her age made her just the kind of woman he was looking for.

He came to the tavern every evening his duty at the hospital would allow. He always came late—on purpose. By his design, Mme. Jardinier and he would be engaged in conversation well past the time when all her other patrons left.

One evening he just stayed. Yvonne was an excellent cook and breakfast was very tasty—almost as tasty as the night before.

Her gentleness, her quiet sense of humor, and her realistic understanding of their temporary relationship was just icing on an already lovely cake.

Yvonne spoke English exceptionally well. She told him she had spent almost five years of her early childhood with an uncle living in England.

A very "French nose" set off her wonderfully expressive face. He liked it. He rubbed his own nose, cheek, ears and chin on it until she collapsed in laughter, protesting his silliness (but enjoying it even more than he).

Their love-making was not athletic. They were like a very old couple; enjoying the scenery along a very long, slow ride over low hills and deep valleys. The hills and valleys were his favorite parts of the trip.

•

He was sent to a field hospital in Belgium to inspect its condition and make recommendations to the Army Medical Corps. While he was there, a stir of excitement ran through the medical personnel when an airman was brought in for treatment. It was the first time anyone there had seen one of "those daredevils" who bet their lives on nothing more than the force of air moving over a wing. As a visiting dignitary, he was invited to assist in the man's treatment.

Corporal Robert Robinson had been flying as a gunner on a bombing flight over Thielt in Belgium when his plane was jumped by a dozen German fighters. Robinson's most serious injury was an elbow shattered by machine gun fire. He had been hit twice more, but those wounds were less serious. He had lost a lot of blood, but his chances of recovery seemed good. As the chief medical officer, he took over Corporal Robinson's care.

The next day, as he was walking by the recovery tent, he noticed two men standing next to Robinson's bed. They were both wearing uniforms he had not seen before, so he stepped in the tent. He was curious but not concerned. As he approached them, they turned to him and came to attention.

He told them to be, "As you were."

He introduced himself as one of Corporal Robinson's doctors. They were Second Lieutenant Talbot and Captain Cunningham, United States Marine Corps.

"Marine Corps?" he almost shouted it he was so surprised.

He knew the Marine Corps had units in France, but these men were airmen, aviators. He tried to explain his outburst.

"I didn't know the Marines had an air division."

The two Marine officers looked at each other quickly, then Captain Cunningham explained it was a fairly new concept and one they were still fighting to establish on a permanent basis. They spoke for almost another half-hour, at the end of which, he had an invitation to "take a little run" with the Captain.

Early the next morning he followed Captain Alfred A. Cunningham as he walked around his single engine plane parked on a grassy, mist-covered field. The Captain moved slowly around his plane running his hand over the heavy canvas that covered its sturdy wood frame, examining everything. He had seen men on the frontier judge the capability of their horses in the same way. He asked the Captain about the plywood sheeting on the front of the plane's fuselage.

"Sir, this is a model DH-4A" explained Cunningham. "The plywood gives the pilot some added protection. The two wings over and under the body give us more lift than a single wing, and the Liberty engine gives us 400 horsepower to get us there and keep us there."

"And to get us back," he said a little prayer to himself.

He climbed into the second place seat behind his pilot. The wings were placed ahead of the pilot and behind the engine and propeller. He had no idea what 400 horsepower meant until the engine was turned over. Seconds later he knew 400 horsepower was a lot of power; seconds after that he was airborne; seconds after that, he knew what drew young men like Captain Cunningham to the skies.

"Sir, look for signs of movement on the ground," Captain Cunningham shouted back to him. "And mount those two machine guns on the ring mount around your seat. You should find them at your feet."

He did as he was told, then loaded and cocked them. He was through with killing, but he wouldn't allow an adversary bent on killing him to find that easy. Captain Cunningham turned back to him at the sound of the bolt chambering the first round in one of the guns. The Captain smiled—one warrior to another. The DH-4A was armed with two more machine guns aimed forward, controlled by the pilot.

"Oh, and, sir," the Captain was shouting over his shoulder again, "try not to shoot off our wings or hit us in the tail."

As an army doctor, he had already met many men who seemed quite capable of shooting off their own tails.

The flight lasted about twenty minutes. They went unchallenged.

Back at the field hospital they spoke again, this time over bad coffee and good doughnuts.

The captain was a handsome man, tall, straight, in excellent physical condition; immaculate in dress and speech—he was very definitely not a "daredevil" but a cool, professional soldier.

He explained, "I had quit Marine flight duty in 1913 because my wife...well, my soon-to-be wife...thought I would kill myself flying around in what she called 'those flimsy looking things.' But I had myself reassigned in another year after convincing her it was what I wanted to do and was the only thing that would make me happy. She's a wonderful woman, and she loves me very much."

The captain smiled as he said it, a little embarrassed.

While telling the story of his career in the Marine Corps, Cunningham mentioned he took his first flight training and made his first solo flight at the Curtiss airplane factory in Marblehead, Massachusetts.

"Marblehead? Did you happen to run into anyone there by the name of Grim? Or have you ever met anyone in the service by that name?"

"No, sir," replied Captain Cunningham.

I can't believe the Grim family would let a big war like this go by without their participation.

"So, what do you think," asked Cunningham, "about the plane and the run? I'm always looking for another good man. We need more men like you in the Marine Aviation Force."

That was one of the things he liked about the captain; he didn't pussyfoot around.

"No," he said, "The best service I can give my country is doing what I'm trained to do, as a doctor. Thanks for the invitation. I'm flattered."

"I'm sorry you feel that way." The Captain did seem genuinely disappointed.

Then he changed the subject. "How is Corporal Robinson doing—how is he *really* doing? Is he going to make it?"

"Yes, but I don't think he'll be able to handle a flying job again."

"That's all right," Cunningham was obviously thinking as he spoke. "I'm going to put both Second Lieutenant Talbot and Corporal Robinson in for decorations. Corporal Robinson shot down one of those German planes before he was hit in the elbow.

He kept on firing with his other arm until he was shot twice more. Second Lieutenant Talbot kept maneuvering the plane until he shot down another German plane before he dove for home."

"I'd say your Corporal Robinson should receive General Washington's merit award, at least."

"General Washington's merit award, what's that, sir?"

"The award for meritorious service. General Washington thought every enlisted soldier who fought well should receive an award. Officers got all the awards, back then. Haven't you ever seen one? It's shaped like a heart with the word 'Merit' set vertically in a field of bluish red. It's about this big."

He touched the end of his index finger to the tip of his thumb to show the size of the patch.

"It's meant to be sewn on a soldier's uniform."

Cunningham was studying him closely.

"A doctor who knows how to chamber a round in a machine gun and who knows about obscure military decorations—you seem to know a lot about non-medical military affairs, sir."

"I've been around," he said as he stood to go.

Captain Cunningham was getting a little too close to his secrets for comfort.

"Well, sir," said Cunningham, also rising to go, "since I can't convince you to join us, can I ask your help in establishing an aviation department in the Marine Corps separate from the Navy's? If you know anyone with influence, it might help a lot."

They shook hands, and he watched as Captain Cunningham strode off to the recovery tent to visit his downed Corporal again. He had no influence with the U.S. government. But he knew someone who did. He wrote another letter to Sylvia Morgan.

•

After the armistice ending the war, he stayed in France for a few more months. He had patients who still needed his medical supervision. Before he left Europe, he learned that Corporal Robert G. Robinson and Second Lieutenant Ralph Talbot had both been awarded the Medal of Honor—the first Marine aviators to be so honored.

He also stayed in France for Yvonne. They both knew he would leave soon. He had to leave and she had to stay. On their last night they lay close together, holding each other and weeping softly.

•

Back in the United States and out of the Army, he again went back to school, this time to document himself as a professional nurse with another set of false identity papers.

Early in 1938 he saw a photo on the front page of a large metropolitan newspaper. It was one of those photographs newspapers were always happy to print—a picture of a beautiful woman. It was an early photo of Sylvia. The accompanying story reported the death of "one of America's most loved and admired philanthropists."

A long biography was continued on an inside page. Turning to that page, he found another photo of her. It was a much more recent picture. In it she was seated at a large desk with two young men, one standing on each side. The caption under the photograph read: *Sylvia Morgan flanked by two of her administrative assistants.*

He calculated her age. She had to be somewhere in her eighties when the picture was taken. It wouldn't have been obvious to a casual reader, but he was sure she had positioned herself at her desk so that the two young men were able to look down the front of her dress.

"To borrow a phrase, my dear..." he said aloud, "...administrative assistants, my ass!"

Richard L. Evans

CHAPTER TWELVE

JOEL

After forty-some years he still knew him: the same black eyes brimming over with intelligence; the same thrust chin; the same little beard; the same long, narrow, hooked nose that got him called "heeb" wherever the Navy sent him. Most of his hair was gone. What was left was very white like his beard. His hair and beard framed a little, white halo around his dark face.
What Jesus would have looked like at seventy-five.
The caption below the newspaper photo read: *Dr. Joel Berger, Ph.D. retired professor emeritus of Psychology at the University of Chicago, now in private practice three days a week at the Mercer Clinic.*
He studied the picture for only a few moments before making a decision. He needed to talk to someone, and his former very good friend, "Joel, the heeb doctor" was going to be it.
He first met Joel under what one would have to call very stressful circumstances—in early 1942. They were both undergoing Marine Corps indoctrination at Camp Lejeune in North Carolina. Basic Marine infantry training was everything they had

been told it would be—and a hell of a lot more (emphasis on the word, "hell").

Joel hated it. He loved it. He even adopted the Marines' standard hair style, high and tight. His head was basically shaved in the back and on both sides with just a short fuzz on top. Joel kept his as long as he could get away with.

They both had completed the training required to be Navy corpsmen—the medical personnel who trained with and then served alongside the "dogface Marines." Enlistment as a corpsman fit his objective of continued service to his country without having to purposefully kill anyone. Although, he had to admit, there were several instances during his Marine Corps training when he would have joyfully killed a couple of his drill instructors. That was before he realized how directed and purposeful their seemingly random cruelty was. Eventually, he became a believer and an admirer of the brotherhood of the Marines—those "Band of Brothers," as they called themselves. He couldn't ever be one, of course—he was Navy.

Both he and Joel were assigned to the 1st Marine Division and shipped out to the Pacific to join the fleet. Guadalcanal, New Britain, Peleliu and Okinawa followed. Later, in Korea, it would be Inchon and the Chosin Reservoir.

The last time he had seen Joel was in 1950 in Korea in the winter in another nightmarish place called Hagaru. Each of them was sure the other had died there. God knows, they all should have died there.

"Corpsman! Oh, God, corpsman!"

How many times had he heard it? How many more times could he stand to hear it? It didn't matter; he had to go—it was his duty—it was what he did.

He heard it first at Guadalcanal: a hot, soggy, rat infested island paradise east of New Guinea on the Coral Sea. Such a nice name, the Coral Sea. Only when he was there, the coral of the sea surrounded the red of the earth—stained by the blood of the dead and dying. It cost them—*his* Marines—but the Japanese were all killed or driven off.

His previous experience at war had prepared him for the Marine invasion of Guadalcanal in only one way: he didn't make friends. Friends got killed. Other people got killed, too, but it was easier to take if they weren't friends.

In 1945 he put away his rotting medical pouches and went back to diagnosing colds and measles at Tripler Naval Hospital in Hawaii. He thought he was through trying to keep severed arteries from spurting blood with one hand while using the other to search for some unbroken flesh to pop with a morphine needle. But in 1950 he had to pull them out again. This time his pouches didn't rot away in the tropical heat and mist. This time they froze.

Yudam-ni was nearly surrounded on three sides by an unknown number of Chinese forces. He was with the 5th Regiment, 1st Marine Division. The days were theirs as they watched units of the Marine Air Wing hit the Chinese positions around them. There wasn't a day he saw those deadly Corsairs swoop in that he didn't give a big "thank you" to Captain Alfred Cunningham for his Marine aviators. The nights, however, belonged to whoever could take them.

That first night at Yudam-ni he heard it again.

"Corpsman! Oh, God, corpsman."

Hand to hand combat in the dark was eerie. So was trying to find his wounded.

Corpsman Joel Berger had served in his same outfits all through the Pacific War. He still held a messy recollection of a time when he refused to leave a wounded man in a burning landing craft at one of their "stops." Joel pushed him off into the sea. He pulled his patient with him and thanked Joel for taking an interest in his welfare.

He had seen his old, long-haired friend move out earlier with part of the 7th Regiment. By now, they should be on the other side, to the east, of a massive icebound lake called the Chosin Reservoir. That was the only side where the Chinese hadn't, as yet, cut them off.

He hoped Joel's boys were doing better than his. With each dawn he would move the wounded from the night fighting out to the airstrip along the other side of the reservoir. C-47s would pick them up and fly them out. The planes would bring in supplies and sometimes, reinforcements. He didn't make friends with the new guys, either.

There were two enemies here: the Chinese and the cold. Of the two, the cold was by far the worst. It was almost December, and the thermometers set out around the perimeter of their defensive lines never read above minus five or minus ten degrees. Everything, all decisions, had to take into account the cold. In subzero temperatures unprotected plasma bags froze.

As he moved among the men fighting on the line at night, he carried morphine syrettes in his mouth, so they would be warm enough to inject. Back at the sick-bay, the head lamps of jeeps were run on cables from the ever-running vehicles to provide sufficient light for field medical work. Most of the time it was an effort not just to move but to think. Frostbite and disorientation from the cold were what bothered him the most. A rifle round or a mortar shell *might* kill him. Exposure to the cold *would* kill him. It was his job to see it didn't kill his Marines, too.

On December 1st they were ordered to move out. The 1st Marine Division was going to make an advance to the rear. Since they were now completely surrounded by the Chinese, the order made perfect sense. They made Hagaru five days later where they met up with the 7th Regiment coming down from the north. They were all going to "get the hell out of Dodge City." He was afraid it would be the last time he ever saw Joel.

The column stretched for almost eleven miles with a thousand trucks and other vehicles. North Korea, as far as anyone in his outfit knew, was nothing but ice and snow-covered mountains. That's all they saw for miles in every direction. The Chinese hit their column repeatedly, and his services were needed nightly and through almost every day.

The scream, "Corpsman!" banged around in his head for months afterward. Some men just stopped moving; they fell in the snow and refused to move. He kicked them, punched them and swore at them. Some he could move; the others just sat and died in the snow. Those he couldn't save were loaded on trucks with the corpses of other dead Marines. The order had come down:

"No Marine was to be left behind, dead or alive."

Fortunately for those still alive, the bodies of the dead were quickly frozen.

He carried his two water canteens under his clothing close to his body. Most of the men also carried their C-rations in their armpits for the same reason, so they would be warm enough to be swallowed. Everyone agreed that C-rations were compatible with armpits.

He came through a particularly nasty part of the roadway called Funchilin Pass. Beyond it near a wrecked power plant, he crossed a very new and very narrow bridge spanning a deep chasm. While he waited for the rest of his unit to cross, he heard two officers nearby talking about it. One of them was a major.

He was saying, "The Chinese destroyed the old bridge to stop our escape. I sure wouldn't want to be caught here with my back to that ravine and no way out. We used prefabricated units dropped from the air and assembled them on the spot. This new bridge section we put together is twenty-two feet long. The ravine is twenty-nine feet across."

There was a pause.

The other officer said, "So, how did you make up the difference, the extra seven feet?"

The major replied, "Oh, just a little miracle."

Then he laughed as he walked away. The name patch on the major's pocket read, Moses.

Five long days and five even longer nights later, he dragged himself into Hamhung. The Chinese attacks had dwindled to almost nothing. He thought they must have succumbed to the unrelenting cold, too. The surviving members of his company were loaded on a Navy transport and taken first to Pusan and then to Japan. The last time he saw Joel had been near Hagaru. A lot of men had died in the snow since then.

He used his G.I. Bill to pay for another round at medical school. Medicine and medical practices were changing so fast, his old training couldn't keep up with them and sometimes even got in his way.

•

When he called for an appointment, he gave the Mercer Clinic his current name and address. Eighteen years had passed since he joined his latest hospital staff, and he was beginning to get those telltale, curious, sidelong looks that meant his unchanging appearance was being noted, perhaps even discussed behind his back. It was time to go. He had already given notice to the hospital administration along with a bogus forwarding address. He would be missed but not followed. Once he left, his whereabouts would be virtually untraceable. He always saw to that.

The receptionist put the five one-hundred dollar bills he gave her in a locked desk drawer and ushered him into Joel's office. It was sparse in furnishings but rich in color. The whole room was a monochromatic tour de force in green. Everything in the room was green: green lampshades, green plants, deep and dark green carpet, multi-hued green draperies and upholstery. Even the ceiling was painted a light tint of green. Joel rose and came around a large mahogany desk to greet him. The desk was the only furnishing in the room that wasn't green.

He observed Joel's initial reaction.

If he recognized his old Navy buddy, Dr. Joel Berger didn't let it get past his professional smile and greeting. He thought he saw just a little narrowing of the eyes, but that was all.

Joel offered him a large stuffed chair and then sat in a similar one a few feet away and almost directly across from it. Joel's pale gray suit was set off by a very narrow, dark green tie. He put on a pair of reading glasses and held out a chart so they both could see it. On it was the information he had given the secretary over the phone the day before.

"Well, Doctor," Joel began, acknowledging his professional status, "you might be surprised by the number of medical doctors I've had as patients over the years."

Joel's eyes studied his face steadily, unblinking, with just a hint of a smile at the corner of his lips.

"No, I don't think I'd be surprised at all. It isn't easy playing God."

He grinned when he said it and thought to himself, *You'd better smile when you say that, partner.*

"I see. Is that what has brought you to me, today?"

"Just the opposite. Not understanding God's purpose in my life has brought me to you today." He thought he might as well get to it right away.

"More specifically," he continued, "why God has denied me a

normal life and death."

"Death?"

"My death has been greatly delayed."

"Are you terminally ill?"

"No, you see, I seem to be terminally alive and well."

Joel said nothing and seemed to be waiting for more, so he continued.

"Joel, I'm the same man you knew in the Navy, and at Marine Corps infantry training, and at Guadalcanal, and at Chosin."

"Uh, huh," Joel looked over his spectacles at him.

"Forgive me, but I don't see how that could be possible."

Joel's eyes were moving over his face with interest.

Joel asked, "The name you've given us on this chart is not your real name, then?" Joel didn't wait for his answer. "Not surprising," he said quickly, "and not," Joel looked him in the eye, "very unusual. Is the name of the man you say I should remember your real name?"

"No."

"No?"

"No, that name was not my real name, either. I have no real name." He gave Joel the name he thought he would remember him by.

Joel nodded and said, "Yes, I knew a man by that name back in my Navy days. Are you related to him?"

Joel still gave no indication that he remembered him by any name.

"No," he replied.

He thought for a few seconds, then continued, "There *is* one name I was given a long time ago. It's probably the closest thing I have to a real name. It's, 'Pele'thi.' It's a Shawnee name."

Joel asked him to spell it for him and wrote it on his chart.

Then he asked, "Are you of Shawnee ancestry?"

"No."

"You said you are 'terminally alive and well.' Is that correct?"

"Yes, that is one of my problems."

"How long have you felt this way?"

"I was born in 1737."

"You believe that you have been alive since...1737?" Joel put a slight emphasis on the word, "seventeen." There was also a slight pause before he said it.

Over the years Joel Berger had heard just about everything. The main reason he had become a psychologist after leaving the Navy was the almost infinite variety of mental illnesses and the unique challenges they offered an agile mind. How many bones could one set; how many pills could one dispense or how many wounds could one suture before the whole repetitious process mummified the brain. One might as well become a bricklayer as become the successful surgeon his father had hoped he would be; one brick or one swollen appendix after another—what was the difference? And here was something new, a new twist of the mind he could help untangle. This fellow with the vaguely familiar face believed he had lived for over...what?...two hundred and sixty-some years.

"How do you know you were born in 1737?"

"I left home and went to sea when I was ten. I had to sign an 'X' for my name to get on a ship. 1747 was the date on the paper. My mother died, and I had to go away. I had to go somewhere else because she didn't own the farm."

"Where was your farm?"

"In the Massachusetts Colony. That was before it became a state. I first sailed out of New Bedford."

There was a pause before Joel continued.

"Why don't you tell me about your life since then?"

He told him about the slave ship, the *Anne*. He told him about the horrors he found on that voyage and his increasing insanity. He told him about the Laudanum and his addiction to opium, and he told him about the start of his nightmares. With the mention of the nightmares, he knew it was time to talk about his other problem, his "gift."

"I have another problem," he began.

He explained about what he could do to cure seemingly incurable diseases with just the touch of his hand and a few words. He told Joel how he had discovered this gift with his boyhood friend, Thomas. Then he described his nightmares: the nightmares where he saw hundreds of eyes around the deceased faces of those he had cured—and who had died terrible deaths soon after he helped them.

"It's almost as if God says, 'No!' every time I use my gift of healing. If God doesn't want me to use it, why was it given to me? And why must I continue to live—its long past my time? I should have died long ago."

Joel looked up from the pad he was using and said, "I'd like to take up the subject of your death in a little while, but let's talk a little more about your life. You say you've been alive since 1737. Can you tell me what has changed in your life since then?"

"That's easy," he said, "The biggest change has been food."

"Food?"

"Sure, food. Look, when you were growing up, did you ever have to worry about your next meal?" The question, of course, was only rhetorical. "No, your family provided that. Then you joined the Navy, and the Navy or the Marines provided your meals. I'd guess you've never been really hungry with no food around in your whole life. You've never come close to starving.

"Okay," he continued, "but that's the past; now let's talk about today. Where are you going to get the food you'll eat this evening?"

Joel waited before he realized he was expected to answer this question.

"That's not something I have to think about. My wife prepares my food."

"That's right; you don't have to think about it. And in your whole life you've never really had to think about it— your food; where it came from; how it was stored or prepared; how it got to you or how you were going to preserve it until you wanted to eat it. These days, we don't have to think very much about where our next meal will come from, other than what to buy at the market or what restaurant to patronize. Or in your case, what your wife is preparing at home. Can you appreciate what a luxury that is? For example, what are you going to eat next Tuesday, a week from today?" He looked at Joel expectantly.

"I don't know." Joel was in the game now.

"In all of my life up until the past, oh, hundred years or so, most of my waking hours had to be devoted to thinking about food. From the first years of my life, everyone I knew—everyone

I've known—had to think about food in the long term. We had to think about what food we could get tomorrow, next week, next month, in the next six months or even next year. Sowing and harvesting times were critical to survival.

"We had to think how to preserve our food, too. You know, in all the long history of the world, more wars have been fought and people killed over getting salt than over getting oil. Salt preserved our food. I got my food by barter, by gathering wild plants or by hunting and fishing. All of those things had their seasons, too. Today we only have to think about one meal at a time—our next one.

"And the variety! The choices! I sometimes wonder what Titus would say if he could walk into a modern supermarket and see the food arrayed there. You can put it in other terms, if you wish—world wide trade, the speed of transportation, scientific advances in almost everything—but it all comes down, for me anyway, to food."

His patient's answer to his question hadn't helped him. Joel decided to take on the important questions more directly.

"All right, tell me about your death. The death you believe God has denied you."

"I'm old and tired and I want death. I want to go into the Kingdom of Heaven. I want to die to this world, but the Angel of Death won't come to me.

'Come lovely and soothing death, Undulate round the world, serenely arriving, arriving, In the day, in the night, to all, to each Sooner or later delicate death.' I want my lovely, soothing, delicate death."

He took a deep breath and continued, "People fear death. People think death is something to be avoided, to be put off as long as possible. I've had people beg me to have their aged parents or spouses kept alive with machines even when they knew— they *knew*—their loved ones were suffering and would have no quality of life. They didn't want to have to deal with death. They didn't want to have to think about death. Death was their enemy—and they couldn't have been more mistaken."

Joel still said nothing.

"It hasn't always been like that. A hundred years ago people still tried to avoid death as long as they could, but they planned for it. They wanted to have what they called 'a good death.' People usually died at home, surrounded by their families and friends. That doesn't happen very much any more. Not in this country. Today, most people die in hospitals or nursing homes surrounded, at the end, by total strangers.

"The average American living today has probably never seen another person die—except as portrayed in the movies or on television. Years ago that probability was the reverse. We saw life end—and I don't mean just a painted face lying in an open coffin—but the final closing of the eyes with a sigh or a death rattle. Death was a common occurrence in almost everyone's life, so it wasn't so much to be feared as to be expected.

"The Indians I lived with had less fear of death than they had of not facing death bravely. Death is a natural part of life. Without death, life has no meaning."

That was it. That was his whole problem in just six words. His long, eventful life had "no meaning."

Joel waited to see if there was more, but he was through.

Finally, Joel said, "You seem to have a strong sense of the value of death. But your problem, as you describe it, isn't death, it's life. Tell me more about your life. You mentioned someone named Titus; tell me about him."

"My life," he paused, thinking about it, "my life is not so much *a* life but *many* lives. My first life was as a boy on the farm. Then I went to sea for over twenty-five years. Then I went into hell on that slave ship. Then I was reborn, redeemed by a man named, Titus. Titus was a negro slave. He became my teacher, my priest, my father—you might say he was even my savior."

He told Joel about Miss Lucille's and about Margery and how Margery taught him more than just how to make love—she taught him *to* love—to receive love as well as to give it. He told how he healed Margery when she got sick and how she died, murdered, soon afterwards. He told him how he himself then became a murderer—how he killed the man who had killed Titus and had to run for his life from the British Navy and join the Revolution.

"By the age of forty I was a slaver, a rapist, a drug addict, an abortionist and a murderer. My only salvation came much later when, as Titus told me I must, I learned to forgive myself."

He continued the story of his lives. He told Joel of his service in the Revolutionary War, about Peshewa and his children, murdered by other Indians. He told him how he had taken revenge on those Indians—how he had seen to it that an entire village: men, women and children all paid dearly for the murder of the only family he would ever have. He had to stop for a while, thinking about his girls.

Joel waited.

"I have murdered many people, some in war, some in anger."

He looked directly at Joel to emphasize his next words.

"I have repented of all those sins—all except the murders of those who killed my family. If I must go to hell for those murders, I will do it gladly."

Joel took a moment to write on his patient's chart, then said, "You mentioned that you are an abortionist. Tell me about that."

"I don't think of myself as an abortionist—not any more. I learned to perform abortions on the prostitutes at Miss Lucille's. In those days, before easy contraception, it was a necessary part of the business. I did it because Titus hated it so. In those days I didn't think it a bad thing or a good thing. It was just something that had to be done.

"Since I've been a doctor, that is, since 1870, I've only performed two abortions, one legal and one illegal. I had to disguise one of them as a 'D & C,' or I could have been prosecuted. In my professional opinion they were both medically justifiable and necessary. Now, I avoid doing abortions if at all possible. Most of my colleagues won't do them under any circumstances. Their reasons are all over the place. Some won't do it on religious grounds; some won't because they're afraid of lawsuits if anything goes wrong; some just think they don't get paid enough for them; and some worry that their medical malpractice insurance will go through the roof if they do them on a regular basis. I get requests for the procedure but turn them down.

"But those people who insist on attacking doctors who do perform legal abortions and who are trying to change the law to make abortions illegal are either too young to remember or have forgotten the bad old days when abortions were illegal in this country. I mean the days when women who weren't rich enough to get on a plane and fly to some foreign country where abortions were legal—and therefore relatively safe—had to take their chances outside the law. Poor women had to seek out abortionists who worked in secret to avoid prosecution—abortionists who might or might not know what they were doing and who worked in largely unsterile conditions. Sometimes women were forced to risk death or disfigurement trying to abort their own fetuses. They were condemned for nothing more than the simple 'crime' of having an unwanted pregnancy."

"All right," Joel said. His tone was noncommittal. "You also said you were a rapist. Tell me about that."

He didn't want to remember the Igbo woman aboard the *Anne*. He told it quickly but held nothing back. There was nothing to be gained by holding anything back.

"That was all part of the hell I found serving on the slave ship. I don't know if it was my insanity that drove me to hurt that woman or if raping her helped push me to insanity. It's all mixed up. The opium, coupled with the alcohol I got when we were in port, made me forget so much of it."

"The opium?" Joel was making another note on his chart. "Yes, I remember you said you were an addict. Is opium the only drug you've used?"

"Yes. The captain of my ship gave me laudanum. I believe he thought he was helping me. That's the only time I've ever used a narcotic or hallucinogenic agent."

"It isn't so unusual for medical practitioners to use drugs to help them." Joel was fishing for more. "Some doctors find the pressures on them to be unbearable."

"No. I would never want to go through that agony of withdrawal again."

He thought it important that Joel understand his intent in coming to him.

"Joel, I'm telling you the complete truth about me—about who I am, about my life, about my hang-ups, about my unusual gifts of long life, about the healing and about the animals."

He noticed Joel's head come up slightly, involuntarily, at the mention of the word "animals".

He continued, "I need help finding the answers to very important questions: why am I still alive, and why do I have this gift for healing, and what has God to do with me? I know the only way you can help me is for me to be perfectly truthful with you. So, in answer to your last, unspoken question, no, I am not now taking drugs of any kind. Except for the nausea brought on when Titus helped me get rid of my addiction to opium, I've never been physically ill in my life. I've never even taken an aspirin."

He knew he needed to get the focus of the interview back on his earlier friendship with Joel—to get Joel to believe he was who he said he was.

"Do you remember back in Navy boot camp when they gave us inoculation shots? Your arms swelled up and hurt for days. You even remarked that I was lucky because mine didn't. It didn't happen to me because my immune system ate up those agents like they were fried chicken on Sunday after church."

It was a strange simile to use with a Jew, but he was sure Joel understood it.

"You say you don't ever get sick because you have this overactive immune system. And you can cure other people by just touching them. Is that right?"

"Yes."

"And you don't want to cure other people because the ones you've already cured all died soon afterward. Is that right?"

"Yes."

"Is it possible that the deaths of the people you tried to help were just unfortunate coincidences? What would happen if you started using your gift to cure your patients? You could cure everyone in the hospital."

"Of course, I've thought about that. But the consequences would be cataclysmic."

Joel took off his glasses, sat back and just looked at him—waiting.

"Okay, suppose I go around healing people, everyone I can. If I'm right about my healing causing them to die soon afterwards in terrible ways, we have lots of awful accidents, or a wave of murders or suicides, maybe even more terrorist attacks. So, what have I accomplished? 'Kill me now, or kill me later.' Further, if those deaths are then blamed on me, what will the world do about me? Kill me? Lock me away where I can't touch and therefore kill any more? No, no, Joel, I can't take that chance.

"And what if they don't die after I've cured them? That would be even worse. Now the world would have a group of people who never get sick: people who aren't ever going to die of cancer, heart disease, AIDS, or any disease at all; people who will never have infections or other complications of surgery; people who will never suffer much from bee stings or snake bite or food poisoning; people, who, God forbid, could pass on their immunity to others. Once word got around that I could give you that kind of lifelong immunity, wouldn't you find a way to get to me? Can you possibly imagine the terrible consequences of that? Not just for me, but for you?"

"I'm not sure I know what you mean by 'terrible consequences?'" Joel replied.

"Okay, suppose I used my gift with you, healed you. If you were careful, if you avoided serious accidents or getting mugged, or some other life-threatening thing, you might live a very long time. And if you also got from me what I've got—an end to your aging processes—you could live forever.

"So, what's so bad about that? There are lots of things that are bad about that. Your whole existence would be turned on its head. You would have to watch all your friends, your wife, your children, your children's children die. Who would you reminisce with about the 'good old days?' Your friends from the good old days would all be dead. As for lifelong relationships, you'd have them for the length of other peoples' lives, maybe, but not yours. You'd be a freak, a sideshow attraction. To avoid all that, you'd have to deal with it like I do: you'd have to hide.

"What would you do for excitement? How could you relieve the sameness, the monotony of living almost without fear day after day, year after year? Unless you had an overriding purpose for your life, you'd almost have to seek danger. You might risk it all just to keep what you have from driving you nuts with boredom. You'd run with the bulls in Spain and dive with the sharks in the Bahamas. And you would seek out war. I know about that. In time, even those things would fail to give you a high. Eventually, the law of averages would catch up with you. Maybe you'd be lucky and kill yourself outright. But maybe you wouldn't be so lucky and just break your neck or your back. Your immune system couldn't repair a severed spine, so you might spend the rest of your eternity in a wheelchair hooked up to a respirator praying for a power failure or a compassionate doctor to end your misery.

"Now, that would be the deal if it were just you. But suppose I healed lots of others, too. Now there'd be a whole society of never-ending lifers. That sounds like a prison term doesn't it, 'lifers?' Well, that's pretty much what it would be. Your entire society would have to be reordered, locked away from normal people, everything turned upside down just as before. What would your new society do about children? Could you allow yourselves to have children who would also live on forever? Not if you think the earth's resources are finite; not unless you'd like to think about starving for eternity. But without children you'd have no particular reason to form families. Each lifer would be on his or her own, forever. Terrible consequences? I'll say.

"Do you see what I mean? If people could no longer sicken, could no longer die from medical problems, they would live much longer. Perhaps we would discover there is no limit to how many years a person could live.

"Joel, you're a very smart man—what happens to our society—to the world's society—when there is no longer any natural cause of death?"

Joel had been thinking and didn't hesitate to answer.

"You said the word: cataclysm."

"Have you noticed how close the major research centers of the world are coming to that condition even now? Some insurance actuaries are saying that anyone born in the United States in the second half of the twentieth century has a fifty-fifty chance of living to be a hundred. Today there are maybe 50,000 people a hundred years old or older in this country. In another twenty years, if those predictions are correct, there could be more than five *million* people over a hundred years old. Can you imagine what will happen when all those people start drawing social security for forty years or more?

"That's not just idle speculation. We already have artificial organs, bioengineering, gene splicing to alter DNA, micro engineering, stem cell research. Those are just some of the things we can see now. With the human genome mapped, the possibility of creating an immune system like mine is already here. Will these medical advances be good things, or are they curses disguised as blessings?

"The real kicker, of course, is who gets it? And, even better, who gets to decide who gets it? Talk about your haves and have-nots!

"Now, you can understand my reluctance—no, the absolute necessity—to keep my gift of healing and my long life a secret. The harm that might result if it were known is incalculable."

Joel looked at him for some moments before speaking. "But you're telling me."

"Yes. I've tried to understand what has happened to me and what it means. I thought another opinion, another more objective view of my situation, might help me. I feel I can tell you my story, relying on the concept of doctor-patient privileged communication to protect me. I know you're an honorable man and would never willingly divulge what I've just told you."

"Yes, you're correct on all points."

"I have to keep moving around. My appearance stays the same, year after year. I look today like I did when we first met in the Navy. Except for a few scars, I look today like I looked back at Miss Lucille's. People get suspicious of me when they notice that I don't change, so I have to leave one job after another. I have no old friends because I must sever all personal relationships every fifteen or twenty years. You're the closest thing I have to an old friend."

Joel's only reaction to that was to raise his eyebrows slightly.

"So, what does all this mean to me?" He took his time to formulate the answers to his own question. "I don't believe I was given the gift of healing to cure masses of people. I believe I have been given long life because I am supposed to be alive to heal just one particular person. That's one reason I usually work in hospitals and nursing homes—that's where people who need healing are. I have no idea who that person is, but I believe God will make that known to me when the time comes. It's the only thing that keeps me from going nuts. God has marked me for his service."

"What?" Joel became very alert. "What do you mean, 'God has marked' you?"

He held out his hands, palms up, so Joel could see the holes in his hands. Joel took off his reading glasses and looked at the hands held up before his eyes.

"The stigmata?"

"No."

He told Joel about the battle at New Bern and how he had tried to commit suicide when he charged the Confederate line with his hands raised over his head, begging God to take him. He told him about Silas who saved his life and about Millicent who pronounced him, "marked by God." He told him about the battle at Antietam Creek where he saw Clara Barton make little miracles of hope and healing. He told him how all of those people turned his life to medicine and to waiting for the coming of the one he must save.

"Then there's this mark," he said, pointing to the scar on his temple. "I believe this is the mark of Cain.

"I first got this when I murdered that British Naval officer at Miss Lucille's. Then it was hit again just as I murdered two more men, Indians. I was struck again in the same place as I tried to murder myself at New Bern. God has protected me from being killed just as 'the mark' was meant to prevent anyone from killing the first murderer, Cain."

Joel waited.

"Do you believe in angels, Joel?" he asked. "I do. I've seen them. They've come to me as people to save me, to guide me. Perhaps people are angels just part of the time when God needs them. Maybe that's what God has in mind for me—to be an angel when the time is right."

Joel stood and walked to one of the two windows in the room, his hands folded behind his back. He looked out at a little ornamental garden.

"You mentioned something about animals. Tell me about that."

He told him how he discovered his gift by accident as he was fishing in a pond. He told him how the other animals behaved around him—how birds would come and sit on his hat and shoulders to keep him company in the forests.

Joel looked out the window the whole time. When he heard a movement behind him, he turned. His patient was at his office door, motioning him to follow. They passed the startled receptionist. She looked quizzically at Dr. Berger, who just shook his head and continued after his patient. They went out the main door and around to the garden Joel had been looking at through the window.

He told Joel to stand perfectly still. By now, Joel was beginning to regret leaving his office with a man who had just told him a whole series of fantastic stories. But it was too late to retreat now. Joel stood, as he was told, perfectly still and watched as his patient scanned the tops of the trees rimming the garden. It was a warm winter day, but there were no birds in sight. Then things got a little hairier for Joel.

As Joel watched, his patient began to sing:
"Mary had a little lamb, little lamb, little lamb. . ."
A squirrel suddenly ran down a tree, raced the few yards across the garden and jumped into his cupped hands in one hop.

He turned to Joel and said, "Hold out your hands just like I have mine."

He put the squirrel gently in Joel's hands. The squirrel nestled down as if it were the most natural thing in the world.

After a few moments he said, "All right, squirrel you can go back now."

With that, the squirrel jumped out of Joel's hands and ran back up the tree.

He looked at Joel who seemed to be somewhat disconcerted and said, "Shall we go back inside now, Doctor?"

On the way back in, Joel looked at his watch and told his receptionist to cancel the rest of his appointments for the day.

They took their seats in Joel's office as before. It took Joel a few minutes to reassemble his notes and a few more to reassemble his dignity. Finally, he fell back on what he knew best.

"You haven't told me about your parents, your mother and father."

"My mother died when I was ten. She tried to support the two of us on a small farm. I never really knew my father. He left us when I was very young. He went into the wilderness."

"You said you did the same thing—you went into the wilderness, too. Did you ever try to find your father?"

"No. I thought about it when I went west after the war, the Revolutionary War, but by then I was in my fifties, so there wasn't much chance I would find him alive."

"No brothers, sisters or other relatives?"

"No. Since my mother died, I've always been alone."

"Not entirely alone."

Joel was back to his accustomed position, looking directly at him as he spoke. "You mentioned several women. Tell me about them."

"You want to know about my sex life?"

"If you want to talk about that, yes."

"Sure. I like sex. I learned how great it could be from Margery, the girl in Miss Lucille's. She also taught me how much better making love could be when it's done with someone you love. I've made love to many women. It's cost me dearly—I had to leave them all—and I loved them all. I also learned the value of loving older women. Almost every woman I've made love to in the last hundred years has been over fifty."

Joel didn't move, but he knew from the slight tightening of the muscles in Joel's jaw that he should go on.

"Older women are better lovers, both in bed and out. They don't have as many serious hang-ups as younger women. A younger woman has to think more of the future and has to think about pregnancy and family and security and well, the list goes on and on. So, when the time comes to leave, when I have to take on a new identity, it's much more difficult to leave a younger woman. An older woman understands quicker and lets me go."

"Do you think that's because older women are more grateful—to have a young lover?"

"No, it's not gratitude. Most older women have been in married or long-term relationships. They've raised their children. They've established their careers or whatever work they do. No, older women are more relaxed. They can just enjoy a man's company without having to question it or examine his motives. They don't ask themselves, 'Will he stay or will he leave me in bad circumstances?' Older women also know more about what works in bed. They know what makes them happy and what makes me happy, and they aren't afraid to go for it. You can't ask for much more than that—except for growing old together. I can never have that. I can never have children or grandchildren. I can't stay to raise children, and I would never abandon my young children. I would never do what my father did to my mother and me."

Joel finished making some brief notes and said, "When you talked about death earlier, you didn't mention anything about your religious views of death. Are you a Christian?"

"Yes."

"Do you believe the one you say you are here to save is the Messiah?"

"No. The Messiah won't need to be saved. He will come to gather us up."

"Then who do you think is the one you must heal? What is that one meant to do?"

"I don't know, but I believe it will be God's work. I also believe that when my job is done, when I have finished what God wants me to do on this earth, then God will grant me my death."

Joel made more notes on the card, then looked up and said, "Is there anything else you want to tell me?"

He hesitated. There *was* something else but it was something he never spoke of—Vietnam. He thought about it for only a moment before deciding he'd said enough.

"No, Joel, I guess that's all."

Joel was silent for several moments, then said, "I'm not sure I can help you as much as you seem to think. I'd like you to see a colleague of mine. Dr. Lin is a clinical psychiatrist, one of the top people in her specialty. If I can arrange an appointment, are you willing to see her tomorrow?"

"Yes."

"Will 2:00 pm, the same time as our appointment today, be suitable?"

"Yes," he said again, "that would suit me."

"Good," Joel said, "I think you've made a wise decision.

Jasmine Lin is a former student of mine. She's a brilliant and sensitive doctor."

Joel stepped through his office door, leaving it open so his patient could hear him tell his receptionist to call Dr. Lin's office.

Just as he feared, Joel hadn't believed him. Indeed, Joel believed he was suffering a serious mental illness.

Sharing the truth had cleared his mind, though. He was surer than ever about his destiny—that he was on the right path. At some time during his session with Joel, he had come to understand that his forgiveness of himself was not enough. He had to accept God's forgiveness as well.

Joel came back in the office and said, "Dr. Lin will see you tomorrow at 2:00. Your initial session with her will first involve a physical examination. You understand, I'm sure, the essential connection between the health of the body and the health of the mind. If you have any recent medical records, please bring them with you. Dr. Lin will also want you to answer some questions that may seem strange to you at first. Please cooperate with her as much as you can. If you want her help, you'll have to help her."

Joel handed him a business card. On the face of the card were printed Dr. Lin's name and medical degrees above the words, "clinical psychiatry." The card also gave her office address and telephone number. On the back of the card, Joel's receptionist had written the next day's date and "2:00 PM."

He stood, shook hands and left.

On his way back to the hospital, he felt relieved. The voice within him spoke clearly now about his long life and healing power. They weren't curses—they were blessings. Blessings he was meant to use in God's service. He had never been lost to God. He would never feel lost again. He was Pele'thi and he could see everything.

At 2:45 PM the following day Joel Berger sat at his desk and looked at the chart he had started during yesterday's interview. It was not unusual for a patient to decide not to continue with therapy after his initial appointment. He was not surprised when Dr. Lin's office called to tell him his patient was a "no show."

He took out his pen and wrote "delusional" in the space marked, "initial diagnosis." His eyes moved to the bottom of the chart where he had written, "Pele'thi" after his summary of the patient's symptoms. He remembered the young man had said it was the "closest thing I have to a real name." Next to it he wrote in parenthesis the words his patient used when asked what his Shawnee name meant in English.

The young doctor had said it meant, "the eagle."

He hadn't gone to the office of Dr. Jasmine Lin the next day as scheduled. He couldn't. He was on a bus over 200 miles away traveling to his next identity as a nursing student and part-time retirement home attendant.

It would be another two years when, diploma in hand, he would sit in the office of the personnel director at Presbyterian Medical Center where he would meet Miss Edna P. Snow.

From the bus the countryside seemed to sweep by in a monotonous blur. He tried to remember if he had ever walked through this country. Years ago he would have enjoyed it. But now it all moved by so fast.

The green trees and fields racing along outside the bus window reminded him of another very green place. He remembered what he didn't want to tell Joel. He didn't want to tell him about Vietnam.

Chapter Thirteen

NAM

War attracted him as no other passion. Death, and therefore life, was magnified by war.

He resigned his latest hospital residency and accepted the rank of Major in the Army Medical Corps. It was early 1967 and the Army wasted no time in shipping him out to service "in country."

He got his first taste of Vietnam just after landing at Tan Son Nhut airfield near Saigon. He was sure as he stepped off the plane that he was drowning. The humidity hit him so hard he thought for a moment he wouldn't be able to inhale. It was hot, too. By the time a ground shuttle delivered him to his medical unit, his uniform was completely stuck to his body, soaked through with sweat. He was assigned to the 25th Infantry Division base hospital at Cu Chi. Mercifully, the hospital was air-conditioned.

What he saw at Cu Chi made it clear the United States was making a major military commitment. The Division headquarters area was bigger than any military base he had seen since Camp Lejeune in North Carolina. He was put to work immediately in the hospital's operating theatre. Most of the wounded were flown in directly by helicopter rescue—medivac they called it. He made a point of talking to the men he treated, not just to give them the healing hope he knew was so vital to their recovery, but to learn how their field medics worked. A good medic could increase a seriously wounded man's chances of survival by ten fold.

Still, even with good care, too many men would carry away the fruits of their war: wheelchairs, prosthesis devices, blindness, deafness, chemical dependencies, even what used to be called, combat fatigue. Everyone, even those that escaped physical injury, would never be the same people their friends and family had known before the war.

In the States he heard people say the American Army was filled with men who had fought the draft and didn't want to go to Vietnam. He heard them called pot heads, psychopaths—murderers of women and little children—baby-killers. He expected to have to deal with them. But he never met anyone like that. He never found one he wouldn't want to have as a son. They were young men caught in a bad situation—between boredom and terror, between duty and conscience—just like other men he'd known in other wars. They were far better men than their countrymen thought they were. They were not Thomas Paine's "sunshine soldiers"—no, not at all.

He was attending to the last of a half-dozen new casualties, the result of a Viet Cong ambush, when a little six-year-old Vietnamese girl was brought in. She was remanded to his care in Cu Chi due to his former specialization in pediatrics. Her name was given on the chart only as An. She had been brought first to the main hospital in Hué where her symptoms had not responded to an initial diagnosis of flu. The Army had flown her to him. By the time he saw her, she was in serious trouble.

She looked up at him with huge dark brown eyes as he examined her.

"Are you my new doctor?" she asked. "I like you better than the other ones. You're nice."

She had his heart even before she finished speaking.

She had the usual symptoms of flu: headache, fever and nausea, but she had also developed a light rash and now complained of neck pain. The new symptoms were very disturbing, so he ordered a spinal tap to test his provisional diagnosis of encephalitis. He hoped he was wrong. Because if he was right, little An would not live much longer.

Leaving the examination room, he nearly collided with a Vietnamese woman standing in the hall. Their meeting was no accident. The woman had been waiting for him and moved to block his path. She said she was An's grandmother.

She was unlike any Asian woman he had ever met. When she spoke, she held her gaze level with his, never looking down or away. She had the prominent cheekbones and long, dark hair he thought typical of Vietnamese women, but her eyes startled him. They were light blue, almost gray—not dark brown or black as he would have expected. He noted that her hair showed no trace of gray, and her face was very smooth with no lines at all. He tried in his mind to judge her age but couldn't do it. This woman certainly didn't look old enough to be An's grandmother. She didn't look old enough to be anybody's grandmother. Her ao dai masked her figure but she was slender—that he could see. She was also taller than most of the women he had met in Saigon.

She introduced herself as Mistress Nguyen Thi-Nu. She was certainly Vietnamese but at the same time very Western. Her English was flawless. She needed to talk about her granddaughter's condition and prognosis.

"My granddaughter's name is Nguyen Thi An, but you should just call her An."

She brought out a note pad with a number of questions. Seeing them, he invited her to join him in the "choke and puke."

"'The choke and puke'?" she repeated what he'd said.

Her expression didn't change with the question.

"Oh, I'm sorry," he said. "That's just an American slang expression for our hospital canteen. Really, it doesn't have that much to do with the quality of the food." *Although, sometimes it did.*

"How wonderfully easy you are with your language," she said. "What a delightful description."

Despite her concern she forced a smile.

"The French are so much more obsessed with keeping their language pure. They make it so much harder on themselves."

He began to speak as he helped seat her. "Everything that can be done for An is being done and will continue to be done. I will see to it."

He ran quickly through An's symptoms and asked her if she knew anything else about her granddaughter's illness. She was as mystified as the doctors in Hué.

"I've ordered a test that should help my diagnosis. I'll have the results in the morning." He hoped he kept his own fears off his face.

They continued to speak for almost two hours, drinking strong coffee, the way she liked it, and eating gobs of chocolate ice cream—the way they both liked it. He kept the conversation deliberately light and the subjects very general. So did she. They both knew the danger in too much clarity. He knew he shouldn't devote so much of his time to Mistress Nguyen Thi-Nu, but even after two hours he didn't want to see her go.

He asked her, "May I see you again?"

She smiled, "I'd be delighted to meet you for dinner this evening. I will wait for you at the base's main gate with a taxi at nine."

That was part of her French background: late dining. He knew he would have to be up again the next morning by 0600 at the latest.

She took him to a good French restaurant. When he asked her about herself, she was hesitant at first, but it soon came out.

She began slowly, saying, "For the past thirteen years I have taught French and English in a parochial school in Hué. I was born in the south in Kien Thien on the Mekong delta. My mother was Vietnamese, but my father was half French. I have his eyes, his grey eyes.

"My father did not have the usual Vietnamese attitude toward women. He sent me to Canada to study. This was unheard of at the time. A son might be sent off to be better educated but a daughter? Never. We were Catholic, so France would have been the logical choice for my education, but France was still trying to recover from one war with Germany and preparing for another. That was 1928. I was nineteen." She smiled, "Now I've told you my age. A French woman shouldn't do that.

"My father sent me to Montreal in the province of Quebec. There were many French-speaking Catholics in that part of Canada. He thought it would make it easier for me. It was there I met my husband. He was also born in Vietnam of French ancestry. He had come to the United States and then to Canada, determined to learn how to build the roads and bridges our homeland so desperately needed. He got an engineering degree from the Universite du Quebec, and then he gave me my 'Mme. degree.'" Another soft smile, then she said, "In one month I was pregnant. Our only child, a son, was born in 1933 and we returned to Indochina as you Americans called it then.

"My husband joined the French fighting the Japanese. After the war he joined the Viet Minh fighting the French. He thought he should fight only one enemy at a time." Another smile, but then it disappeared as she continued, "He was killed at Dien Bien Phu in 1954. Our son grew up in my home near the Mekong. Then the Viet Cong came to Kien Thien to recruit converts to their communism. When they learned that my son and his family were Catholic, they forced him, his wife and their two boys to kneel in the middle of the village and then shot each of them in the back of the head. Little An escaped only because she was with me in Hué. Perhaps you can understand my great concern for my granddaughter's health."

During her entire description of these events, some happy, some horrific, Mistress Nguyen Thi-Nu's expression barely changed—only a few quick smiles lit her face. She looked directly at him seemingly without emotion. He understood her demeanor perfectly. Some hurts are just too painful to be given any purchase. To allow any to stand brings them all up and takes away one's sanity.

Suddenly she reached out to him, placing her hands on his. He had been holding his own emotions back as she told of the tragic deaths in her family—the executions of her son and daughter-in-law and her other grandchildren. He didn't realize he had been clenching his fists tightly in front of him on the table.

"It's all right," she said.

She said it repeatedly, keeping her hands on his until he was able to relax. Neither of them really believed it was "all right."

As they left, she gave him a number where she could be reached in the morning. He had again hidden his fear for An. There was no point in alarming her before he knew himself what the test would show.

•

He read the report first thing in the morning and knew what he must do. An needed a miracle, and she needed it very soon before the encephalitis took her life. He had already made up his mind. After hearing Mistress Nguyen Thi-Nu's account of her family's destruction, he would do whatever he could to save An.

He took her tiny hand in his and put his finger to his lips, so she would not speak while he said the words he hoped would not condemn her to die in some other way.

By early afternoon An had recovered enough to have a meal, and she began speaking to everyone, mixing French words in with the English she spoke in her sweet, little-girl voice. He thought she was adorable. The nurses all thought so, too.

He dined again that night at another French restaurant with An's grandmother. The good news of little An's remarkable recovery put Mistress Nguyen Thi-Nu very much more at ease. He drew her out with more details of her life, including her given French name, Catherine. He was well-prepared with a bundle of lies to tell about himself. Lying was so easy for him now; he was sure he could pass even the best lie detector test. He had learned to pretend his life was very dull—it stifled any penetrating questions. They agreed to dine the following night as well. He was to come to the apartment she had just rented on Hai Ba Trung in Saigon.

He was anxious. He came early.

They dined alone. This, their third evening together, went well with more good, if controlled, conversation and a good wine. Mistress Nguyen Thi-Nu, now "Catherine," was an excellent judge of wine. Her company had already convinced him he was an excellent judge of women. Dessert having been served and eaten, they rose from the table, and he turned to leave. He got to the door before he realized Catherine was still standing at the table. She said nothing. He said nothing. He came back to her, not hesitating, but testing each step as he took it. His last step took him into her arms.

He kept putting off An's discharge from the hospital. Everyone could see she was well—perhaps, too well. She would not be kept in her room. She spent each day racing, jumping or crawling all over the place while entertaining the men in the recovery wards. Naturally, she became "Annie" to everyone in the hospital.

He stood watching her one morning as she made her rounds, stopping at each bed and speaking to each man. She would stay and listen as long as a man wanted her attention. Then she would pat him tenderly somewhere she thought wouldn't hurt him and go on to the next survivor. She was a tiny angel moving among them making the same little miracles of healing he had seen Clara Barton make at Antietam. By the end of her first day on the ward, she had six new mothers, too. Every nurse was her *mere*. He managed to keep her at the hospital for three more days for "observation." That gave him three more nights of "observation" with Catherine.

Their love-making was restrained at first. She was so small and slender he was afraid he might hurt her with his strength. It soon became clear to him, however, that restraint was not what she wanted. She had kept herself from any sexual relationship since the death of her husband. But that was in the past—fourteen years ago. Now she wanted it all. She wanted it both rough and easy. So did he.

Some things, they say, come back to you even after you haven't done them in a long time—like riding a bicycle. Catherine had no trouble riding her new "bicycle." Most older women know something about love-making that only very few young women know. Catherine was well-aware that the most sensual of his sexual organs was not to be found between his legs: it was between his ears. She worked his mind, holding back at times to build his hopes, then overwhelming his emotional circuits with a rush of pleasure. It was both cruel and wonderful. He tried to do the same for her.

Catherine also knew things two people could do for each

other in bed, as well as out, that were entirely new to him. She surprised him. His initial training in the "moves d'amour" had come from Margery, a professional. Other women he had known had added a twist here or there, and Sylvia had engaged him in what he thought must have been every possible move and position in every sex manual ever written. The sex manuals hadn't added much to his repertoire. But Catherine was a woman who could make the most commonplace of moves newly exciting.

As experienced lovers they anticipated each other. She anticipated his needs and he hers. They came to a point after their first hour together when her anticipation of his anticipation of her anticipation got so ludicrous they both started laughing wildly together. After that they each gave to the other without thinking, their passions rising and falling through the night—and through all the next three nights as well.

"You are a great surprise to me," she said on their third night. "For one so young, you know so much about l'amour and so very much more about a woman than a man should know. I might expect this from an older Frenchman...but from an American, never! I am very curious about where you learned these things? And how have you come to mix such skill with so much delicacy? Or is it that I have underestimated American men. The ones I...well, let us say...the ones I encountered while I was in Montreal were clumsy and concerned with all the wrong things—when they thought to be concerned at all. But you! I have never known a man with so much...I don't know the word...perception? Yes, that's it—you know what I want before I know it myself."

He turned it back on her, telling her it was her expertise that brought them to such mutual pleasure. He knew she didn't believe it, but she was too well-mannered to press it further. Besides, he had begun pressing her in a way he knew she would never question—considering the place he was pressing. All military men learn that sometimes the best way to defend one's position is to attack. This was particularly useful when one knew the other's area of greatest vulnerability. Mistress Nguyen Thi-Nu was well-aware of all his areas of vulnerability as well, and he loved the way she exploited every one of them.

He couldn't justify keeping An any longer. She had been under his care for a week. As soon as An realized she would be leaving, she climbed up on her bed, stood up and held her arms out to him. At that height she was almost as tall as he. When he came to her, she put her arms around his neck and kissed his forehead on his scar.

"Make it all well," she said by way of explanation.

Then she gave him the same look she gave all the wounded men in the wards and said, "I love you, Major Doctor."

He held her tightly for a moment, then put her down until her feet could touch the floor. He would have given her a playful smack on her backside, but she was too fast for him. She ran away down the aisle squealing with delight at her narrow escape.

"You girls are all alike," he said as they walked together laughing through the hospital.

At the door Mistress Thi-Nu gave him her hand, and they exchanged only a formal "au revoir."

People were watching.

•

"Major! Sir, take this weapon!" the sergeant screamed at him. Master Gunnery Sergeant Leary, USMC was yelling at all the officers in the BOQ as he passed out M-16 rifles. "Grab a couple of clips from that ammo box over there and get in the passageway with the others."

He did as he was ordered.

Over his shoulder he heard, "I'm not taking that, Sergeant."

It was the voice of a Lt. Colonel from Cuong Thien way down south of Saigon.

"I've got to get back to my unit. Find me some transportation."

Sergeant Leary had neither the time nor the inclination for any insubordination at that moment.

"You ain't going nowhere tonight but straight to hell if you don't take this piece right now, *sir*! And that's *Master Gunnery* Sergeant...*sir*."

It was clear the sergeant was not in the habit of taking any shit from anyone. He put a final point on it.

"Them VCs are at the gate!"

His own commanding officer was off somewhere "to hell and gone," so it had fallen to Master Gunnery Sergeant Charles Alpheous Leary, as senior NCO, to organize the defense of his immediate area with only a little disparate group composed of himself, one lance corporal, two Marine privates, and four others who were supposed to be enjoying a vacation—all, God help him, officers.

The other three officers had come to the ancient city of Hué to enjoy some R & R during the truce at the Tet holiday. From the sounds in the street, they had all made a serious miscalculation. Instead of "rest and recreation" they were in for some "rifles and rations." Or, more likely, just "Rest in Peace." His own motivation for coming to Hué was ostensibly to check up on An who was living in her grandmother's home in the city. The truth was, he knew An was all right. What interested him more was checking up on her grandmother. But that passion had been replaced by a new one. Now he just had to stay alive.

Sergeant Leary pushed him out on a terraced walkway on the ground floor of what had once been a cheap hotel. Leary was giving instructions as they went.

"Those little shits out there will know this is an officers' barracks and will want us real bad. Your field of fire is the wall in front of us and particularly that gateway in the wall between us and the street. If they try to come straight through it, you've got to stop them. If they come over the wall, pick them off. And, whatever you do, keep firing."

Leary paused, looking at his insignia. "You're Army Medical—a doctor? You don't have any reservations about killing these bastards, do you?" Sergeant Leary didn't have time to wait for a reply. "Sir, have you ever qualified with an M-16 rifle?"

It was a bad time to say so but no, he hadn't. Sergeant Leary gave him the short course, the fifteen second version: ammo, clip, trigger, safety, sights, semi- or full-automatic.

"And, sir, try not to shoot your ass off. And, goddamn it, don't shoot me."

Where had he heard that before?

He knelt behind a concrete barricade placed in front of the hotel to prevent drunken officers from driving vehicles directly into their rooms. Sergeant Leary placed two of his Marines at the ends of the building on either side of him and then left. He presumed the rest of the officers and the other Marines must be defending the perimeter of the building area. He took comfort in the company of two qualified riflemen as he swept the street wall from left to right to be sure there were no obstructions in his field of fire.

The lights in the barracks had been shut off, and there was precious little light coming from any where else. Only brief flashes from exploding mortars or artillery shells lit the sky. The wall was about four feet high and made of some sort of ancient masonry. The uneven slabs cast little shadows over the whole surface. It would be a difficult background to target a man. He settled his sights on the open gateway twenty yards in front of him. He decided to fire the M-16 as a semiautomatic—just one shot each time he squeezed the trigger. He liked controlling his fire.

The sergeant's question was still in his ears: *"You don't have any reservations about killing these bastards, do you?"*

Did he? The last time he killed anyone had been well over 150 years ago. He had been through four major wars since then without killing anyone. Some of the people he *had* killed, he killed because he felt he was forced to. Some he wanted to kill. He had murdered both the British officer and the Blackfoot brave in a rage. He also willingly killed the Indians who killed his family. The rest he killed in self-defense. So why would killing the Vietnamese, who might be coming through the gate to kill him, be any different?

A sudden increase in the sounds coming from the street broke through his thoughts. There was always a lot of noise in the streets here—cars, motor bikes, military vehicles, bicycle horns and street vendors—lots of people shouting. But this noise was gunfire, rapid and repeated gunfire. And it was very close.

Four armed men suddenly ran through the gate and spread out in a line, raking the barracks with bursts of fire from automatic weapons. Glass began breaking behind him, and a number of rounds slammed into the concrete barricade in front of him. A building off to his left suddenly caught fire and flared up, illuminating the courtyard. In the firelight he could see the men were all wearing olive-colored pants, matching short-sleeved shirts and pith helmets: NVA!

What in hell was the North Vietnamese Army doing attacking in force south of the demilitarized zone? Wasn't there supposed to be a cease-fire for the Tet holiday?

Another burst of gunfire shattered a wooden post near his shoulder. He stopped thinking about it and began killing again. He went left to right: pop...pop...pop...pop. That was how it started. It would be days before it was over.

•

"This is great! This is really great!" The Lt. Colonel from Cuong Thien was very pleased. "Eighteen killed—what a great body-count."

He watched the Lt. Colonel move happily about. He also saw the look on the face of Sergeant Leary and knew if the sergeant had his way, there would be nineteen dead bodies—and one of them would be an American lieutenant colonel.

The actual conduct of war is a strenuous business. It is a young man's business. The dead, spread out in the courtyard between the barracks and the street, had been very young men.

Young men...dying for...what?

Unfortunately, he thought he knew. These men died for an idea. They died for an idea much like men he served with in other wars. But was the dried blood and swarming flies on the bodies of eighteen young men worth it, worth it to them—to him? Was he now like one of the Hessians he faced in the American Revolution, just a soldier hired to put down a revolt against a colonial government?

No, he knew that wasn't true. It might seem like it if one didn't look at it too closely. But it wasn't true. He thought the motives of his beloved America were honorable, even if the Vietnamese government they were here to preserve might not be. At least both of Vietnam's present governments were free of their former French officials. They were no longer ruled by people from half a world away. His countrymen were not here to continue foreign control of the Vietnamese people; they were here to prevent the spread of an idea—an idea that would make them all slaves to a flawed ideal.

Master Gunnery Sergeant Leary was giving orders again. "We gotta go and we gotta go now!"

"But where do we go from here?" It was the Lt. Colonel asking.

All the officers had agreed that Sergeant Leary should take complete charge of the situation. He knew the area and the capabilities of his men better than anyone. Leary was also the only one of them who had been in direct combat with the Viet Cong before the first night of the Tet assault, now three nights ago.

Leary responded, "I'd like to hook up with the Marines down in Phu Bai, but that's ten miles to the south. And there's no telling how deep the shit is down there. There's a South Vietnamese Regiment holed up across the river in the old Citadel. Our best bet is to get over there and join them. We may have to fight our way to the railroad bridge to the west to get across the river, but that's our best chance to survive. Them VC seem to have taken over the rest of the city."

He had a question for the sergeant himself. "What's going to prevent the South Vietnamese from shooting us when we get there?"

Leary smiled. It wasn't a pleasant smile, but it was an improvement over Leary's usual dour expression.

"We don't have no radio communication capability, so I used the telephone. They'll be expecting us to come in from the west."

"The telephone!?" The Lt. Colonel was incredulous.

Sergeant Leary explained, "The Vietnamese phone system usually ain't worth a shit. But it was all I had so I called them up. The number was in my travel register—damned if it didn't work."

Sergeant Leary was a bit incredulous himself.

The street ran alongside the Perfume River. They moved cautiously in single-file, divided in two groups. Master Gunnery Sergeant Leary led the first group. He led the second. Leary didn't know quite what to think about an Army doctor who could kill men so efficiently. But talent was talent, and Leary had been around long enough to take advantage of it.

Smoke was everywhere, and at times it was hard to breathe without coughing. He was sure so much smoke meant many parts of the city must still be burning, but that was good for them. The smoke covered their movements. They were almost across the river before they were challenged from the south shore. A burst of gunfire rattled off the bridge's steel superstructure over their heads. No one was hit.

An ARVN soldier who stepped from cover at the end of the bridge led them over narrow, and very temporary, walkways spanning two smaller water courses. When The South Vietnamese soldier took the point, Leary and his lethal doctor both moved back to protect the rear.

As they crossed the last walkway, a flare burst above them, and he could see the water courses were long and straight—moats. For the next hour they alternately crept across open, grassy spaces and moved around or through a series of walled buildings. Some of the walls they passed were more than fifteen feet tall and were constructed of large squared-off stones fit tightly together. He remembered reading a brochure that said the Citadel covered some four square miles—a small city within a city. He believed it. He was tired.

Finally, they were safely inside part of an old fortress.

The Citadel at Hué was built to repel ancient armies using ancient weapons. Now it would have to withstand modern mortars and artillery shells. The enemy was already inside the outer walls and firefights erupted close by their entire escape route. Until he was actually in a walled compound, he wondered if they might not have been safer in Phu Bai.

The First South Vietnam Division was commanded by Brigadier General Ngo Quand Truong. He liked Truong immediately. The General was a man who didn't just command respect, he earned it. And he earned a lot of it. Even Master Gunnery Sergeant Leary who was very skeptical about any military service other than the United States Marine Corps, in general, and about officers, in particular, admitted a few days into the battle for the Citadel that General Truong was, "a guy I'd go anywhere and fight for."

He gave Leary back his weapon and took up duty as a doctor

again—as *the* doctor. He was the only trained physician present. The two regular Vietnamese doctors never made it back to the ARVN compound when the shooting started. No one knew where the Viet doctors were. Several ornate tables were cleared and made as sterile as possible using alcohol. They had plenty of alcohol. He was in business; but unfortunately, business was so good it was about to break down his door—or blast through the roof. Many wounded men waited for his help. He was surprised at the number of wounds containing fragments of rock until he realized that the NVA artillery was blasting at the walls around them, breaking off sharp slivers of stone.

There was little time for rest, so there was little time to dream. It was a good trade-off for him. Ten more days of almost continuous combat kept everyone in the medical area going at full speed.

The NVA must really be desperate to take this place. Their losses must be horrendous.

Both his body and his clothes became quite "ripe." The food was cold, and everyone stayed wet from the early spring rains coming through shell holes in the roof—all the comforts of combat as he remembered them. He changed his clothes after bathing in a bowl of water for the first time on the tenth day. On the eleventh day of the siege a new sound came to them. Units from the U.S. Marines and South Vietnamese Army were driving the communists out of Hué.

He moved outside, joining the advancing troops. Almost immediately an old, familiar odor came to him, the same odor he first learned to associate with modern combat back on Guadalcanal: a mixture of cordite, diesel fuel, burned flesh and fresh blood. There are some things old soldiers never forget. That odor was one of them.

It took almost another two weeks before the entire city was secured. American and South Vietnamese causalities fell even as those of the enemy rose.

The dead lay everywhere.

He was officially attached to the South Vietnam Regiment under General Truong, assigned to assist with the immediate treatment of civilian casualties in Hué. In another few days the fires had been put out and the buildings searched, one by one, to secure the city. But it wasn't long before it became apparent that something was still very wrong in Hué.

He tried to get word to Mistress Thi-Nu, but the messengers all came back saying they couldn't find her. Her home was intact, but there was no one there. She wasn't the only one missing. Many people had fled the city—which might explain some of the missing—but not all of them. There were far too many who could not be accounted for.

General Truong had assigned an interpreter to help him with his Viet patients. Captain Quy spoke several local Viet dialects, as well as French, some Chinese, and enough English to be of real help. The Captain, like the General himself, wasn't physically imposing. But Leary, that supremely competent judge of military muscle, pronounced Quy, "a very tough cookie." That put him at the top of Leary's rating scale. The General had also managed to get Leary and his Marines assigned to his American detachment. They were to protect their only doctor from any remnants of the enemy forces.

Among the injured were a few who had been tortured and thought killed by operatives of the Viet Cong. They had survived by digging themselves out of shallow graves after being left for dead.

"There were many others," they said.

They led them to several mass graves covered by only a few inches of sandy soil. He soon went from treating the living to exhuming and examining the dead.

He hadn't seen anything like it since Bloody Lane at Antietam. In one mass grave near a school lay more than a thousand bodies, piled on top of one another, ten deep in places. The dead were removed and laid out on a paved street next to the grave so that relatives could take them away for proper Buddhist burial. As more and more were found and laid on the road, his fears for An and Catherine grew. He went to the grave several times each day to see for himself what the beasts who called themselves men had done. He had killed here, too. But he killed only when given no other choice. Most of the victims in Hué had been civilians, trussed with wire, securing their elbows together behind their backs. Then they had been bludgeoned with rifle butts or bats, smashing their skulls and necks, their bodies then thrown into the pits and covered—covered to hide the cruel evidence of an unspeakable evil.

Captain Quy told him that the Regiment had discovered lists containing the names of most of the people found in the graves. The Viet Cong had come into the city with those lists determined to deliberately murder certain groups of people: foreign nationals and their families, civilian and military personnel, government employees, policemen, religious leaders and professionals, particularly teachers and medical people—anyone who served the people. It explained what had happened to the Viet doctors caught in the city. The Viet Cong had held parts of Hué for almost twenty-five days—plenty of time to accomplish their objective.

He was walking along the edge of one of the pits watching the ARVN volunteers working to remove the dead when something stopped him. It stopped his heart, as well.

No!

But he recognized her ao dai before his legs gave away and he fell down. Captain Quy and Sergeant Leary helped him to his feet as Catherine's body was lifted gently by the men working in that ghastly place. An's body was under her grandmother's. Even little An's arms had been wired behind her back. Catherine must have had to watch her killed just before her own murder.

He sat down again on the street. It was almost an hour before he could say or do anything. His body recovered with his mind.

"They have no family," he said. "I'll have to see to their burial myself. They're Catholic. Where can I find a Catholic priest?"

Captain Quy was at a loss, but Sergeant Leary said, "There's a monastery down near Phu Bai. There should be a priest there. I'll get on it, sir."

Leary was gone so fast he couldn't be sure he'd heard his, "Thanks, Top Sergeant."

He said it again when Leary returned with a body bag and a light truck. "USMC" was stenciled on its bumper. If you need something important from the military, you can't go wrong giving the job to a senior NCO—they're the people who can always get things done.

They couldn't leave until he could certify all the causes of death in the mass grave. That took another full day. He moved through his duty while living in his nightmare. He couldn't be sure when he was dreaming and when he was waking. It was just the same.

They left for Phu Bai early the second day. Lance Corporal Jacobs drove with Captain Quy up front should there be any problem getting through the guards on the road. He and Sergeant Leary rode in the back with the body bag. They had put Catherine and An in together. Even together their slight forms made almost no noticeable bulge in the bag.

They all rode in silence.

The monastery near Phu Bai had a peculiar look. He didn't understand what it was until he was out of the truck and walking toward it. It was an attractive building, built of stone with elaborate wooden treatments around tall windows. What made it peculiar was that there was nothing in the windows except a lot of light. The light came out through the windows because the back of the building didn't exist. It had been blown away along with a major portion of the roof. A very tall and very thin man came to them from one side of the building. From his dress they guessed he was the priest. Father Xavier had already spoken with Captain Quy before they left Hué. The Reverend Father did not speak English, so all communication had to be in French.

The funeral mass began soon after their arrival at the monastery. He couldn't help but think how strange it was that four men, Leary, Quy, Jacobs and himself—a Southern Baptist, a Buddhist, a Jew and whatever sort of Christian he was—were the only mourners at a Catholic funeral. They had most of the bases covered, anyway. Nguyen Thi-Nu and Nguyen Thi An—Catherine and "Annie," still in the body bag, were buried together in the small cemetery beside the monastery.

After the service he had Captain Quy translate another of his wishes to Father Xavier. The Father indicated that one of the monks who had survived the attack was a talented stone carver. He gave the father a drawing he had been working on. Payment was made in advance for a stone monument for the new grave.

Father Xavier also accepted a contribution to the monastery to help rebuild its roof and walls.

Before they left, the Reverend Father gave Captain Quy another piece of information which the captain translated for the rest of them. There had been another priest and five more nuns living there. Before the Viet Cong attacked Phu Bai, they came to the monastery because there were many refugees here. Most of the refugees along with Father Xavier and four nuns escaped but the others were captured and killed. From the description given by Father Xavier, the nuns were killed in the same way the victims in Hué had been killed. The other priest, however, denounced his captors, and for that insolence he was not beaten to death but was simply buried alive.

The least tolerant religions in the world are those whose dogma will not survive in the company of a gentle and loving God.

•

Once back with the 25th Infantry, his commanding officer, Colonel Kirk, suggested he take a furlough. The colonel was afraid his experience in Hué might make the difficult, medical decisions he had to make each day even harder.

He declined the offer. He knew the best way for him to honor the dead was to live his life as it should be lived, as the healer he had become. The newly wounded men coming in needed his skill, and the men in the recovery wards needed his hope and his laughter. The laughter was hard at first, but as the months passed, it became genuine again. His dreams returned, too, and as he feared, the nightmare now had another face—a very little face. But the face in his dream was not what he expected. An's face in his dream was not her face in death—it was the face she had shown the wounded men in the hospital—the same face he remembered when she said she loved him.

Most of his regiment was moved out of Vietnam in 1971. He stayed a little longer to oversee the removal of all of his patients to hospitals in Japan or back to the States. However, just before he was to leave, he got a military hop back to Phu Bai.

He discovered the monastery had not been completely restored. The back wall was only partly rebuilt. He found the cemetery on his own. The stone cutter commissioned by Father Xavier was more than just good; he was an artisan. The winged angel carved into the little monument was even better than the one in the drawing he had left with the priest. It had An's face—the same loving face he saw every night. He went away sure that Catherine and An had their own little angel looking over them for eternity—whatever that might be.

•

His plane touched down at O'Hare International, and he walked into the terminal. He had heard the stories of other soldiers returning from the war who were spat on and cursed as "baby killers." His reception was the opposite. He was studiously ignored. Yes, eyes were turned momentarily to his uniform—he saw them—but they looked quickly away. It was as if people wished he were invisible. And so that's what he was.

He picked up his bag and took a taxi to his hotel. His orders were in his pocket. Fort Sam Houston, Texas, would be his next temporary home. He was in no hurry to get to the hotel. The dreams would always be there waiting for him when he tried to sleep. There would be his usual nightmare, the one with all the faces of the dead. There would also be another—a new one: "Nam."

Chapter Fourteen

CHAREE and PENNY

Dr. Virginia Louisa Carnegie, M.D., was very unhappy. She was losing, and she was a sore loser. She hated to lose any of them, and she really hated to lose this one. Despite everything she could do—every weapon she could use—Charee Norris was dying.

Little Charee, so bright, so vivacious and such a joy to know was dying. Curious about everything, Charee wanted to know how everything worked and why her "Doctor Louisie" wanted to be a doctor, and what she did, and how she did her hair, and did she have a boyfriend, and did she like working in the hospital, and…and…on and on it went. Charee was also very intuitive, so today, "Doctor Louisie" reminded herself, even if she was very unhappy, to "put on a happy face."

Virginia had just started her examination when he burst into the room with a big smile and a "How ya doing my Charee, my darling sweetheart?"

Dr. Carnegie looked up, unsmiling from across the bed.

Virginia was something of an enigma to him—and he suspected he was one to her as well. They were both devoted to their calling, saving as many as they could. She told him he could call her by her first name after he offered the same to her. She was a crackerjack doctor. She was also an object of desire for every man working in the hospital. Dark curly hair, blue eyes and tall, even at forty-two, she had a figure most women would kill for. Women also envied her hair.

"I'll bet all she has to do in the morning is run her fingers through it a few times, and she's set for the day," they thought. They were right.

He was the lone exception to her pack of male admirers. On at least one occasion she had gone out of her way to attract his interest in a non-medical way. She was unattached and took a lover briefly from time to time. But it never lasted; she was too devoted to her work to give up the additional energy living with a man required. Her reaction, when he didn't respond to her flirtation, was confusion and mild embarrassment. She knew he wasn't gay. It was rumored he was seeing a mystery woman, someone who worked right there at Presbyterian Medical, but no one knew who it was. He thought she was pretty, all right. She just wasn't his type. She wasn't old enough.

He retreated to the door of Charee's room immediately, apologizing for the interruption.

"No, please come in," she said.

He did, and together with Charee, he had a great time entertaining "Dr. Louisie" with their songs and corny jokes.

Only the children could call her, Dr. Louisie. He thought that was a shame since it fit her so well. She was pert, fun to talk to, interesting and usually smiling—but not today. Today, she was very unhappy.

The remission and cure rate for juvenile leukemia patients was much higher than it had been thrity-five years ago when he was a practicing pediatric specialist at another, far away hospital, just before he went to Vietnam. He knew Dr. Carnegie was the best that PMC had to offer, probably the best to be found anywhere. He also knew that no matter how good an oncologist was, he or she wasn't going to win them all. As he left, he gave them both his best, million-dollar smile.

He didn't know why Charee attracted his attention more than the other children. They were all in need of the same thing. They needed hope, and he tried to give it to them every time he saw them. But something drew him to Charee. That was why, two hours after he left Charee's room, he stopped short just as he was about to pass the visitor's lounge on the oncology floor.

Glancing in, he saw Dr. Carnegie sitting with a man and a woman explaining something to them. They were black. Since Charee was the only black child in oncology at the time, he was sure they must be her parents. He took a chance and stepped into the lounge. The chance he took was that Virginia might toss him out on his ear—not physically, of course but in a way that would hurt a lot more. She was very protective of her turf—that is "her" children. He stopped just inside the door. Both the man and the woman saw him and looked his way. Virginia turned her head, saw him and smiled.

In like Flynn.

He introduced himself. Virginia introduced them as Mr. and Mrs. Norris, which they immediately corrected to Derrick and Valery. Derrick stood and they shook hands. They were aware of his interest in Charee and the lift he gave their daughter whenever he came into her room. Charee had already extolled his virtues. He extolled hers and said he would like to know more about her. He couldn't have asked at a better time.

He could see Charee in her parents. Valery was tall, maybe a little taller, he thought, than Derrick. Charee got her looks, her dignity and her quiet gentleness from her mother. She got her energy and her laugh from her father. Derrick was a bull.

Derrick spoke first. He was so frustrated; he was on the edge of madness. He was the father; he was the provider; he was the protector of his family against all harm—but he could do nothing to save his only child. He needed to talk about her. He needed to bring her into the room, to keep her from the leukemia down the hall. Their story came out in small pieces with Derrick and Valery taking turns telling it.

"My business," Derrick said, "is D. K. Norris and Son, Contracting. I'm the son. My grandfather started his own business pouring and finishing concrete back in the 1920's. When I came along, the old man retired. He spent his whole life digging foundations and building forms to control concrete. That takes a toll on the body. My father sent me to college, so I could come back and make the business better. That's where I met Valery."

They exchanged soft smiles. It was something they did often.

"My business is doing well now." Derrick said.

He and Valery needed to keep talking. If they kept on talking, things wouldn't change. Things wouldn't get worse.

Dr. Carnegie said quietly, "Tell us about yourself, Valery."

Valery Norris said she had trained as a social worker.

"Derrick and I were married right after he graduated. I was already working. I finished my undergraduate work a year ahead of him. We both wanted children right away, but after a year we were told we probably would never have any children. I went back to school and earned a master's degree in psychology. We applied to adopt a child. The very next day the doctor called and said the rabbit died.

"I stopped working shortly before Charee was born and didn't go back. I wanted our daughter to have the best childhood any child ever had."

She stopped for several seconds, swallowing and controlling tears. Then she continued.

"We were unhappy with the school where Charee started kindergarten. By the middle of the first grade we could see that Charee wasn't progressing as she should. I went to Charee's class and sat for a whole week observing what was and what wasn't happening. What I saw was incompetence piled on top of indifference. We moved two months later to a suburban neighborhood close to a school with a good reputation. Charee is doing so much better. I read with her almost every evening. Charee is very bright, and she wanted to read on her own. In her new school she has to work hard to keep up with the other children. Charee thinks that's great."

Valery had to stop. She touched away a tear.

Derrick took it up. "My Valery won't tell you this, but she volunteers four hours a day at Charee's old school. She believes the other children deserve a good education as much as Charee."

Derrick's pride in his family was obvious.

"My father met me at the hospital right after Charee was born," Derrick continued. "We stood together in the hall where we could see the new babies behind the glass. Dad said, 'Well son, I see your apple doesn't have a stem.' Can you believe my old man?"

"But," Valery came in very quickly, "you won't find a prouder or more loving grandfather anywhere."

Derrick lowered his head, smiling and said, "Yeah."

They were both smiling, again.

"Charee was an angel," Valery continued. "She slept through the night almost from the start. She was such a happy child, always exploring, always so curious: she wanted to know about everything. She…until the leukemia came…" Her voice trailed away again.

He noticed that Valery had spoken of Charee in the past tense. Was she preparing herself for the thing no one wanted to talk about?

Neither of them wanted to speak. They were both fighting to get back to a normal voice.

Finally, Derrick broke the silence and said, "Tell them about the squirrels and the birds."

Valery looked up smiling, glad to have a happy memory to share.

"When she was only four and a half, I put her out in the backyard on a beautiful spring day. It was warm enough that she didn't need a coat. The phone rang, and I went to answer it. I was gone less than two minutes, but when I came back and looked out the window to check on Charee, she was sitting on the grass with her knees tucked up under her, and a squirrel was sitting on top of her head!"

"No! You're kidding." Virginia was very much into the story.

He had almost forgotten she was in the room. Everything else in his world had just stopped. His arms and legs were suddenly numb. He had to remember to breathe.

"No, I'm not kidding," Valery continued. "It jumped from her head to one shoulder or the other and then back up on her head again. I went to the door and stepped out on the stoop. When the squirrel saw me, it jumped down and ran up a tree, making this little barking noise. It sounded like it was scolding me."

"Was Charee hurt?" asked Dr. Virginia, always on duty.

"No, but she turned to me and said, 'Wasn't that a funny squirrel, Momma?'

"Then she asked what she should do. I didn't want to frighten her about the squirrel. She seemed to enjoy it so. I told her to try to whistle and see if the squirrel would come back. She was just learning to whistle, and the only thing she knew how to whistle was *Twinkle, Twinkle, Little Star,* so she tried that.

"The squirrel stayed where it was, but in no time all these birds started flying around her and then landing on the ground near her. I was scared, but Charee just laughed and clapped her hands. She was having a wonderful time. Then she held out her hand with one of her fingers stuck out, and a bird flew up and landed right on her finger."

"What happened?" asked Virginia.

"The bird started chirping and chirping almost as if it were singing just for her. You know, I think it was." Warm tears filled Valery's eyes.

The room grew silent once more.

Again, no one wanted to speak.

He couldn't have spoken if his life depended on it. A shiver had run over him from his head to his toes and back up again. His body was numb but his brain was racing.

Charee had the same power of communication with animals I have! Was that why I feel drawn so powerfully to this little girl?

Derrick recovered first. He moved enough to put his arm around Valery and squeezed her shoulder gently.

When he spoke, his voice was still husky.

"We appreciate all that you've done…are doing…for our little girl." He paused. "We're Christians you know. Charee comes from a Christian home. Whatever happens, it's God's will, and we will have to accept that."

"Thank you for sharing your Charee with me." He willed himself to stand up and go to the door. Virginia followed him out of the lounge.

In the hall she said, "Two weeks ago, Derrick confessed to me something that happened at home. He told me he had come home early from work one day and when he opened the door, he heard Valery screaming. She was in Charee's room. She was just standing in the center of the room screaming. Derrick had to hold her for fifteen minutes before he could calm her down. He said all he could do was cry with her. I've seen it before. More and more, they're being forced to confront their own helplessness."

He nodded.

She forced a wan smile, "Thank you so much for talking to them. I think they really needed to talk about their little Charee, and you knew just the right questions to ask."

He didn't remember asking any questions. It was funny, when all you did was really listen to people, to concentrate on what they said, they came away thinking you were the greatest conversationalist in the world.

He watched Dr. Carnegie walk away down the hall.

If only I could meet you again twenty years from now, Dr. Louisie.

He turned away from her and left the visitor's lounge behind him—the lounge where Derrick and Valery Norris waited for the only thing that could save their little girl—a miracle.

He found her slumped over in her bed. Charee had completed another round of chemo and was feeling the effects of those killing drugs in both her body and her soul.

"Come on, my Charee."

He raised her up to a full sitting position being careful to steady her head with one hand, so she wouldn't feel the vertigo and nausea of a quick head movement. Her head was completely bald. All her hair had fallen out with earlier rounds of chemotherapy.

"I have a special treat for you today. Your mother told me how special you are with animals."

He went to the window and slid the movable panel to one side, then pushed the screen back enough to reach out with his hand. He whistled softly, only once. Charee watched as he held out his finger, keeping it parallel to the windowsill.

A half-dozen little birds flew to the sill. Three of them hopped up on him: one on his finger, one on his hand and one on his wrist. He spoke a few words so softly that she couldn't hear what he said. Two of the birds hopped down, and he drew his hand back through the window and carried the little bird to her. The bird was still clutching his finger.

He nodded to her and she whistled.

Twinkle, Twinkle, Little Star.

The bird hopped off his finger and on to her head. It began to chirp as it took little leaps, fluttering up and down all around her smooth head. Charee laughed and laughed. Her laughter was soon joined by another laughing voice.

Neither he nor Charee had heard Nurse Maria slip into the room. Maria had observed the whole thing and was now laughing softly with Charee, her face a little red with embarrassment. She knew that opening a window was against hospital policy. And bringing a wild bird into the room must be against the rules, too. But she had also seen in that brief moment the wonderful effect the singing bird had on Charee and was reluctant to scold him for his breach of policy.

The moment was magic.

After another few minutes, he again held out his finger and whistled softly. The bird flew back to him, and he carefully put it back out on the windowsill, closing the screen and glass panel behind him. Nothing was said about it, but there were smiles all around.

It was almost the last time he saw her smile.

•

They both arrived at the staff entrance door at the same time. To a casual observer, their meeting might seem accidental, a mere coincidence. It wasn't. He had watched Miss Edna P. Snow closely and knew her schedule well. He knew when she would reach the staff door after leaving her office and that the weather that evening would give him an excuse—an excuse he might, or might not, need.

It was 6:30 and time for a new shift to come in at Presbyterian Medical. A late spring rain backed by a vicious wind was driving the downpour into an almost horizontal torrent. She asked him where he was going. She couldn't remember the address he had given on his employment application. It didn't matter. Her car was parked near the door. Miss Edna P. Snow, who almost never acted on impulse, impulsively asked him if he would like a lift. He would.

Later, when she remembered the rest of the evening, she was sure she should have known what would happen. She was attracted to him from the beginning. She, of course, assumed she was more than twice his age, and that made her retreat from personal contact. But her attempts to hide her interest failed.

From the first day, even during his initial interview with her, he knew. He had observed and judged people for years. Whenever their eyes met, she dropped her gaze quickly. He also noticed the slight flush in her cheeks, the heightened pulse rate in her neck and the huskiness in her voice. Several times each month they met, seemingly by chance in the wards. But their meetings were never by chance.

He knew.

They dashed from the hospital door to her car. She asked for directions to his home. He gave her back her own address. She paused only long enough to suppress a shallow gasp, then drove. By the time they had again dashed through the rain from the car to her apartment door, they were both wet. Once inside he put their coats over the edge of the tub to dry while she made coffee. They sat at her small kitchen table. No one had called her anything except, Miss Snow for years. She told him to call her, Penny.

They spoke for hours. Or, more precisely, she spoke while he listened. He concentrated fully on what she told him, interrupting only to clarify a statement or encourage her to continue. That evening she told him everything—the story of her life. He continued to listen to her as he prepared a simple meal for them, moving easily and confidently around her kitchen.

At last, he put on his raincoat. The rain had stopped, but he put it on anyway. At the door she held out her hand. He brushed her hand aside and took her in his arms. Their lips met, almost but not quite, by surprise. He took off his raincoat and put it back over the edge of the tub.

Her memory of the next few hours is flawed. She never actually lost consciousness but slid in and out of a pleasant stupor. He concentrated on her body in the same way he had listened to her story—completely. His love-making was not at all like anything she had ever experienced—not even when she was "making love, not war" years ago. He took his time. His hands moved over her and around her carefully and deliberately, never hurrying but never stopping. He caressed everything he could reach—and he reached everything. He spoke, when he could, voicing his appreciation of her smoothness, her softness, her aroma and her energy. Penny became acutely aware of his touch—the feel of his hands, his lips, his knee gently pushing her legs apart, his fingertips everywhere, and his tongue. Even the heat of his breath as he moved over her stimulated her in ways she didn't think possible. Finally, he announced the end of their first round with a long, low moan. They were both covered with a fine film of moisture—but not from the rain. It wouldn't be long before they worked up some more.

•

The fourth floor juvenile oncology ward at Presbyterian Medical was a highly polished stage dominated by Marcella and the Chiquitas. Marcella, although not yet forty, was the oldest nurse by seniority on the ward. Oncology nurses typically transferred to other services after only a few years. Her seniority, alone, would have dictated her role as leader, but she would have been a dominate figure anywhere. Her broad smile and booming laugh were counterpoints to the deadly serious business of the ward. She stood several inches over six feet tall, and no reasonable person would guess her weight at less than 280 pounds—and no one was foolish enough to suggest she might be overweight, not even her own doctor. Bright colors sometimes could be seen peeking from beneath her nurse's uniform—a reminder of her African heritage.

The other nurses called themselves, "Chiquitas." A year ago an irascible old racist—the grandfather of a patient—noting that almost all the floor nurses were of Hispanic origin, had started calling every one of them, "Chiquita." They soon began referring to each other in the same way, twisting the ethnic slur for their own amusement. What began as an inside joke shortly became a recognition of sorority and a source of pride. Even nurse, Amy Fogelberg, R.N., was proud to be called, "Chiquita."

Miss Edna P. Snow was happy to employ as many qualified Hispanics as she could find. Their sense of personal honor led to good work habits. She could count on them to be punctual, dependable, trustworthy and well-groomed. They were usually sociable and friendly, easily relating to the rest of the staff and were a boon for the patients. Her "Chiquitas" (she would have eaten glass rather than call any of them, "Chiquita") were a source of special joy for her.

Although they often spoke to each other in Spanish, they were as proficient in English as any on the staff—and their handwriting was far superior to most of the doctors'. So it was not unusual for Miss Snow to take a shortcut through their ward as she did on the morning after the big rain storm. She nodded and spoke her usual, "Good morning."

Marcella, the most intuitive of all the nurses, took one look at the secret smile on Miss Snow's face and her bouncing gait as she passed the nurse's station and said, "Umm, umm, umm, I do believe that our Miss Edna has herself a boyfriend."

The Chiquitas present all immediately leaned over the counter to check out the retreating figure swaying down their hall. Soft smiles were punctuated by a chorus of Chiquita giggles.

•

Months passed pushing summer into fall and fall back into winter again. They had agreed to keep their love trysts a secret. Penny pushed the idea from day one (or night one). She told him it was undignified and would hinder her work if they were made "an item." He knew better. She just didn't want the words, "cradle robber" following her around.

Their secret was made even sweeter by the speculation running through the staff at PMC about the identity of the man in Miss Snow's life. Limericks appeared on the walls of some of the staff bathrooms feeding the mystery. The wags that supplied them almost always made the last words of their little poems, "Miss Snow's beau." He fueled the speculation himself one day while surrounded by two shifts of nurses—one going, one coming on. He suggested it had to be one of the older doctors or even one of the hospital directors. The next day that news came back to him at least a half-dozen times. He smiled even more than usual.

Spring had begun to get a grip on the landscape. They were preparing to celebrate—in secret, of course—their one-year anniversary together. They were both trying to think of something special to do that they hadn't already tried. That didn't leave much.

That same day a large manila envelope arrived at the Center—Priority Mail—addressed to her. Penny glanced at it casually, noting the return address as that of a "Dr. Joel B. Berger." It took her several minutes to recall who Dr. Berger was. She had met him at a hospital administrators' convention two months earlier. They had attended a three-hour seminar outlining current, legal regulations governing employment practices in the public sector. She thought he was employed in mental health somewhere but couldn't be sure. By the time she remembered that much, she saw she was going to be late for several job interviews and left the package unopened on her desk.

A week later, she took it home intending to look at it later that evening. She put it on a little table in the hall—and promptly forgot about it.

He was always particular about what he said and what he did in his personal relationships. His unwillingness to share the truth about his gifts required him to be vague about his past. He kept his secrets well. Women, particularly his lovers, always wanted to know much more than he was willing to divulge. He made up stories to satisfy Penny's curiosity, remembering to relate them to the lies he had included in his application to work at PMC. Secrets and lies were now as natural to him as breathing.

Late one evening, after a particularly strenuous round of mutual body exploration, she lay resting at his side. She reached to touch him and idly took one of his hands in hers. If he hadn't been just on the edge of sleep, he would have taken his hand away, but he carelessly let it go. Penny let out a little squeal and twisted her body quickly to turn on the bedside lamp. She examined his hand where her fingers had probed the hole in his palm. One secret gone; it was time for another lie.

"What happened to your hand?" She was concerned, "Does it hurt? Are you all right?"

"No, it doesn't hurt any more." He had prepared several stories to explain his hands should it ever be necessary.

"It happened when I was just a kid, when I was seven years old. I was playing in a neighbor's yard, and someone had left a garden rake on the lawn with the teeth up. I was racing around, you know like kids will, and I fell on the rake. I must have tried to break my fall with my hands and they hit both ends of the rake. See?" He held up his other hand so she could see both his palms. "I fell on both hands. My mother almost fainted when she saw all the blood when I ran home. But that was a long time ago. They don't hurt anymore."

Penny took both of his hands in hers and kissed his palms.

"I will kiss them everyday to make sure they're all well."

She had to smile at herself—a mature woman talking like a little girl.

A woman in love\was so eager to believe anything her lover said.

It made it so easy to lie to her. He hated it though; lying to someone you loved, hurt—and he loved her. He loved her secret sweetness, her eagerness to go wherever their love-making took them, her intelligence and above all, her trust. Miss Edna P. Snow didn't trust anyone else, not even herself. But she trusted him. Maybe that was why he wanted to tell her something that wasn't a lie—something that was true about himself.

"I have another name," he said, "one you won't find in your files at the hospital. It's a name I was given years ago."

He paused for dramatic effect.

"Okay, okay, tell me!"

The idea that she would know a secret name for her man was so deliciously mysterious.

"Pele'thi." He pronounced it slowly. "It's a Shawnee Indian name."

"What does it mean?" She was getting really excited. "What does it mean in English? No, wait. Don't tell me! I know what it means...it means...it means...stud muffin!"

She squealed with joyous laughter at her own joke.

"Why, you little minx," he said laughing as he rolled over pinning her under him, "I'll show you just how right you are."

•

It was Friday evening. She waited for him to come off his shift. It had been an exhausting day for her. The entire morning was taken up with a general staff meeting and the early afternoon by another meeting in her personnel section. She hadn't even had a chance to get to her office. She left the hospital early because she wanted to have a surprise ready for him: a lamb chop dinner she cooked herself. He was such a good cook; he always prepared their meals. Friday evenings were special because they were both off. But that evening he didn't come home. At 10:00 pm she called the hospital and asked them to page him. There was no response. She didn't sleep at all that night.

Early Saturday morning she was at her desk checking the hospital's computer listing of patients. Nothing. She pulled up the data base for all the medical facilities in the entire metropolitan area. Still nothing. She went through all the wards where he was a regular. No one had seen him since Thursday. She went to his apartment and let herself in with his extra key. Nothing was around to suggest he had ever lived there, no clothes, no toothpaste in the bathroom, no food or drinks in the refrigerator, nothing. She talked to his landlady. He had given her thirty days notice and paid a full month's rent Thursday morning. He told her to donate his security deposit to the American Red Cross. He had left a forwarding address. It was hers.

She spent the rest of Saturday and all Sunday in mourning. Actually, it was worse than mourning—she didn't know what had happened to him or why he had left. Most of his clothes were gone—the two dresser drawers she had allocated to him were empty. She even did something she hadn't thought of doing for years. She prayed. She prayed he was safe and that her questions would be answered.

On Monday she went back to work, but she couldn't find the

energy to do anything. She had heard the term, basket case, but until now she couldn't appreciate the depths to which her spirits could fall.

Her mind was so consumed with thoughts of him she failed to open the top center drawer of her desk. If she had, she would have noticed that its lock had been jimmied. That was the drawer where he knew she always kept the keys to her filing cabinet and where he had left a note explaining (only in general terms) the reason for his sudden departure. Most of the note was devoted to his extreme regret at having to leave her. He *did* love her, and he would miss her more than he could say.

She went home at the end of the day and began to prepare a meal she was sure she wouldn't be able to eat. She brought home some work she needed to catch up on, including all the things she wasn't able to do during the day. She put it on the small table in the hall beside some other things she had brought home earlier in the week, intending to catch up with that, too.

She changed out of her dress and into a robe. As she passed the hall table again, she noticed Dr. Berger's envelope on top of the old pile of work. Now she remembered Dr. Berger. He had promised to send her some profiles of certain psychological types to help her identify undesirable applicants. She decided to start with those files first, right after dinner.

"Maybe, it will take my mind off...things," she whispered to herself. She couldn't even bear to think about his loss.

Dr. Berger had sent her about twenty charts from his files. He had taken great care to place a blank sheet of paper over the part of each chart giving his patient's name and other personal data so it didn't show on the Xerox copies he sent her. Only his diagnosis and notes were legible. His observations, he thought, would suggest keys to recognizing potential problems.

She had read through about half the files making notes as she went when her eyes fell on a chart containing a few lines that looked like they had been written quickly without organization.

She froze. Her heart froze. Her brain froze.

Her eyes froze, too—only her hearing continued to function, but all she heard was a terrific roaring in her ears.

She had read about halfway down the chart when she saw,

"...he has holes in both palms of his hands from, he says, bullet wounds suffered during a battle in the Civil War (the stigmata?)...claims to have lived since 1737...says he seeks work in nursing homes and hospitals but has to leave every fifteen to twenty years because of his unchanging appearance...thinks he is a 'healer,' that he can cure even the most severe sickness with just a touch...believes he has a mission to save a particular individual but doesn't know who it is..."

At the bottom of the chart she read, "'Pele'thi' (the eagle)."

Joel Berger had not thought to mask the name because it was not with the personal data at the top of the chart.

There could be no doubt. Despite her desperate attempts to deny what was plainly in front of her, there could be no doubt.

She sat staring at the chart for a long time. She didn't like it, but her prayer had been answered. She knew he was gone and would not be coming back.

•

It had been the previous Wednesday evening when he spotted the big, manila envelope on the hall table. He was curious. When he looked at it more closely, he saw it was addressed to Penny and that it was from Dr. Joel B. Berger, Ph.D. He didn't try to open the package. He didn't have to. Even if there was nothing in it about him, the fact that she knew Joel made his continued presence at PMC a shaky proposition.

He knew he had to leave even though he hated the idea. His relationship with Penny should have lasted at least another ten, maybe even twenty years. He would miss her as much, or more, than any of the others.

Thursday morning he went to his old apartment and gave thirty days notice to his landlady who was genuinely sad to see him leave. Why not? He continued to pay the rent for an apartment he hadn't used for months. That had to make him her quietest tenant.

Then he went to his main bank. He emptied his safe deposit box, putting the contents in a large gym bag joining the spare underwear and the few shirts and pants he had removed from

Penny's apartment while she slept that morning. The safe deposit box held only a few items: Titus's Bible with Margery's cross inside, two envelopes, one containing his discharge letter dated August, 1789 from the American Army, the other holding birth certificates, drivers' licenses, social security cards and two bundles of cards bound with rubber bands.

The birth certificates were new. In some ways computers and vast databases made it more difficult for him to assume new identities, but in other ways they made it easier. He used the computer system at Presbyterian Medical to access their medical records and documentation areas. Years before at other hospitals, he was forced to find records of children who had died at birth or as infants to use as birth records for his aliases. This time he had the luxury of creating entirely new, bogus records using rather common names he made up himself. Then he printed birth certificates using the hospital's own blank forms and adding the false records to their data base. Any future employer would find those records waiting to confirm his lies. The safe deposit box also held his most recent passport and $2,000 in cash.

Next, he went to a personal bank representative to close out his checking account. There were still two small checks outstanding, so he left enough to cover those checks plus another $100. He took the remaining balance in the account, just under $300 in cash. The bank representative, a Miss Gwen Wertz, said she would be glad to send whatever was left in the account, after the checks and bank fees were paid, as a donation to the Red Cross. He asked her to do it as a personal favor. She was also quite willing to do him a world of favors that had nothing to do with banking if only the young doctor with the interesting scar on his forehead would ask. She thought she communicated that willingness clearly, but he turned to leave.

Too bad, he's gay.

Still, she was a little sad as she watched him walk out of the bank.

He made two more stops that morning. Two other banks held certificates of deposit in two different names. The bundled cards were his identifiers at each bank. He cashed in his CDs after signing the certificates agreeing to pay a ten percent penalty for early withdrawal. He always filed and paid his federal and state income taxes. But this time the IRS would have a couple of tax skippers they would never find. By the end of the day his gym bag contained a little over $32,000 in cash and cashier's checks.

As he slid the bag in the back of the hall closet, where Penny never looked for anything, it struck him that his gym bag contained all his worldly possessions. He remembered Titus quoting Lord Jesus as having said, "Lay not up for yourselves treasures upon earth...But lay up for yourselves treasures in heaven...For where your treasure is, there will your heart be also."

Titus would be proud of him. He never owned anything he couldn't carry on his back. He never owned a boat or a wagon or a car. He did have that horse out West for a few years, but no one owns a horse; the horse owns you. He never owned land, not even the place where Peshewa and his girls lay buried. He had no furniture, no radio, no computer, no personal telephone. Everything he owned was in that gym bag. His treasure was now in Penny's place—where his heart was.

He was very attentive to Penny that Thursday evening. She didn't notice anything unusual—he was always very attentive.

By early morning he was gone. There was nothing unusual about his leaving at that time, either.

•

He came into her room just before he was to go on his regular Friday shift. It was still very early in the morning, and the dimmed room lights made the lighted panels on Charee's support systems seem to glow more brightly than ever. He looked down on her still form. She lay on her side with her face away from him.

He began to sing softly just under his breath, "Mairzy doats and dozy doets and little lambzy divey . . ."

He had taught her the little novelty song from World War II weeks ago when her eyes could still brighten with delight. Now, she could barely open them.

He continued singing, "A kidely divey, too, wouldn't you?"

She stirred and turned her head toward him, looking over her shoulder. She recognized him. A little smile turned up the corners of her mouth. She moved her hand from where it had been resting on top of her hip and took his hand in hers.

Twenty minutes later he slid into the back seat of a taxicab and said, "Airport."

•

Her mind began to work even though her limbs had gone almost numb. Penny looked at Dr. Berger's chart again.

She read, "thinks he is a 'healer,' that he can cure even the most severe sickness with just a touch…believes he has a mission to save a particular individual but doesn't know who it is…"

"Damn!" It was very unusual for her to swear. But she did it again, "Damn him to hell!"

She wasn't entirely sure who she was damning more: Dr. Berger or the man who said he was Pele'thi. At the moment they were both on her shit list: Berger for revealing too much about his patient and that "S.O.B. Shawnee bastard" for deceiving her, for using her, for…

"Oh God," she thought, "for loving me…and most of all…for leaving me."

Her mind really began to turn over now. Hadn't he mentioned someone on the oncology floor, someone who needed some special prayers, some special help? Yes, it was a little girl, a little black girl with leukemia who wasn't going to make it. What was her…Charee! Yes, her name was Charee. He talked about her a lot in the last week.

Now both her mind and her body were racing. She changed back into her dress and touched her hair in the mirror only briefly on her way out the door.

She was back at PMC in no time—out of the parking lot and up the steps running to the elevator. There was only one nurse on duty at that time of night. She remembered her name, Maria.

"Maria, you have a patient whose name is Charee. Charee… what is her last name?"

Maria answered, "Charee Norris."

"Yes, that's her. What room number?"

Richard L. Evans

"Number 414, but Miss Snow..."

Penny turned and was running toward room 414, so she didn't hear the rest of what Maria tried to say. She got to the door and stopped for a few seconds to catch her breath. She pushed it, and the door opened easily, silently. The first thing she noticed was the quiet. There were no low hums or clicks coming from the monitoring systems. There were no lights. She felt along the wall for the light switch and turned it on.

The bed was empty.

She heard the door move behind her. Maria had followed her down the hall and into the room.

"Miss Snow, I tried to tell you, the little girl, Charee...is gone."

Penny turned around and the look on her face prompted Maria to continue quickly. "No, no, it's all right. Four or five nights ago she was so sick Dr. Carnegie called her parents to come to the hospital because it looked like the end. But when they got here, Charee was perfectly well. She was just sitting up in the bed singing this funny little song, 'Mares Eat Oats,' or something like that.

"They took her home today. You should have seen it. We were all so happy. Everyone was crying—everyone except Charee—she couldn't understand what all the fuss was about. It was like...I don't know how to say it. It was a miracle."

> *And God shall wipe away all tears from their eyes; and there shall be no more death, neither sorrow, nor crying, neither shall there be any more pain: for the former things are passed away.*
>
> **REVELATION 21:4**

EPILOGUE

The reservations clerk at the Britannia Hotel in San Jose checked the passenger list for the airline flight that had landed forty-five minutes earlier. One of the passengers, an older woman with a reservation at the hotel, had fallen in the terminal and was being transported to what was reputed to be the best clinic in Costa Rica. The driver of the hotel van had called to give her the name of the guest.

The injured woman was a Miss Edna P. Snow.

At the clinic Penny was immediately helped to an examining room. Her injured wrist was immobilized and a cold pack applied to reduce the swelling. Then her personal medical information was recorded by a medical tech. The name on the tech's badge was "Marianna." Marianna was a beautiful woman. Penny guessed she was somewhere in her thirties. Marianna rose to leave, saying the doctor would be right in.

She had just opened the door when Penny heard his laugh in the hall. No one who had ever heard it would forget his laugh.

Marianna turned back quickly and caught Penny to prevent her from falling again, this time in a faint.

She hadn't seen him in twenty years, but it didn't matter. He was the same: the same easy way with people; the same peculiar scar on his temple; the same smile and of course, the same laugh. She wondered if his "bedside manner" was the same. She hoped so. He looked a little heavier but that was all. He was still handsome.

He was not as shocked as she was to meet again. He had read her name on the admittance roster minutes before coming into the room. She wasn't sure her throat would let her say anything but she had to try.

"Well, doctor," she got out, "I guess we'll have to stop meeting in places like this."

What, after all, does one say in such a circumstance?

He embraced her gently as she sat on the table, being careful not to move her hand and wrist. His scent triggered old, suppressed emotions, and she nearly fainted again. Mercifully, he released her and removed the ice pack to examine her wrist.

"I tried to explain why I left in my letter—the one in your desk. I'm so sorry I had to leave you the way I did."

He looked straight into her eyes. His voice was much softer.

"I'm sorry I had to leave you at all."

This wasn't going to be easy.

"Are you still with PMC?"

"No, they have a policy of mandatory retirement at age seventy. That was seven years ago. I've been traveling ever since. Have you been in Costa Rica long?"

"I came here straight from PMC." He had started to say, "straight from you," but he held it back. "I recertified as an M.D. here."

"I tried to trace you. You knew I would, I'm sure."

"You had no luck, though."

He didn't wait for her confirmation. His smile was even gentler, now.

"I'm very good at covering my trail. I tried once to count up all the different names I've used in my life. I couldn't do it. There were too many."

"Including, 'Pele'thi'?"

She wasn't going to let him off easily, not just yet. He could only smile, now truly embarrassed.

"I had a little talk with Joel Berger before he died," she said. He certainly remembered you. I also checked with the American Red Cross and the medical school at the University of Pennsylvania. Since I couldn't give them a name, they couldn't help me. Then I searched through military records going all the way back to the Revolutionary War. No luck. You're a slippery bastard."

"Then you believed me—you believed me even though Joel didn't."

"I saw how you were with the patients at PMC. And I knew you as my...I knew you well enough to know you were telling the truth. Of course, I believed you."

"I hope, someday, you will find it in your heart to forgive me, too"

"You gave me the happiest days of my life. I forgave you years ago."

Now it was his turn to find it hard to speak. He decided to move on.

"I've changed. Can you see it?"

Of course she could see it.

"You've aged. A little gray hair at the temples, a little extra flesh around the neck."

The scar on his forehead was much lighter, almost as if it were fading away. She could barely see it anymore. She thought that a little strange, but what wasn't a little strange about this man?

"You look to be in your mid-forties. How old, exactly, are you?"

"I was born in 1737. It took me 240 years to go from being twenty-five years old to being twenty-six. But I'm going to make it all the way, now. I'll probably live to be over 300, and then I believe God will grant me my death. I asked God for this blessing, and He has given it to me."

"I sure can pick 'um, can't I?"

But she was smiling now. They were both smiling now.

They spoke for another ten minutes, catching up on people he remembered from PMC. Then they came to the things each really wanted to know.

"Have you been following Charee Norris?" he asked.

They both had watched the Norris family.

"Derrick's business is thriving, and Valery has been elected to her local school board."

It had been easier for Penny to keep up with the Norris'. He had to rely on e-news accounts.

"And what about our superstar-to-be?" he asked.

"You mean Charee."

They both had a compelling interest in Charee Norris.

"She's out of med school and moving up in the political world. The word is she'll run for Congress in a safe district next year. The current occupant of that seat is not very happy about it, but he's being pushed out. Where do you think she's headed?"

"I'm not sure, yet." he said. "She's smart. I'm sure she knows she can't achieve that much from a pulpit or a medical research post. Her best chance is from the floor of the House or the Senate." He paused, then said, "Or the White House."

"The White House! Our first black *and* our first female President?"

"Yes, I believe so."

"Well I'll be a...do you really think she can do it?"

"I think she has the most potent, political ally anyone could have. After all," he said, "'In God We Trust.'

"I suppose Joel told you about my so-called *gift* of healing." He paused, "I didn't use it with Charee. I started to—I held her hand and started to say the words I learned from my father hundreds of years ago. But then I remembered something else another man, a black slave, who was much more a father to me had said. That man told me to ask God to guide me to what God wanted, not what I wanted.

Holding Charee's hand, I started to speak, but her hand went cold; her pulse stopped. I was too late—I had lost her. In The Lord's Prayer we ask that, 'Thy will be done.' That's what I prayed for. I had said those words hundreds of times but never listened to them, never really meant them. It was only when I gave up myself that God gave me a new life—one like other men. And God gave Charee new life, too. Her pulse returned and her breathing became deep and regular. I saw her healed. God's will was done.

"I was almost out the hospital door when I saw Charee's parents coming toward the building from the parking lot. I ducked back in the doorway. As they passed by, I saw so much grief on their faces, I rejoiced. I knew their grief would all be washed away. Oh, how I would have loved to have been there to see it happen!"

Penny reached for his arm with her good hand and held it. For a moment they were both silent. They knew it was time for the other thing between them.

He said, "You know, I've always had the help of angels. I believe in angels—I've seen them. I've even lived with them. My first angel was a girl named Margery. She said no matter what happened, she'd always be with me. She was right. She's with me now. My second angel was Titus, the black man I told you about. He showed me my life could have a sanctified purpose, that I could make a difference in the world. There have been others, too."

When he spoke again, his voice was different, softer.

"You're one of my angels, you know. Without your love and your strength I'm not sure I would have had the courage to ask God to heal Charee. When I decided I had to leave you, I knew I couldn't just leave Charee, too."

He took a deep breath. "Do you remember the bad dreams that used to wake me in the night?"

She nodded. Of course she remembered holding him and telling him that, "Everything was all right, now."

"I still have them, but they're not *bad* dreams anymore. I used to feel sorry for myself—that I couldn't have any old friends. But I was wrong. All the people in my dreams *are* my old friends—and they're always with me."

There was another awkward pause. It was time for her big question.

"How's your love life these days?"

She tried to make it sound casual—not fooling either of them.

He wanted to spare her as much as he could.

He said it quickly. "I've had many lives. The way I am now—

this is my last life. When I was sure I was aging, that I was finally going to die, I wanted the family I thought I could never have. It's the sureness of death that gives life its meaning.

"The lovely woman who took your medical information, Marianna, has been my wife for the last fourteen years. She's a wonderful woman and as good a wife as a man could have. We're very happy together. This time I can stay. This time I can live out my life with the same person."

Penny fought her rising tears. It was certainly not what she hoped to hear.

"Joel Berger probably told you about my preference for older women. That might make you wonder about Marianna. But I couldn't have children with an older woman. Even with the recent advances in bio-obstetric extension, I couldn't ask an older woman to bear my child."

"Do you have your family, yet?"

Her voice was steady. She was thankful for that. And she was surprised by the depth of her love for him—she really wanted him to have his family, even if she couldn't be part of it.

"We have a son. He's quite a boy. He's...wait."

He helped her off the examining table, cradling her arm and led her to a large window at the back of the examining room.

The clinic was built atop a low hill in an open forest. It had a lovely view. Looking out the window, she saw a small cleared space down the hill at the edge of the forest. There was a boy just coming out of the trees into the clearing. He looked to be about eight or nine years old.

The man she once knew as Pele'thi was standing at her elbow, still holding her arm when he said, "There he is. There's my son."

The boy was walking fast, moving easily across the clearing. Penny saw several birds perched on his shoulders. The boy and the birds seemed to be singing to each other.

"Those birds with him," she asked, "are they pets?"

"No, no, those are just wild birds."

She watched the boy as he moved along, fascinated by his singing with the birds.

Then suddenly, the child stopped and reaching down, picked up a small animal. Penny saw it clearly. It was a squirrel. The sight took her back to her conversation with Dr. Berger, to something that had happened during his session with this strange man.

She became aware of his voice telling her something from behind, breaking through her thoughts. He was saying, "He's eight, almost nine, now. He's such a happy boy—always smiling, always singing. Everyone seems to love him. He'll grow up to be the kind of man who speaks to dogs."

Printed in the United States
21161LVS00002B/1-51